For All the Right Reasons

Elaine Coffman

For All the Right Reasons

WHEELER
PUBLISHING, INC.
ROCKLAND, MA

★ AN AMERICAN COMPANY ★

Published in Large Print by arrangement with The Ballantine Publishing
Group, a division of Random House, Inc., in the United States and Canada.

Wheeler Large Print Book Series.

Set in 16 pt Plantin.

4|99

Library of Congress Cataloging-in-Publication Data

Coffman, Elaine.
    For all the right reasons / Elaine Coffman.
        p. (large print) cm.(Wheeler large print book series)
    ISBN 1-56895-637-1 (hardcover)
    1. Large type books.
I. Title. II. Series
[PS3553.O39F67   1999]
813'.54—dc21

99-010598
CIP

The heart is half prophet.
Yiddish proverb

CHAPTER ONE

Brownsville, Texas, 1848

The war was over.

The man sitting astride the stout little buckskin scratched the rough stubble on his face and tried to decide if he was glad. He was glad there would be an end to all the killing. But the end of this war meant there would be no need for the army that had fought so bravely under General Zach Taylor, no need for the men who had misplaced two years of their lives. For two years the Mexican War had filled the void in his life. But now it was over. What would become of him now?

His name was Alexander Mackinnon. He and his twin brother, Adrian, were the youngest of the Mackinnon brothers, who numbered six in all. There were only five of them left now, since Andrew, the oldest brother, had been killed by Comanches back in '36. *Twelve years.* Andrew had been dead for a long time. Andrew Mackinnon, the oldest and the first to die. During the two years of heavy fighting, Alex often thought he would be the next to go. He pondered upon that for a minute and shook his head sadly. It was a grim thing to admit, but he figured the only significant thing about his death would be that it would reduce the number of living Mackinnon brothers to four.

The war with Mexico had been grueling, but

1

short, and it had occupied Alex and his twin, Adrian, for a couple of years, giving them something to do besides starve to death. But now it was over and they weren't exactly sure what they would do next. It wasn't that they hadn't planned ahead, or that they were so foolish as to believe the war would never end. They simply had never given much thought to what they would do when it did.

An aimless little wind came out of nowhere, stirring up a spiraling cloud of dust—a dry reminder of how long it had been since this part of the world had last seen rain. Alex pulled the bandanna from around his neck and wiped the sweat from the inside of his hat, then stared at it for a minute, as if he were trying to place just where he'd seen that particular hat before. He pushed and poked the crown, trying a new shape or two, before he put it back the way it had been and put it on his head. He turned in the saddle to watch Adrian ride up the road toward him, his horse up to his hocks in dust. After six months in Brownsville they had been mustered out of the army and were free to go. Adrian hadn't been in any particular hurry, but Alex had been itching to head out since the day they arrived—which wouldn't have surprised anyone who knew them, since it was commonly known that the Mackinnon twins were rarely in agreement about anything. It was the gospel truth that Alex Mackinnon was acting as anxious as a new bride, even though he had no idea where it was he wanted to go. Only one thing was certain: Whatever it was that he was looking for wasn't going to be found in Brownsville.

Alex shifted in the saddle, the leather creaking as he took one last look at Brownsville. He stole another look at the stubborn sun high in the sky and was thinking that for the past three hours it hadn't moved. Adrian had almost caught up with him now, and Alex waited, his faded blue eyes staring out over the alkali flats, seeing no movement except the chalky dust Adrian stirred up and the quick, darting run of a chaparral through the sparse stand of brush. Behind them, across the Rio Grande lay Mexico and a chapter of their life that had already been written. Ahead of them lay nothing but the grassy coastal plain and beyond that San Antonio. And then where? He wasn't sure, but he knew the rest of their story lay in that direction.

Alex felt tired and a lot older than his nineteen years. He looked at Adrian and wondered if he felt the same. It was hard to tell what Adrian was feeling just by looking at him. Alex knew his brother as well as anyone, knew that he had a temper hotter than a blacksmith's fire, and it was as likely to explode as a hammer cocked back over forty grains of dry powder. Alex felt fortunate he had been spared that, for he was one of those men blessed with a sunny nature, the ability to take everything in stride, in spite of the insults life hurled at him.

And hurl them she had.

Life hadn't been particularly kind to him and

he had been forced to grow up in a hurry. None of this had been his fault. If there was blame to be laid, it would have to be on the Comanches, for they had been the ones responsible for the deaths of his mother, father, and brother, and the kidnaping of his six-year-old sister, Margery. But even as he blamed the Comanches, he knew it was somehow wrong to do so. They had killed part of his family, true—and orphaned the remaining five Mackinnon boys that ranged in age from eight to fourteen. But the Comanches had been struggling longer than he had, fighting a battle that had already been lost, just like the Mexicans had done. Somehow it didn't seem right to whip a downed horse.

"What put you in such an all-fired hurry?" Adrian asked as he pulled even with Alex and reined in. The bay he was riding was breathing hard, his arched neck glistening with sweat. Another mile or two and he would be lathered. Alex felt his thirst return.

Alex's silence didn't seem to bother Adrian. "You mad about last night?"

Alex shook his head. "Nope."

"Then why wouldn't you loan me two dollars for that whore?"

"She wasn't worth two dollars."

"You ever bedded that particular whore?"

"Nope."

"Then how in the blue blazes could you know if she was worth two dollars or not?"

"Good Lord, Adrian, that woman was ugly enough to turn a train down a dirt road."

"So, who's looking at her face?"

"You couldn't be that hard up for a woman," he said. "Nobody could."

"That was my decision. Don't you think I have the right to bed whatever whore I choose?"

"Not with my two dollars."

"I would've paid you back. You know that."

"Now you don't have to."

Adrian knew it was pointless to continue this discussion. "I still say we should've lit out in the morning instead of leaving at midday. It's too hot to breathe." He eyed the parched country around him and dusted the alkali chalk from his thigh with his hat. "We seem to be the only fools out and about. It's a sad thing to admit, but I think horned toads and scorpions have more sense than we do." He cast his eyes over to where Alex sat still and quiet in the saddle.

Alex was thinking about something else and didn't say anything for a spell. He was thinking in reverse, reflecting on how he and Adrian had campaigned with General Taylor back before the war with Mexico was officially declared. It was May of '46 when they crossed the Rio Grande and occupied Matamoras after the battles of Palo Alto and Resaca de la Palma. By the following February they had marched nearly 300 miles into Mexico and won the Battle of Buena Vista against overwhelming odds.

And now a year later the Treaty of Guadalupe Hidalgo was signed, giving the United States Texas, California, and the territory of New

Mexico. At last the war was over and they could go home. Problem with that was, they weren't sure exactly where home was—unless they considered it to be the old Mackinnon homestead over in Limestone County. Best anyone could recollect, there wasn't much there to draw them back.

Nothing except the Simon sisters.

CHAPTER TWO

The whore in San Antonio wasn't worth two dollars either. But she was a damn sight better looking than the one Adrian wanted to bed in Brownsville.

It was early evening and still hotter than a burning stump. Alex was thinking it was too hot to breathe, let alone talk, but the whore next to him had her pump primed. He couldn't understand it—wholesomes or whores, they always wanted to talk afterwards.

"During the war I could get five dollars without even trying," the whore called Lily said, giving Alex her never-fail petulant look.

Lily yawned and Alex looked at her lolled back on the bed, calm as a brood sow in mud. He slapped her on the fanny. "You should still be getting five dollars," he said dryly, "because you still aren't trying."

Lily gave him a sly look and said nothing. Lord have mercy, but he was a looker. Enough to make a woman sit up and howl. She had forgotten how beautiful a young man's body was—the smooth, taut skin, the absence of flab, the tight muscles. Lord! Was there anything that felt any better than to run your hand over the smooth curve of a tight butt, or to feel a hard, flat stomach, or to know the strength of strong thighs? Of their own accord her eyes moved reflectively over his splendid body and she gave her undistracted attention to his smooth chest and slim hips as he lay on his side facing her. Yes, he was as splendid a specimen of manhood as she'd ever seen, and she'd seen plenty. Her gaze lingered on that part of him she found the most splendid of all. He was so big. But a lot of men were big. The difference here was, this young, healthy animal knew what to do with it. That was the difference. He not only had one as straight and hard as a bullet, but even now, after the way he'd satisfied her like she could never remember being satisfied, he still wasn't flat. It wouldn't take much, she speculated, to have him raring to go again. The thought of making love with him again curled like a clenched fist low in her belly. She reached over and took him in her hand. "Honey, you shore look like you're ready to sprout again."

She had no more than finished what she was saying when his hand shot out and clamped around her wrist and she released him, looking as peeved as all get out but saying nothing.

"What makes you think I want another poke when I didn't get my money's worth on the first one?" He released her and rolled to his back. When he stretched his legs out the bed creaked. He folded his arms behind his head and stared at the water spots on the ceiling.

"How 'bout I give you a free poke this time?" Lily rolled over beside him and draped herself across his chest, one finger lazily tracing the outline of his lips. "Whadda ya say?"

"I say the last one should've been free."

She was feeling a little guilty, but she wasn't up to letting him know that. She had simply forgotten herself. She couldn't remember that ever happening to her before. She had been whoring since she was sixteen and for twenty years she had always been able to separate herself from what she was about. A man's body was like a map. There were places to take it slow and easy, others to take off like a scalded cat, and a few places you could stop and dally along the way. But she had forgotten she was supposed to pleasure him, that she was supposed to know when and where to dally and when to forge ahead. This time it had been pure pleasure for her. "Wasn't all my fault. A woman needs a *little* cooperation," she said, "besides a battering with *that*."

"I didn't hear you complaining a minute ago."

"That was a minute ago." Her fingers trailed lower, touching him.

He pulled her hand away. "If I'm going to do all the work you should be paying me two dollars and you damn well know it."

And she did. But being found out didn't sit too well with Lily. A minute ago she had been itching to get him aroused again simply because she had enjoyed his particular brand of lovemaking. But it had moved past that now, past desire and on to determination. She wanted him and she was going to get another poke or die trying. There were other ways for a woman to get what she wanted.

Alex could see she was in a good pout now and he wondered why he was being so hard on her. He reflected on that for a moment. He had had worse looking women, and a lot less talented, too. He remembered their shared passion of a moment ago. Maybe she was right. Maybe he hadn't been as cooperative as he could have been. Fact was, he didn't really have his mind on sex right now—at least not the way the whore wanted. It was something he had learned to do without really thinking about it; something he did by rote, just as a man can button his shirt without giving much thought to what he is doing, if he's had enough practice. The whore had satisfied him. He had found release. Wasn't that enough? Why should this time stand out as different from any of the other of a hundred or so pokes he'd had in the past? He couldn't seem to get his mind on what he'd come in here for. It wasn't that he was bored. It wasn't that the woman was a whore. It was simply that she wasn't the woman he wanted. She wasn't Karin.

He had been thinking about Karin a lot lately. Maybe that was because of the war being over. Perhaps that was why he'd been so restless in Brownsville, why he'd been so difficult for Adrian to get along with. It had been over three years since he'd seen Karin Simon. He'd been no more than a peach-faced kid of sixteen back then, but he knew what he felt for her was real even then, and that it would last. In spite of what Adrian had said about him forgetting her.

"Honey, you sure are acting troubled. You got something you want to talk about? I'm a good listener. No charge for that either."

Alex looked her over with interest and curiosity, then shook his head. He was tempted. He couldn't remember the last time he wanted to spend some time with a woman just to talk. But there wasn't time for that now. There were things he had to do, pieces of his life he had to put back together, and the desire to get started was strong. Sometimes it was so strong he wasn't sure if he was being pulled or pushed.

"You sure you don't want to talk a spell? I ain't got nothing to do particularly."

"No troubles," he said, "and no time for talking. I'm anxious to get home." And that was the truth. He was getting as anxious as Adrian. *Maybe that's what's wrong with me.* He was restless and reflective and those two combined always made him just a little moody. He looked at Lily's concerned face. Whores were a sympathetic lot, usually too good-hearted for their own benefit. He gave her a slap on the rump and rolled from the bed. Going to his money, he handed her five dollars. She took it, then noticing how much it was, said, "This is five dollars."

"I thought you said you could get five dollars without even trying."

"I did, but there ain't no war goin' on now."

His look turned reflective. "There's always a war of some kind going on," he said, "and we've all got our prices."

Lily started to say something else, but Alex had his customary look; the look of a man who has moved on somewhere else. She studied him—the handsome face, the long lines of his fine naked body. Like a lot of men, he was neither modest nor proud about his body. She felt her secret places throb as she remembered the way he had peeled out of his clothes and stood over her, naked and sleek and hard. Her eyes dropped lower—he sure had something to be proud of. His body told her a lot about him, about his extraordinary vitality, his correctness, how he accepted himself and made no excuses. A man's body could tell as much as his eyes, if a person knew how to read it. Her eyes went over him again. Yes, this one was fine looking, and young, tall, and slim, with a head of the thickest black hair she'd ever seen on a man. And Lord have mercy, but those eyes of his were enough to set a woman trembling. The palest blue she'd ever seen, and so direct, yet touched with something she could only call sadness. Against that tanned face it gave him a certain haunting quality, and women were always drawn to men who possessed that haunting quality. Not that it was to their betterment, for if Lily had learned anything during her twenty years of whoring, it was how to judge a man. A man with that haunting quality was difficult to move off center. Once he got himself locked in on something he was as hard to pull away as a bulldog with a mouthful of leg. Some men were content to play the cards they'd been dealt, while others like this one went through life like a swiftly flowing river that stays true to the course. No matter how many obstacles were put in a river's way, it always managed to go around or batter its way through until it reached the place it was supposed to go. This young man had his course pretty well charted out unless she missed her guess. Lord help anyone that tried to stand in his way.

Her eyes traveled over him once more. "Why don't you come back to bed?"

Alex glanced back at the bed. She was lying on her back. Her lips were wet and parted. So were her legs. He gave the area between her legs a frank look. She saw his body react and smiled. "Come on, sugar. You don't want to go just yet."

For a second he considered doing just that, but he knew the real ache wouldn't be satisfied any more than it had been the first time. He gave her a reluctant smile and shook his head, watching the warm glow fade from her eyes.

After Lily left, Alex was still feeling odd, a combination of restlessness and dread. As far as he could remember he'd never felt those two emotions at the same time. The piano from the saloon across the street was loud and out of tune, but it drew him to the window just the same. His body was bathed in sweat, and the breeze that billowed the curtain felt good on his heated skin. He stood before the window, as naked as a scraped hog and wondered if anyone could see him. Probably not. It was dark outside and there was no light in his room. It really didn't matter anyway, for he didn't really care. There were only two kinds of women down there on the streets: the ones who had seen a man naked and the ones who hadn't. If they'd seen a naked man before then the sight of one more wasn't apt to shock them any. If they hadn't seen one, it was probably high time they did.

He thought about that for a minute, thinking that sounded a little detached even for him. And the more he thought about it, the more he felt that was a good description of the way he felt: detached. When had he become so indifferent to things around him? Had he seen so much killing, witnessed so many lives being snuffed out in a twinkling that he no longer held ordinary things in very high regard? Maybe this was true. He had no way of knowing the answer right now. It was something only time could tell.

His body cooled, the whiskey having done its work at soothing his brain, Alex moved away from the window and went back to bed. He sat down and poured himself another whiskey and downed it as quickly as he had the other three, then lay down, watching the shadow of the fluttering curtain as it moved on the opposite wall. The old need filled him, possessing his thoughts. Sex was only a temporary stand-in, he knew that. Women. Fighting. Getting drunk. They all had their way of working on him, but none of them helped for long. He sighed and leaned back, his arm across his eyes, but no matter how he lay or how much whiskey he consumed, the old feeling was still with him. But it wouldn't plague him for much longer. *Soon,* he thought. *Soon I will see her again. How many more days before we reach our old place? Does Karin still live across the creek? Is she sweet on anyone? Is she married?* He closed his eyes and called up memory after memory, wondering if Karin thought of him as often as he thought of her.

"Alexander Mackinnon?" Karin's heart pounded at the sound of his name. "Stars above! Whatever made you think of him like that—right out of the blue?" Karin looked across the kitchen table at her sister. Sometimes she didn't understand Katherine at all. One minute she could be laughing her head off, astounding everyone around her with her funny side, only to turn as gloomy and dark as a moonless night when the mist rolled up from the creek. Karin was thinking her sister had been showing a lot of this gloomy side of late, poking around in her mental cobwebs, dragging out old ghosts, stirring up dead memories. It was enough to make a body shudder, like someone was walking on your grave. Take tonight for instance. Why would she dredge up Alexander Mackinnon's name all of a sudden? He'd been gone from these parts so long that Karin had grown tired of waiting. Alex was a looker, for sure, but she wasn't the kind to wait for a man forever—no matter how good he looked. Besides, she wasn't about to take her ducks to a market that poor. Oh, his name still made her heart turn flips, but she had decided her heart could learn to turn flips for a rich man as easily as a poor one. "What made you think of Alexander Mackinnon all of a sudden?" she asked again.

Katherine got that far-off look in her eyes. "Mr. Carpenter stopped by on his way back from town. He said three of his kids are down with the chicken pox."

By this time, Karin was looking completely dumbfounded. "And *that* reminded you of the Mackinnons?"

"Well, of course it did," Katherine said, giving Karin a direct look. "Don't you remember how we all had the chicken pox at the same time... you, Alex, Adrian, and I?"

"Saints preserve us! How can you remember things like that? I don't even remember having the chicken pox, much less who had them with us." Karin looked reflective, and just a little irritated. How on earth did Katherine manage to remember all the nonsense she had salted away in the back of her mind? It was all she could do to remember what dress she planned to wear tomorrow. Sometimes when Katherine got like this and started dumping all these questions and bits of poppycock in her lap, Karin felt like someone had just handed her a shovelful of hot coals and she couldn't decide if she should drop it or light out running. "The chicken pox," Karin repeated slowly, her voice trailing off in reflection. "I think I do remember something about that, but stars above! That was seven or eight years ago." Karin stood up and began poking her sewing into her basket. "We've got enough to worry about right now without dragging our past along with it, especially when it's of no value whatsoever. Like hauling garbage, if you ask me. Now, why would a body want to haul a bunch of worthless garbage around when he didn't have to?"

Katherine didn't have an answer for that one. "I don't know, but sometimes I just can't help thinking about the way things were back then, back when mama was alive."

It was galling to Karin, always being reminded of how much Katherine had loved their mother, or how much their mother had loved Katherine. Karin had loved her mother too, but never in the same way that Katherine had. Katherine was like that. She didn't love, she cherished, and when she cherished someone, that person could do no wrong in her eyes. She was loyal to a fault and no matter how hard you tried to convince her of something lacking in someone she cherished, she would have no part of it. Because of that, Karin had, on more than one occasion said that Katherine had a stubborn streak a mile high and a mile wide. But that never did stop Katherine from cherishing. That kind of loving was bigger than Karin could swallow. She knew everyone had different ways of going about things, but if she were really and truly honest she would have to admit that it made her feel that in matters of the heart she always took a back seat to Katherine. She didn't want to be relegated to any back seat right now, unless it was in Carter Turner's new buggy. She was feeling too happy and in like with herself to be put in her place by anyone, let alone her dreamy-eyed sister. "Well, there are more important things than the old days to think about now," she said.

Katherine snipped the last threat and looked sadly at her coarse brown skirt lying across her lap. There were now three lines where the hem had been. "I'm going to wear this skirt out hemming it," she said wistfully, that far-off look in her eyes again. "I wish it would wear out completely."

"You should be wishing for a new skirt, or at least that you stop getting taller. You're already half a head taller than most of the men around, and men are scarce as hen's teeth since the war. You keep shooting up tall as a bean pole and you'll never get a man to marry."

"I'm not that tall, and I've told you before I'm not going to marry anyway."

"What do you want to do? Stay here and grow as hard and unforgiving as this measly piece of land?"

"I don't feel the same way you do. This is our home. I love it here. I don't find it any harder or any more unforgiving than life."

As much as Katherine loved the land, Karin hated it. Once, when they were thirteen or fourteen and walking home from school after a rain, Katherine said in that enraptured way she had of speaking sometimes, "Oh, how I love to smell the earth and its wetness. Don't you?" To which Karin had fervently replied:

"No, I don't, and please don't say that in front of anyone. They'll think you're as daft as old Mrs. Tribble. I can see it now. I'll be the laughingstock of the countryside. Everyone will be telling stories of how you go around with your nose plowing the dirt like a pig."

Karin eyed her sister across the table, feeling her irritation reach new heights just remembering something like that, and the way Katherine had just looked at her in a sympathetic way and said, "Then I'm sorry you don't. You see the roses Karin, but you never smell their lovely scent." Her tone of pity had been something Karin didn't understand. But then, she had never understood Katherine. And their father hadn't understood her either. Only their mother had.

Years ago, Katherine and Karin had hidden in the broom closet one evening, listening to their parents talk over a slice of pie at the kitchen table after supper.

"That Katherine," their mother had said, "she is a sight for sore eyes." But that hadn't bothered Karin any, because their father had said, "I suppose she is—it's a cinch she's nothing like Karin. Karin is the picture of perfection." Karin had looked smugly at Katherine, but Katherine didn't look put out in the least. Karin didn't understand that at all. Didn't Katherine comprehend that it was much better to be called the "picture of perfection" than "a sight for sore eyes"?

All this remembering made her tired, so Karin gathered up her things, and dropped her sewing basket in its usual place beside the hutch in the kitchen and went outside for a walk. She was feeling left out again, just as she always did when Katherine got reflective and stirred up old memories in her own head. She couldn't understand how her sister did it, how she managed to call up so much from the past. She walked toward the creek, hearing the bullfrogs in the distance.

Alex Mackinnon.

Lordy, Lordy, it had been a while since she'd thought of him. She tried to remember what he looked like, but aside from being way too thin and having a badly cropped shock of black hair and a face as handsome as the devil, she couldn't conjure up much. And when she tried, the image of Jester Brewer's face kept coming to the front of her mind. Jester was the banker's son and quite the most eligible bachelor in Limestone County, and he had been paying quite a bit of attention to her lately. He wasn't much to look at, but money did a whole lot to offset a homely face. A girl could do worse than Jester Brewer. Yes sirree, she most certainly could.

Karin walked for quite a spell, until she saw the light go off in Katherine's bedroom. She made her way back to the house, glad Katherine had gone to sleep. She didn't like to talk about the past like Katherine did. And why should she? The past was dead and buried, just like their folks. Pointless, it was. Just plain-as-pig-tracks pointless. The past held nothing for her, just as this dirt farm held nothing for her. It was a stopping-off place, nothing more—a place to bide her time until she could pinch and scrape and save enough to buy herself a one-way ticket out of here. A ticket to as far away as her money would take her. Maybe as far away as New York City, or San Francisco—or at least St. Louie. She'd go anyplace, as long as it was a big city and away from here. Away from this farm. Away from Limestone County.

Away. *That's* where her future lay, and for that reason she was only interested in the future. Her future.

Katherine wasn't asleep, but she didn't feel any more like talking than Karin did. She was lying in bed asking herself why she had mentioned anything about Alex Mackinnon to Karin. Karin thought she was crazy as a loon as it was. What would she think if she knew just how often Katherine thought of Alex? Or worse, the kinds of things she envisioned whenever his memory paid her a visit. She closed her eyes, calling up another memory.

Katherine remembered when she and Karin were growing up. Back then life in the rolling hills of Limestone County had been easier on them. Papa's eyes were sharp as an owl's and their mama was as pretty and healthy as a body could hope to be. Back then the corn was as tall as the eaves on the house and life had held so much promise. "Count your blessings," their mother always said. "If you don't thank the Good Lord, He might just see fit to take it all away."

And Katherine had counted her blessings, and she had said her prayers every night, thanking the Lord above for giving her all that He had seen fit to give her, praying life would always be this way. But it hadn't been, and just as mama had feared, the Lord had seen fit to take it all away, and Katherine couldn't understand why. She only knew that He had seen fit.

"Our job isn't to question the workings of the Lord, for His reasons aren't ours," Katherine could remember her mama saying after they suffered through a hard winter and the spring rains washed all the newly planted crops away. When the rains had finally stopped, their mother had said, "There's better times a coming."

But better times must have decided to go someplace else, because that summer their five-year-old brother Billy had died suddenly from

21

a snakebite, and that fall, when she'd just learned to walk, baby Audrey had toddled into the bull pen and had been gored to death. Mama had never been the same after that. One day she would be as normal as sunshine, and then all of a sudden she would turn strange. Several times, when Katherine came into the house, she would see her mother standing over Audrey's tiny, little bed singing a lullaby, and when she saw Katherine she would smile and place her fingers over her lips and say, "Shhhh, baby Audrey is sleeping."

The minister, Rev. Archibald Haynes, had said the same thing the day they buried Audrey. "She isn't dead, but sleeping. Sleeping in the bosom of Abraham."

Two years ago her mother had gone on to sleep in the bosom of Abraham along with Audrey. After her mother's death, Katherine had wondered just how long it would be before her father went that way as well. Jonathan Simon had been as thin as a split rail and couldn't see the hand in front of his face. Most of the time he just sat on the front porch and stared straight ahead, as if his cloudy eyes could see the world crumbling in decay all around him. He had been doing just that the day he died, and the only thing that looked different when Katherine came in from chopping the Johnsongrass out of the corn, was the way his head slumped down between his shoulders. It had been a little over three weeks ago that they had buried him beside their mother, just a few feet from Billy and little

Audrey. Sometimes Katherine wondered if she would be buried there as well. What would her marker say? *More than likely, it will say: Katherine Simon, spinster,* a voice inside her head replied.

Of all the things in her past that haunted her, it was thoughts of Alex Mackinnon that filled her mind at night the most. Thoughts of how she had always loved him. Thoughts of how he loved her sister. Katherine Simon, spinster. It did have a familiar ring to it.

She was only six the first time she could really remember being drawn to Alex Mackinnon. It was the day the Mackinnon boys all returned home with their father to find their home burned and their mother and brother killed. The Simons had dropped by, offering the boys and their father John a place to stay while they rebuilt their house. Katherine could remember as vividly as if it were yesterday, the way Alex had looked that day when his pa had talked to hers. She remembered too, how John Mackinnon had backhanded Alex and knocked him to the ground when he saw the tears on his face. "Your ma is dead and it's time you acted like a man. Don't ever let me see you sniveling like a baby again." That was the last time she saw John Mackinnon, for he was scalped a few months later, leaving his boys orphaned.

After that, Alex seemed to have grown up overnight. It had always been a little bit strange to her, as she watched Alex and Adrian grow over the years, that it had been Adrian, not Alex, who had turned so cynical. Alex was anything but cynical. He had grown up with a grin on his face and a twinkle in his eye, and Katherine would go to her grave remembering the way Alex laughed; how he threw back his dark head and laughed, the sound of it rumbling up from somewhere deep within, rolling across the pastures like a clap of thunder. It was like no other laugh she had ever heard. She guessed if Alex had any faults at all, it was that infuriating habit he had of teasing girls until they screamed. "I don't know how you can stand him! He torments the daylights out of me," Karin had once told her, but the way she had said it sounded like having the daylights tormented out of her was something Karin rather looked forward to.

Since they were neighbors, the four of them, Katherine and Karin, Alex and Adrian had walked to and from school together. Since the day they had all come down with chicken pox at the same time, they had always looked upon that occasion as something quite special about their friendship, something that set them apart and made them unique. It was after they recovered that they had taken oaths to marry one another when they were grown. Only problem with that oath was, they hadn't been too specific as to just which Mackinnon married which Simon.

And for a while it didn't seem to matter.

Katherine and Alex had always held a special fondness for one another, feeling themselves linked by a bond that did not exist between Adrian or Karin. However, as time passed, Katherine began to feel Alex's pranks and capers were too irritating for words. "Stop pestering me!" she would shout to Alex as the four of them walked home. Her harsh words only caused him to pester her all the more, and soon he began teasing her about her freckles, telling everyone at school that she had swallowed a ten dollar gold piece and it broke out in pennies. One day she had had enough and clobbered him with her spelling book, and sat for a spell on the naughty stool in the corner. On more than one occasion she had refused to speak to him. Gradually he had stopped his teasing.

About the time Karin and Katherine had felt the first tingling of budding breasts, Katherine began to realize she wasn't feeling as much resentment toward Alex as she had been, and was ready to forgive and forget past injustices. She had given it much thought and decided to welcome his teasing again when she realized that Alex hadn't really stopped his teasing. He had simply stopped teasing her. The tricks, the pranks, the jokes he used to play on her, he was still playing—only now they were being played on Karin, and it appeared to Katherine that Karin didn't find it half as irritating as she had.

The first sting of rejection came when Katherine realized she had lost Alex to her sister. A thousand times she cursed herself for bringing that book down over Alex Mackinnon's head, and for driving him away. Yet it really wasn't a book slammed on top of his head that had made Alex take a sudden interest in Karin Simon.

Katherine rolled over in the bed and punched her pillow with a frustrated sigh. *What am I doing thinking about all of this? Like Karin said, you can't go back, so why torture yourself?* Katherine looked at the long shadows on her wall and knew the moon had climbed higher in the sky. It was growing late. She needed to sleep. Tomorrow was going to be another long hard day, when there would be too many chores for her to do and too little time to do them in. But the thoughts wouldn't go away. *What is wrong with me?* Why was she tormenting herself this way? She flopped over in her bed again and squeezed her eyes together tightly. It was no use. She could still see the white flash of Alex Mackinnon's smile as he rode by, his black horse thundering across the pasture toward the pecan grove that stood along the creek, the far-away melody of his laughter coming back to haunt her, carried by the wind.

It must have been a night not for sleeping, but for memories, for about the same time Katherine was tossing in her bed, Alexander Mackinnon sighed in his and rolled over, his hand coming out to grope for the lantern. Finding it, he raised the wick, filling the room with a dull golden glow. He looked at the bottle of whiskey, the empty glass, and wondered why he hadn't been able to drown his thoughts. He looked at the dark liquid in the bottle, the way the lamplight shimmered on the top. He recalled the way the sunlight danced like a thousand scattered spangles on the surface of Tehuacana Creek in the summertime. The glossy green leaves arched out over the water like a woman's parasol, filtering the sunlight that sparkled on the water's surface, sending shadows across Karin's milk-white skin.

Karin.

Her name whispered across his mind like a spring breeze heavy with the scent of woodbine, the memory of her coming with the force of a kick in the belly. How well he could see the Simon place, just as he'd seen it so many times before—just across Tehuacana Creek from the grove where his mother and brother Andrew were buried. How old were they when he and Adrian had begun wandering down to the grove, under the pretext of seeing after the graves, when all they wanted was to spy on the Simon place, hoping and praying they'd catch a glimpse of Katherine or Karin?

And one day that prayer had been answered. Lord preserve him. How well he could remember that particular afternoon when he'd caught more than a glimpse. Oh, he remembered all right—as if it were yesterday.

It was one of those hot, dry days that come, one after the other, during the long, scorching Texas summers. Katherine and Karin had been helping with the chores, Katherine doing laundry in a wooden tub on the back porch, while Karin was working the garden. When Karin finished chopping weeds, she gathered black-eyed peas, okra, summer squash, beets, and a few green onions, none of which were a particular bother, except the okra, which left her skin red and itching.

The back door banged behind her since her arms were too full to stop it. Her mother was stirring something in a pot that simmered on the stove and didn't bother to turn around. "Just put them on the table, angelkin."

"I washed them in Katherine's tub outside. You want me to cut anything up?"

"No. I'll see to them in a minute. Why don't you go look for your pa? Supper will be ready before too long."

Karin started out across the pasture intending to look for her pa, but her arms were itching and burning like fire from that okra, and the thought of washing them in the cool waters of the creek was just too tempting. She could always say she had looked for pa and simply couldn't find him.

She changed direction and headed for the dark fringe of trees that lined the creek. A minute later, she broke into a run, feeling as happy and carefree as any girl her age could feel. She had planned to run until she reached the cool strip of shade that followed the creek, but she had to stop when she got a stitch in her side. By that time she had decided she didn't want to run anyway. It was too hot, and she was breathing harder than a plow horse. Stopping to walk, she caught her breath, walking on, counting the number of steps to the creek. She had reached four hundred and thirty when she stepped into the shade. A bluejay scolded her noisily and she laughed, mocking his scolding chatter. Overhead a gust of wind rattled through the dark glossy leaves and the branches drooped gently, swaying the woodbine that trailed like long May-day streamers to the ground. As she walked, she pushed the trailing vines back to let herself pass, feeling like she had entered her own private hideaway as they closed behind her, looking as thick and matted as they had before she entered. In the shade, the ground was cool and covered with vines and rotting logs grown over with lichen, and near the tree trunks last year's leaves still lay moldering on the ground.

She reached the water and paused, thinking how quiet and still everything was. Overhead the sun was still shining through the arch of trees and all about her the sky was a clear, cloudless blue. Everywhere the world was still and cool and perfect as a picture. Even the surface of the water seemed subdued as it reflected the blue of the sky and the white brilliance of the sun in shimmering sparkles of light. The stillness was broken when a fish flipped out of the water, his silver sides flashing for a moment before he fell back and disappeared out of sight.

She stood for a moment looking at the water, then moved to its edge and began scrubbing her stinging arms with wet sand. As she rinsed them she spied a log that had fallen across the creek. The water in the middle of the creek was deeper and cooler and she decided to walk out there and bathe her feet that were blistering hot. She took off her shoes, then her stockings, leaving them on the bank. As she made her way across the log, she decided to dramatize the moment, closing her eyes and imagining herself to be the greatest ballerina in all of Russia. Balancing herself on one leg, she raised the other in a perfect point. She stayed in flawless balance for several seconds, enjoying the moment to the fullest. Then something happened that should never happen to any ballerina, and certainly not the greatest in all of Russia. She lost her balance. In a twinkling of a moment she felt herself falling through the air, having no time to prepare herself for the landing that was to follow.

She hit the water with a loud splash, a wall of silvery water rising high into the air all about her. The water closed over her face and she fought her way to the surface, realizing by the time she reached it, just how lovely the cool water felt.

Once she was in, she decided to stay in. She made her way to shallow water, where she could plant her feet firmly on the sand, and began removing her clothes. Each article she removed got a fair washing before she stood on her toes to drape it from the low-hanging branches that stretched out over the water. Normally, when the sisters were allowed to swim, they kept their undergarments on, but today, Karin decided not to. *Katherine wouldn't take all of her clothes off,* a voice said. *Who cares? Katherine is only fifteen.* Karin, who at sixteen was a year older than her sister, was feeling just a little daring. It was summertime, she was young and the world seemed to hold still just for her. She removed all her clothes, even down to the hair ribbon holding her long hair back with a bow at her nape. Once she was free of all her cumbersome clothes, Karin waded back to the deeper water, where she cavorted like a young seal, swimming and diving and floating on her back. She laughed and splashed water on a frog watching her from the opposite bank, and tossed a dead branch at a turtle that was swimming her way.

On the opposite bank, a dry-mouthed Alex watched, barely aware that his good fortune to see Karin like this was doing strange things to his body. Alex had never seen any more of a woman's body than her face and hands, and to catch a quick glimpse of water-slicked white skin now and then left him breathing hard. When Karin finished her swim and walked from the water, standing at the creek's edge while she sluiced the water from her body with her hands, Alex noticed another reaction his body was having, farther down. Watching her hands move with swanlike grace over her body, he thought he had never seen anything so beautiful. Everywhere he looked she was as smooth and white as satin, except for the pale twisted ropes of hair that hung down her back and the darker clustering of curls that glistened with droplets of water between her legs. He swallowed hard when she tossed her head, her breasts bouncing and drawing his eyes to the firm young points that looked as soft as a kitten's nose. He couldn't breathe. He couldn't speak. All he could do was watch.

Along the water's edge, the grass stopped growing, and as if drawn by the promise of moisture, a colorful blanket of flowers seemed to compete for the space. Standing in the shallows, Karin gathered a bouquet of red and yellow and white blossoms, adding sprigs of clover in bloom. She tossed a few clover blooms out into the water as well, and watched as they floated beneath the log and meandered around the bend and out of sight. As her eyes followed the tiny white blooms under the log, she saw the reflection of a face looking at her from the opposite shore. Her first thought was to cover herself and run, but something about the moment, the silent intrusion into her privacy, gave her a feeling of power. She had never held anyone's rapt, undivided attention before. It was a challenge to her to see just how long she could.

Turning toward the opposite bank, she knew she was giving the man an unobstructed view of everything he had come to watch. Something warm and intense throbbed low in her belly, and her eyes searched the dark foliage that grew along the opposite shore. Then she saw him, not just a man, but a man she knew. Alex Mackinnon. A moment later she turned and made her way back to the log to let the sun dry her hair.

As she lay there, pulling the silky strands of hair through her fingers, Alex thought she was the most beautiful creature he had ever laid eyes upon. And when she was dry and began to put her clothes on, he knew he could never love anyone like he loved Karin Simon.

CHAPTER THREE

It was a few weeks after the incident at the creek when Katherine Simon stood in front of her mirror giving herself a critical look. "I'm too short and too plump," she said, as she looked at her reflection even more critically than she had five seconds before.

Ellie Simon put her head through the door to see who her daughter was talking to. Just as she thought. Katherine was at it again. Talking to herself. Ellie stepped into the room. "You're too plump and short for what?" Ellie asked, giving her a quizzical look, fighting the urge to smile.

"For anything. I look like a toad. A speckled toad," Katherine added, reminded of her freckles. "Why can't I be thin like Karin? And born without freckles."

"Karin is a year older than you," Ellie said, wondering if she should remind Katherine she wasn't born with freckles either, that they had come along later. She decided against it. That would lead to another round of questions.

"Yes, and she was thin last year, and the year before that."

"You'll grow out of it."

"When?"

"Before too long."

"And these freckles?" she asked, pointing to her nose.

Ellie smiled, giving her a fond look. "Seven or eight freckles is hardly enough to be overly concerned about."

"Well, what about this neck?"

"What about it?"

"I don't have one!" Katherine wailed.

"Oh, Katherine. You have a neck. You most certainly do."

"No, I don't. See?" Katherine pulled the collar of her dress apart to emphasize her point. She even went so far as to stretch her neck. "You see? I was right. There is no neck here. My head is sitting on top of my shoulders. I'll probably go through life being called 'No neck Simon.' "

Ellie clucked her tongue. "Shame on you, Katherine," she said, wagging her finger at her. "You shouldn't poke fun at yourself."

"I suppose you're right," Katherine said morosely. "I should let everyone else call me 'No neck Simon.' "

"Has anyone called you that?"

"No, but they will."

Ellie laughed. "I hope the Good Lord isn't listening to you right now. What would He think?"

"He'd probably agree with everything I'm saying."

"Oh, Katherine," protested her mother. "Honestly, I think you're just looking for something wrong. You have a neck. You have a lovely face. Your figure will come. Right now you're between stages, no longer a little girl, but not quite a woman."

Katherine groaned. "What if I'm stuck there? What if I never become a woman?"

Ellie's laugh was a little heartier this time, and her words a bit more understanding. "You'll become a woman whether you want to or not. That's one thing you can't stop."

"Who's trying to stop it? I'd give my three favorite peacock feathers to hurry it along."

Ellie watched Katherine step away from the mirror, over her hastily discarded night-gown, past her unmade bed, stepping over the dress she wore yesterday, to stop and pick up one of her precious peacock feathers that had fallen from behind the crosshatched picture over her bed. She leaned over the bed and placed the feather in its proper place along-side the other two.

Ellie sighed and gave Katherine a fond look. Her daughters were only a year apart in age, but a decade apart in womanly things. Ellie watched Katherine slump on her bed, her hand coming to rest on the bedside table where an opened book lay. She touched that book as if the words could be absorbed through her fingertips. And perhaps they were. Perhaps they went straight into her blood and flowed directly to her heart, for everything about Katherine seemed to come from the heart. And that is where the greatest difference between Katherine and Karin lay. Katherine had a depth and sensitivity that Ellie feared Karin would never possess. While Katherine knew the plot of every classic by heart and could quote poetry or scripture until the cows came home, she had not the faintest inkling about fashion, and showed no interest in learning. She could grow anything, knew every flower by a dozen names, as well as its history, and she had a way with animals and people, not to mention the fact that she could cook circles around half the women in the county. But when it came to knowledge about women's clothing, Ellie had to agree with Katherine. It did indeed look rather hopeless. "Grow where you are planted, Katherine," was the only advice she had to give.

"Wonderful," Katherine said, throwing up her hands in disgust. "I could be one of those beans that sprout on the outhouse floor and all my mother says is, 'Grow where you are planted.'" She went on to add, "Why couldn't I sprout in a rich man's garden like Karin?"

"Karin isn't any richer than you are."

"Oh, but she is. She is. She always looks like she is rolling in money."

Once again, Ellie was inclined to agree with Katherine.

Money for the Simons was scarce as hen's teeth, but Karin always managed to look like a rich man's daughter. She worked hard, but where Katherine was always spending her money to buy something for a friend or member of the family, Karin was frugal and saved her money, using it to buy fabric and notions for a new dress from time to time. When

Karin got a new dress, she took care of it. She took care of all her things. Ellie looked around Katherine's tumble-down room. Across the hall, Karin's room was neat as wax. Ellie let her eyes rest on Katherine. There she stood, in a dress that wasn't very old at all, but she had worn it when she should have saved it, and now it was soiled and tattered, looking much older than it actually was.

In spite of these differences, Katherine didn't have a thing to worry about as far as her mother could see. More than once Ellie had scolded Katherine and told her, "You should never be jealous of Karin. You have too many lovely things about you to ever be jealous of anyone. And don't forget what it says in the Song of Solomon: 'Love is strong as death; jealousy is cruel as the grave.' "

"And it says in the Book of John that 'the truth will set you free.' "

Ellie knew when she was whipped. She knew better than to get into a quoting battle with Katherine, for in truth Ellie knew she wasn't as well armed as her daughter when it came to that. Wisdom was a mother's strongest ally. Ellie decided she would be better off if she stuck to that. "If you want to quote scripture, how about: 'heed the wisdom of your mother'?"

That closed Katherine's mouth. At least for the time being.

Watching her daughters grow to maturity, Ellie saw early on that Katherine was the kind of girl that was slow coming into womanhood, while Karin seemed to reach it overnight. She looked at Katherine's stocky form, the straight torso with hardly any indention for a waist, the small breasts, the softly rounded hips. Then she looked at her face.

Of course every mother crow thought her baby crow to be the blackest, but Ellie Simon couldn't find any fault with that face that looked back at her so earnestly. Katherine had huge green eyes that were almost hidden beneath a thick fringe of lashes. And her freckles were the same color as her rich mahogany hair. Right now that hair was braided rather haphazardly, but when she was older and realized how blessed she was to have such thick, shiny hair, she wold learn to fix it in something besides sloppily done braids.

Katherine saw her mother was giving her the once over. "I know I look like the back end of hard times and you have every right to be ashamed of me. Next to Karin, I must be a terrible disappointment." She dropped her head in her hands, looking like the picture of hopeless despair. "What mother wants to hatch one graceful swan and one mud hen?" Lifting her head a bit she looked dejectedly at her mother. "See? You're laughing." Then to the ceiling she said, "How's that? My own mother laughs at me. I am a mud hen! I knew it. I knew it."

"Oh, Katherine, for heaven's sake. I'm not laughing *at* you, but at what you said. Honestly, you'd make a marble statue laugh. You've never been a disappointment since the day you were born. You will be a beautiful woman one day, and don't you ever forget your mother was the first person to tell you that."

Katherine couldn't fathom that. Beautiful? *Me?* How could anyone expect a person with frog-green eyes, hair the color of saddle leather, no neck, and a nose with more speckles than a robin's egg would turn out to be anything but ugly? And on top of all that, God seemed to have forgotten that there were *certain* things that identified a woman right off that should be making their appearance about now. Did the Good Lord intend for her to have a bosom or didn't He? And if He did, just where in the world was it?

Her mother understood what was going through Katherine's mind. And not just because she was an understanding sort, which she was. No, it was more that Katherine reminded her so much of herself at that age, for Ellie had been as awkward as a newborn colt and as homely as they came at Katherine's age. She had told Katherine that before and it didn't seem to help. Far as she could see, it wouldn't be listened to any better the second time around.

"Where is Karin?" Ellie asked, hoping to get Katherine's mind off her looks and lure her attention to something else. "I found that bit of lace she was looking for."

"Karin is doing what she always does. She is outside making a fool of herself over Alex Mackinnon."

Ellie groaned. She had lured in the wrong

direction. *Just where is all this wisdom I'm supposed to be having?*

"Honestly," Katherine went on, "I've never seen two people who see each other every day act like they've been separated for years. What could they possibly find to talk about for so long? Karin doesn't even know enough words to talk more than ten minutes." She sighed wistfully. "It must be terribly boring for an intelligent person like Alex Mackinnon to sit there hour after hour listening to Karin recite the same trivia over and over. You'd think he'd welcome a change and a challenge."

An understanding smile stretched across Ellie's face. "Now, don't you go criticizing too strongly, Miss Vocabulary. You'll be making a fool of yourself over some young man before too long, or I'll miss my guess. I've seen the way Adrian looks at you. He'd be making a fool out of himself too—if you'd only give him the slightest bit of encouragement."

"Adrian!" Katherine exclaimed. "I wouldn't give Adrian all the hay he could eat!" Seeing that hadn't had much effect upon her mother, she added, "Mother, Adrian is past boring."

"I don't understand that. He's smart as a whip. And I think he's an adorable boy."

"Then you talk to him!" Katherine said and stomped from the room.

Ellie shook her head, as if to say she saw Katherine had a tough row to hoe ahead of her. How much simpler things would be if Katherine would just fancy Adrian instead of Alex. But the heart had its reasons, although reason, she well knew, played a very small part.

"Adrian!" Katherine said with a snort, hitching her skirts up and throwing her leg over the bannister to slide down, still fuming when she hit the bottom. "I'd sooner be sweet on papa's mule as Adrian Mackinnon." Adrian might be Alex's twin, but the two of them didn't look anything alike, and even if they had been born identical, she would still love Alex. And that was the gospel truth, for as much as Katherine adored Alex, she ignored Adrian. Whenever she was around Adrian, she was as cool as a February wind, in no way thawed by Adrian's fond intent or his desire to please her.

Katherine went down to the barn, ignoring her cat to sit on an overturned bucket. But the cat was persistent. The third time she wound herself around Katherine's legs, Katherine sighed and said, "Okay, you win," and plopped Georgia on her lap. *Alex and Karin. Karin and Alex.* Sometimes all of that was downright nauseating. Just how much was a body supposed to tolerate anyway? The two of them acted like they were joined at the hip, or at least that they were the only two people in the world. It wasn't fair. Hadn't she considered herself in love with Alex Mackinnon for as long as she could remember—way before Karin paid him any mind at all? And what in the blue blazes made Alex so silly over Karin? It was she, Katherine Simon, that Alex used to pay attention to. Didn't he tease her about her freckles? And didn't he put a garter snake in her paint box? But as time passed and she grew older, her woman's intuition grew as well. It was a crushing blow to realize Alex considered her nothing more than his friend.

Katherine looked up to see Adrian walk into the barn, the sunlight tinting his brown hair with the reddest gold. That was another thing she didn't like about Adrian. His hair was too close to the color of her own. Of course he didn't have her green eyes. And he didn't have Alex's pale blue ones either. Katherine decided then and there that she didn't particularly care for dark blue eyes either.

"Hello," he said. "Your ma said I'd find you in here." Adrian stopped a few feet from her and looked at the face that played such havoc with his heart.

"As you can see, my ma was right."

"What are you doing?"

"Honestly, Adrian," she said with teeth-gritting irritation that dripped from every overstressed syllable, "even *you* should be able to see that I am holding the cat."

Adrian thrust his hands deeper into his pockets, not understanding her at all. He had come looking for Katherine because he wanted to visit and you can't visit properly when the person you want to visit with won't visit back. "I don't suppose you'd want to go for a walk down to the creek. There are lots of pecans on the ground."

"Whatever for? Mother has had me gathering pecans all week. That is *work*, Adrian. *W-o-r-k*.

Besides, I just gathered pecans this morning. Now, what makes you think I'd want to traipse down to the creek to gather more?"

"Oh," he said, looking a bit unsettled. "Well, I guess I'll be going on home, then."

"All right."

"Bye, Katherine."

"Good-bye, Adrian."

Adrian ran into Ellie hanging out clothes in the backyard. "Did you find Katherine?"

"Yes, ma'am. She was in the barn, like you said."

"Did you have a nice visit?"

"Not especially."

"Was Katherine rude to you, Adrian?"

"No, ma'am."

Ellie breathed a sigh of relief.

"But she wasn't very friendly."

"Oh, dear," Ellie said.

"That's all right, Miz Simon."

"Honestly, I don't know what's come over that girl of late. Cross as crabs, she is, without a kind word to say to anybody." She watched Adrian walk toward his horse. "I'm awful sorry, Adrian."

"Thank you, ma'am." Adrian mounted his horse and rode away. Ellie watched him for a spell then shook her head and went back to hanging out her laundry. A short while later Katherine came out of the barn. Ellie looked up just in time to see her walking her way. "Why such a long face?" Ellie asked.

Katherine gave a mournful sigh, one that sounded somewhere between pining and lost hope. "It's because of Alex. No one will ever understand how much I love him. I don't think I was ever destined to be happy. I know he will ask Karin to marry him and they'll probably live right across the creek for the rest of their lives and raise a dozen sons and daughters. And what about me? I'll be an old maid, for I'll never love anyone as I love Alex." Her expression turned even more forlorn. "I can see it all now. They'll even ask me to be in the wedding and I'll have to walk behind Karin and carry her veil, smiling at the people on each side of the aisle, never allowing them to see that beneath my new bridesmaid dress there is the brokenest of hearts."

"Is *brokenest* a word?"

"I am taking poetic liberty, Mother. Most broken heart just doesn't have the right flow to it. When you are speaking of a broken heart it is imperative that the words flow."

"Oh, I see." Ellie had to hand it to Katherine. She had a sense of the dramatic and a flair for drama that any actor would covet. She quickly picked up a tablecloth and began spreading it out to dry, hoping it would hide the spasm of twitching that had suddenly seized her face. But it didn't help. Thankful that Katherine didn't tarry long after her eloquent speech, Ellie buried her face into the tablecloth and laughed so hard she developed a serious case of the hiccups that lasted four hours.

It was her own fault, Ellie supposed, for she had always encouraged her daughters to talk about things. Katherine was by far the most responsive, the real talker in the family, and hearing Katherine go on and on, Ellie would often lay her mending aside to muffle a cough she faked to hide her smile. Whenever Katherine got on one of her soapboxes about one issue or the other, Ellie would sometimes take the opposite position, just to offer her a challenge. It got to be a sort of game between the two of them—Katherine making a point; her mother challenging it, then Katherine would plunge ahead, giving a multitude of reasons and even more quotes of why she was right to feel the way she did, knowing all the while that the more determined she became, the more her mother enjoyed it.

It was much the same between Karin and their father, for he was as close to her as Ellie was to Katherine. As she grew older, Katherine would often find herself imagining what it was like in her parents' room at night. She could almost hear her father say, "That Karin, she's a real little princess. I'm glad she's not the wild ragamuffin Katherine is." And her mother's reply, "But Katherine has a wise and loving heart and a strong spirit." But most of all, they were both loved by their parents, Katherine soaking it up like sunshine that made her grow straight and strong, Karin looking on it as more of a blessing that made her feel special and set her apart.

It was only a few days later that Katherine lay across Karin's bed watching her dress. She was trying to figure out just why it was that

Karin always looked so neat and lovely, and why she always looked like a flag forgotten on the pole outside the post office during a windstorm. She watched Karin put on her yellow muslin dress and patiently button the row of tiny buttons that ran down the back. Katherine sighed. She didn't have the patience to button that many buttons, especially when she considered that in a few hours she'd have to *unbutton* them all again. *All this fuss getting dressed when she has to know she'll just be taking everything off in a few hours. It just doesn't make any sense.*

Katherine wrinkled her nose as she watched Karin move to stand in front of her mirror and brush her hair one hundred strokes. Katherine was betting she didn't give her hair a total of one hundred strokes in two weeks. It was a wonder Karin's hair didn't fall out and leave her head as bald as a plucked chicken. But there it was, going up on top of her head, as perfect and shiny as a spinning top.

"Do I look all right?" Karin asked, whirling around, a look on her face that told Katherine she knew she looked beautiful and was dying for Katherine to tell her so.

"Yes, and you well know it."

"Don't be such a crab," Karin said, picking up her parasol. " 'If you can't say something nice...' "

" 'Don't say anything at all,' " Katherine finished in a mimicking tone.

Without another word, Karin hurried from the room.

Katherine waited until she left, then made a face and did her best to sound like Karin, " 'Don't be such a crab.' Bah!" For a while she lay where she was, her eyes moving around Karin's room. How did Karin keep her room so neat and clean while hers always looked like a storm had just blown through? She grimaced and rolled over. One of the five dresses Karin had tried on fell to the floor. Draping herself over the side of the bed and coming to her feet, she picked the dress up and almost tossed it back to the bed when she held it up in front of her. Maybe she would look as pretty as Karin, if she put on her dress.

Katherine had a quick vision of Karin throttling her.

She put the dress on, giving a few of the buttons down the back a go, and then tying the sash. She moved to the mirror and brushed her hair, intending to go all the way to one hundred, but when she reached twenty, her arm gave out, so she stopped. After four or five tries, she had her hair on top of her head and jabbed full of Karin's pins, but it didn't look quite as good as Karin's, resembling more a wind-blown haystack than a shiny new spinning top. She tilted her head to one side. The knot of hair slid that way as well. Katherine shoved the knot back in place and studied herself critically. She had done everything she had seen Karin do. Why didn't she look as pretty?

A few minutes later she went downstairs to find her mother. Maybe she could tell her just what she had done wrong. Her mind on finding her mother, she didn't notice as she walked by the parlor that Alex and Karin were there, sitting at the piano. And why should she have noticed. Pianos were for playing, and if a body wasn't going to play the piano, they ought not be sitting on the piano bench. There were chairs for that. As she passed she heard Karin's shriek of laughter. "Oh, this is too much," Karin said, laughing. Then, between gasps for breath, she said, "Alex, will you look at that?"

Alex looked up and grinned. Katherine was a mess. Her dress was way too short, and a tad small. The pale pink color was horrid on her, and the back was misbuttoned—at least where it was buttoned—and the sash was trailing the floor behind her. And her hair! What on earth had she done to it? It looked like she'd been caught in an updraft. Either that or someone had hit her in the head with a cow pattie. But in spite of the sight she presented, Alex liked Katherine and he didn't have the heart to laugh at her. For a few seconds her eyes met his and held. Although he didn't say anything, Katherine knew he was telling her that their friendship was something special and secret.

But that didn't make any difference at a time like this as far as Katherine was concerned. To have her sister ridicule her like she was, and knowing Alex was privy to that was the same as if Alex had laughed his fool head off. Her face red with humiliation, Katherine whirled and ran up the stairs.

"You shouldn't embarrass her like that," Alex said.

"Then she shouldn't go traipsing around like someone just fired her from a gun." Karin thumped a crumb from her skirt. "Besides, she won't be upset for long. She never is."

"She won't? I've always thought Katherine stayed mad longer than anyone I knew. I think she's still mad at me for putting that snake in her paint box."

"Oh fiddle! She just wants you to think that. Actually she likes to pretend she's mad just so she'll get attention."

Alex frowned. "Humiliating someone isn't giving them attention. I don't think..."

This was starting to get Alex's attention off of her and onto her sister, so she gave Alex a gentle whack with her fan. "Hush up, Alex. You don't know my sister like I do, and what's worse, you are ignoring me."

Alex gave her a blank look, but he hushed up.

"Now," Karin said, "where were we?"

Looking down into Karin's beautiful blue eyes, Alex gave her a smile that Katherine would have given two years of her life to see bestowed upon herself. "You may know Katherine better than I do, but I like her and I hate to see her hurt."

That sent Karin into a pout. "Will you stop all this palaver about Katherine? Heaven knows why you're always so eager to champion her cause," she said. "She's always making a fool of herself in front of you and we both know the reason why. She'd give her eyeteeth to have you for a beau."

"I'm not championing her cause. I just don't like to see anyone hurt and embarrassed. And I think you're wrong about Katherine having heart flutters over me. We're friends, that's all."

"You go on thinking that, Alexander Mackinnon. You go right on. Don't bother to listen to me when I tell you Katherine is smitten over you and would do anything in the world she could to have you." She whacked him again with her fan. "One of these days you'll see I was right."

Deep in his heart Alex knew of Katherine's fondness for him, and more often than not, she did make that known to the point of embarrassing herself and him. At first he had found her pestiferous ways quite irritating, for she did have a tendency to show up at the most inopportune times, and she frequently stalked him with all the finesse of a Comanche hot on the trail of a stray steer. But of late his feelings about her childish adoration had changed from irritation to amusement. She was just so damn comical in the ways she went about it that he couldn't help harboring a fondness for her.

Only last week she had gotten some nasty rope burns on her hands trying to reach the hayloft by climbing up the rope so she could spy on him and Karin. And a week or so before that he and Karin had sneaked off to the pecan grove, and he had been about to put his hand on Karin's breast when a branch overhead groaned suspiciously. Looking up he had seen those familiar green eyes staring down at him. Grabbing her by the ankle, he gave her a yank that sent her tumbling into his arms. He carried her to the path and set her on her feet none too gently, telling her he would give her dainty little posterior a good dusting if he ever caught her spying again.

Since that day, she had stopped her spying, but she seemed to have taken up a new crusade in its absence. Now she seemed determined to make him notice her whenever possible, sometimes intentionally and sometimes not—like today. Katherine had always been smart as a treeful of owls, but she had never bested him at school—at least not until three weeks ago. He had smugly assumed that to be because she couldn't. But now he wasn't so sure. Over the past few weeks she had bested him in the spelling bee, been responsible for his essay taking second place to her first, and had driven him to his chair in defeat when she finished her sums a good five minutes before he did. When Karin made a cake, Katherine baked a cake and a pie. When he took Karin riding, there went Katherine streaking by them, riding like someone had set her horse's tail afire. When Karin took him to help her gather wildflowers for the dinner table, Katherine showed up at the house ahead of them with enough flowers in her arms to put flowers on every table in Limestone County. On and on it went, the list growing longer every day, until Alex found he was actually looking forward to seeing just what Katherine would do next.

Alex wasn't the only one of the Mackinnon brothers that was waiting on Katherine. But instead of waiting to see what Katherine would do to win Alex's favor next, his brother Adrian was waiting to see when she would come to her senses and fall out of her state of infatuation with his brother. And that presented a problem for Adrian, because being Alex's twin, the brothers had always been very close. But now Adrian could no longer talk to Alex, at least not with the same ease and frankness he had always been able to employ in the past. The truth of the matter was that Adrian resented Alex, partly because of Katherine's attachment to him, and partly because of Adrian's fondness for Katherine, both of which Alex was aware of and had never missed a chance to tease his brother about.

"My little twin is in love," Alex said to Karin one afternoon as they walked toward her house from the creek. He had just looked up to catch sight of Adrian leaning against the fence. Even from where he was, Alex could see Adrian was watching Katherine bring the milk cows up from the pasture.

When Alex and Karin stopped beside Adrian, Alex let out an exaggerated sigh and said, "Adrian is in love and hankering from afar." He glanced at Katherine, then back at Adrian. "Why don't you hop on over that fence and help her with the cows?"

"Shut up, Alex," said Adrian.

Alex laughed and turned to Karin. "Wouldn't

you like to have that sweet face looking at you like that?" He gave Adrian's face a pat.

Adrian slapped his hand away. "Alex, I'm warning you."

Karin stepped closer and gave Adrian the once over, patting his face as Alex had done. "He does have a sweet face, doesn't he?"

Adrian clenched his jaw, feeling his fists itch with the desire to smash Alex's pretty face. Instead, he turned quickly away from the fence, knowing, even as he turned, that there was something deeper here than just brotherly teasing. Alex seemed angry at him.

"Oh, do look, Adrian. I've made Alex jealous."

Adrian turned back, as Karin spoke to him. "Do you think I should ask his permission before I pat your sweet face?" Karin's tone wasn't as gentle and teasing as before. Adrian didn't say anything, but Alex did.

"Why don't you behave yourself?" Alex lashed back at her.

"Why should I? You aren't." She saw Alex's face getting redder and redder. "Don't tell me you're afraid Adrian might show some interest in me?"

"My brother has more sense than that," Alex said angrily, then stomped off.

Karin came over to where Adrian was standing. "I really do think you have a sweet face, Adrian. To be Alex's twin, you two really don't look anything alike."

"We aren't that kind of twins." His voice was not cordial in the least. He did not like Karin and she knew it.

"Adrian, don't be angry at me."

"I'm not."

"Thank you, sweet Adrian."

Adrian didn't get a chance to say anything else. Karin leaned toward him and kissed him softly on the lips. "Why waste your time wishing for something you can never have? It's your brother she wants, can't you see that?"

"I've got eyes," he said hatefully.

"Darling Adrian, don't be cross. It doesn't become you." She gave his cheek another pat.

Adrian slapped her hand away, then turned, giving her his back.

After she left, Adrian looked out across the pasture, seeing Katherine was looking at something. It didn't take long to figure out what. At the crest of a gently sloping hill he could see Alex staring off into the distance, his hands rammed into his pockets, completely unaware that Katherine was looking at him with such longing in her eyes.

Adrian was never able to understand why Alex couldn't see how selfish and spoiled Karin was in comparison with Katherine's gentle and compassionate nature. Adrian guessed it was always the fate of the younger sibling to get the short end of the stick, for that seemed to be the fate he and Katherine were resigned to.

He watched Katherine until Alex had disappeared from sight and Katherine stooped to pull a flower, inhaling its sweet scent. He saw her close her eyes and wrap her arms around her middle as if she were hopelessly in love.

As Adrian turned and walked away Karin's words kept sounding in his head. *To be Alex's twin, you two really don't look anything alike.*

That was one of the few things Karin had ever said that Adrian agreed with. He and his brother were not identical, nor were they anything alike. They didn't look alike, think alike, or react alike. In fact, about the only likeness to be found was in their build and their love for fighting. They were both strong and stubborn, both wanting their own way, and that was a constant source of irritation and friction between them. Of the two, Alex was the gentler, more easygoing brother, while Adrian was too cynical for his own good and prone to be rather opinionated. He was a bit of a perfectionist in comparison with Alex's sometimes sloppy disregard for the things around him. But the biggest source of annoyance for Adrian was the fact that he was born a few minutes after Alex. He went through life feeling Alex had a distinct advantage over him.

Needless to say, most of their disagreements weren't settled verbally. It had taken a strong father and older brothers to keep the two from killing each other in the all-too-frequent fights they had had when they were younger. After their father John and older brother Andrew were killed, the twins were held in check by the remaining three brothers, Nicholas, Tavis, and Ross. Strangely enough, in spite of the constant bickering and fighting between them, they were fiercely loyal and close to one another. If they had thought about having a motto, it would have been: "I can do it to my brother, but nobody else can."

As time had passed, the friction, the tendency for the twins to disagree violently was still there, but the number of fist fights diminished. Alex and Adrian still found themselves locked in frequent battles, but usually of a nature that could be settled by talking, with a good fist fight thrown in every now and then—if for no other reason than to just clear the air.

But today Adrian wasn't feeling like talking. For weeks his ire had been rising toward Alex and some things needed settling. It had been quite a spell since they'd had a fight and cleaned the slate, and on top of that, fighting had gotten to be such a habit with him and Alex that he couldn't conceive not having one every now and then.

Early the next afternoon, Alex, having finished his chores, was riding over to the Simon place when he saw someone standing all alone in the middle of the pasture. From this distance he couldn't tell if it was Karin or Katherine, but figured it had to be one or the other. He turned his horse in the woman's direction. When he drew close enough to speak, he didn't, for there was something about the way Katherine was standing there looking like the tight bud of a four o'clock before the flower opens in the late afternoon. Something was wrong.

He rode closer, and dismounting, spoke her name. "Katherine?"

She was turned away from him, but he could tell by the way her body was all hunched forward that she had been crying. Seeing her like this, with the sun so brilliant all about her, she seemed no more than a vapor, a fairy spirit that guarded this particular pasture. "Katherine?" he called again and stepped to her side. He saw then what had caused her distress. Lying before her like a crushed petal was a fawn, its huge brown eyes open and starting to cloud, a gaping hole just behind one ear where the blood had already dried.

"Why?" she sobbed. "Why would anyone shoot a fawn?"

He put his arm around her shoulders and drew her against him, feeling surprised that she wasn't as hefty as he expected. In truth, she was more narrow in the shoulders than Karin. He looked down at the gleaming head, not red and not really brown, but a color that lay somewhere in between. Another thought struck him: Karin would have never noticed a dead fawn in the pasture, much less paused to grieve over it. "Don't cry, Kath. It won't do the fawn any good."

"I know, but it's so little. See? It still has its spots. Why would anyone kill it?"

"Maybe something happened to the mother and they killed it to keep it from being orphaned." He began looking around, then spying an area not too far away where the grass had been trampled, he took her hand. "Come on."

He pulled her along with him like a child would pull a toy on a string, and she followed just as silently. "See?" he said, pointing.

She followed with her eyes. "Blood."

"Quite a bit of it. See, here's where it came down. Then it was pulled over here. There are tracks here. Two horses. And the marks of a man's boot. He must have killed it then loaded it on the other horse here."

"A deer?"

"Probably a doe. He must have discovered the fawn in the grass where she'd left it hidden." His arm came around her. "Poor Kath, don't take on so. It was a mercy killing. The hunter didn't want the fawn to slowly starve to death."

"It was murder!" she sobbed against his shirt.

"After you've had time to think on it, you'll feel differently."

She pulled back and looked at him, the sight wrenching his heart. "No, I won't. I won't ever forget the way it looked, Alex. It was so sm-sm-small." Her tears were coming harder now, running down her wet face in great droplets and splashing on his hand. He drew her closer, feeling her shoulders shake, the trembling that overtook her. He dropped his chin on the top of her head and began rubbing her back.

He had been rubbing for some time when he realized she had stopped crying. For the briefest moment he felt reluctant to let her go. There had always been this strange bond between them, a closeness he couldn't explain. There were times he almost felt like he was one side of a coin and Katherine was the other side, but that sounded so idiotic that he would dismiss the idea as soon as it came. It was Karin he loved. But he did have a strong feeling of some unexplainable sort for Katherine. Drawing back and cupping her chin with his hand to lift her tear-streaked face, he wiped the tears with his thumb. "Better?"

"Not better," she said with a shaky voice. "Just all cried out."

He laughed and gave her a quick kiss on the head. "Tell you what. Why don't you ride Tarnation on over to your house. I'll just take my shovel," he said, removing the small spade from his saddle. "I'll give that little friend of yours a decent burial, then I'll come on."

"I can walk."

"I know you can," he said, dropping the spade and sweeping Katherine up into his arms. He carried her to his horse and put her in the saddle, handing the reins to her. She started to say something, but he gave Tarnation a swat. "Go on, now."

He watched her lope across the pasture on Tarnation. He remembered the day Tarnation was born. Katherine had been there and the two of them had wiped the jet black colt dry. "I want you to name him," he had said to her, but before she could answer, Karin walked in, wedging herself between them.

"I've got to go," Katherine said, rising to her feet.

"What about a name?" Alex asked.

"You can name him Tarnation, for all I care!" Katherine said hatefully, and left the barn.

Alex had done just that.

Now, he was shaking his head as he watched her and the black gelding go over a hill and out of sight. Then he turned and picked up the spade, walking back toward the place where the fawn lay. He saw Adrian coming toward him.

"That was touching. What were you doing, rehearsing for *Romeo and Juliet*?"

"Ease up, Adrian. I'm not in the mood for your cynicism."

"What are you in the mood for? Pawing one sister while you're bedding the other one?"

"What's gotten into you? I wasn't pawing anyone, and what I do with Karin is my own damn business, but I haven't bedded her."

"Just keep your filthy hands off Katherine. She's not like Karin. She's decent."

"Is that what's eating you? Because all you know is *decent* women? You know what I think? I think you're as randy as a seasoned buck, but you don't know how to go about getting any woman to ease it for you. Why don't you go into town like I do?" He shrugged. "It's your choice. But if you choose not to, don't go around taking your troubles out on me. I'm—"

Alex never got to finish that sentence, for

Adrian's fist came out of nowhere to crack his jaw, driving him to his knees. "Okay. Okay," Alex said, coming to his feet and wiping the thin trickle of blood from his mouth with the back of his hand. "You've been itching for a fight for weeks. We might as well get this over with."

Adrian cracked the other side of his jaw. This time Alex didn't say anything. He simply dove at Adrian, locking his arms around Adrian's knees and sending them both to the ground.

An hour later they buried the fawn as well as their battered bodies would allow and hobbled down to the creek and fell in, clothes and all, both of them covered with blood and caked dirt, aching in places they didn't know they had, their mouths too swollen to talk, their bodies too weary to want to. For over an hour they had simply lain there, in the shallows of Tehuacana Creek, letting the cool water ease their soreness.

When they finally headed for home, their older brother Nicholas was driving the last nail into a shoe he was putting on his horse and he saw them coming. Giving the shoe one last tap, he dropped the mare's foot and led her into the paddock. "Looks like I'll have to see to that brushing tomorrow," he said, giving the mare a scratch between the ears. Then he turned and walked toward the house, reaching it just about the same time Adrian and Alex did.

Taking one look at them, Nicholas threw back

his head and laughed. "What was it this time? Did you run into a tree?"

"Shut up, Nick," they said in unison, hobbling into the house and slamming the door against the sound of Nick's rolling laughter.

Little did they know then, as they slammed that door that day, that it would be the last time they heard Nick laugh.

But it was. A few days later, the two oldest brothers, Nick and Tavis, announced they were leaving.

"Leaving? You mean leaving here? Our home? Leaving us?" Adrian asked.

"Where are you going?" asked Alex.

"Nantucket, to look up Ma's brother Robert," Nick said. "I've always had a fondness for the sea."

"You've never even seen the sea," Alex said. "How can you have a fondness for it?"

"I've never seen God either."

"Uncle Robbie? You're going to live with Uncle Robbie?" asked Adrian. "How will you get there? You don't have any money."

"If we waited until we had money, we'd be too old to go," Tavis said.

And Tavis was right.

After the deaths of their mother and father, things hadn't been easy for the Mackinnon brothers. Poverty has a cruel set of standards which tends to be inflexible. Another bad thing about poverty, although not contagious, it tends to prove long lasting and eventually fatal. And like some life-threatening illness, once poverty struck, one rarely recovered from it. And so it was with the Mackinnon brothers.

Little by little they had been forced to sell parcel after parcel of their land, until there wasn't much of the original farmland left. It had become a way of life for them to eke out an existence, harvesting just enough good crops to cancel out the bad ones, raising a few horses, butchering a few beefs, but nothing more than just getting by. But for five young, strapping men who were chomping at the bit to see if life had more to offer them, this wasn't enough. After struggling for years to make a go of the farm, one by one the brothers began to realize the futility of it all, and they began to drift away.

Nicholas and Tavis were the first to go, leaving for Nantucket and the home of their mother's brother to pursue their lifelong interest in shipbuilding and the sea. Before he left, Nicholas was invited to Scotland to inherit a title from their father's recently deceased brother. Nick turned it down flat, then said to Tavis, "I guess you're next in line. Do you want to go?"

"Nope," was Tavis's reply.

"Ross?" they both said in unison, then remembering that Ross was the most heathen of the lot, and trying to visualize him as a Scottish lord they fell against one another laughing and said, in unison once again, "Not Ross."

So Nicholas sat down and penned a letter back to Scotland, declining for himself and informing their kinsmen that he had already asked the next youngest, Tavis, who declined as well. As an afterthought, he added, "You'll have to find someone else, as our other brother Ross has other fish to fry, and neither of the twins would take to the task without the other one."

Not long after Nick and Tavis left, Alex and Adrian were forced to face reality. If their brothers couldn't make a go at farming, they couldn't either. It was time to call it quits. A hitch in the Texas Rangers seemed the only choice since troops were needed to patrol the border along the Rio Grande between Texas and Mexico—a border plagued by unrest that eventually led to a declaration of war.

It was some time after Adrian and Alex signed up for a hitch in the Rangers that another letter came from Scotland. This time the offer was for Ross, and Ross, having nothing better to do, and having a marriage-minded woman with an irate papa on his back, accepted. He left immediately, which the neighbors thought was a good idea, since they personally knew of two weddings in two different counties being planned by papas who thought they had Ross backed into a corner.

"When the nest is on fire, a wise bird takes flight," Ross had often said to his brothers. His brothers thought Ross wise beyond his years.

The following Sunday, the minister heard Ross Mackinnon had left for Scotland. His only comment was, "I have heard it is possible for a wild colt to become a sober horse. I pray that will be the case with Brother Mackinnon. Perish the thought that we should end up going to war with Scotland when they realize what we've sent them."

CHAPTER FOUR

It had been almost four years to the day since Alex and Adrian had ridden away from Limestone County. A lot of things can happen to a man in four years. Things that change him. Things that make him grow up overnight. It even happens sometimes that some time away can make a man forget, but that didn't happen to Alexander Mackinnon. A few months with the Rangers and a hitch in the army had not dulled his feelings for Karin Simon, far from it. A lock of her golden hair, that he had taken the night before he left, had been a constant reminder of the fair-haired lass he had left behind, but had not forgotten.

The sun was hot upon his shoulders, the warm midday breezes cool upon his brow as Alex rode up the road toward the old Mackinnon homestead. Adrian rode up next to him, easing his horse into a slower gait. Like Alex, he let his body roll along with the rhythm of his horse, his thoughts focused on what lay just ahead. "It seems like it's been longer than four years, doesn't it?" Adrian said at last.

Alex nodded, watching Adrian lean over and

spit in the Johnsongrass that was as high as the belly of a horse. Adrian had taken up the habit of chewing tobacco during the war, something that Alex found irritating as all get out, although he couldn't say just why that was. Like Adrian said, it wasn't causing him any pain, but Alex found it as galling as watching someone rub his belly and belch, or pick his nose. He had been after Adrian to give it up, but Adrian was as stubborn as they came. "I'll give it up when some sweet little thing asks me to," Adrian had said only yesterday.

Adrian spit again, glancing at Alex, as if he expected his brother to make some comment. Alex didn't say anything. He didn't feel much like talking today, and that was unusual for him. It was also unusual for him to be so reflective. But coming home can do that to a man.

Leaving the main road, they turned up the road that led to the Mackinnon place, having their first glimpse of one of the few things they could call their own—their land. As their pa always said, "A man who has land is lord of something, even if it's only a horned toad." The road was overgrown now, the ruts no more than grassy indentations, and what had once been a sturdy, well-built fence that ran along the road was no more than a few sections of broken-down posts with a scissortail or two sitting on top. But it was home and that was all that mattered.

All around them the yellow-green grass

was a sea of ripples as it sloped down toward the creek that would be running slow and sluggish this time of year. It felt good to be home, to feel you belonged to something enduring. A scissortail sitting on a post took sudden flight as they passed and Alex looked in time to see its fine colors of gray, salmon pink, and black. Alex watched as the bird climbed higher, its folded scissor opening as it did.

Absorbed with the long familiar land about him, intoxicated with the fresh smell of spring that lay all about, Alex felt like he was dreaming, yet he knew he was awake. He looked out over an ocean of pale silver-green grasses four feet high, flowers of every color interspersed in the ravines and along watercourses where the grasses did not grow. Dear God, the memories this weedy old road stirred. Well he could remember a time when the fences were strong and straight and the road was well-metaled with two deep ruts, and fat cattle grazed that silver-green grass for as far as the eye could see. The pastures were empty now, a silent testimony to the passage of time. Yet, as he looked toward the sun he could see its brilliant heat turned the grass the color of shimmering flax that reminded him of the color of Margery's hair.

Margery. The youngest of the Mackinnons and the only girl. The pageant of his years here at this place seemed to take over his consciousness, unfolding steadily in pictures that brought the past so vividly before him. Margery came first, her long blond hair a tangle of curls around a sweet cherub face, her eyes blue and laughing, her cheeks as pink as a summer sunset, her chubby fingers locked around a wilted bunch of buttercups. Margery. She had been only six the day the Comanches raided the little private stockade known as Parker's Fort and stole her away. That had been twelve years ago, but the memory of it was still fresh. Twelve years. Dear Lord above! She would be eighteen now and more than likely the wife of some Comanche brave who did little more than fill her belly with half-breeds. Maybe it was a blessing his ma and pa were dead. They would have never been the same after little Margery was gone.

Alex let his eyes wander in the direction of the pecan grove that lay along Tehuacana Creek. He couldn't see the grave markers, but he knew they were there, knew what they said: *Andrew Mackinnon, son of Margaret and John. Margaret Mackinnon, wife of John.* And on the last marker, because their father had already been buried when they received word that he had been killed and scalped, they had simply written, *Here lies the memory of John Mackinnon. Born in Scotland. Died in Texas.* They knew their mother would have wanted it that way.

In spite of the pain a return to the past holds, there were good times tucked into his memory as well—times that had been meadow-sweet. He could almost hear the shrill laughter of his brothers running barefoot along the creek in the summertime, feel the breath-taking shock of that first plunge into its cold water. And then the sun would be on them again, warm and brilliant and they would feel as languorous as a bull snake at midday. He remembered sitting on the back porch on afternoons that were so hot a body could do little more than sit and watch the chickens peck, and the way the sun would set, a peachy-orange color against a twilight sky of the purest royal blue. He had never seen that exact color of twilight in any other place he had ever been. How well he could remember cold winter afternoons around a crackling fire, and the way he would grow sleepy listening to the sound of his mother's voice reading from a book; and there were long rambles along leafy lanes and across dry, rustling cornfields on frosty autumn afternoons. This was the land that had taught him so much, the washes and draws, the deepest parts of the creek and the most shallow, the open fields and the secret hollow, the bare, stripped trees in winter, the leafy undergrowth in summer, the rich smell of the heavy black land when it rained, all giving up their secrets that helped him to look shabby poverty in the face and say, "Someday, I'll rise above it."

He was glad life had been unembellished, hard, and stripped of convenience. He had lived with the barest bones of existence and they had taught him something. This was his land, his home, the place where he had been tripped by logs and chased by bees; the place where he learned to recognize the rubbings of a deer in velvet, or the hair-infested droppings of a bobcat. It was where he had lain in a meadow of sweet clover and studied clouds and funguses on stumps and been amazed at their caricatures. It was where he learned to ride like an Indian, swim like a fish, work like the devil, and say, in spite of all life threw at him, he'd do it all again in a minute, if he had the chance.

Of all the memories that called out to him from this place, none were as strong as the memory of Karin. Karin with the brightest blue eyes this side of heaven. Karin with hair as cool and pale as a moonbeam. Karin, so lovely, so misunderstood. Sometimes he felt as if he were the only person in the world who understood her and her often prissy, determined ways. He couldn't fault her for wanting more than life had seen fit to give her so far. There was no harm in that. Folks that didn't know her thought her to be selfish and vain, but she was hardworking and frugal, and she knew what she wanted. There were times he felt as if some of her ambition, her desire to better herself had rubbed off on him, for the poverty he had left behind held no appeal for him, and like Karin, he wanted something more. Only one really big difference that he knew of stood between them. He loved the land, and drew his strength from it. Karin saw it as something you walked on. "For God's sake, Alex. It's only dirt!"

He shook his head at the memory and

almost laughed. How many times had he heard her say that? And how many times had he taken her in his arms and kissed her, saying, "Sweetheart, this *dirt* is going to give you everything you ever wanted, everything your adorable heart desires."

Karin was too practical to be taken in by visionary dreams. "I don't survive on fairy tales," she had said. "I don't soar on imaginary wings. Life isn't a dream. It's fact, Alex. Cold, hard, cruel fact."

"Why are you so unhappy with your life, with what you have?"

"Because I have to be, don't you see that?"

"No, I don't, but that doesn't mean I'm not going to do my best to give you the things you want. This land, this soil that I love will make me a wealthy man one day."

"And if it doesn't?"

"Then we'll still have each other."

"It isn't enough, Alex. I love you, but it isn't enough." She had turned the loveliest, tear-filled eyes up at him. "I read something once, something St. Augustine said. I wasn't much more than twelve or so at the time, but it struck me so hard, I never forgot it. A year or so later, I came across it again, and this time I copied it down and hung it over my bed. I read it every night and every morning: *What you are must always displease you, if you would attain to that which you are not.* That's why I'm unhappy with who I am and what I have. It isn't because I look down my nose at others, or that I think I'm a little better than anyone else. I simply detest this life, this existence, this groveling in the dirt for a few measly potatoes. I want to wear beautiful gowns and eat at places I can't even pronounce the name of. I want to be able to walk into a fine store and buy anything I want, without having to ask the price and listen to the snickers of others when I put it back. I know you don't understand, Alex, and I don't know what to say or how to explain it so that you will." She had laughed a little—a dry, sad sound. "I understand that you don't follow what I'm saying, for God knows I don't always understand it myself. I only know it's something I want above all things, something I will stretch and claw and reach for until I get it."

"There's always a chance you won't."

"Then I'd rather be dead."

"I don't know how you can say that. Only a fool talks that way."

"I can say it, because it's true. If I thought this"—she looked around her and indicated the house with a wave of her hand—"was all that I would ever have, I would take Pa's gun down and place it against my breast and pull the trigger."

When he had started to speak, she had taken his hand and led him outside to stand on the porch. "Look out there, Alex. Look as far as you can in any direction you desire, and tell me what you see."

"I see the land."

"You see? We are so different, Alex. You look

out there and see the land, but when I look, I see the stars."

Had anything changed for her? He found himself wondering if she still saw stars. He wondered if she had thought much about him all these years he'd been away. He hadn't written, but there had been no chance, not when he was always on the move, fighting a war in Mexico. At least that offered some consolation. With the war going on, there weren't many eligible men around. Not that he was interested in whether or not there were any men left in Limestone County, mind you, but it did mean that Karin, more than likely, hadn't found a star to hitch her wagon to.

He was still a bit uneasy, though. A woman as beautiful as Karin—as beautiful and determined. He wouldn't put it past her to marry some old fool in his dotage, as long as he had money. No one around Limestone County had much more than the Mackinnons or Simons— another point in his favor. Maybe, just maybe, if his luck held, she might be waiting for him, just as she had been that night he had come by her house to say good-bye.

His thoughts spun backward, to the last time they had been together. He had asked her to wait for him, to give him a chance to prove himself when he returned. The moment he had spoken those words, he wished them back. Karin hadn't said anything. She had simply looked at him, her eyes meeting his. For some time they had looked at each other, her beautiful blue eyes snared for a moment by his, and unable to look away. He had known even then that her heart must be hammering as fiercely as his own, had known that the blush that stole to her cheek spoke for a woman full of yearning.

Well aware of her hesitancy, of her love for him on the one hand, of her long-held desire to better herself on the other, Alex had moved in swiftly. His arms had come around her, drawing her small-framed body hard against his, as his mouth sought and found hers. Lord, he remembered just how soft her mouth was—soft and responsive, and he had parted her lips gently and easily, his tongue surrounded with her warm sweetness. Even now, he could feel the way her fingers had moved swiftly to the back of his head, digging into hair that was a little too long, her nails raking his scalp. His hands had been so frantic to press her closer, as if by doing so he could mold her against him and bind her to him forever; flesh to flesh, bone to bone, woman to man, mate to mate.

As it always did whenever he was around her, he had felt himself growing rock hard, knowing too that she had felt the rise of his desire, firm and strong, against her belly. His hands had moved from her shoulders to the small of her back, rubbing, caressing, learning the shape of that which he held so dear. His body straining for fulfillment, his mind reeling with need, his hands had come around to caress her breasts. It was as it had always been, that night being no different from all the others—first the talking, then the kissing, the touching, the wanting, and for Karin, the fear. She had broken away. "Alex, please. We can't..."

"Why the hell can't we?"

"Please, Alex. It's our last night together. Don't let's be angry with each other. Let us both have something more to remember than anger, or..."

"Or what? Go on, say it."

"I wasn't going to say anything."

"The hell you weren't. You were going to say the *groping*, weren't you?" He shook her. "Well? Weren't you?"

"All right, damn you! What if I was?"

"Thank you, at least, for your honesty."

"It isn't like you think, Alex."

"No? Then how is it, sweetheart? Tell me how it is for you when I touch you. Does it repulse you? Does it frighten you? Does it make you wish I would hurry up and go away?"

"No!" she screamed. "It makes me want you to do all the things you want to do."

"Then why, for the love of God, aren't we doing them?"

"Because it's too soon."

"Too soon for what? I'm leaving at first light. We sure as shootin' can't do them by mail!"

"It's too soon for us to know what the future holds for us, Alex. You're leaving to join the Rangers. There's a war brewing. Anything can happen. You could change your mind. You might be caught up in a stupid, senseless war and get yourself killed. Or you could meet someone else."

"Or you could."

"I know that. That's why we can't. I've made a vow to myself. I won't give myself to any man without marriage."

"I've offered you that and you've refused."

"I didn't refuse, Alex. You were talking about the future. I said I'd give you my answer when you came back." Her arms had come around him then, soft and sweet and sure. "I love you, Alex."

"I love you too."

That had been the last thing he had said to her. The next morning he had ridden away. Now, almost four years of his life had passed since that night, and he still meant those words as much as he ever had. Problem was, did she?

His horse faltered and pulled him out of his reverie. He glanced at Adrian, seeing their return had the same effect upon him. For some time, the brothers rode in silence, following the neglected road, passing a pond on their left—a pond where Alex and Adrian had spent many an hour fishing for catfish and catching nothing but perch. A sad smile lingered on Alex's face as he remembered the first few times they had fished for their supper after their ma and pa had died. Their older brother Nicholas had appointed the twins, as the two youngest, to be in charge of the garden and catching fish, while the three older boys worked the fields and tended the livestock. How many times had he and Adrian thrown out their lines with their mouths watering for a big, juicy catfish, only to pull in perch after perch after perch, and tiny ones at that. Not knowing how to clean a perch, they had simply gutted them, lopped off the heads and dipped them in cornmeal to fry. He chuckled softly, remembering the way Tavis had take a bit bite and immediately spit fried perch all over the place. "What's the matter with you?" Ross had asked.

"You try it and find out."

Ross took a bite, and like Tavis, spit fried perch all over the place.

Nick was laughing now. Then giving the twins a questioning look, he said, "You boys did scale those perch, didn't you?"

"Scale them?" the twins said in unison.

Nick threw back his head and laughed, a deep rolling laugh that he swore later had left his sides aching and tears in his eyes. Alex had never been reminded of it before, but now it came swiftly to him, just how much Nicholas was like their father, and just how much he missed both of them.

Rounding a bend in the road and coming up over a rise, they came in sight of their old house and drew up, content to just sit in the middle of the road and stare. It didn't look as fine as it had in his memory, or as new. At one time it had been a handsome, dignified place with a neat yard surrounded by a picket fence covered with woodbine and Virginia creeper, and their mother's rocking chair on the front porch. But after their mother and brother were killed by the Comanches, the house had been burned, and only the chimney and a small part of it had survived. They had helped their father to rebuild it, or at least make a good start, but their father had been scalped before it was finished and the brothers had finished the rest of it, using the original fireplace and two of the bedrooms. They soon found that they weren't the craftsmen their father was, and the old place had never looked quite the same. In fact, Nicholas had said it looked old and dejected the day they finished it.

"Well," Alex said at last, "we aren't going to get much done if we sit here staring like two imbeciles who forgot where they were going." Adrian nodded and they kicked their horses into a faster gait and headed for home. Once they reached the yard, they tied the horses to the sturdiest section of run-down fence, Alex reaching the front porch before Adrian. He tried the door handle, but it didn't give. Then he remembered Adrian had locked the door the day they left. He turned toward his brother.

As twins often do, Adrian sensed what his brother was about to ask him. He shrugged. "Don't even ask," Adrian said, coming up beside him.

"You're the one who locked it. You had the key."

"You forget that Ross was still hanging around these parts when we left. Besides, we both said we weren't coming back here."

"*You* were the one who said that, not that

it matters. Hell, we're both doing and saying a lot of things we never thought we would," Alex said.

"True," said Adrian. "I guess kicking in a front door can be one of them."

"Right," Alex said, and kicked the door. It gave straightaway, the old rusted hinges pulling away from the jamb, the door falling inward with a loud crash that sent dust rolling upwards in billowing clouds.

"That," Adrian said dryly, "will be the first thing on the list of repairs."

Alex stepped inside, his eyes going over the dingy interior with care. "It's going to be a long list," he said, shaking his head, for he saw how thick the dust was lying on everything, saw the cheerless, desolate look of a long abandoned dream. They stepped back outside, waiting for the dust to settle. "Why don't you ride on into town and get some of the things we'll be needing while I try to get this place cleaned up and habitable?" Alex said.

Adrian looked at the crumbling ruin around him. "Looks like you've got your work cut out for you."

After Adrian left, Alex checked the place out, seeing just what he could find to work with. A quick survey turned up nothing, no broom, no soap, no nothing. Ross sure wasn't much of a homebody if he'd left the place looking like this, but then he remembered how Ross was always one to lay his head on a woman's soft bosom rather than on a pillow stuffed with corn husks.

A few more minutes of searching turned up one dehydrated bar of lye soap, but it was harder than Adrian's head. The furnishings would serve, but the mattress needed a good dusting and a few hours in the sunlight. The linens in their mother's chest smelled of age and dampness and would need airing as well. There wasn't much here to get started with. But he knew where he could find the things he needed.

He rode across the creek, through the pecan grove and across the pasture, scattering a curious herd of cattle. As he drew near the Simon place he could see the passage of time hadn't been particularly kind to them either—scrawny as all get out, they were. Cows that bony couldn't give much milk. The state of neglect made him wonder if old man Simon had passed away. The place was a mess. And the more he looked, the more dilapidated everything seemed. The chicken coop leaned so far to the left a sneeze would topple it over, and an old plow, rusted and abandoned, was almost hidden behind a tall stand of grass and weeds. Where a fine smokehouse once stood, a half-rotted buggy lay turned on its side. At one time, a whitewashed picket fence had surrounded the house, but now only a portion of it remained. One long section leaned drunkenly outwards, one section was missing entirely, and a third section had evidently given in to its drunken leaning and fallen flat—and that had happened some time ago too, for the grass and weeds that grew between the pickets were a foot tall. A few feet from the back door a lazy old sow lay on her side in the mud, a dozen squirming piglets nursing hungrily. But the dark-haired woman on the porch was as fine as dollar cotton. *Who the hell is she?*

Katherine stood on the back porch shaking the crumbs from an old red and white checkered tablecloth when she saw the man on horseback coming up the road. Seeing no one she recognized, she was about to turn away when something about the man called out to her. She watched him for a moment, her face a curious mixture of apprehension and elation as one by one pieces of familiarity fell into place. She gasped, her hands clenching the tablecloth and pressing it against her stomach as if by so doing she could make the sharp pain of recognition and remembrance go away. Her eyes grew wide with disbelief. Her heart pounded furiously. The color disappeared from her face. Alexander Mackinnon. His very name had been so much a part of her thoughts, while the man himself was the very essence of her dreams. And now he was here, no longer a thought, no shining image from her dream. He was real. He was alive. He was home. And her heart leaped from the joy of it. Alex. Dear, beloved, Alex. No more would she have to wonder if he still had the power to steal her breath away. The magic was still there, at least for her.

At least for her. At least for her. At least for her. A sobering thought, for it reminded her that it was her sister he was coming to see, not her. But none of that mattered now. He had come home and her heart was singing in response. She could sooner sprout wings and fly than she could still the trilling in her soul. *Oh, joy! Oh, happiness! Oh, he looks so good. Dear Lord, I look so bad.* Her hand came up to smooth the sleek lines of her hair.

He drew up just a little shy of the porch and sat on his horse just a few feet away, looking her over. He was still as beloved to her as before, still as lean and handsome as ever. Her eyes went over him anxiously looking for signs of change and finding few. He was older, of course. And more filled out. But there was something more, not a change exactly, but more an attitude of seasoning, of being weathered. The boy that left here four years ago was no more than unripened fruit, but the man who rode into her yard moments ago was no green boy. The four years he had been gone and the things that had happened to him during that time had ripened him and given him a patina that only comes with age. She saw his eyes were still the color of a cloudless sky on a sunny day, and his smile was as crooked as ever. *Ahhh, Alex,* she thought. *You're still so perfect in every way.*

"Alexander Mackinnon! I can't believe it's you!"

"Hello, Katherine." He grinned. "It's mighty glad I am to see you remember me, lass, for in truth, I didn't recognize you until you spoke." Alex couldn't manage more, for it had taken him more than a moment to realize this unbelievably striking woman was Katherine

Simon. There was little of the freckle-faced, copper-haired girl he remembered in the woman that stood before him now. The Katherine he remembered was a chubby, awkward girl trapped somewhere between child and woman. *This* Katherine was an exceptionally beautiful woman, tall and slender with dark, heavy hair. Where had all that red gone? A moment later she stepped forward, out of the shadow of the porch and he saw the red was still there, only the coppery color had darkened. Her hair was a deep rich auburn, not the dark brown he had first imagined. Because of the heat she had pulled it straight back from her face. On any other woman this would have been stark, but on her it merely emphasized her high-boned cheeks, the pure tones of her skin. Her nose was slender and straight, her mouth full and soft, but as it had always been with her, her expressive green eyes were her most arresting feature. She was both familiar and foreign, earthy and exotic, and so essentially female that he could not keep himself from staring.

But Katherine didn't really notice. Perhaps this was because she was guilty of the same thing, for she was finding it hard to keep her eyes on anything but him. For a moment or two, she allowed her fancy to run wild with imaginings of how he would have greeted her if things had been different, if it had been her he had ridden over to see. But her practical, sensible side soon took over. Her mind was still going at a full gallop, but the words she wanted to say hadn't as yet reached steady plodding. So when she opened her mouth to speak, the only thing that came out was the same thing she had said before. "I still can't believe it's you," she said, shaking her head in a dazed way.

Before she could draw another breath, he grinned at her again and said, "It's me." A moment later he was coming down off his horse.

Oh, it was him all right. Long and lean as ever, making her think about things she had no business thinking about. Alex wouldn't have a moment of peace as soon as the womenfolk in these parts got a glimpse of him. Here was the kind of man women baked pies for, and faced raging floods and tornadoes to deliver them. She watched him walk toward her. His body had filled out some, but he still had that loose, easy way of moving, and his features were still strongly cut and bronzed. He was the same, and yet the changes in him were remarkable. His eyes were still "take my breath away" blue, and his hair the same rich, dark brown that looked black out of the sun, but it was longer than she remembered, and she longed to touch it to see if it was as soft as it looked. Gone was the slim youth in hand-me-downs that were always way too short. Although his clothes were well-worn, they were clean and fit him well—a little too well, in her estimation, if a lady was expected to keep her mind on practical, sensible things. His youthful curiosity was gone and in its place was confident ease. Maturity had given more definition to his face and it most certainly added emphasis to his maleness. Something within her seemed to rush out to him, all the love and longing she felt for this man coming forward so swiftly she felt herself sway. She reached out to grip the porch railing for support.

Unable to think of anything else, she said, "How's Adrian?"

"Ornery and mule-headed as ever. He's back, too, but he went on into town to get some much needed supplies. There's not a dad-blasted thing left at the old place." He grinned. "I'm supposed to be getting our place cleaned up and ready to live in before he gets back."

She laughed at that, and he thought he had never heard a woman's laugh that sounded so musical, save his mother's. "Have you *seen* your place?" she asked, the hint of a smile lingering on her fine mouth.

He couldn't help grinning, thinking he probably looked like a pure fool smiling at everything she said. "That's why I'm here. I need to borrow a broom."

The corners of her mouth lifted in the most delicious way, and the light in her eyes was pure devilment. "A broom," she repeated. "For riding?"

He laughed. "For sweeping. I only ride when there's a full moon."

Her smile was bigger now. "Then you're in luck. I think there's one tonight—at least that's what the *Farmer's Almanac* says."

"Good! You wanna come with me?"

For the rest of my life. "No. I'm sticking to mules these days."

"Brooms are safer." *And so is Adrian. Don't look so fetching, Katherine.*

She laughed. "You're right about that, especially if the mule is Clovis."

"Clovis...isn't he the one that..."

"Bites," she said, suddenly looking self-conscious, "and eats everything in sight." She smoothed her hands over her apron. "Well, look at me! Not a bit of manners in my head, making you stand out here in the hot sun like this. Come on in, Alex, and get yourself out of that blistering, hot sun. I'll see if I can't scare up a few things for you."

He followed her inside, noticing immediately that the mess he saw on the outside did not come inside. The inside, humble as it might be, was spotless. They went into the kitchen, and he looked around the room, seeing it had changed so little in four years. It was a good feeling to know something in his life of changes had remained constant. In a way, he supposed that was a good description of Katherine. Constant. Best he could remember, it took a lot to get her riled—but Lordy, Lordy, Katy, bar the door if she ever got mad. He noticed she was watching him, and he gave himself a mental shake, his eyes going around the room. "It's nice to see the old place still looks the same," he said, wondering where Karin was. He was about to ask, when Katherine said:

"You must have been wearing blinders

when you rode up if you can say this place looks the same. It's a dilapidated wreck, Alex, and you know it."

"It isn't too bad," he said.

"It isn't too good," she answered and they both laughed.

He stood in the doorway for a moment taking it all in. The same white muslin curtains he remembered still fluttered at the window, but now a yellow ruffle had been added. The trestle table with its four chairs was the same one he remembered, and even the pie sitting there seemed familiar. He remembered how Katherine always loved to cook and what a little homemaker they always teased her about being. Evidently she was still as domestic as ever. His eyes went back to the table. How many times had he, Karin, Katherine, and Adrian sat there hunched over their school lessons, working beneath the dull glow of an oil lamp? And how many sums had they calculated while Ellie Simon busied herself over a pie or chicken and dumplings? The oil lamp was gone now, and so was Ellie Simon, but the memory of those times was still sharp and as fresh as that pie Katherine had baked.

Katherine saw Alex look at the pie.

"Apple," she said. "You want a slice?"

"No, thanks," he said, but his stomach growled in protest.

"I'll tell you what, why don't you go hitch Clovis to the wagon and I'll gather a few things that you'll be needing?"

"I don't need to borrow your wagon," he said. "I can take the things on horseback."

"Maybe so, but you can't take me and my basket both on horseback." When he started to protest, she slapped her hands on her hips and said, "Alexander Mackinnon, if you think for one minute I'm going to let a dear friend I haven't seen in almost four years go home and clean his own house you've got another think coming!" Turning away from him, she added, "Now get a move on, you hear? We've got work to do." She opened the cupboard and took out some neatly folded cup towels and placed them on the table, talking all the while. "A fine neighbor I'd be, knowing Alex Mackinnon was fresh home from the war and me not lifting a finger to help. If I let that happen, Ellie Simon would roll over in her grave and don't I know it."

He grinned, remembering how Katherine always talked to herself. He watched her pull a basket down off the top of the pie safe, catching sight of him out of the corner of her eye. "Well? What are you waiting for, the second coming?" Not giving him a chance to respond, she kept on talking. "Now, you get on outside and hitch up Clovis." When she heard his chuckle she said, "And don't forget he bites."

"I won't. I still have a scar on my shoulder to prove it, remember?"

Her hand came up to spread, fanlike, across her chest. Lord, she did remember, but that had been so long ago, when Clovis was the most adorable little mule, nothing but long ears and big eyes, not much bigger than a billy goat. One afternoon Alex had tried hitching him to a small wagon he and Adrian had built. But Clovis wasn't having any part of Alex or his wagon. And when Alex persisted, Clovis took a plug out of his shoulder. Alex was ready to take a strap to Clovis, but Katherine took one look at Clovis, all long-eared and black with the biggest, most repentant brown eyes she had ever seen and begged him not to. The memory brought a smile. "Lord have mercy, I do remember, but, land sakes, that was a long time ago. Why, Clovis was just a baby."

"And it's probably a good thing too. If he had been any bigger I would've lost half my shoulder. I should've taken that strap to him," he said, giving her a soft look, "but I was afraid you'd hate me forever if I harmed a single hair on his ornery, stubborn hide."

Her voice was as soft as his look. "I could never hate you, Alex. No matter what you did."

Their eyes met, neither of them looking away and the moment stretched between them, heavy with tension. Katherine felt her body tense, her muscles coiling tightly. She wanted to look away, but something held her. It was as if Alex had the power to reach out to her across the distance that separated them. Strange as it was, she felt as though he was making love to her from where he stood, wordless and methodical, as if he knew her body better than she. A thrill of delicious excitement ran over her, from her scuffed old shoes upward to the coil of glossy auburn hair secured at her nape. A penetrating warmth spread slowly through her, touching her in the most private of places, touching, awaking, softening, until she wanted to cry out. *Alex... Oh, Alex, if you only knew. It could be so beautiful between us.* But he would never know that. Or would he? Perhaps he knew it now. Perhaps that was why he looked at her as he did, coaxing and drawing her toward him with the power of his eyes alone. Perhaps he knew, deep within the innermost part of his being, deep within that part of him over which he had no control, perhaps this very moment, softly slumbering within his unconsciousness he knew—and yet, he didn't know at all, and probably never would. Alex was a man of conscious mind, one that loved with a will. He had no harmony with the reasons of the heart, reasons the mind knew nothing of. She knew Alex loved Karin with every conscious fiber of his being simply because he willed it so, and Alex was a man of strong, determined will. He would not, could not love her ever, simply because he did not will it. What he willed between himself and her was friendship, and all the wishing in the world wouldn't change it. And that was that. "Well," she said, feeling both self-conscious and brokenhearted at the same time. Her hand came up to smooth the side of her hair and she did her dead-level best at forcing a weak smile. "Just look at me standing here like a stepped-on bug, when there's work to be done." *Dear God! The pain! The pain of loving this much and knowing it can never be. The pain of having so many tender looks, so many love-whispered words waiting in deep, dark silence to be shared, and knowing they will always remain tiny forgotten seeds tucked away and unremembered, never given the chance to sprout, to flourish, to bloom. Dear God! The pain.*

She hid the painful swelling that comes before tears behind a halfhearted cough and turned her back to him, wishing with all her might that he would quietly walk away.

He watched her turn away, feeling an emptiness he had not felt since his mother died. He stared at her slim back for a moment, then shook his head to clear the confusion from his mind. It had been too long since he'd had a woman, he told himself. *Get a hold of yourself, man. This is Katherine, not Karin.* Hell, as randy as he was, he'd probably flirt with a broom, if it had a dress on. *This is Katherine, Alex. Katherine.* But each time he told himself that, a tiny voice inside him said, *I know. I know.*

He felt awkward for the first time he could ever remember—at least around Katherine. For Katherine had always been the kind of girl he could be at ease around, the kind of girl that was as comfortable as a pair of favorite old shoes. *So why am I feeling awkward and shy as a schoolboy?* He rubbed the bridge of his nose, feeling the pinch of tension at the base of his neck. He inhaled deeply, then turned away. "I'll be back to carry everything outside as soon as I'm finished."

She nodded, but she didn't look up when he left, for in truth she wasn't even aware of when that was, for Katherine was also a person of strong will and determination, and she had already given her attention to the task at hand.

She had packed the last of her supplies in the basket and was just closing the lid when Alex returned, telling her that "beast of a mule" was hitched.

Seeing the swelling redness and the way Alex was rubbing the back of his hand, she couldn't resist. "Beast? You mean Clovis? Why he's as mild as a moonbeam," she said, remembering how much she had always enjoyed teasing Alex, and seeing a good jabbing about Clovis as a good opportunity to start up again. "You don't mean to say he gave you trouble, do you?"

"Not because he didn't try. Now, I'm serious, Katherine. I don't think you should keep that mule. He's too unpredictable to be around women."

"Like a lot of men I know." Katherine laughed and picked up her bonnet along with her basket and stepped outside. Alex followed her, glancing at the table as he passed. The pie, he noticed, was gone, and that was curiously uplifting. He had just settled his eyes on Katherine's hair, thinking it was like slumbering coals that burst into flame the minute she walked into the sunlight, so vivid and intense were the red highlights that had seemed no more than a trusty warm brown moments before. Something about the masquerading of her hair set him to thinking. Too often things appeared to be what they were not. Wasn't this true of people as well? He was thinking Katherine was a lot like her hair, for the memory he had of her was also trusting, warm and brown, while the woman he found upon his return had shattered before his very eyes, splintering into fragments of impassioned color that were both powerful and unforgettable. He would have trailed that thought a little farther had not the musical tones of sweet, feminine laughter penetrated his thoughts. He looked up to see Katherine bent over, convulsed with laughter. So consumed was she, that she could not speak. But she could point.

Alex followed the line of her pointed finger and stopped short. His horse was still tied to the fence. Clovis was still tied to the tree, But somehow, Clovis had managed to stretch his leather lead to the limit, and with his neck extended to what had to be full capacity, he was able to reach the backside of Beedle, his horse. Beedle was in a doze, his eyes half-closed, his head dropped as he soaked up the sun. And that must have made him feel pretty obliging, for he took no mind of the fact that Clovis was somewhat fascinated with his tail. 'What in the hell is going on?" Alex shouted, unable to believe what he was seeing. When he had ridden over, Beedle had a long tail that flowed down to his hocks—something the horse tied to the tree did not have. Alex narrowed his eyes. The horse looked like Beedle. And he was sporting Alex's saddle. But the horse Alex saw was a broom tail if he'd ever seen one— with a tail that barely covered his rump. Clovis had chewed a good foot and a half off the end of Beedle's tail. With an exasperated curse, Alex cleared the porch and crossed the yard in a few swift strides, yanking what was left of Beedle's tail out of Clovis's mouth. With a muffled curse, he led him out of range, examining his tail and mumbling to himself when he had him a safe distance away. Katherine watched Alex tie the gelding to the back of the wagon, while she tried to keep her expression calm and pleasant, which was awfully hard seeing as how mental pictures of Alex mounted on a bobtailed horse kept coming into her mind.

Alex was no fool, and he had a pretty good idea what she was thinking that put that expression he found so provoking upon her face. His brows drew together and he glared at her. "One of these days someone is going to shoot that blasted mule right between the eyes and I can't say I'll be too sorry when it happens."

"It wasn't all Clovis's fault," she said, feeling just a little put out and bristling.

"I don't know how you can say a thing like that. Who can you blame but that mule?"

"How about that thick-witted horse of

yours? As far as I'm concerned anything dumb enough to stand there while his tail is being chewed off ought to walk around looking like a dust mop." She collapsed into fits of laughter and couldn't say more, even when she saw the dark as a thundercloud look on Alex's face.

"Katherine..." He had been about to vent his spleen a little more when Katherine turned her face toward him. He had expected to see her face twisted with anger, or at least a bit miffed, but he saw only devilish humor, followed by a wash of pink color that spread over her face when she caught his eyes upon her. Every peppery, quick-tempered word he had been about to hurl at her vanished. Never before could he remember losing track of his breathing—it was, after all, a simple process of taking air in and letting air out. But somewhere in between the taking in and the letting out, he was so distracted that he lost a breath when everything about him seemed to shut down. Something strange was going on here. He blinked his eyes to clear his mind, opening them to a clear view of her profile—the stubborn chin, the full lower lip that pouted just a little as she lost herself in concentration, the unbelievably long lashes, the dairy-fresh texture of her skin. His eyes dropped lower, following the long graceful line of her throat as it gave way to the sharp detail of her breast. It hit him with a jolt, just what he'd caught himself thinking. He jerked his eyes away. *Get your mind on the road, Mackinnon. Or Beedle's tail. On anything but what it's on. This is Katherine, not Karin. Katherine, you fool! She's nothing but a pest. Remember how she was always spying on you? Have you forgotten all the dumb things she used to do? She can't be quiet more than five seconds. She irritates the daylights out of you. And she couldn't be serious long enough for a man to get a romantic thought in his head about her. She is going to be your sister-in-law, for God sakes! What do you think you're doing?*

Through the debris of shattered resolve, she saw his brilliant blue eyes studying her curiously, searching, probing, concluding. It was as though they had just met for the first time, and he was finding her every bit as confusing as she was finding him. For indeed, that is the way she felt—that they were two strangers facing each other across a great void. Deep within the eyes that studied her she sensed interest, but on the same level, something she could only call ridicule.

She opened her mouth to say something, but he cut her off. "You're the talkingest woman I've ever come across," he said trying to sound as cross as he felt, and knowing it just wasn't so. He was still a bit peeved about Beedle's tail and was placing the blame on her, unwarranted as it was, although he wouldn't have admitted as much to Katherine if his life depended upon it. But he could still see her mouth quirking at the corners.

He helped her into the wagon, tying Beedle to the back, then climbing in beside her. Giving Clovis a slap with the reins, he guided him in a wide, sweeping turn, then headed down the road that dipped and curved as it ambled on down toward the creek.

Katherine had always been too garrulous for her own good, and went right on talking. "I remember Mr. Peabody had a peacock that the cows chewed the tail off of—'course Mr. Peabody is half-blind, and never did notice. But it gave everyone else a good laugh to see that peacock strutting about with his tail fanned, not knowing his beautiful feathers were gone and all that remained were a few bare shafts bent over at the end, like cornstalks after the harvest. But you shouldn't worry that anyone would laugh at your horse like they did at that silly bird, because he doesn't look half as bad as Mr. Peabody's peacock, and *nobody* would dare to poke fun at you even if they did feel the urge to laugh at your horse. I dare say half the horses in the county would be sporting bobbed tails in a week if you kept right on riding yours around." Katherine paused a moment, feeling such elation to be sitting next to Alex like she was.

Feeling intensely irritated and wanting to shut her up before he said more than was prudent, Alex said, "Where's Karin?"

As for shutting her up, that did the trick. Katherine's next words died in her throat and her elation fell flat as the road they were on. All the exuberance was gone from her voice when she said, "She's taken a job in town at a dressmaker's."

The sudden return to reality put an end to her fancy and Katherine went on to tell him in businesslike terms all about their father's death and how Karin had taken the job in town to help out. She told him how Karin made the money they needed to run the farm and she did the running of it. "We're like an old married couple," she said. "I stay home and tend the house and garden, Karin makes enough for us to hire a little help with the plowing. Of course she's as frugal as ever. It amazes me how she manages to save some of her money, each time she gets paid."

"Still saving, huh! I guess that means she still has all those fancy ideas about going to St. Louie, or San Francisco."

The cows were still as curious as before, following the wagon as far as the fence. The road made a sharp turn around the corner post of a pasture, then dipped sharply toward the creek. A minute later, they crossed the creaky old bridge that spanned the creek, the wheels of the wagon clicking against the old, wooden planks, making a strange, harmonious rhythm to blend with Katherine's laugh. "She still wants to leave this place, but she's lowered her sights some. Why, just the other day, she was talking about Dallas or New Orleans."

Alex was looking at her strangely, as if she'd said something she shouldn't have. Just as strange too, was the fact that for a woman who loved to talk, Katherine couldn't think of a blessed thing to say.

"She always did love pretty things, and she always saw getting away from here as a way to have them," Alex said, amazed that he was feeling a sense of loss over the disappearance of Katherine's bright chatter.

The old Mackinnon place was in sight now, and Alex slapped the reins against Clovis's back. Clovis kicked once, then picked up the gait. Alex didn't look at Katherine as she spoke.

"She still loves pretty things, and she still works like a field hand to have them."

They pulled up in front of the Mackinnon place, stopping short of the swaying porch. Katherine snatched her basket and was out of the wagon before Alex could tie up Clovis and come around for her. "Don't snub Clovis too close," she said, hurrying up the front steps, "or he'll pitch a fit."

He watched her walk into the house wondering just what it was about her that fascinated him. He had been wrong to become irritated at her over what that mule had done, as if she were personally responsible for the behavior of every mule about. *You've been away from women too long,* he told himself. *You'd stare at any woman.* But he knew that wasn't the case. Katherine wasn't just any woman and she certainly wasn't anything like she had been before. And the magic of it intrigued him.

She disappeared inside and Clovis began acting up, so Alex didn't have any more time to think about Katherine. By the time he let Clovis know who was boss and snubbed him, a good fifteen minutes had passed. When he reached the house he found Katherine in the kitchen. She had her basket unpacked, her bonnet off, and her apron on. He watched her as she busied herself with taking the rather pitiful assortment of dishes and utensils out of the cupboards. "There's enough dirt in here to plant a garden," she said.

Alex picked up the bucket she had placed on the table. "I'll get you some water."

When he came back a few minutes later, he could see results already. Everything had been dusted and put back into place. He watched silently as she pulled a chair over to the cabinet and stood on the counter so she could dust the top shelves. Her waist didn't look big as a minute from where he stood. "Where do you want the water?" he asked.

She didn't miss a beat. "Just put it on the table." She was down before he could blink an eye, grabbing the broom and pushing it toward him. "You wanted to borrow a broom, I believe?"

He eyed the broom. "Did I say that?"

"You did," she said, shoving the broom into his hands. "You do know how to use a broom, don't you?"

"I've a fair recollection," he said. He laughed then, his hands going around the broom, his fingers brushing hers. He gave a slight tug. She flinched and pulled her hands away.

He watched her step away, color dotting her cheeks as she turned back to what she had been doing, leaving him to wonder why he didn't leave instead of standing there. He had no answer for that. He looked at her slim back as she tackled the grimy kitchen window. He had known Katherine all his life and she had always been his friend, someone he could talk to. But now, he felt as awkward as hell. He looked at the broom in his hands. He looked at Katherine's back. With a puzzled look on his face, he walked slowly from the room.

By the time he finished sweeping the rest of the house and walked back into the kitchen, Katherine had everything in apple pie order. So much order, in fact, that he was amazed. Everything in the room had been dusted and rubbed down. The wood on the cabinets was darker than the cupboards due to the rubbing of lemon oil, and he guessed the table too, although he couldn't see it for the blue and white tablecloth she had spread over the top. There were even flowers in the center—a few buttercups mixed with heavily scented stems of woodbine poking from a chipped enamel cup.

"You work fast," he said.

She eyed the broom. "I can't say the same about you."

He grinned. "And why is that?" he asked. "And here I was thinking I worked every bit as fast as you."

She laughed at that. "I work," she said. "*You* play."

"Were you spying on me?"

"I didn't have to." He made a face and she laughed harder.

"I'll teach you to make fun of my housekeeping." He made a dive for her. She shrieked and danced around the table, her eyes alive and sparkling with life. Wagging her finger at him, she spoke in her sassiest way, "I know you, Alex Mackinnon. You were never cut out for housework."

"You're right about that," he said, laughing, his eyes looking her over. "But neither were you."

"Oh, posh!"

He made another lunge and she darted around the kitchen table, but she wasn't as quick this time. His arm came out and curled around her waist, yanking her back against him.

"It's true," he said, the smile disappearing from his face as his eyes looked her over even slower this time, from the top of her glossy auburn head to the tips of her worn shoes peeking from beneath her well-worn hem, hitting all the points in between. She was about to say something else, but seeing his eyes upon her as they were she could only stammer.

She had never felt such a bumbling fool in front of him. "You'd better let me go," she said in a breathless way, "or Adrian will be madder than an old wet hen when he returns and finds you've been playing while he was away."

"Yes," said a feminine voice from the doorway. "You'd better let her go."

CHAPTER
FIVE

Alex whirled around, his face lighting up. "Karin," was all he said, but it was enough to send Katherine's spirits plunging.

Karin was standing in the doorway when Alex first saw her. He sucked in his breath, sure everyone in the room could hear it. Karin. After all this time. Karin, still as beautiful—no, a hundred times more beautiful. There she stood, fashionably dressed in lavender silk that was gathered and tucked in the most flattering lines around a figure an angel would covet. She had always been a real looker, but now she had a woman's maturity, the poise and confidence of a woman that knows what she wants and how to get it. Her hair was still as golden as he remembered. Her skin as fair. He watched her smile, and the pure intensity of it left him breathless, unable to feel the way his heart wrenched.

In three long strides, Alex crossed the room and took Karin in his arms. While Katherine busied herself with taking a few things out of her basket, Alex whirled Karin around and around, until she said, "Alex Mackinnon, if you don't put me down, I'm going to be sick."

Katherine looked up, seeing Adrian was standing next to Karin. Feeling the heat rush to her face, she wished she could disappear. Adrian, bless his dear soul, must have sensed this, for he said, "Well, bless my bones, Alex! If I'd known something this pretty was going to be cleaning the kitchen, I'd have sent you to town." He let his eyes travel over her and then let out a long whistle. "How are you, Katherine?"

"Passable," she said. "And you?"

"A lot better since I parked my sore eyes on you. You're looking...well, blast it, Katherine, you're downright beautiful."

She smiled, thanking him with her eyes even before she spoke. "Why, thank you, Adrian. Although I don't believe a word of it, and I haven't forgotten what a flatterer you are, it's wonderful to hear."

"It's the gospel truth," he said.

"Well, whatever," she said, picking up her dust rag. "Here I am wasting time when there's work to be done."

"Why don't you take a little rest, Katherine?" Alex said. "I'm going to take Karin for a little walk. I don't feel right about you doing all the work."

"Oh, that's all right, Alex. You'd do the same for me, if I had a beau here I hadn't seen in nigh on four years." Katherine took the last towel out of her basket, closed the lid and turned back. It was then that she noticed she and Adrian were alone, for Karin and Alex had left the room. "I'll see to the back rooms now," she said, leaving without looking at Adrian again.

Some time later Katherine was working in Adrian and Alex's old room, her knee braced on the mattress as she leaned across it to tuck the patchwork quilt in between the wall and bed on the other side.

"I always thought you'd look good in my bed," Adrian said, giving her a sad, twisted smile when she jumped a country mile and exclaimed:

"Adrian Mackinnon! You scared the living daylights out of me! You should know better than to sneak up on a body like that!" Katherine backed off the bed and turned toward Adrian.

But Adrian couldn't say anything. Katherine was truly the most beautiful woman he had ever laid eyes upon. Even now, with her hair coming down out of its knot, her face dotted with perspiration, a smudge or two of dust on her cheek, she was pure perfection. She was seductive and tempting as hell with the sun glinting off her hair, her mouth round and open with breathless surprise, her eyes wide as she looked him over.

But it hadn't taken him a second to see she still had eyes only for his brother. That thought made him smile sadly, his hand coming out to cup her cheek. "If I had you," he said softly, "I would be the happiest man on earth."

A pain wrenched her heart and at that moment, Katherine wished with all her might that she could somehow come to love Adrian. But he was like a brother to her and the thought of anything more seemed a violation, almost sacrilege. That was just it. She did love him. Like a brother. "Oh, Adrian, I wish..."

His fingers came up to silence her. "I know," he said with a look of regret. "We both seem to want the same thing—I want you and you want to want me. They sound so close, but in truth, they're oceans apart."

Tears ran down her face and her heart reached out to him. Strange, but at that moment, she felt closer to Adrian than she ever had. "I wish I knew what to say."

"I know."

"Oh, I hate this! I hate it! I hate this feeling," she said, pressing her fists into her stomach as if by so doing she could make the hurt go away. "I hate it because it's so painful." She reached into her pocket for her handkerchief, bringing it up to her eyes.

"Yes," he said softly while looking away, "it is." With a long, exhaled sigh, he said, "You can't imagine what it's like to love from behind prison bars, knowing you'll never be freed."

Her look was sad, regretful. "We seem to have a lot in common, you and I."

"No, sweet Katherine, we don't. To have loved but been rejected is like being sent to bed with no supper; it's nothing more than a bee bite to one's spirit. But to love and be overlooked is to die slowly by starvation, like soap that wastes away, giving up a little of itself with each washing."

"Oh, Adrian, why must life be so miserable?" she asked in a dismal way while hunting for a dry spot on her handkerchief.

"I'm not sure, but I don't think even God goes through eternity without feeling some pain. Now dry your eyes and stop sniveling."

"I never snivel," she said, the sound coming through blocked nasal passages.

He smiled, taking the handkerchief from her and blotting her face, then putting it to her nose. "Blow," he said, and she did. "Ahhh, Katherine, what a torment you've always been." He folded the handkerchief and handed it to her, watching her poke it back into her pocket. "Life's a road with one bump after another, but you're going to make it. Have no fear about that."

"Sometimes I wonder."

"Say now," he said, "aren't you the girl that gave the address to the eighth grade class? 'Misery bridled becomes strength,' I believe was your title. A bit dramatic, if I remember, but well done."

"You remember that?" He nodded and she gave him a tentative smile. "You'll make it too, Adrian. I know you will."

He grinned and chucked her under the chin. "Of course I will. I've never doubted it. One of these days I'll be something to see all right, a real sight for sore eyes, and then you'll look at me and say, I wish I had loved him when I had the chance."

"Oh, Adrian, I've already said that."

The silence was empty, chilled, and obstinate. Katherine realized with dismay that what she said was true. Oh, how she did wish she could love Adrian as she loved his brother. She watched him look like he was about to speak, then turn and leave. After he had gone she remained behind for some time, sitting on the side of his bed, looking around the bare room where Alex and Adrian had slept so many nights.

When she had done all she could see to do, Katherine packed her basket and went outside, thinking she had a dozen things to do when she got home. There were chickens to feed, eggs to gather, cows to be milked, vegetables to tend, and... She drew up short. Clovis and the wagon were nowhere in sight.

She decided Karin must have taken him, and because of her excitement, her haste to get home and fancy herself up for Alex, she simply forgot. She sighed, looking around. Katherine knew it wasn't a conscious decision on Karin's part to be hateful or mean. She was the high-spirited kind that too often found herself swept up into the ecstasy of the moment. Whenever that happened, she just never thought that far ahead, never considered that there might be someone else to take into account before she acted. At times, Karin could act like she was the only living, breathing soul that walked upon the face of the earth.

With a sigh of resignation, Katherine thrust out her hip and balanced her basket against it and set out walking. Walking was something she was accustomed to, but today, she would have preferred to ride. Thankfully, it was a short distance—as the crow flies. She guessed she should count her blessings, instead of complaining. Wasn't the weather custom-ordered and hadn't Alexander Mackinnon come back home? What more could she ask for? By the time she was through the gate, she decided to go as the crow would fly and cut across the pasture instead of taking the road, thus saving herself quite a bit of shoe leather. Her green eyes were serious as she set out across the pasture late that afternoon.

It had been a hard week and a long day and Katherine was plumb tuckered out— bone tired as her mother would have said. But soon, the blue haze that scarfed the green slopes, the softest of breezes that whispered, elflike, through the pecan trees, the rippling splendor of a hundred varieties of swaying grasses and wildflowers that dotted the fields with bright color soon proved they were of stronger interest than thoughts of fatigue. Helping her renewed good cheer along was the fact that Katherine was not the kind of person to be bogged down in drudgery of any form for very long. Trying to keep Katherine's spirits low would be like trying to hold Clovis's nose to the ground—it was possible, but not for long. Soon, the tired, worn slump to her shoulders slipped away, and Katherine, her feet moving more lightly now, her eyes dancing over the flowers ahead, would pause to pick a handful here and there, poking the ones she could no longer carry in her basket.

As she covered the distance between the two homesteads, her mind floated about as fast as the splendid mass of white fluffy clouds overhead, and soon she was speculating once again on the possibilities of Alexander Mackinnon coming to his senses and loving the one woman in the world capable of loving him as no other woman could. It was plain as a sheet that the woman she spoke of was not her sister Karin.

If she were prone to stick to the obvious and forego fancy—something that must be said in all honesty Katherine rarely did unless she was forced to—it wasn't too likely that Alexander Mackinnon would ever come to his senses as far as loving Karin was concerned; but one never knew what odd little quirks of fate, what sudden, unannounced twists lay in the road of life just ahead. Stranger things had happened, to be sure. Katherine had more than enough rose-tinted pictures of what life between herself and Alex would be like if fate would just see things her way, and she was lost smack in the middle of the most delicious scene a few months hence, as Alex carried her into his bedroom and dropped her in the middle of his bed, quickly stripping her wedding finery from her body, including everything from something borrowed to something new, all the way down to the last pearl earring. Just exactly what he was going to do once he had stripped her of her finery was still hidden in the rose-tinted fog, but Katherine knew as certain as the Texas flag had one star that it would be something more thrilling than the touch of his hand upon hers. She was submerged in the vision of Alex paying homage to her body, as the good reverend was fond of saying, all the while hopeful that *paying homage* meant more than simply lighting candles at her feet, when suddenly her reverie was shattered by a loud war whoop and a splash.

Not being one to ignore what was going on around her, Katherine directed her steps toward the pecan grove that ran along the creek, which happened to be where the whoop and splash had come from.

Fighting her way through the tangle of woodbine, Katherine parted the twisted maze of vines in time to see the water-drenched head of Alexander Mackinnon break the surface. A quick glance told her Karin was nowhere around, so that must mean Alex had come here to take a bath, as the Mackinnon boys were known to do when the weather was warm. In the past, Katherine and Karin had kept plenty of distance between themselves and the creek whenever the Mackinnons went for a swim. However, Katherine was of a more curious nature now, and besides, she was already here, wasn't she?

Stupefied, she watched in awe as Alex swam to and fro, crossing the small stream several times before leaving the water—if leaving the water wasn't too tame a phrase to describe the manner in which a full-grown, splendidly developed, naked-as-the-day-he-was-born male steps from a watery cloak into full view. He was close enough that Katherine could see the tiny golden hairs that covered his body in all the places hairs of another type did not grow.

Saints above and angels too! She had never seen, nor imagined anything like it. Her heart was thumping so loud she was certain he could hear it, and her head had built up so much pressure, every ounce of blood in her body must have rushed there. She had a sudden inkling of what *paying homage* was all about, for she had a feeling she wanted to do just that, and it was no mere urge. He moved as fluidly as water running over rocks to his clothes, then turned to look across the creek when he heard something on the opposite bank. *Saint Sebastian! He was beautiful from every angle.* How had she always thought the female body would far surpass that of a male? One look at the firm, smooth skin stretched over softly rounded muscle told her this was not so. When he turned full toward her and she saw that part of him no mere fig leaf could hide, she was surprised that she felt many, many things, but afraid or embarrassed was not among them. *Oh, Alex, you are beautiful.*

Afraid to breathe lest he might hear her, Katherine remained in the exact position she had been in until Alex dressed and left. Once he had gone, she crawled from her tangled bower and hurried home, not distracted in the least this time by any of the finery mother nature had put in her way. As she walked home she tried to conjure up some sort of remorse, some form of shame for what she had done, but none seemed to be coming, and it was a good thing, for in truth, she didn't rightly feel she had committed any sin or done any wrong. For where was the wrong in staring at the naked body of one's beloved? Had it been

Adrian's body she had seen, or any other male for that matter, she would have been embarrassed. But with Alex, things were different. How she wished—wished with all her tender young heart, that Alex would one day look at her as she had looked at him.

Katherine climbed through the fence, where the road forked off to the Simon place. Suddenly, something down the road a piece caught Katherine's eye. Clovis and the wagon were angled across the ditch that edged the road. Coming closer, she could see Clovis was grazing the tender green shoots of grass that grew so lush where the water from the last rain had collected. One look at the lead rope told her Karin hadn't taken the wagon on home as she first thought. Clovis had chewed the rope in two and wandered off on his own.

Giving him a scolding, she climbed into the wagon and started down the road. When she reached the house, she saw Karin coming out the gate, carrying the shovel in her hand, and looking on the verge of a fit. Katherine was about to inquire about the shovel, when she put her hand over her mouth to hold back her laughter, for suddenly the idea of a fit being something one could throw seemed odd, even funny. Rocks one could throw. Clovis threw his shoes. Dice could be thrown, and horseshoes, too. But a fit? She wondered how that phrase came to be.

Katherine never did get to pursue that thought further, for Karin rounded on her the moment she pulled the wagon to a halt. The sight of Katherine's apparent good humor sent her into a red rage—a *red* rage being the worst possible sort of rage.

"I see you found him," Karin said. Her voice sounded threatening.

"Where are you going with that shovel?" asked Katherine.

"I was going to knock some sense into that stupid mule's head. Alex walked me home, and not long after he left I heard the wagon come into the yard. When you didn't come in after a spell, I came out to see where you were. I saw the chewed rope and tried to get that beast into the paddock. He bit me and took off like a ruptured duck in a hailstorm."

"So you went after the shovel."

"Yes, and I'm still tempted to use it."

"You going to see Alex tonight?"

Karin looked astonished. "Of course I am. That's why he walked me home—so I would have time to dress. He went on down to the creek to clean up."

Katherine started to say, "I know," but caught herself just in time. She looked at her sister. Karin looked like she was on the verge of crying. "You go on in and get yourself all gussied-up. I'll see to Clovis."

"I should say thank you, but it's your fault we've kept that blasted mule. I don't know why we don't sell him."

"Because we aren't."

"Well, never mind that now." Karin threw up her hands in despair. "I'll never be ready on time. Nothing I have looks right. I can't find my crimping iron. My hair is a fright."

"I think you look fine, just the way you are," Katherine said, meaning every word she said.

Karin assumed her most astonished look, and said, "Honestly Katherine, you act as if Alex's coming over were something he did every day."

The mention of Alex sobered Katherine and she listened patiently to Karin's rage. "I can't believe all this is happening to me at a time like this," she sputtered, "when I did so want to look so special. I don't know why you can't understand that. Sometimes you amaze me, Katherine. Yes, you do, and this is one of those times. I don't mind saying, I am amazed, Katherine. Simply amazed. Here, all this time, I thought we shared things, sorrow, pain, poverty, and what few pleasantries that come our way. But I see I was mistaken. You aren't capable of understanding matters of the heart." With that, Karin plopped the shovel in the wagon bed and turned around, stomping back to the house.

The slamming door startled Katherine out of her stupor and she headed Clovis toward the barn. A few minutes later Katherine stepped into the kitchen and put her basket on the table. Karin was heating her crimping iron.

"I see you found it."

"Yes," was all Karin said, but her eyes swept over her sister. "Look at you! What did you do? Crawl home?"

Katherine looked down, not seeing anything particularly wrong—nothing a little soap and scrubbing wouldn't take care of. "Are you going to stand there looking like that until Alex comes and you humiliate me in front of him? Honestly, Katherine! He will be here soon. You act as if you'd like nothing better than to have him catch you looking like something the cats dragged up and the dogs wouldn't take."

By this point in time, Katherine had heard all of Karin's fit that she intended to. She flew up the stairs, wishing quite frankly that sisters had never been invented. But when she came back down some time later, she thought she must have passed muster, for Karin was all smiles. "Thank you," she said, "you look ever so much better." When Karin smiled, the whole world seemed to light up, and Katherine felt the resentment fly right out of her heart. After all, Karin loved Alex too—not the way she loved him, but she loved him, nonetheless.

Katherine wondered if she should tell Karin that she had fully intended on changing her clothes, even before Karin threw her fit, but she was distracted by the dreamy expression Karin had upon her face as she looked at her reflection in the mirror. Turning back toward Katherine, Karin said, "Is it my day or yours to cook supper?"

"It's yours," Katherine said, knowing what was coming next, and deciding to volunteer before she was asked. "But I'll cook tonight so you'll have more time."

"Oh, thank you. What would I do without you? You are truly the dearest of sisters." She started from the room, then stopped. "I do want to look splendid tonight. What should I wear? The yellow muslin or the pink?" She smiled and whirled around, giving Katherine a hug. "The pink, I think. Alex always liked me in pink."

"Alex always liked you in anything you ever wore," Katherine said, but Karin wasn't listening. She had gone to the ash pail and taken out a bit of charcoal, then moving to the faded and cracked piece of mirror that hung on the wall over the washstand, she rubbed a bit over her pale brows and in the crease of each eye. "There," she said, standing back to look at herself. "It makes my eyes look ever so much larger." She turned toward her sister. "Do we have any of that paper left, the paper with the red roses?"

"I think there's a bit of it left in the bureau drawer."

"Oh, good!" Karin looked at her reflection again. "I do think I'm a little pale... the excitement and all. A little dab of the rose paper dampened and rubbed on my cheeks should give them a nice bloom." Without taking her eyes off herself, she said, "Oh, I almost forgot. You really need to mend that fence next to the barn. Clovis has been at it again. He ate all the irises along the fence on the other side of the house."

Karin's sigh brought Katherine's mind back from Clovis and the irises to Alex. "I simply can't believe Alex is back." She turned to look at Katherine. "And you said he wouldn't come back."

Katherine followed her into the parlor. "I said there was nothing left around here for Alex or Adrian, and there isn't."

"Apparently you forgot about me," Karin said. She pulled the fringed shawl off the back of the sofa and wrapped it around her shoulders, turning her head this way and that in front of the mirror before discarding the shawl. "Oh, Katherine, I don't know what to do."

"About Alex?"

"Yes. You know, it's funny, the way I thought I was over him, but the minute I saw him standing there with you in the kitchen, I knew he still held all the old magic. Now I just feel a little crazy, like I want him, but I don't want him." She looked at Katherine. "That doesn't make any sense does it?"

"Not really."

"I love Alex. I really do. I know I haven't acted like it while he's been gone, but I'm not the kind to pine for anybody. I didn't know if he would even come back. I couldn't be expected to sit around longing for him, could I?"

"No, I suppose not. What difference does it make? You didn't pine for him."

"I know, but it's strange. The moment I saw him, I knew I'd marry him in a twinkling if..."

"If he weren't so poor?"

"It sounds so cold and calculating when you say it like that."

"It is cold and calculating." Katherine saw the hurt look on her sister's face and regretted her harshness. Karin couldn't help being the way she was any more that Katherine could. They just wanted different things, that's all. Katherine felt cruel for being so judgmental of her sister. At least Karin was honest and admitted what she wanted. And she wasn't afraid to go after it or work hard.

Karin wasn't just a hard worker, she pursued money relentlessly. She was dogged in her determination, ruthless with her own person, scraping and saving every penny she could get her hands on, holding down a job in town, then spending her evenings doing sewing and mending, sometimes even cooking for anyone willing to pay the coin. She detested her poor conditions and had decided years ago to do something about it. Everything she did was part of her plan—the way she dressed, the reason she worked so hard, the motivation behind the men she chose—except Alex, that is. Katherine thought about that for a minute. She guessed Alex had managed to get his foot in the door when Karin was younger, before she was so dogged and determined to better herself. Now he was like an old habit. Old habits were hard to break. How well Katherine knew that, for she had loved Alex most of her life. In spite of that, Katherine's heart went out to her sister. She didn't envy Karin any. Sooner or later, she would have to decide. A man like Alex wouldn't wait forever, no matter how much he loved Karin.

"I'm sorry," Katherine said. "I shouldn't have said that."

"It's all right. I suppose, in a way, you were right. I know Alex has no way to support himself, let alone a wife. And for that reason I know I could never marry him. I suppose I keep hoping something will happen, something that will make him a wealthy man."

"That's not very likely to happen."

"I know that, but what else can I do? There certainly aren't any prospects around here to speak of, save Carter Turner. Every woman in five counties is after him."

"That's not a very nice reason to keep seeing Alex. Anyway, you know Carter is sweet on you."

Karin ignored Katherine's stab. "Carter may be sweet on me, but that won't make his mama like me any better."

"Mrs. Turner doesn't like you?"

"She doesn't like anyone that she sees as a threat."

"How do you mean?"

"Lavinia Turner isn't about to let Carter marry any of the women that are after him, including me."

"Why not?"

"Because she comes from one of those fancy Boston families—you know, the ones that know their ancestors all the way back to Adam."

"If things don't work out with Carter,

someone else will come along," Katherine said.

"They won't come here, but that doesn't matter. I'll go to them. That's why I've been saving my money. Before too long, I'll have enough to leave this place and I will, without letting my shirttail hit my back."

"Does Alex know you're still so set on leaving here?"

"He asked me that today."

"Did you tell him?"

"Of course I did. I may be a lot of things, but I won't lie to Alex."

Katherine nodded. "What did he say?"

"He said we weren't as far apart as I thought, that he wanted a lot of the same things I did. He's changed a great deal, Katherine. I suppose the war did that to him. He doesn't want to be poor any more than I do, but he still loves the land, still has hopes of being a farmer—a rich farmer."

"Perhaps he will be."

"Perhaps. Who knows? In the meantime, I won't change my plans. I won't ever change them. I told Alex that. He asked me to give him a chance to get the farm on its feet. He still thinks he can make that place pay."

"So you're going to keep seeing him?"

"Yes, at least until I get enough money to leave here."

Katherine's heart fell to her feet.

Alex came for Karin at eight. It was Katherine who answered the door, but the minute she led Alex inside, Karin came down. Suddenly feeling like a third leg, Katherine watched Alex devour her sister as she walked into the room. A moment later she watched the way he glanced down into Karin's wide-set eyes. At that point, Alexander Mackinnon smiled a smile that Katherine Simon would have chopped off five fingers to have seen bestowed upon herself. She made her excuses about needing to see to the kitchen and left, knowing even as she did, that neither one of them realized she had done so. So much for her plans to get Alex to notice her.

Alex didn't waste any time taking Karin outside. Katherine had barely finished mouthing her words when he took Karin's hand and led her out into the warm, fading light of late evening. "You want to take a ride? I cleaned up the buggy, just in case."

Karin nodded, and Alex followed her through the gate, taking her in his arms as soon as they reached the buggy. Karin's eyes flashed back toward the house. "Not here, Alex. Katherine might be watching."

"So? We're not doing anything wrong."

"Help me into the buggy, Alex. Let's get away from here so we can be alone."

Since that was exactly what Alex had in mind, he didn't waste any time. He guided the buggy into a turn and headed it down the road, taking the fork that led away from his own place. "I suppose we can just ride down the road a piece," he said.

"Anywhere, just as long as we're away from here awhile."

"I know it's been hard on you," he said, "trying to run the place since your pa died."

"Katherine mostly runs the place, since I'm working in town. I help out with the money for things we need." She laid her head against Alex's shoulder. He shifted in the seat, bringing his arm around her, drawing her closer. Lord! Did she ever smell sweet. Just like flowers.

"You're right," she went on. "Things have gone from bad to worse since my folks died. Sometimes I think Katherine is fooling herself when she thinks she can keep on running this place, even after I've gone."

At that reminder, Alex fell silent. After a bit, he said, "How'd your pa die?"

"He just wore out, Alex. Just like mama did. And this is what did it to them," she said, waving her hand out across the stretch of land that sloped away from the road on either side. "Maybe that's one of the reasons I want something different, why I can't forgive this wretched land, this place."

"You can't hold a grudge against land."

"I can, and I do. This place takes and takes and takes. It never gives anything, not even hope."

He turned the buggy down the road that ran up to the old McCracken place. There was a nice little tank of water just below the place where the old barn had stood. Of course that barn had blown away long before Alex left, but he was hoping the tank was still just as pretty, with its drooping branches of willows that skimmed the water's surface. The catfish were probably working the top of the water this time of day. He almost mentioned that to her, then remembered Karin wouldn't be interested in such as that.

"It should be nice and cool down by the tank," he said as they crested a rise and he could see the tank still looked as lovely as he remembered it. He guided the buggy around one side of the dam and down into a grassy spot between two big trees, one a hackberry, the other a cottonwood.

When he pulled to a stop, he asked, "Do you want to get out and walk for a bit?" She nodded and he swung down from the buggy and tied the horse before he came for her, holding out his arms. She stood, placing her hands on his shoulders as he drew her down into his arms. She fit as perfectly as she ever had. Alex didn't wait. He couldn't. He whispered her name once, then stopped anything she was going to say with his mouth against hers. "I want you," he said. "I've always wanted you."

"Kiss me, Alex. Kiss me and don't stop."

His mouth covered hers again, harder this time. In response, her arms came up to slide around his neck as she pressed forward, aligning her body fully against his. His tongue was in her mouth now and she kissed him with all the unleashed passion she felt. It was so good to be with a man again, a real man, even better to be with Alex, for there had been no one like him, hadn't been and probably never would be. Her thoughts vanished like vapor when she felt his heart pounding so fiercely against her own. His manner wasn't gentle now, but wild with yearning, his tongue tangling with hers, teasing, daring, showing her what he felt. Her body swayed. The blood pounded painfully in her head. His hand came up to squeeze her breast and she wanted nothing more than to guide his other hand to its mate. Her last thought, before she broke away, was, *Oh Alex, Alex. Why can't you be a rich man?*

"What's wrong?" he asked.

She didn't want to get into another discussion about the future. She didn't want to be reminded of the past. For just a little while she wanted to be young and free and in love. "Nothing," she said, giving him a playful shove and darting around the buggy. He caught her before she got very far. She was laughing and so beautiful it hurt him to look at her. She took his hand in hers. "Come on," she said. "Let's walk before it's too dark to see anything."

"Walk?" he croaked.

"Walk," she said, laughing. "Honestly, Alex. Have you forgotten how to behave around a lady?"

He laughed, feeling a little sheepish. "I guess I have. It's been a while since I've been around a real one."

"I'll not pursue that vein, for fear of what I'll hear. Do tell me about your travels... about the war too, if it isn't too painful for you to talk about it."

They walked around the top of the tank and he talked, telling her of his short time with the Rangers, the longer time with General Taylor. She asked questions and seemed interested, but when he began to talk about New Orleans, or Mexico, her face lit up. She fired questions at him until he finally said, "Whoa there, little filly. You're asking questions faster than I can take it all in." She laughed. He noticed she slowed down a bit, but she didn't stop asking questions. For over an hour they walked and talked, until it was growing too dim to see.

"I guess we'd better find our way back to the buggy."

"When we get back home, I'll give you a slice of sweet potato pie."

"I'd rather have a bite of you," he said taking her in his arms and kissing her.

She kissed him back, but not before she said in a breathless whisper, "I believe you."

"Do," he said, "for it's the gospel truth."

CHAPTER
SIX

Katherine sat at the kitchen table the next morning, feeling as wrung out as a piece of chewed twine. She didn't know why.

The sun was warm and shining through

the window as bright as polished brass. The peach tree near the back porch had burst into bloom overnight, a flush of rosy white, blushing like a bride and the object of worship for a dozen adoring bees. Earlier this morning a tour of the garden had shown her the row of turnips she had planted were coming up, and the black-eyed peas were already sprouting a few blooms.

A smart rap at the back door did little more than turn her head in that direction in time to see her nearest female neighbor, Fanny Bright, step through the door.

Fanny was an institution of sorts in these parts—a woman with a keen, perceptive mind and a quick wit who said what she thought and damn the consequences. She had the patience of Job, the luck of the Irish, talked up a blue streak, had a remedy or a bit of advice for everything, and never met a stranger. She was a short, plump woman, all curves and no angles; her brown hair was streaked with gray and was always braided into two braids that criss-crossed over the top of her head and were secured with two or three wire hairpins that looked like they had been poked there in a hurry. She had a sweet round face and two of the merriest blue eyes a body could ever hope to see. The loveliest things about her were her mouth that always smiled and the most jovial words that were always coming out of it. For it could be said that Fanny Bright didn't have a pessimistic bone in her body. With a name like Fanny Bright, how could she?

Fanny stopped dead in her tracks and took a ponderous look at Katherine. "Bless my soul! You're looking as dazed as a duck in thunder."

"I don't know how you can say that," Katherine said with a dejected sigh. "I'm feeling as sharp as a briar."

"And you're lying like a rug when you say that," Fanny said, then made herself at home. First she went to the cupboard and got herself a cup, then moving to the stove, she poured herself a cup of tea. When she reached the table she put her teacup down then dropped into the chair across from Katherine with a plop. "Whew! It's hotter than two fires out there." Fanny looked around the cheerful kitchen that was flooded with early morning sunshine, then at Katherine who sat glumly in the only spot the sun didn't touch. "You distrustful of sunshine?"

Katherine thought about that. "Maybe I should be—anything that irresponsible can't be trusted."

"Irresponsible?" Fanny dwelt on that for a minute before deciding the sun could be called irresponsible, for it was just as apt to shine as not, and it wasn't too particular about who it shined upon. "Lord! You're sour as clabber this morning. And here I thought you'd be grinning like a fool now that the Mackinnon boys are back."

"They're *not* boys."

Fanny's brows went up and her lips twitched in understanding. "Oh, ho! So they've grown up, have they? I must say I'm mighty relieved to see you noticed."

"A body would have to be blind not to." *Or at least refuse to peek through the woodbine down at the creek.*

"Now don't go getting your tail over your back. I ain't taking no shots at you." Her head tilted sideways as she studied Katherine thoughtfully. "I think you need a good shot of castor oil."

"I need something," Katherine said, "but it isn't castor oil."

"Well, like you said, a body would have to be blind not to notice those Mackinnons." She saw Katherine wasn't softening up much, so she said, "So you noticed. What's wrong with that? It's springtime and in the spring you know what a young man's fancy turns to."

Yes, my sister, Katherine thought, but she said, "No, what?"

"Why, courting and all that."

"All that what?"

"All the things that go with courting—making eyes, holding hands, kissing..."

"Humph!"

Fanny laughed. "Don't tell me those rascally Mackinnon twins are back and you haven't been kissed yet?"

Katherine shot her a glare. "Kissed? Me?"

"Of course *you*. What's so strange about that?"

"Fanny, I haven't been kissed in so long I don't remember if you're supposed to suck or blow."

When Fanny's laughter subsided a bit, she wiped her eyes with the corner of her apron, then said, "Don't worry your pretty little red head about that none. It'll all come back to you I reckon, when the time is ripe."

"If it gets any riper I'll go to seed."

"My, what an obstinate, bull-headed creature you are. And when you have so much to be thankful for. Shame on you, Miss Pessimist." At that moment the sun seemed to shift and come into the room more fully, striking Katherine and bathing her in light. "Give up, my girl. This isn't going to be a bad day, in spite of all you're doing to make it so."

Katherine shrugged, feigning indifference.

"Well, have it your way for as long as you can, but I'll lay you money this is going to be a good day."

Fanny Bright was still sitting at the kitchen table having her third cup of tea and talking up a blue streak when Karin walked in looking as fresh and fashionable as a display in the front window of the seamstress shop where she worked.

"Good morning, Fanny," Karin said, walking to the tea kettle and pouring herself a cup, favoring her right hand a bit.

Fanny nodded. "Top of the morning to you, Miss Priss."

"What's the matter with your hand?" asked Katherine.

Karin shot her a look and mumbled something Katherine couldn't quite understand.

"What?" asked Katherine.

"I said it was Clovis."

"Clovis?" repeated Fanny Bright. "You mean that mule? The one that bites?" She eyed the purple place on Karin's hand. "Rub a little horse liniment on it and it'll be good as new."

Karin wrinkled her nose. "That stuff smells terrible and it reminds me too much of Clovis the biting mule."

"Clovis the biting mule," Katherine said slowly, remembering how Karin had come after Clovis with the shovel last evening.

Karin put the teacup down and plopped her hands at her waist, her eyes hot upon her sister. "Sometimes I would swear that you put that mule up to it."

Katherine looked flabbergasted. "How can you say something like that?"

"Because he never bites you, *that's* how come."

"He would if I gave him the chance. Clovis bites anything that doesn't move fast enough. You just have to be more careful."

"Maybe you just need to mend that fence so he won't get out. Next time I'll just let him eat your stupid old irises."

"I thought you said he already ate them."

"Oh, do be quiet. You're just trying to get me flustered and the Good Lord knows I'm flustered enough as it is. Here I've got miles and miles of lace to sew on a dress for that crabby old Mrs. Witherspoon and I can't even hold this teacup, much less a needle."

"You want me to come with you? I could sew the lace," Katherine said.

"No, thank you. I'll manage. If you want to do something helpful, keep that blasted mule away from me!"

Katherine started to say that she didn't remember forcing Karin to have anything to do with Clovis, or that there was some unwritten rule that said she had to mend all the broken fences, but Fanny must have sensed the tension, for she said, "My, you're a sight for sore eyes this morning, all gussied up pretty as a teapot and looking as anxious as a pullet expecting her first egg."

Karin perked up, forgetting her injured hand. "Why, thank you, Fanny. I am rather expectant this morning, but not for eggs," Karin said very seriously, not realizing how laughably grandiose she was acting.

The table began to shake with Fanny Bright's half suppressed laughter, but Karin didn't notice as she looked at her sister, and said, "If you have any more plans of ruining my day, I will ask you to kindly refrain. I plan on having a good day." She looked at the watch pinned to her bodice. "Oh dear, if I don't hurry I'll miss my ride with Mr. Carpenter," she said, then walked from the room closing the door a little harder than usual behind her.

"She might be planning on having a good day, but she won't. At least not in that dress, she won't," Fanny said. "It's sticking to her tighter than bark to a tree. She'll be purple faced and passed out in the back of Mr. Carpenter's milk wagon before she gets halfway to town.

A body can't breathe in a dress that tight. And a body needs to breathe."

But Katherine wasn't so sure. Karin always wore dresses with the bodice and waist so tight she looked constricted, but it never seemed to bother her.

Things settled down rather tranquilly after that day, Karin up each morning wearing a brand new dress and hurrying off to the dress shop, Katherine busying herself with housework, tending the garden and the few animals they possessed. When summer finally came it was hot as a furnace and even Clovis seemed somewhat mellowed by the force of it.

Often Katherine would be bent over a basket of freshly washed laundry, or stirring a pot of simmering squash on the stove when suddenly Alex Mackinnon's tantalizing features would swim before her very eyes. She would soon tell herself that it would do her no good to dwell upon the features of a man in love with another woman, no matter how handsome or beloved he was.

Life was growing harder for them day by day. Katherine began selling more and more of the produce she grew in the garden, and more of the eggs and butter she normally kept for herself and Karin. When Karin complained, Katherine reminded her that since the Mackinnon brothers had returned she hadn't given one bit of the money she earned for their upkeep. "The way I see it is you can have food on the table or new dresses on your back, but you can't have both," Katherine said.

Karin was eating the same thin vegetable soup they had had for supper for the past three nights, but when Katherine spoke, she slammed her spoon down and leaped to her feet. "You're being spitefully mean," she shouted. "And I know why. Just because Alex is paying court to me is no reason to starve me to death. There are ten women to every man in town and none of them are as fine as Alex. I have to look nice, I thought you of all people would understand that. I shouldn't have to suffer because you're so jealous!" Karin left the room and Katherine, having lost her appetite, threw the rest of her soup into the slop bucket for the hogs and went outside to work the garden while it was cool.

It was dark almost an hour later when Alex rode up and dismounted, tying his horse to what was left of the dilapidated fence that had, at one time, circled the house. He was about to go inside when he saw the faint outline of someone in the garden. He headed that way, seeing Katherine chopping weeds like her life depended on it. "It's a little late to be working out here isn't it? How can you see what you're doing?"

Katherine jumped and turned toward him. "Great gobs of goose grease! You shouldn't sneak up on a body like that! What are you trying to do? Make me faint?"

Alex grinned. He had a mental picture of Katherine fainting. Karin, maybe. But not Katherine. She had too much mettle for that. "Why don't you go on up to the house?" He stepped closer and put his hand on the hoe to take it from her. "You can do this tomorrow."

But Katherine held on firmly. "I've other things to do tomorrow," she said. "Now kindly go fetch my sister and leave me to my work." She gave the hoe a yank, but Alex seemed as determined as she.

"You're no match for me and you know it. Now, you can stand out here all night playing 'yank the hoe' or you can be sensible and come inside with me."

I'd love to go inside with you, if you'd promise to stay with me. Katherine glared hotly at him, glad there was still enough light for him to see just how put out she was. It wasn't the first time since his return that she found him horning in on her affairs, always butting in with his advice on how to do this or that, or what he thought needed to be done. Only yesterday he'd taken a look around the yard and said it needed a good cleaning. And the day before that, he'd come by when she'd been harnessing Clovis. She was just putting the blinders on Clovis—because that helped control his biting a bit—when Alex walked up and said, "That leather needs mending."

"I can see that, but I don't have any leather to mend it with and no money to buy any."

"I've got some leather you can have."

"We aren't running a charity here, Alex. You better be keeping your leather for your own mending. Unless I miss my guess, you're only a couple of steps farther from poverty's door than we are."

"Katherine, why won't you accept my help? I've offered several times to come over here and clean this place up for you."

"I'll do my own cleaning, thank you, and I've told you that before."

"There are some things a woman can't do. The henhouse needs rebuilding, the fences are desperate for repairs, the bed of your wagon is going to rot through any day now."

"When it *rots*, I'll fix it. Not before." Here he was again, pestering and butting in with his advice. It was getting to where he gave more advice than Fanny Bright. Of course Fanny said it was because Alex liked her and that might lead to something more.

She couldn't say that he was really interested in her, but he did have an uncanny knack for turning up at the darndest times, just to pester her. It was unnerving to have him always about and underfoot as much as an overcurious cat. The way he looked at her sometimes, as if he thought he was seeing her for the first time and yet felt he knew her from somewhere and was trying to put his finger on it. When he looked at her like that, she understood why Karin always wanted to look pretty for him, for she was conscious of the way she looked in her faded dress and her heavy work shoes. She despised herself for feeling awkward around him, for being self-conscious when he caught her looking less than her best. And now he was looking at her like that again and she felt her face heat up in response, her pulse throbbing strangely in her throat.

He reached up and placed his hands over hers on the handle of the hoe. "You're a hard worker," he said, pulling her hands from the hoe and letting it fall to the ground.

"I suppose I am," she said a little harshly. "In these times, isn't everyone?" She pulled at her hands but he held them fast.

He turned her hands over in his, his thumbs brushing lightly over the thick callouses at the base of her fingers. "Some work harder than others."

A shiver rippled up her arms and she shuddered. She felt choked by the nearness and dearness of him and wanted nothing more earnestly in her life than to be released so she could run. How embarrassing to have him catch her working late like this, how humiliating to have him see the callouses and other signs of neglect and hard work when she wanted him to see her as soft and lovely as he saw Karin.

As if sensing her anguish, he released her hands and leaned over, picking up the hoe and handing it back to her. "Hit me over the head with it if you like. I didn't mean to embarrass you."

"You didn't," she said hotly.

He sighed. "Always so quick to defend herself, a mother hen with no chicks."

"Thank you for the reminder," she said so icily he laughed.

"There's nothing to be ashamed of, Katherine. I admire your spunk and your drive. Work is an honest effort that has a lovely face."

"Work spares me from starvation, Alex. It's not as noble a thought as yours but one more dear to me." She looked back toward the house. "I'm sure Karin is beside herself wondering where you are. Don't you think you should see to her?"

He shook his head in wonder. "You're more stubborn than that mule of yours," he said, his voice laced with humor.

"Perhaps," she said, "but at least *I* don't bite."

"I'm not too sure," he said, turning toward the house. "I'm not too sure."

She watched him walk away until he disappeared around the house. She didn't feel much like chopping weeds after that. But she lingered outside for a spell, sitting on the back stoop and watching the lightning bugs and listening to the coyotes yelp in the distance. She stayed there until she saw Alex and Karin start down the path for their customary walk. When they were well away from the house, she went inside and saw to a few chores before going up to her room.

For a long while she stood before the small oval mirror that had belonged to her mother. She stared at herself, leaning closer and drawing the lamp closer as well. She hadn't been too careful about wearing her bonnet lately, mostly because of the heat, and now she could see the consequences. Her face was lightly tanned and sprinkled with a few new freckles. She ran her hand over her cheek, wondering how long before it would be dry and wrinkled and leathery like most of the hard-working women in these parts. She held up her hands, inspecting the darker skin there as well. Her nails were short and broken, rimmed with dirt and rough as cobs. There hadn't been money for anything as frivolous as softening cream, so she had taken to smearing her hands with saddle oil or lard and rubbing it in. She remembered how soft and delicate Karin's hands had looked at supper.

Picking up the lamp she walked to the rocker in the corner and picked up a book, *Flora of the Southwest,* and began reading about herbs and wild edible plants. But it was difficult for her to concentrate tonight, for the touch of Alex's hand upon hers was still strong in her mind. Sometimes the ache she felt for him, this tightening in her chest she called love was so overpowering she wanted to cry.

She closed the book and undressed, pulling the worn cotton gown over her head, and crawled into bed. Tomorrow she would pull the calf off the cow so there would be more milk to sell. Tomorrow she would pick peaches and make a pie and preserves. Tomorrow she would have to find the time to go down to the creek and fish, for they hadn't had any kind of meat in over a week. Her mouth watered at the thought of a fat old catfish frying to a crisp golden brown in her cast-iron skillet.

Katherine heard Karin and Alex return, the soft, hushed tones of their voices, the creak of the porch as they stepped across it, the silence that followed. It was always this spell of silence that was the hardest, for she imagined the kinds of things they were doing. Katherine always saved her prayers for the silent spell and she rolled over baring her heart to the Lord. She was still praying when she heard the click of the door as Karin stepped inside. A few minutes later Karin's voice whispered across the darkness. "Katherine? Are you asleep?"

"No, I'm not. I was just finishing my prayers."

"I'm glad because I wanted to tell you that I'm sorry about the way I acted today."

"I know," Katherine said. It was dark inside the room and Katherine couldn't see Karin's face, but she had seen it enough times before to know exactly the way she looked. Upon first entering her face would have been rapt and radiant, only to turn mournful and penitent the moment she started speaking.

"Oh, but I feel so bad about it," she said with a quiver in her voice. "I behaved terribly. I hurt your feelings I'm sure. I don't know why I always want to rail at you about everything, even poor old Clovis. I guess it's because I'm a dreadfully wicked and most ungrateful person. You're so good and kind and giving. Say you'll forgive me. I shall die of sorrow if you don't, and I'm sure you wouldn't want that on your conscience."

The sincerity was unmistakable, but Katherine knew how well Karin enjoyed her *periods of penitence*—how she seemed to revel in the thoroughness of her abasement, how she drew strength from occasional walks in the valley of the shadow of humiliation. "It's all right."

"Say you forgive me, please."

Katherine sighed, feeling older than her years and tired. "Of course I forgive you."

Karin hurried across the room and kissed Katherine on the cheek. "Thank you. I'm sure I shall sleep ever so much better now."

"Yes, I'm quite certain you shall," Katherine said dryly, but Karin, not being overblessed with perception, missed the implication.

Breathing an exaggerated sigh of immense relief, Karin said in a swoonlike state, "I can't tell you how relieved I am. 'Let not the sun go down upon your anger,' as the Bible says.

"Yes, that's what it says all right."

"Oh, my dearest, sweetest Katherine, you are a veritable pillar of strength to me. I do want you and me to always be this close. I should die of sorrow if we weren't." She walked back to the door. "Good night."

"Good night," Katherine said as Karin closed the door.

For a while after Karin had gone, Katherine lay there reflecting on Karin's burst of contriteness, which wasn't by any length of the imagination, her first. Bursts of contriteness, periods of penitence, bouts with guilt were as much a part of Karin as her blue eyes and blond hair. Karin was what Katherine called a bit temperamental and excitable and was, more often than not, guilty of jumping to conclusions, unjustly placing blame, or sometimes being just downright disagreeable, or just plain selfish. And just as predictable as these outbursts were was the remorse that always followed. She was like a child in that respect, or so Fanny Bright said, for she thought she could say the first thing that popped into her head, no matter how hateful, or heap accusations until she was blue in the face and that those things should all be forgiven the moment she appeared the least bit repentant. Many times Katherine wondered what Karin would do if she said simply, "No, Karin, I don't forgive you."

True to her resolve the night before, the next day Katherine pulled the black and white calf off its mama, and put it in another pasture with two young heifers. After cleaning the house and sweeping both porches, she picked a bushel basket of fresh rhubarb, cleaning and slicing it, putting the choice slices aside for a pie and what was left in a pot, adding sugar and setting it to simmer slowly. She made the pie, putting a fancy lattice top on it and put it in the oven. She had no more than opened the oven door and leaned over to take it out when Adrian poked his head in the back door.

"Ye gods and little fishes! Sweet Katherine, seeing you like that makes me feel friskier than a flea on a fat dog."

Katherine came up quickly, banged her head on the low-hanging shelf over the stove and burned her hand. How she managed to hang on to the pie she would never know. Her temper rising faster than the temperature, she slammed the pie down and rounded on Adrian.

"I was not put here on this earth for the sole purpose of making you feel friskier than anything, and I'll thank you kindly not to make reference to any positions you might happen to catch me in in the future. Now, I realize you might have thought you were paying me a compliment, and I am not above receiving such. I think a compliment from time to time is quite permissible and often very nice, but a remark like you just made is neither permissible nor nice. I have never, by any scope of the imagination given you permission or any encouragement to make such comments to me. It is beyond me how you always manage to find the time to go flitting around the countryside poking your head in kitchen doors unannounced and scaring the drawers off half the women in Limestone County. You came close to making me drop my pie and I can tell you right now that if that had happened it would be too wet to plow around here as far as you're concerned. I'm not telling you these things to offend you, but simply for your own good. You are going to get yourself shot or arrested if you don't start knocking before you walk into a body's house. It's only been a year or so ago that old Mr. Hawking over near Waco was surprised by a neighbor who just walked into his house one evening. Mr. Hawking can't see worth a flip even with his glasses on, and that night he didn't have them on, so when this neighbor walked in, old Mr. Hawking mistook him for a no-good and pulled his old blunderbuss down from the peg over the fireplace and blew a hole in his neighbor big enough to drive a hay wagon through. Now, if that's the kind of end you want to come to, you just keep on going as you have been and I'll promise to cry at your funeral." Katherine stopped talking when she saw the way Adrian was doubled over with laughter.

"Katherine, you have talked a full five minutes by your clock. I don't think I've ever seen you go on so."

"You've never come bounding into my house like an intruder before either. Now, state your business so I can get on with mine."

Adrian was grinning at her. "I'm on my way into town and thought I'd stop by and see if you need anything."

"Even if I did, I don't have the coin to pay for it, so you'd best be on your way."

"Would you like to go with me for fun?"

"Fun? Adrian, if I didn't know you better, I'd swear you'd been working in the sun with your hat off. You call riding into town in a bumpety old wagon in this blistering heat fun? Out of curiosity, I'd like to know just what you think would be fun about that?"

"I thought I'd entertain you with a few stories."

"I get all the stories I want at church. Besides, I've heard all your stories a thousand times."

"I've learned a few new ones since I was away."

Up went Katherine's brows. "I'm sure you did, but they're probably not the kind of stories you should be telling a lady."

He laughed. "I'd buy you a lemonade in town."

"I just had a glass of peach nectar and that was quite sufficient, thank you."

"I could show you the picturesque points along the road to town."

She gave him a sour look. "I've been going down that road for nineteen years and there isn't a part of it I haven't committed to memory years ago. And furthermore, there isn't a picturesque point on that road between here and Waco and you know it."

He grinned. "You can't blame me for trying."

"And you can't blame me for taking the broom after you like I would do any other pest," she said, making a dive for the broom. Adrian laughed and headed out the door, running to the wagon and climbing up the wheel to the seat, Katherine giving his backside a good dusting on his way up.

She was smiling at him when he picked up the reins and said with a grin, "I swear you're getting as cantankerous as that old mule of yours."

"Clovis isn't cantankerous. He just likes to bite...and eat irises," she added.

Adrian guided the mare in a circle and turned the wagon. "I'm off, then. Sure you won't change your mind?"

"Have you ever known me to change my mind?"

"There's always a first time."

She laughed. "Maybe so, but it isn't going to happen today."

"You should have been a banker," he said. "You're all business."

"And you should have stayed a child. All you want to do is play."

"Only with you, Katherine," he said softly, then he slapped the mare and headed toward town.

Katherine shook her head and walked back to the house. The rhubarb had cooked down sufficiently and she ladled it into jars. While they cooled on the kitchen table, Katherine took her fishing pole from the back porch, picked up a bucket and walked toward the garden to dig worms. When she had enough worms squirming around in her bucket, she headed on down to the creek, anxious to spend an hour or two in the cool shade along the water.

Her hook baited and in the water, Katherine sat down on a large rounded rock and waited. The creek was slower now than it had been earlier in the spring. She studied the glassy surface reflecting the sun like a million tiny mirrors, the darting movement of a dragonfly as he dipped down to the water repeatedly. There wasn't a breath of air coming through the trees and the heat was stifling. Laying her pole carefully to one side, Katherine loosed the collar of her dress and opened a few buttons and removed her bonnet. Then she removed her shoes and inched her way along the rock until her feet were in the water. She sighed blissfully. Indeed, it was much cooler this way, she thought as she picked up her pole.

"From what I can see from here, I don't know why you don't have at least a dozen fish jumping on your line, just to be the first one you catch," said a deep, rumbling voice behind her. "Caught anything yet?"

Katherine whirled in surprise, and seeing Alex step through the trees and come up beside her, she released the breath she had so hastily drawn in. "It must run in your family," she said. "Every blessed time I see you or Adrian it's *after* you've come sneaking up on me and scared me out of a year's growth."

His teasing glance slid over her from the top of her dark head with its fiery red highlights to the small feet dangling in the water. "You're not much bigger than a minute already. I'm afraid losing a year's growth would make you disappear completely."

"There are times when that thought is almost appealing."

"Really? Why would you say that?"

She tilted her head to one side and thought about it. "Oh, I don't know. Haven't you ever wished you could just disappear?"

"Only if I could reappear someplace else. I wouldn't want it to be anything permanent."

She laughed. "Oh, neither would I." Then her features fell back into place. "What are you doing down here this time of day?"

"I had my heart set on a fish dinner." His

eyes drifted over to where her pole dangled over the water. "Same as you, apparently."

"Well, I hope you have better luck than I'm having. I've caught one pathetic perch that wouldn't fill a gnat."

"Where is he?"

"I threw it back with a message to find the biggest catfish in the creek and send him my way."

"What are you using for bait?"

"Worms."

"That's why you're catching perch."

"What do you catch catfish with?"

"Blood bait."

"Blood bait? Ugggh! It sounds horrible." He laughed. "It is."

"What's it made of?" Seeing the glint in his eye, she added, "Besides *blood*."

"A fellah would have to get up before day-light to snag you, wouldn't he? How do you manage to always stay a jump ahead?"

"Luck, I guess. You were going to tell me about blood bait."

"Not much to tell. I mix a little flour, corn-meal, and blood and let it sit for a few days."

"And then what? Throw it out?"

He laughed. "I've been tempted. Here, I'll get mine and show you." He turned away. "I'll be right back."

She watched him rattle his way through the trees, wondering why he was so much noisier going than he had been coming. A minute later he reappeared with his pole and a bucket. He climbed onto the rock beside her and pulled a small tin out of the bucket. "Blood bait?" she asked.

"As fine as can be found anywhere." He twisted the lid. "Your first introduction to blood bait can be somewhat overwhelming," he said, pulling the lid off.

The foul odor almost gagged her, and Katherine had always prided herself on having a strong stomach. "Merciful heavens! I wouldn't eat *anything* that ate that. Put the lid back on. *Please!*"

When he ignored her plea, Katherine picked up the hem of her skirt and brought it up to cover her nose. "You aren't going to put your hand in there, are you?"

"Now you can't be that squeamish. I've seen you clean hogs, remember?"

"Not even hogs smell that bad. That smells worse than a gut wagon."

"It has to smell bad so it won't lose its potency in the water."

"That wouldn't lose potency in an ocean full of water. How are you going to get it on your hook?"

He pinched a hunk and replaced the lid before rolling it into a ball and shaping it over the end of his hook. "Want to try some?"

"No, thank you. I'll stick to worms."

"And perch," he said confidently and cast his hook into the water. They fished in silence for a few minutes, then Alex said, "How about making a little wager?"

She narrowed her eyes at him in a distrustful way that made him laugh. "What kind of wager?"

"Something for the one who catches the most fish."

"Perch included?"

"They're fish, aren't they?"

"Size makes no difference?"

"They have to be big enough to be seen with the naked eye."

She laughed. "What do you want to wager?"

"Ladies first. Tell me what you'll forfeit if you catch more fish than I do."

"I thought I'd win something if I catch the most."

"We've changed the rules a bit."

"I'm to give you something if I catch more fish than you do?"

"Right. So, what are you going to give me?"

"A rhubarb pie."

"Fresh?"

"Baked today."

"No slices taken out of it, either."

It was her turn to laugh. "Not unless they've been taken since I left it to cool on the kitchen table. Now, what about you? What do you give me if you catch the most fish?"

"A week's labor."

Her face fell. "Pick something else."

"I accepted your terms, you have to accept mine."

Katherine didn't respond right away, because Alex's cork went under water and Alex yelped, springing to his feet. Giving the pole a yank, he exclaimed, "It's a big one, I'll have to draw the line in by hand."

Katherine watched him work the line to

the bank and land a nice catfish that weighed at least a pound. While Alex ran a cord through the fish's mouth and gills, Katherine quietly pulled her hook out of the water, hoping he wouldn't see.

"You giving up already?"

"No, I was just checking my bait."

Alex nodded toward the worm wiggling on her hook. "Everything looks in order to me," he said, laughing when she slung the worm back into the water.

"Oh, be quiet!" she said.

"You're going to sling that worm right off your hook if you don't ease up a little."

"Is there anything else you want to point out that I don't do right, Mr. Know-It-All?"

"Nope."

"Good, then I'll thank you to remain quiet if you're going to sit here."

"Now, where were we? Oh yes, you had just accepted my terms."

"I did nothing of the sort!"

"It doesn't matter anyway. You were free to offer what you wished with or without my approval, just as I am. Now, I'm going to give you a week of my labor, and the *only* way you can stop me, Miss Stubborn, is to out-fish me."

Just about that time, Alex let out another yelp and Katherine saw his cork go under water. "Are these fish friends of yours?" she grumbled as she watched him pull in another catfish that outweighed the other one by at least half a pound.

He cast her a teasing grin and picked up the tin, offering it to her. "Wanna try a little blood bait?"

"Go to the devil!" she said, scooting farther away from him when he laughed outright.

A few minutes later he landed another catfish. And another one not long after that. When he pulled in the fifth one, Katherine, who had never looked so dejected and glum said, "Pass me the blood bait."

For a full minute Alex couldn't lift his own head, let alone the tin of blood bait, for he was weak from laughter. But one glance at Katherine told him she didn't think it was a bit funny. "Sorry," he said, the picture of contriteness, and handed her the tin. "Want me to put it on for you?"

"And lick your fingers when you're through!" she snapped. "I'll bait my own hook, thank you."

"Suit yourself," he said, leaning back to watch.

He would have never thought to see a woman tackle blood bait like Katherine did and he had to hand it to her. She was a trooper through and through. He had to admit she was a little green around the edges by the time she got the hook baited and into the water, but she did it. He had a quick glimpse of Karin doing the same, and recognizing how unfair that was, quickly dismissed the thought. Karin had other qualities that warmed his heart.

The thought of Karin made him a bit reflective and he remembered the way she had been yesterday when he'd dropped by and caught her in a sunny yellow dress and crisp white apron. She had a feather duster in her hand when she answered the door, and he had asked her what she was up to. Her answer had been, "As you can see, I'm dusting."

He had followed her into the house and she fixed him a cup of coffee, telling him to take a seat on the sofa while she dusted the furniture. In one of her playful moods, she had taken a swipe or two at him, then, laughing, she began dusting him in earnest. He was laughing so hard, he sucked two loose feathers down his throat and almost choked to death. Once he'd quit choking, she had kissed him, telling him how sorry she was. He grabbed her duster and began pulling feathers out, tossing them about the room.

"Alex, whatever are you doing?"

"Trying to suck a couple more down my craw," he'd said, laughing. "I like the way you tell me you're sorry."

"Oh Alex, you don't have to swallow feathers to get me to do that," she'd said. She kissed him, just to prove her point.

But his heart went out to Katherine a few minutes later when she caught her first catfish, and it was bigger than any of his. Never had he thought she could be as lovely as she was at that moment when the fish cleared the water. "Saint Sebastian!" she exclaimed. "It's bigger than yours! It's a bloody alligator!"

"No, Katy, my lass, it's not. But it is as hefty

a catfish as I've ever seen. I bet it's at least four pounds."

"Fanny Bright told me she's heard of catfish growing to weigh twenty or thirty pounds."

"Not in this creek," he said. "Around here I wouldn't think you'd catch one over seven or eight pounds, if that."

Alex caught another fish a few minutes later. The fish seemed to quit biting after that. It was late in the evening when Alex stood and said, "I guess that's going to be it for today. Word seems to have gotten around about us. I don't think we'll catch any more now." He looked at Katherine, feeling a tenderness for her. She never had been one to take losing well, being of the school that thought hard work would put her ahead. But some things just weren't won, no matter how hard you worked.

He offered her his hand. "Come on," he said jovially. "I'll give you a chance to get even next week."

Katherine sighed, placing her hand in his. "Oh! Wait! I've got to put my shoes back on."

He pulled his fish and Katherine's out of the water while Katherine put her shoes on. When she finished, she watched him. He looked so handsome and so tall. She remembered how they had played "Vikings raiding England" when they were children, and how he was always the Viking. In truth, he looked the part even now.

"Wake up," he said, and Katherine's head

snapped up to see him standing over her, his hand extended.

"Oh!" she said, feeling her face flush. She allowed him to pull her to her feet, feeling the loss when he had her on her feet and withdrew his hand.

"Come on. I'll walk you home. We'll clean our fish there."

They walked and he talked, and Katherine paid hardly any attention to what he was saying. She was lost in the sound of his voice, so deep and full of authority. She wanted him to go on like this forever. She wanted so many things. But her house was looming larger in the distance and the closer they drew, the more she felt the old prison walls close in. When they reached the house, Alex stopped and looked at her a moment in a very intent way. For a split second she thought he was going to say something, but then she saw he had apparently thought better of it. It was strange how many times this happened, when she had the feeling he was about to say something to her, to share some thought or other that would draw them closer, and then he would stop himself. *Just once, I'd like to see him let the moment carry itself without any interference.* He couldn't be that indifferent to her, no matter how much he loved her sister. He simply couldn't.

CHAPTER
SEVEN

Apparently Fanny thought two weeks was just too long to go without seeing her friend, and she wasn't going to let one more day pass until she dropped by Katherine's for a hot cup of coffee and some warm conversation. Up at the crack of dawn, she lit out one morning, making a beeline for the Simon place. Once she arrived she wasted no time opening the back door and sticking her head into the kitchen, calling out her customary, "Yooo-hoo, anybody home?" Before anyone had a chance to tell her if they were home or not, she let go with another blast. "Yooooou-hooooo! Katherine, are you here?"

Karin cringed. "Yooou-hoo," was something she found supremely irritating, and quite unnecessary, since somebody was most always at home. Katherine rarely went anywhere, except for church or church socials, and Fanny attended these as well. Once in a while Katherine would make a trip into town, and more often than not, Fanny accompanied her when she went. Therefore, in Karin's mind, all this caterwauling was unnecessary. She had said as much to Fanny, of course, on several occasions, but things of this nature, things that were as plain as peanuts to Karin, didn't seem to settle in as logic in Fanny's mind.

From somewhere upstairs Karin's voice floated down. "I'm up here, Fanny. Katherine is in the barn, I think. Feeding."

Fanny nodded. That sounded reasonable. On Fanny's arm was a willow sewing basket. Inside the basket was a dress she was sewing and wanted Katherine's help getting fitted. She placed the willow basket on the kitchen table, poured herself a cup of coffee, and sat down at the table to wait for Katherine. After waiting fifteen minutes—she knew it was precisely fifteen minutes because she had checked the clock over the stove when she sat down—she pushed back her chair and went outside to look for Katherine.

Katherine was in the barn, just as Karin said she would be, but something strange was going on. Fanny stopped just inside the door, killing a little time and watching Katherine, who stood in the middle of the barn with a milking pail in one hand and a milking stool in the other, but she didn't look as if she had milking on her mind. In fact, she didn't look like she had *anything* on her mind. There she was, staring straight ahead like she was seeing a vision—as if she was there but she really wasn't there. Fanny waved her hands in the air, just to see if Katherine noticed, but she didn't let on like she had seen a thing. Truth was, she didn't bat an eye. About this time, Fanny was wondering if Katherine had fallen from the barn rafters and knocked the starch out of her drawers, for the only time Fanny had seen anyone look so stupefied was when a hired hand she once had fell from the rafters of her barn. The poor man ended up walking around in a daze for two full days.

Fanny's look of interest had turned to one of disbelief. She was still watching Katherine—who had stopped looking like she was seeing a vision and started talking to herself. Fanny wondered if she had gotten hold of some loco weed—the kind that made cows act crazy as a bullbat. She ceased all speculation, however, when Katherine carried the milk pail and stool to the stall where Clovis was penned. When she placed it on the floor in front of the mule's stall, Fanny was shaking her head.

Still unaware of Fanny's presence in the barn with her, Katherine turned and walked to the stall where the cow was penned. Going into the stall, she fastened a lead rope on the cow and led her outside. Fanny followed, still shaking her head.

Katherine was still mumbling to herself as she led the cow to the wagon, going around to the front and stopping in front of the singletree. She looked at the wagon, and then she looked at the cow. Her face had the most peculiar look on it, like she had just crawled out of bed and didn't have the fuzziest idea how she had gotten dressed and into the barnyard with this cow. Fanny couldn't stand the suspense any longer.

"You planning on hitching that cow to the wagon?" she asked.

Katherine still had that dumbfounded expression on her face. "I thought I had Clovis," she said in a half-dazed way.

"Clovis is still inside. I think you planned on milking him."

Katherine's expression was still dumb-founded.

Fanny laughed. "I almost wish you had tried," she said with a chuckle. "It's a small wonder to me why you insist on keeping that mule—with him giving milk and all."

Katherine didn't say a word.

"Are you all right?"

She nodded. "I'm okay."

"Katherine Simon, you are acting mighty peculiar. Is it something you ate? I don't mind telling you I was mighty surprised to see you take that milking stool toward Clovis. For a minute there, I thought you were going to hitch that cow to the wagon."

"You aren't any more surprised than I am," Katherine said. "I feel like I've been in a state of surprise for weeks now. I hardly know who will be staring back at me each morning when I look in the mirror. I feel like I'm living with a stranger."

"Well, hankering for a man can do that to a body. I always say, love can make the most clever woman into an idiot," she said.

"What about men? What does love do to them?"

"Since they're already idiots, it can make them appear almost clever."

Katherine laughed and gave Fanny a shove. "Oh Fanny, you are always a bright spot in my day." Then, on a more serious note, she said, "I'm not hankering after anybody."

"Humph!" was all Fanny said.

Two days passed before Katherine went

into town and saw Alex. He was there before she arrived, picking up a wagonload of supplies he'd ordered for the farm. Katherine was passing the general store when Alex came out with a keg of nails. With a grunt of exertion, he heaved the heavy keg into the wagon bed, then turned, his eyes catching a glimpse of Katherine as her wagon drew even with his. He grinned at the sight of her and tipped his hat. She dipped her head in recognition. "Morning, Alex."

"Morning, Katherine."

She was driving that cantankerous mule of hers, the sun splaying about her, warm and bright. Her dress was plain and white, her hair hidden beneath a calico bonnet, her cheeks a flush of pink. His first thought was that she looked like the pinky-white bloom of a peach tree, only this blossom wasn't hummed over by a myriad of bees. But the blossom coming down the boardwalk just over Katherine's shoulder sure was, for he caught sight of Karin sashaying down the street all prissy and sassy-looking in a lovely dress of wild-rose pink, so soft and frilly he ached to take her in his arms, just to see if she felt as good as she looked, knowing damn well she did. Her hair was wound around, all fancylike and tied back with a shiny, satin bow, and she twirled the prettiest little pink parasol over one shoulder. Every man on the street looked his eyeful, most of them making fools out of themselves, tripping and stumbling all over the place trying to speak and tip their hats at the same time, something few of them could do with any ease. Even old Hooter Peabody let fly with a wad of chewing tobacco, just so he could mumble "Good morning, Missus."

Of course, Hooter Peabody didn't look before he spit, and the ill-aimed wad splattered, dark and oozing on the ruffled skirt of Mrs. Claiborne Claiborne, who promptly smacked him a good one up beside the head with her parasol.

Alex laughed and shook his head. Knowing that amused look wasn't for her, Katherine followed the direction of his stare, catching a glimpse of Karin, who lit up like a Christmas tree when she saw him.

A pain so intense she almost doubled over stabbed into the heart of her, and Katherine clucked Clovis and moved slowly on down the street. Her first stop was the post office, then the bank, the blacksmith, and lastly the shop where Karin worked. Karin, she was told, had gone to lunch.

That must have been true, for when Katherine headed her wagon out of town, she passed Alex and Karin standing beside the rain barrel in the alley between Doc Lesley's and the hotel. It was the sound of Karin's laughter that drew Katherine's head in their direction—just in time to see Karin dampen the corner of her handkerchief and blot Alex's mouth. Katherine winced when Alex's hand came up to cradle Karin's hand, his eyes locked on her face.

Their heads and shoulders dappled by the sunlight filtering through the Virginia creeper that covered the balcony of the hotel, they stood breathtakingly close as Alex leaned closer and whispered something in Karin's ear.

At least it looked like a whisper from where Katherine sat, but it was nothing more than a soft nuzzle laced with kisses. Karin laughed. "You make me feel like a confection and you a starving man."

"I am a starving man," he said in a faint, nibbling whisper. "Starving for you."

Karin rested her forehead against Alex's chest. "Oh Alex, Alex. What am I going to do about you?"

"Love me," he said. "Just love me."

"I always have," she said. "For as long as I can remember."

And that was true.

A few minutes later she was back at work, watching Alex through the shop window as he rode out of town. Lordy, Lordy, he was a looker—by far the most handsome man she'd ever seen, even dressed in the faded blue shirt and worn pants. It wasn't the clothes, but the body in them she thought, trying to analyze just why he appealed so much to her. Looking at the lean face that possessed a hint of almost barbaric handsomeness, she let her eyes rest on the proud aquiline nose, the full lips that she knew could speak with such determination and passion. No man had ever attracted her as he had. No man had ever been so much of what she wanted—with one exception. Alex was poor. Dirt poor.

Oh, he went on to talk about how he and

Adrian had saved their army pay and were using that to buy the things they needed to fix the old place up, and how they were going to put in a good crop this year and how prosperous they'd be the next. But whenever Alex took off in that direction and began talking about the life they would have there, the way the old place would look fixed up, she would find her mind wandering back to thoughts about getting away from Limestone County. It had become almost an obsession with her.

Just as she was about to turn away from the window, Karin saw Nathan Bradbury ride into town on his sleek chestnut. He was a tall, slender man, very attractive and well-to-do by small town standards. He was older than she by at least twenty-five years, not that it mattered any to her, but one thing about him did matter. Nathan was married. Whenever she saw him, she noticed the fire for her was still in his eyes. She remembered too, the way he had sought her out at a church social, following her until she was alone and some distance from the others, then coming to her, pressing his case and professing his desire for her.

"Mr. Bradbury, I will pretend you didn't say that. Everyone knows you're a married man."

"And everyone knows my wife is an invalid. They also know you are a very ambitious young woman." His arms came around her. "I can give you everything you want, everything you've ever desired: a nice home, clothes, a fancy carriage."

"And a bad name." She pried his hands

away and twisted out of his grip. "I'm not a trollop, Mr. Bradbury. I may be poor, but I don't sell myself."

"You will," he said confidently. "I've seen your kind before. The brothels are full of women like you, women who were starry-eyed young girls once; girls too young and foolish to be realistic until it was too late. You'll come around. Your kind always do."

Karin felt like crying. "You stay away from me, you hear? You stay away from me and my sister. We may be poor, but we aren't trash."

He laughed. "I have no designs on that outspoken sister of yours," he said. "She could be a pretty little thing well enough, I suppose—if she put her mind to it, but she's too clever with her own way of thinking, too plain and plodding. She wears adversity like a mantle of strength. She has too much will to survive for me, too much faith in herself."

"We both do," Karin said hotly, lifting her chin.

Again he laughed, his hand touching her face. "You have too much will to get ahead, too much faith in what you think it will bring you. You'll stick to the straight and narrow for a while, and when what you want doesn't come along, you'll sell your soul, if you have to, to get it. Your sister isn't a woman to compromise. She would die first."

Karin swept around him, feeling his hand clamp down on her arm. "You think about my offer," he said. "There is no one else around that can give you the things you want. I know that. And so do you. You'll change your mind, and when you do, I'll be waiting."

"You can wait until the cows come home," she said. "I won't ever change my mind about that. I'll have the things I want, no matter what you say. The difference is, I'll have them my way."

Even now, almost three years later, the sound of his mocking laughter haunted her. But in a way she owed Nathan Bradbury a debt of gratitude. After that day, Karin had begun to have a feeling that she would show him. She would show them all. She would be a grand lady, one day. And a rich one. Some might call her cynical and calculating, but that didn't matter to her. Her blue eyes turned sapphire dark, glittering just as coldly. She would *show* them. She would. She would.

The sound of a child's laughter pulled her thoughts back to the present. As she followed the sound of the laughter, she saw Betty Jo Dillingham come out of the mercantile, her three-year-old son laughing so loud, the baby in Betty Jo's arms started crying. It was awful to stand there watching Betty Jo with her children, because it reminded Karin painfully of her brother Billy and the baby sister she really never got to know, little Audrey. She stared almost lovingly at the children for a moment, then thought of her family, of the lives that were so dear to her, lives that had been snuffed out as insignificantly as a candle. She hated this place. Its cruelty. Its harshness. The unforgiving way it took and took and took, and when there was no more to give, it took your life as well. God damn Alex Mackinnon to perdition for being what he was. How much easier it would have been to harden herself against him if he weren't so desirable, so handsome, so much a part of her past.

It was because of this, because he was so much a part of her past, that she was more determined than ever that he would not—not ever, be a part of her future.

CHAPTER EIGHT

Over the next few weeks Katherine rarely saw Alex, and when she did he was fawning over Karin or behaving in an uninterested, impersonal manner toward her. How could she have ever thought him anything but different? It would have been easier to accept his going out of his way to ignore her—at least that would have said he was aware of her existence. But to treat her like she was transparent as glass was another matter entirely.

Only that morning she had awakened earlier than usual and lay staring at the ceiling, thinking of Alex. A cold weight settled in her heart. She wondered if she would ever be able to let go of the love she held for him, or would it continue to control and dominate her life as much as it did her thoughts until she was so old it no longer mattered. *Katherine Simon, spinster.*

She squeezed her eyes together as tight as she could.

How much longer? How long would the feeling torment her? When would it ever end? Tomorrow? Next year? Ten years from now?

It wouldn't be today. That much was certain. For already thoughts of him had robbed her of an hour of precious sleep and set the somber tone for her day. For a moment she allowed herself to think about her future. What if Karin was right? What if this place never got on its feet? What if it was never possible to do more than eke out a measly existence? One day, Karin would walk through that door and say she had saved enough to leave here. What would she do then? What would happen to her when she was too old to run this place by herself? *Something will work out,* she told herself. *It always has.* But what if it doesn't? *I'll worry about that tomorrow. Right now, I have work to be done.*

Overcome with the futility of it all, she threw back the covers and removed her gown. She pulled on a worn muslin dress that had faded from amber to a washed-out yellow, deciding to wear only one petticoat because of the heat. She moved to the pitcher and poured water into the basin, washing her face and hands, then drying them, studying her face in the mirror.

What is it about Karin that he prefers over me?

Was it her china doll appearance? The blue eyes? The blond hair? The way she always looked perfect and pampered, not a hair out of place? Did her conversation delight him? Did the sound of her laughter thrill him? Were her jokes so terribly funny?

Katherine braided her hair, continuing the critical study of herself as she did. Would Alex like her better if her hair was blond? She didn't know how to make her hair blond. What if she dyed it black? Would he like black? But then she looked at the rest of her. Everything seemed wrong—too many things to change, that much was certain. Comparing herself to her sister, everything about her was a complete opposite. The wrong colored hair. Her skin too dark, her hands too rough, her walk too determined. Her face was too exotic, her eyes too green. Her laugh was too genuine and came too easily to be controlled. She was too tall, too filled out, too everything.

She wound the braid on top of her head and fastened it down with pins. Then she looked at herself and said quite frankly, "Katherine Simon, what has gotten into you? You never felt inferior to anyone in your life, especially Karin. She isn't better than you. She's just different. And on top of everything else, Alex probably can't help loving her any more than you can help loving him. Maybe it would be just as hard for him to force his feelings for you as it would be for you to force your feelings about Adrian."

That was a sobering thought.

She went downstairs, still wishing that she

could at least know what Alex thought of her. *Maybe it's better you don't know. Maybe you should be glad he's indifferent.* She carried those thoughts with her to the garden, where she picked a mess of turnips and turnip greens, returning to the house to wash them and put them on to simmer. She threw the waste into the slop pail, then carried a bucket of soapy water into the parlor, telling herself as she went that she wanted more from Alex than indifference. She would have dwelled upon that thought a bit longer, but Karin picked that moment to flutter into the room like a leaf swept up before the wind. "It's too hot to be stuck in this inferno of a house." She fanned herself furiously. "I'm going to take a walk down by the creek to cool off."

"A walk?" Katherine asked, dropping the rag she was using to wash the windows into the bucket beside her. She glanced out the window, seeing the dark clouds banking in the distance, then back at Karin. "I don't think this is a good time to be taking a walk. We're in for some bad weather. Just look over there," she said, pointing toward the dark gray shadow that stretched itself like a lazy cat across the horizon. "I've been watching it for some time now. It's getting closer and darker."

"It could be hours before those clouds reach us, and there's always the possibility they won't reach us at all."

"I think it'll be here before you know it," Katherine said.

"And if it is?" Karin said, giving her umbrella

169

a snap. She twirled it over her head. "What's a little rain? It's nothing but water. I've been wet before."

"It's bad luck to open an umbrella in the house."

"Oh, posh! I don't believe in all that poppycock. You're too superstitious." Karin untied the apron at her waist and dropped it over the back of the armchair. "Ta, ta," she said, going out the door.

Katherine watched Karin sashay across the yard and out the gate, then turned back to what she was doing. A few minutes later, she finished washing the windows, thankful she had decided to clean the inside today, because of the rain. She took one last look out the window. It was going to rain, and it would be a good one at that—a real gully-washer. She smiled to herself, remembering that Fanny always called a good rain a "turd-floater." It sounded perfectly all right coming from Fanny's mouth, but Katherine couldn't bring herself to say anything more than gully-washer. She picked up the bucket and carried it into the kitchen. She needed to make a quick inspection of the rain barrels to be sure they were still in position to catch all the runoff from the roof. After she put the bucket away she gave the turnips and greens a quick stir, dipping the spoon in the crock of bacon fat and stirring it into the greens for added flavor.

Clovis began braying. At first Katherine didn't think that strange, but after he continued much longer than usual, she decided she'd better have a look. She opened the back door and stepped outside, breaking into a run the moment she did, for something was wrong. Clovis was braying and kicking, working himself into a frenzy that he seemed to be taking out on the fence. And well Katherine knew that fence was held together by prayer and precious few nails and wouldn't withstand too much of his pounding. She reached the corral just in time to see Clovis kick like the mule he was, splintering the already weakened boards, then whirl and break through them with a mighty crash. The cause of the disturbance, a bull snake about three feet long, crawled swiftly between two boards to disappear inside the barn.

Katherine stomped her foot in frustration as she saw the last of Clovis's tufted tail as he rounded the chicken coop and disappeared from sight. "Go on then, you stupid, stubborn... Oh, what's the use?" she said, throwing up her hands and giving the dark horizon one last look. She would have to go after him, for Clovis was as necessary to their livelihood as the air they breathed. Without another thought, Katherine hitched up her skirts and hurried into the barn where she scooped up half a bucket of oats and dropped a lead rope inside, then headed in the direction Clovis had taken, her skirts gathered in one hand, the bucket in the other, for Clovis wasn't a mule to be lured by harsh threats or sweet, soothing words. Only one thing would get him close enough to snap the lead rope on his halter and that was the rattle of oats in the bucket—if she found him, that is.

Once she was in the open field, she spied Clovis heading toward the trees that lined the creek. She prayed Karin would see him. She caught herself, realizing what she'd just thought. What difference did it make if she did? Karin wouldn't come within a mile of Clovis if she didn't have to.

She didn't think about Karin again as she hurried across the field, feeling the wind picking up and catching the scent of rain in the air. She tripped once, spilling some of the oats and driving a cocklebur under her fingernail when she dropped down to scrape up the spilled oats. She stood again and took off in a slow, steady lope, seeing Clovis disappear behind the heavy green branches of trees just ahead. *Finding him will be like finding a needle in a haystack,* she told herself as she reached the trees and ducked beneath a low branch.

The thicket was dark and cool, the leaves rustling as the wind picked up. She made her way slowly, searching the shadows, hoping to see Clovis looking back at her from beneath his long black ears. *Just before I box them!* She could see him now, his neck stretched out as far as it would go as he tried to reach the more tender leaves that grew higher on the tree. He was standing in a thin strip of a clearing that ran down to the edge of the creek. A sliver of light cut through the tops of the trees to fall across his broad back which was turned toward her. It also fell on the broad back of Alexander Mackinnon standing just a few feet away. She started to call out to him, to ask for his help in catching Clovis. She guessed he didn't hear Clovis over the sound of the wind blowing through the leaves overhead. But he must have heard something, for at that moment he turned, his eyes going first to Clovis, then to Katherine, who took no notice, for her eyes were immediately drawn to her sister who stood in front of him, her bodice unbuttoned and her naked breasts gleaming pale and creamy against the deep walnut of Alex Mackinnon's hand.

Katherine made no sound, save the thump of the bucket dropping to the ground, the swish of oats as they spilled out. She whirled around as silently as she had come, running blindly, seeking the cover of trees and the relief from humiliation they offered. The moment she ducked out of sight, she broke into a harder run, feeling no pain from the tangled vines that scratched her arms and face, the dead branch that ripped her clothing. Just as she reached the clearing, a blinding flash of light slammed into a hackberry just a few feet from her, splintering the wood and sending it flying. A deafening clap of thunder seemed to split the earth apart and Katherine felt a tremendous jolt that knocked her backward. It took her a moment to come to her feet, and when she did, she was stunned and wobbly legged, her sense of balance confused. When she reached the open fields, she broke into a run, stumbling and falling over the ruts she had hired Eli Whittaker's boy to plow, getting up again to run and stumble and fall again. By the time she had reached the center of the field, great gray drops of rain were falling and a jagged bolt of lightning ripped at the sky overhead, throwing flashes of light all around her, the splitting crack of thunder coming only seconds later.

"Katherine... Katherine."

The sound of her name being called out to her only hastened feet that were already flying. The sound of her name came again, closer this time, mingled with the thundering sound of hoofbeats drawing up close behind. The sound of her name reached her again, sounding as if it were coming from just behind her as she ran through the open gate. When she reached the porch, she did not slow down but hurled herself against the door, turning the handle as she did, feeling herself falling, then the warm, steadying strength of an arm as it whipped around her pulling her back against a body that suddenly had a name.

Adrian.

She knew it was Adrian the moment he touched her, for if it had been Alex, she would have felt the jolt of his touch as surely as if she had been struck by lightning.

"Katherine, my God! What's the matter? What's happened?" He whirled her around, his voice dropping as he cradled her wet body against him. "No," he said, then louder, as if the agony of it were ripped from his throat. "Oh, Lord, girl. What have you done?"

Katherine looked at his face, the droplets of rain clinging to his lashes, then she looked down at her bodice that was soaked in blood.

The sound of her own voice sounded strange, detached and hollow, as if it were coming from far, far away. "It's all right. I haven't been shot," she said, remembering the loud crack of what she had thought to be thunder, the force of it knocking her to the ground. Then she said, "I don't think I was shot."

"There's one way to find out," he said, ripping the sleeve from her dress and splitting the shoulder seam with his knife. "Don't," she screamed, slapping at his hands.

"Katherine, this is not the time to be modest. You're hurt. I've got to see how bad."

"I don't want you—"

"I have to," he said, cutting her off and catching both of her hands in one of his. "I'm the only person here."

He pulled the dress down, slicing the shoulder of her chemise, baring the wound. A jagged splinter of wood had pierced her flesh, imbedding itself deeply. Looking down and seeing it Katherine felt light-headed. Adrian swept her into his arms and carried her up the stairs to her room. Once there, he lowered her to her feet. "Do you think you're going to faint?"

She shook her head. "No, I'm just dizzy," she said, feeling a stab of pain for the first time. He caught her just as she slumped, feeling her body like a dead weight in his arms.

He carried her to the bed, hearing the door downstairs open just as he laid her down. "Up here!" he shouted. "Quick."

Alex was first in the room, followed by Karin.

"Katherine!" Alex said. Then to Adrian, "What happened?"

"I was too far away to see exactly, but she was deathly close to a tree when it was struck by lightning. Just as it struck I saw her fall. I thought for a moment it struck her. There's a good-sized splinter imbedded in her shoulder that must have been driven in when the tree was struck."

Karin was bathing Katherine's face with a cloth. She turned to Alex. "We need a doctor."

"I'll go," Alex said.

His face drained of all color, his hands trembling, he looked at Katherine one last time, then hurried down to his horse.

Everything seemed vague after that: bringing the doctor to the Simon place, the hours of waiting downstairs, the sound of the doctor's voice saying, "It was a nasty wound because of all the splinters I had to dig out after I removed the large one. But she's sleeping quietly now. I've left instructions for the opium drops with Karin. What she needs now is rest."

Adrian stared in surprise at his brother as Alex cursed softly under his breath and hurried from the room. Doc Lesley followed Alex out, and Adrian walked to the window, watching the doctor climb into his buggy. As it pulled away, he could see Alex walking toward his horse tied to the fence. Just as he reached for the reins, Adrian had a glimpse of his agonized face just as he smashed his fist against the top rail with enough force to break his hand.

Alex's hand wasn't broken, but it was good and sore for several days. It had healed completely by the time Katherine was up and about, tending to her chores with the same determination as ever, and a little soreness.

She didn't see Alex for two weeks, and Karin refrained from looking her in the eye. At night Katherine went to her room and collapsed tiredly on her bed. The pain in her shoulder always returned late in the evening, but it wasn't severe and she reminded herself she had lived with worse. Once she was in bed, she would think of Alex, just as she always did, something that came so repeatedly, like the steady *tap, tap, tap* of a hammer. And then she would remember what she had seen that day down by the creek. After the first few weeks, the shock lessened. Then came awareness—not so much the awareness of what she had seen, but more the awareness of what it all meant; awareness that Alex Mackinnon would never belong to her as he belonged to her sister; awareness that she had read so much more into his friendly presence than was actually there; awareness of the fool she had been.

The hideous reminder rose like a scaly dragon before her. *Fool...Fool...Fool...*

And fool she was. Wouldn't anyone agree? Wouldn't anyone who knew say that's what she deserved for wanting the man who belonged to her sister? Didn't the Bible warn against coveting thy neighbor's wife? Wasn't that about the same thing as coveting thy sister's lover?

But to see them together like that! Why? Perhaps that was her punishment. Perhaps that was what was needed to jerk her back to her senses.

Never again would she allow her mind to fill with hope. *Don't absorb yourself with his every word, his teasing looks, the humorous jabs he all too frequently takes at you. Alex is a nice person,* she kept telling herself. *He was being nice to you, Katherine. N-I-C-E. That's not the same as being romantic. It's not the same as being attracted. It's nothing like being in love. What it is like is friendship. That's what you are to Alex. A friend. Nothing more.*

It was the third week after her accident when Karin came into her room one night, shortly after Katherine had gone up. "I know you must think I'm a horrible person," she said, sitting on the bed and crying into hands that were cupped over her face. "And you're right! I am a horrid person. I know it. I could never be good and kind like you, Katherine. I don't know why, but I can't."

"You aren't horrible," Katherine said wearily. "And I'm not as good and kind as you think."

Karin came off the bed in one dramatic sweep of rose and lavender cotton, dropping to her knees in front of the rocker Katherine sat in, her golden curls, spilling over her shoulder. Grabbing Katherine's hands in hers, she looked up at her sister through tear-blurred eyes. "I know I was wrong to let Alex take those kinds of liberties with me. I promise it won't happen again, Katherine. I promise."

"I'm not your mother, Karin. It isn't for me to tell you what you can and can't do. Whether this was the first time, or the fiftieth, it isn't my affair. You don't have to answer to me. I just don't want you to do something you will be sorry for the rest of your life. I want you to be sure Alex is what you want."

Something about the way Katherine looked must have said she doubted this had been the first time, for Karin wept bitterly into her sister's lap. "Alex has never touched me like that before, Katherine. I swear he hasn't. Please say you believe me. Please."

"Karin..."

"Please."

"All right. I believe you. But that really shouldn't matter."

"But it does," she said, still weeping. "What you think has always mattered to me. I just don't want you to think I'm a bad person."

"I don't."

"Not even after what you saw? Not after the way you were hurt?"

"Not even then." Katherine stroked Karin's golden head, wondering why she always ended up feeling more like Karin's mother after one of these discussions than her younger sister.

Karin's head came up, her delicate hands wiping the tear paths from her face. "I promise it won't happen again."

Katherine sighed. "Karin, do you love Alex?"

"Please," Karin said, struggling to her feet. "Please don't ask me that."

"Why not? It seems like a perfectly logical question to me."

"It may be logical," Karin said, wiping the tears from her face and looking like the perfect picture of composure, "but logical or not, I don't want you to ask me."

"Why?"

"Because I do love Alex, but in a way I don't think you would understand. Because I feel I'll lose no matter what I say."

"I don't know how you can say that. Alex loves you, and..."

Karin came to her feet and walked a few feet away. "I know he does, but I also know things won't ever work for us."

"How can you be so sure?"

"Because I see what's going on over there. I pass by their place every day. I see how hard Alex and Adrian are slaving—no, how they're killing themselves working that run-down old farm all by themselves. All this talk—and it's little more than that—just talk. They won't make that place pay—ever. I've known it from the beginning. It will suck up every penny they saved and give them nothing in return."

"They may surprise you. They've got more than thirty acres under cultivation right now, and the spring rains have been abundant. They'll have enough hay to feed those thirty cows they bought from Karl Webster, and then some. Why, just the other day Alex was telling me about that fine, prizewinning bull he's trying to buy from George Tatum's widow."

Karin threw up her hands. "Stories, all of them. Nothing more than dreams and stories. There's nothing realistic about any of it. It won't work, Katherine. I'm telling you, it won't work."

"Then nothing has changed for you, has it?"

"How do you mean?"

"You haven't changed your mind about leaving, have you?"

"No, I haven't. Why should I? Tell me one thing that's happened that would make me reconsider."

"Alex is back."

"And still as poor as a church mouse."

"If you feel that way, why do you keep him hanging on? Why don't you tell him? Why keep him hoping?"

Karin turned away, giving Katherine her back. "I have told him. It isn't my fault he's so stubborn. I told him again last night, told him I could never spend the rest of my life here."

"What did he say?"

"The same thing he always says. He asked me to wait a little longer, to give him more time. But it's so hard, and I'm so confused. I love him, but I don't want to. I want him, yet he isn't what I want. Does that make sense?"

Katherine nodded.

"You know yourself there were never too many men around and now, after the war there are even fewer. Alex is so *nice*, and I'm so very tired of being poor." Karin turned back toward Katherine, wringing her hands in front of her. "Oh, Katherine, you don't know what it's like to be poor."

Katherine looked dumbfounded. "I don't know what it's like? Aren't you forgetting that I'm as poor as you, that I live in the same run-down house, that I eat the same pathetic food as you do? How can you say I don't know what it's like to be poor."

"Because you don't, not really."

"That simply isn't true."

"It is! I know it is, because you know how to withstand troubles, Katherine. You're like an oak tree with deep, strong roots, able to withstand all the things mother nature throws at you, while I'm like the water plants that grow along the creek. I bloom and look pretty as long as everything is in perfect balance, but when it isn't I wither and die."

"You aren't that shallow, Karin, no matter what you think. You're just upset about what happened. I don't hate you and I don't think you're sinful or awful for what happened. I just want you to be certain about whatever you choose to do. Alex is in love with you. Don't give him false hope."

"You know, it's almost funny. I know you love Alex more than I could ever love anything."

"I don't! He's a friend, nothing more."

"Oh, Katherine, it's so obvious. Of course you love him, everyone knows: me, Adrian, even Alex."

"Alex has never said a word to me."

"He wouldn't. He likes you, values your friendship too much to hurt you. He always thought you'd outgrow it, or find someone else to love."

"It isn't fair for you to say that. You have no right to talk that way. *If* I was in love with Alex, it wouldn't be some silly, childish infatuation I'd outgrow."

"Don't be angry. I probably shouldn't have said what I did. Heaven knows I don't have any room to talk. Look at me! Here I am in love with Alex, yet telling myself it can never be. That's what I meant a while ago when I said you love Alex more than I could ever love anything. I can't love like you do, Katherine. It isn't my whole existence, my entire being. In my way, I do love Alex. I know I should stop this thing between us, because it isn't fair to him and he'll only be hurt in the end. I should let go, but I can't seem to." She pressed her knuckles against her temples. "Oh, why is life so wretched? Why am I the way I am? All my life I've felt I had to do something to stand out, to draw attention to myself. You were always so smart, Katherine, so self-assured, so confident. Life was always a challenge for you. You were always good at everything you did. You won all the races, you made better grades, you could cook and sew and quote poetry. I never thought I would have a chance to compete with you. And then one day I realized I had something over you. I was pretty. I had a figure. I was becoming a woman, while you were nothing more than a plump child. That was my one chance to outshine you, and I took it."

Katherine felt a deep sadness for Karin, for she had no idea Karin felt this way, even though she knew what her sister said was, in essence, right. She had always bested Karin in school, so often that Karin would wail, "But it's not fair! She doesn't pay attention at all. She's always staring out the window, her mind a million miles away. She never studies, while I'm always poring over my schoolbooks. Why does everything come so easy and natural for her?"

"It isn't fair," Karin wailed again, and Katherine remembered how her father's hand would come out to stroke the lovely golden curls on Karin's head, and how much she wished he would do that to her. *I don't care,* she would tell herself. *I have my mother.* And that was true.

Katherine stood. "Why don't you go finish putting the buttons on your new dress. I'll check on the progress the stew is making."

While Katherine set the table, someone knocked on the back door. When she opened it, Alex was standing there. Seeing him, her body tensed, a shiver of awakening flesh leaving a trail of goose bumps. She looked at the hat in his hands, his clothes sweaty and dirty, as if he'd just come from the fields. Even this way he looked tempting—honest, hardworking, and bronzed by the sun. Seeing the way she looked at him and imagining her thoughts, he said, "I apologize for my appearance. I've been plowing since sunup. I only came by to bring Clovis home."

"Oh no!" Katherine frowned. "Did he get out again?"

"I'm afraid so. I found him heading down the road toward town. I penned him, and I figured out how he was getting out. I replaced a few worn boards and tightened the lock. That should do the trick. If it doesn't, let me know."

"I will. Thank you, Alex. I appreciate that. Sometimes I swear Clovis knows how vital he is to the work around here. He always knows just how much he can get away with." Her voice trailed off as his eyes fastened on hers. She felt torn in two. One part of her screamed to have this pretense done away with. She wanted to be free to shout her love from the treetops. The other part, as always, worked hard to appear impersonal and uncaring.

"Katherine," he said softly, looking a little uncomfortable.

"Yes?" She looked at him, feeling her insides twist painfully. He smiled, a little hesitant, unsure. Normally, his smile would put her at ease, but today, even that gave her no peace.

"About what happened that day at the creek—the day you were hurt."

She didn't say anything. There were no words to express her thoughts, her feelings. She didn't speak because she couldn't. Nor could she think. Everything within her seemed to shut down. Nothing seemed to exist for her in the entire world, nothing save this most beautiful of men standing grimy and uncertain before her, and her desperate need to have him close, to feel his hands touch her in places that

185

had known no man's touch. The tension was strong enough to reach out and strum like a guitar. So much love for him welled inside her, she knew it had to be shining brilliantly in her eyes. It was something she wanted desperately to hide, and she looked down, trying to concentrate on the worn ruffle on her apron.

"Please," he said. "Hear me out."

Katherine held up her hand. "I'd rather you didn't mention anything about it. What goes on between you and Karin—" Her voice faltered and she was afraid she couldn't go on. With supreme effort, she managed to say, "It's none of my affair, Alex. There's no reason to discuss it."

"I just wanted you to know..."

"You owe me no explanation. As far as I'm concerned, it's forgotten."

"Katherine, I know better. I know..."

"I said it was forgotten, Alex. Let's leave it that way."

"All right," he said looking hurt. "If that's the way you want it."

"That's the way I want it."

"I'll be heading back, then."

Katherine nodded and watched him turn and walk away. She closed the door, then leaned her back against it, her hands spread flat against the worn wood. She closed her eyes and listened for the sound of his footsteps as he turned away, her mind screaming, *Oh, Alex...Alex...Alex...* Knowing as she thought those words he would never hear them or the other words she longed to say: *Alex, I love you.*

Alex walked home, his hands shoved deep into his pockets, a thoughtful expression on his face. Why should it upset him that Katherine had seen him with Karin? Why did he feel this hammering need to talk to her, to set things straight, to explain? And why in the name of hell did it bother him that Katherine was so obviously hurt, no matter how much she let on that she wasn't? He tried to rationalize all this by telling himself that it was no more than brotherly concern, that Katherine had always been as close to him as a sister, that his concern was only brotherly concern. Only problem with that was, he couldn't explain away the tiny knot of frustration over Katherine that twisted his gut, nor could he, in all honesty, ignore the small kernel of attraction Katherine held for him.

He had always been fond of Katherine, but he was wondering if that's all it was. "You just need a woman," he told himself, recognizing how frustrated he was over Karin's refusal to sleep with him, her stubborn determination to be a great lady.

He sighed, wondering, *Why couldn't I have fallen in love with Katherine? It would have been so much simpler.*

But he hadn't fallen in love with Katherine. It was Karin he loved. Karin with eyes as blue and clear as glass beads, and hair as golden as the pollen sac on a bumblebee. Karin was the one who brought out the feelings of a man in him, and it was Karin he thought of as a woman—a woman he wanted to touch and make love to. Karin was always soft and gentle; always knew what to say to make him feel ten feet tall, while Katherine could level him with one silencing look. And she could, and had, on more than one occasion, cut him to the core with a pointed comment driven home. No, Katherine with her quick wit and sharp tongue, her no-frills talk, her plain dresses was not for him.

Alex saw Adrian was still hard at plowing, and he hopped the fence to join him. The farm was in worse shape than either of them had thought at first. It was like a great hole into which they dumped three years of army pay. He would never give Karin what she dreamed of this way. He stared out over the barren fields trying to imagine them green and fertile. Hard work would do that. Hard work would give him what he wanted.

For the next month, Alex drove himself without mercy. Adrian noticed it. Katherine noticed it. Karin most certainly noticed it. Alex was avoiding her and it didn't sit too well with her. While Alex wasn't what she wanted in the end, he certainly filled the hours in between. She didn't want to lose the bird in the hand until she found one in the bush.

In plain English, Karin was bored.

One sultry afternoon Adrian dropped by, asking Katherine to ride into town with him, knowing that she would refuse, just as she had refused the other thirty or so times he had asked her. It almost knocked him off his perch on the wagon seat when she dropped the pillowcase she was about to pin on the line back into the basket and said, "Why Adrian, I'd love to go with you. How lucky I am that you asked, because I have a list of things I need that is almost as long as the road from here to town."

After Katherine had finished hanging out the clothes, she had fetched her list and her bonnet and climbed into the wagon. That last bit had surprised him, not because Adrian was used to Katherine letting him help her do anything, for she wasn't, but he had hoped that since she had softened somewhat about riding to town with him, that perhaps she had softened about other things as well. In truth, Katherine had simply seen Alex Mackinnon coming down the road on his buckskin and desired to put as much distance between herself and him as possible.

Alex met Katherine and Adrian just as they were leaving. When he drew even with the wagon he pulled Beedle up, then pushed back his hat, using his thumb to do it. "Whew! It's hotter than blazes out here. Why aren't you two cooling your heels in the shade somewhere instead of broiling out here in the sun?"

"Lord, I'd rather be doing that," Adrian said, then looking to Katherine he asked, "wouldn't you?"

"*If* I had time," Katherine said stiffly and looked away.

The brothers exchanged glances and Adrian shrugged his shoulders.

"Where are you off to?" Alex asked.

"Town," Katherine said. "Karin is milking in the barn," she said before he had a chance to inquire. Tugging her bonnet over her head, she said to Adrian, "If you want me to go with you, Adrian Mackinnon, we'd best be going. You may have all day to dawdle, but I don't. I'll swan! I could walk to town faster than this, not to mention how we look like a couple of pure fools dawdling in the middle of the road like we are."

Alex laughed at the way Adrian hopped to it and had those horses moving before a body could say armadillo. Tugging his hat down low over his eyes, Alex turned Beedle toward the Simons' barn, wondering what Karin would be doing when he found her, because he didn't believe for a minute that she would be milking if she didn't absolutely have to.

He found her sitting on the ladder that led to the loft, holding one of the barn kittens— a cute fuzzy little gray thing that sputtered and hissed when he reached out to pet it, then jumped from her lap. When he teased her about not doing her chores, she informed him that she had already finished milking. Alex looked at her, thinking it was something he could do for the rest of his life. His gaze rested on her glossy golden head, not finding a hair out of place, then traveled over the perfect, doll-like features, dropping lower to enjoy the curves of her body, remembering the way she had looked that day so long ago when he had watched her swimming naked in the creek. The memory of it shot through him with a jolt. Karin stood, calling the kitten, and admonishing Alex when it ran outside. "I've always heard animals were a good judge of people and that kitten doesn't especially like you. Maybe there's a lesson in that for me."

"Well, Clovis likes me," he said, flashing her a smile.

"That's reason enough to send you packing. I hate that mule. I don't know why Katherine insists on keeping him."

"Probably because he's a good mule. One of the best in the county. She's had more than her share of offers from folks wanting to buy him."

"And she's a fool for not taking any of them. I wish someone would ask me. I'd sell," Karin said, sounding just a little put out, and in fact, she was, for Alex had interrupted her at a time when she was deep in thought, and those times did not come too often.

Alex laughed. "Now stop complaining, sweetheart, and give me a kiss."

"And if I don't feel like it?"

"You will," he said, grinning, his arm coming out to curl around her waist as he led her along with him to a dark abandoned stall. He stopped, backing her against the wall and turning her toward him, his eyes moving slowly over her face as if he were committing each of her features to memory. He kissed her softly on the neck. "This is all I've been able to think of since that day at the creek."

"That should have never happened, and it won't happen again."

"Yes it should, and it will again." He drew her closer with one hand, the other hand coming up to tilt her chin up. The moment their eyes locked, she felt his warm breath as his face came closer, his lips, soft and inviting, sliding over hers until she forgot all about her words of a moment ago. It always happened this way. When she was away from him she would make up her mind that there would be no more kisses, no more groping hands, but when she was with him nothing seemed to matter but the taste and feel of him, the words he whispered so hoarsely in her ear.

Feeling his control slip and nearly mindless with wanting, Alex pressed his knee between hers to the point she was almost straddling him. And that was her undoing, for she groaned, putting her hands around his head and pulling him down to kiss her again. His lips blistering a trail to her ear, he said, "Come up the ladder with me."

"Up the ladder," she said in a dazed way.

There were times he felt he wanted to shake Karin and this was one of them. He kissed her again. "Listen to me, Karin. I want you and I know you want me, and unless you prefer this stall to the clean hay piled in the loft, then get yourself up there."

"Alex, I told you…"

He didn't let her finish. Just listening to her voice stirred him. He pressed himself closer, backing her against the wall again, his mouth coming down to cover hers. She groaned, "Oh Alex," then kissed him back with everything she had, and Alex must have thought that was plenty, for he groaned in response.

"That's it sweetheart." His hand dropped to one side and began inching her dress up until he had his hand on her smooth, warm thigh. "Easy, my love, if you won't come into the loft with me, at least let me touch you."

She was debating that when he kissed her again, his hand moving up the outside of her thigh, then moving over. "Alex, someone might see us."

"They won't."

"But Katherine might walk in."

"She's gone to town."

"Adrian, then."

"He's gone too, so you might as well give in, unless you're worried about what Clovis might think if he sees us."

She couldn't help laughing at the idea of that. Lord, what was wrong with her, ever doubting that there could ever be another man that charmed her more than Alex. Any further thought vanished as Alex's hand found the place he sought and Karin moaned softly, a picture of Adrian coming suddenly to the front of her mind.

"Karin? Karin, where are you?"

"Oh, dear God," Karin said, pushing Alex away. "It's Fanny Bright!"

"There are times I swear she isn't," Alex said with a trembling sigh, feeling as frustrated as all get out.

"You swear she isn't what," Karin said, putting her clothes in order.

"Bright."

"Well, never mind that. I just hope I can get myself presentable before she walks in here. Now you give me some time to get her lured into the house before you come out, you hear? That's the last thing I need—her catching the two of us in here together, or to see you sneaking out after me."

Fanny called again, and Karin answered, hurrying from the barn, not giving Alex so much as a last look. Alex waited until they walked inside the house before leaving.

That night Karin lay in bed thinking that she didn't enjoy kissing and flirting with Alex the way she used to. She found that strange, but not shattering, for she had never been one to stick to anything too long. There were just so many things to do and see, and the same was true, she supposed, of men. How could she know Alex was the one, when she hadn't seen more than a handful of others? What if she married Alex—and then met another man she liked better? She closed her eyes and rolled over, seeing Adrian's face again, and she found herself wondering why she was suddenly thinking of Adrian so much. But once the thought was there, she couldn't shake it. What would it be like to kiss him? And, furthermore, what would it hurt?

This idea was firmly planted like a seed in the back of her mind and over the next few days Karin watered it liberally. Whenever Adrian was around, she began to fuss over him, lowering her lashes, brushing against him, not enough that Alex would notice, or even Adrian, at first. When Adrian didn't respond, Karin became a little more persistent until she saw him walking toward the creek one afternoon, a fishing pole slung over his shoulder.

Adrian did not share any of Karin's curiosity. In fact, he had grown almost to the point of despising Karin for what his brother was too blind to see, that she was making a fool out of him.

Hearing the rustle of leaves behind him, Adrian turned to see Karin coming up behind him. "Have you caught any fish?"

He gave her his back. "A few."

She ducked her head to come under a low branch, then, when she was on the other side, she moved with a swaying walk to Adrian's side, peering at his string of fish in the water. "How many do you have?"

"Two." Adrian turned toward her, his face controlled, his words not very warm. "But that isn't why you walked all the way down here, and we both know it."

"It isn't?" she repeated, giving him a smile. "Why *do* you think I came?"

"I think you came to get the answers to some questions."

"Like what?"

"Like how I compare with my brother."

She gasped. "Adrian! How can you say such a thing?"

"Because it's true, and you know it as well as I."

She toyed with a lock of his hair. "And if it is?"

He pulled his head to one side. "It won't do you a bit of good."

"Why is that?"

He turned toward her, his face a mask of red fury. "Because I don't like the way you lead my brother around by the nose. Because I don't like the way you pretend to care for him and make eyes at me every chance you get. Because I'm not half the man my brother is around women and you wouldn't be happy with me for a single minute."

"You hate me, don't you?"

He sighed. "No, I don't suppose I hate you exactly, but I could shake you until your teeth rattled. I suppose I've known you too long to hate you. We've always been friends. I remember how much I used to like you before you began to change. I don't like what you've become."

"What do you mean?"

"I can remember a time when you weren't so hoity-toity, a time when you would run barefoot and swim naked, a time when you didn't fuss over the way you looked or worry if no one noticed you."

"We were children then."

"Yes, and some of us grew up. You just changed."

She sat down next to him, feeling the need to look beautiful, to show off, drain away. "I haven't become anything. I may want things that are different from you and Alex and

Katherine, too, but inside, I'm still the same person." He shot her a look and she said, "Oh, I know what you think, what everyone thinks. But I haven't slept with your brother. We haven't even come close."

"You give the impression that you've done a hulluva lot more than come close."

"Do I?" She tossed a pebble into the water. "Oh dear! I scared away the fish."

"It doesn't matter. I think they've stopped biting anyway."

She drew her knees up under her chin. "I know you think I'm using Alex, but I'm not, Adrian. I'm really not."

"What are you doing, then?"

"I've been perfectly honest with Alex. There are things I want, things I can't get here, things Alex can't give me. He knows that." Karin lapsed into silence, staring at the flat surface of the water without really seeing it. She was seeing Miss Minnie Perkins, the oldest spinster in Limestone County. Ninety years old, and in her fourth rocking chair. Dear merciful God, what if that happened to her? Over the years that Alex had been away, three young men had cycled through her life, each one looking promising at first, then dwindling to nothing. Of the three, one joined the army; one went back east to school; one was pushed into marriage with a wealthy Dallas girl.

There were times she thought about catching the next stage and taking it as far as the money she had would take her. She told herself that she was simply a woman who needed more in her life than a place like Limestone County, Texas, could offer. She told herself that marriage was a way to put Limestone County behind her; that it was possible to love a rich man just as easily as it was to love a poor one. Basically, men were all alike—some were like fleas, hopping from place to place, while others were like ticks and once they latched on they sucked you dry. Alex didn't seem to fit either one and that puzzled her.

It was at half past four in the afternoon a week later that Karin was tying a wide taffeta bow on a new bonnet displayed in the window of the seamstress shop. She tied the bow once, then backed off a ways to look at it, then yanked the ribbon, and retied it. This went on for a few minutes, tying and retying, until she felt she had it right. And the moment she stepped back and smiled with satisfaction at her handiwork, she glanced up to see Alex Mackinnon grinning at her from the other side of the window. He took the watch from his watch pocket and opened the lid pointing at it, then looking at her in question. She held up ten fingers and mouthed the word ten minutes. He nodded and pointed to the place he now stood, telling her in that wordless way that he would be waiting for her there in ten minutes' time. Karin nodded, watching him walk away before she turned back to what she was doing.

Ten minutes later when she locked up the

shop, Alex was waiting for her, just as he'd said. "This is a surprise," she said, relieved when he took her packages from her.

"I'll toss these into the wagon, then we can take a stroll through town."

Karin looked at the main street of Groesbeck, which happened to be the only street, and said, "It'll be a short one."

Alex laughed. "True, but we need to talk."

She nodded, feeling the knot of apprehension curl inward in her stomach.

"I've been thinking," he said.

"About what?"

"I think I was wrong to come back here thinking I could make a go of things. Adrian and I—Well, we've tried, but it just isn't working."

"You haven't given yourself much time, Alex."

"Time isn't the problem. I could spend the rest of my life here trying to scrape a living from this unforgiving place and still have no more to show for it than I do now." They reached the wagon and Alex placed the packages beneath the seat, then turned, taking Karin's arm and guiding her up the street. "There are so many things I want for us, things we can never have as long as I stay here."

"Are you trying to tell me that you're leaving?" She laughed. "Now you sound like me."

"No, I'm not leaving. At least not right away." His laugh was dry and crackling.

"That's the hell of it. I don't know where I'd go even if I did leave. I only know I won't ever be anything more than a poor dirt farmer as long as I stay here."

"And I don't want to be a dirt farmer's wife." She saw the way he looked at her. "I know Katherine would say there were worse things than being a dirt farmer, that you were young and strong and in time..." Her eyes were pleading. "I can't think of anything worse than being a dirt farmer, Alex. Absolutely nothing."

It surprised her when he said, "I know. Sometimes I feel the same way. If I keep going like this, in time I'll be dead, just like half the men around here will be because they're killing themselves at a hopeless task, hoping to perform miracles."

"I suppose you'll just have to make the most of it and not give up hope until an opportunity for something better comes along."

"What if that opportunity never comes? Or what if it does and I can't make myself latch onto it? I've always loved the land. You know that. I can't see myself doing anything that would take me from it. But it's no use. Adrian and I have buried every cent we had in this place, and for what? A few dehydrated sprigs?" He looked up at the sky, a red, molten ball beating down without mercy or moisture. "We haven't had a good rain in a while, and you know what that means to a dry-land farmer." He fell silent, staring off for a moment. "God, I hate this—this feeling so god-damn helpless. You can't imagine what it's like to work your fingers to the bone, plowing and planting, and then watching every seed, every tiny green sprout break forth with promise, only to wither and die beneath this hell-born sun."

"Then you'll have to do what others do that aren't farming. Get a job."

"Doing what? Shoveling manure in the livery? Counting pennies at the bank? Hell, I wouldn't last a week." He shook his head. "Maybe you're right. Maybe that's what I should do, but somehow I can't seem to make myself walk through a door that the hand of poverty is holding open." He sighed and they walked on in silence, passing a store or two, a few people they knew who spoke or nodded in passing. Everything was closing down for the day, folks turning their thoughts toward home and more than likely, what was for supper. Alex and Karin reached the end of the board sidewalk and taking her arm again, he helped her step down and cross the alley. Once they were in the middle, he sighed and took her hand as if it were some sort of apology, and drew her aside, down the alley to stand behind the protection of some stacked crates. He took her in his arms and kissed her softly. "I know I confuse you. I asked you to trust me, to give me time, and you did. It tears me up to know I've failed you, that I can't give you the things I was so certain I could."

"You haven't failed me, Alex, because I

never believed you could do those things, not because I doubted you, but because I know what a cruel mistress the land can be."

He looked down at the sweetest angel face that looked back at him with wide, beautiful eyes. "No matter what you say, I made so many promises, promises I couldn't keep—save one." He pulled her against him, cuddling her head against his chest and resting his chin against the top of her head. "I promised to always love you, and that hasn't changed. You do know how much I love you, don't you?"

She nodded.

"It's been pure hell for me to keep my hands off you and to keep from taking you to my bed. I want you so bad I can't sleep at night, but that will have to wait a while, I guess."

"I wish I knew what to say, how to help you." She laughed and took his hand. "We're a strange pair, aren't we, Alex? The blind leading the blind. Here you are, wanting above everything to spend the rest of your life here, yet fate seems determined to drive you away, while I want nothing more than to get as far away from this godforsaken place as I can, yet every door out of here seems shut in my face. Here I am, terrified I won't ever get away from here. And you? You're worried you won't be able to stay."

CHAPTER
NINE

Katherine was sitting on the back porch crying when Alex rode up.

He didn't know she was crying at first, but by the time he got close enough to see her sitting there, her legs crossed like an Indian, her skirts tucked in the circle of her legs, her bare toes peeking from beneath her frayed hem, her head resting in her hands, he heard the soft, muffled sounds of her crying.

Funny, Karin could cry and he took it in stride, but seeing Katherine—something about the forlornness of it pierced him to the soul. Perhaps that was because tears came to Karin frequently and with apparent ease, while Katherine was the kind who kept such emotions private. "Sweet Katherine," he said, coming up the steps and dropping down on one knee beside her, "why are you crying?"

"Just go away and leave me alone," she said between sobs.

"I can't leave until I know why you're crying, so you might as well tell me. Has anything bad happened?"

Her head shot up and her lip quivered. "Not unless you consider what that careless, inconsiderate, pestiferous mule did as bad."

"Clovis?"

"Do you know any other mule around that fits that description?"

He shook his head. "Well? What did he do?"

"Come here," she said, climbing clumsily to her feet and clutching his arm, "you can see for yourself." She led him around the side of the house to where a makeshift wire was stretched from the house to the chinaberry tree, a wire she used to hang out her laundry, just as she must have done earlier today. Only now the clothes weren't on the line, they were scattered about the yard, trampled and dirty, the basket overturned and half of it missing. His eyes lingered on the frayed edges of the basket. "What in the..."

"He ate it," she said, almost choking on the dismay in her voice. "He was eating what was left of it when I came out here and found what he had done." She looked around the yard at the tossed and scattered laundry and her lip quivered again. "Just look at what he's done," she said, the tears coming of their own accord in spite of her efforts to hold them at bay. "Do you have any idea just how long it will take me to get this mess all cleaned up and the laundry rewashed? And some things," she said, picking up a pair of bloomers that had been shortened to a provocative length, "are beyond repair. He ate the legs out of these," she wailed. "Now they're fit for nothing except the rag barrel."

He tilted his head to one side and studied the chewed bloomers, a vivid picture coming into his mind—a picture of Katherine wearing nothing but those lopped-off bloomers and a mass of long, mahogany hair. His eyes went over her slowly. Was she as leggy as his vision of her, or was it simply because of the bloomers' indecent length?

Alex saw the hopeless look on her face and patted her arm, looking around. "Where is he now?"

She wiped her eyes with the corner of her apron. "Sulking in a stall in the darkest corner I could find in the barn."

He laughed. "He won't like that. I better see to him before he tears the stall apart."

"He won't get the chance to tear anything this time. I snubbed him so close he can't even blink, and I plan on leaving him there."

Alex pushed his hat back and looked around the yard at the scattered laundry. "Well, it's a mess for sure, but you can't punish him forever. He's just a dumb—"

"Don't you dare tell me he's just a dumb animal," she shrieked. "He's smarter than two dictionaries and meaner than an acre of snakes! I'm the only person in the world that's nice to him and this is my thanks!"

Alex forced the smile that threatened to stay hidden, his arm slipping around her shoulders. "Well, if it helps any, I don't think he meant it as something personal against you."

"He doesn't care one way or the other. That's the problem. And he's stubborn as—"

Alex grinned, looking down at her. "A mule?"

Her face seemed to transform right before his very eyes, the anger and frustration melting away to be replaced by a smile held in tight check. Alex threw back his head and laughed, and the tight grimace eased itself into a bright smile, Katherine's bubbling laugh joining his a moment later. She elbowed him sharply. "It's not funny, Alex."

"I know," he said, "but I figured I could laugh if you did."

"I might as well laugh," she said, looking around at the destruction scattered about the yard and sighing in a sad, dejected way, "it's the only enjoyment I'm going to get out of all of this."

"Now, this sounds mighty strange coming from someone I remember always telling me that I would *get out of things just what I put into them*. Don't you feel that way anymore?"

"Of course I do! It's just that what I'll be putting into all of this is nothing but back-breaking work. It'll take me a while to gather everything up, then I'll have to spend a whole day doing laundry I've already done."

"I know."

"Heaven only knows when that peddler man will be back this way with another basket like that one I had, and it cost me two bits! There are a million things I need that I could buy for two bits."

"I know."

She clamped her hands on her hips and glared up at him. "You keep saying the same thing over and over. *I know. I know.* Is there anything *else* that you haven't told me that you *know*?"

"I know you're the most adorable woman

I've ever seen and if I wasn't already head over heels in love with your sister, I'd be after you faster than Clovis was after that laundry basket."

"If you didn't love my sister, do you think you really could love me?"

The question jarred. "Don't ask such silly questions. Everyone loves you," he said, not really answering her question.

He watched the teasing light of humor fade from her eyes. "And you're in love with my sister, so those were really wasted words, weren't they? We both know where you stand."

The life had gone out of her voice, and he knew why. He knew how Katherine felt about him. It was something that soaked into him like a hard rain—welcome and refreshing at first, but coming too hard and too fast to handle. He didn't want this complication in his life, and he didn't want to spoil the friendship he had always had with her. Most of all, he didn't want Katherine to be hurt. *Don't love me, Katherine. It hurts too much to know I can't give you what you want.*

"Yes, we do," he said softly, "but that doesn't mean I can't help you gather these things. Then I'll see to that pen Clovis keeps breaking out of, although I think we've got more mule on our hands than pen. You need a new one."

A teasing light came into her eyes. A second later, he heard it in her voice. "A new mule, or a new pen?"

"I'm afraid I'd get my ears boxed if I said

anything against that mule of yours, so I must be talking about a new fence."

The humor was gone from her voice now. "I know, but there isn't money for that now."

"Maybe..."

"Thank you, Alex, but we aren't at the point of accepting charity just yet."

After the laundry was carried to the house, Alex went to see about Clovis. A few minutes later he came back to the house, finding Katherine sitting on the back porch again, her bare feet on the top step, her chin resting in one hand that was braced against her knee, the other hand lying limp in her lap.

"I left Clovis in the barn. The wood in that pen of his is so rotten a fly could break it if he happened to land on it. No wonder he gets out all the time. Adrian and I will be over tomorrow with enough lumber to rebuild it." He was waiting for her to refuse, to remind him that they weren't charity, but the fight seemed to have gone out of her voice as well as her. He sat down beside her. "Where's Karin?"

"She was here for a while, but Beau Ridley dropped by and took her over to his place to measure his aunt for new dresses."

"Who is Beau Ridley?"

"I guess you could say he's the new boy in town. He's been coming here every summer for three or four years. He visits his grandmother, Mrs. Carpenter."

"Why would Karin go riding with him?"

"I don't know." She looked at him squarely. "I can tell you're just full of questions, and

I'm telling you I don't know anything more than Beau Ridley has a rich papa, and a new conveyance."

Seeing that didn't sit too well with him, Katherine lifted her head so she could look him in the eye. "Did you and Karin have a fight or something?"

"No, just a little discussion. Why?"

"I was just wondering."

"Was Karin in a tizzy when she got home?"

"No, not that I noticed."

He looked over at her, seeing her profile as she stared out into the yard, seeing the way her hair had all come down and was littered with leaves and twigs. He made some comment about her holding that pert little nose of hers up in the air too much and getting her head in the trees and her hair full of leaves and such. Then he took her by the shoulders and half-turned her so the back of her head was in front of him. Using his fingers, he began pulling twigs and leaves from her hair, smoothing out the snarls and tangles as he went. Afterward, he massaged her scalp with his fingers, laughing at the way she sighed and dropped her head forward, resting her chin on her folded arms that were braced against her bent knees. While he braided her hair, she remained motionless, her eyes closed, musical notes of satisfaction drifting upward from her throat. He smiled, feeling the muscles he had held so tightly in check all afternoon relax. It was strange, this friendship he had with Katherine, how he always felt so at ease around her, so easy. He sure as hell couldn't picture himself sitting on the back porch with any other woman, braiding her hair. Not even Karin.

"I think I had something to do with Karin's going over to the Ridley place," he said after a while.

Katherine looked at him. "You sure you two didn't have words?"

"I told you, we talked."

"That's good. Talking can put a lot of things right."

"Then why do I have the feeling we're more at cross-purposes than ever?"

"I don't know. I always thought you both wanted the same thing."

"We do."

"Then how can you be at cross-purposes?"

"Because we don't seem to be wanting them at the same time."

"Uh-oh! That spells trouble." Things grew quiet between them, but around the yard the creatures of late evening were just starting to tune up. Before long the bullfrogs down by the creek would start to croak, and over in the thicket, the hoot owl would do his part, the distant yelp of coyotes rounding things out a bit. "I assume you were discussing marriage."

"No, we weren't."

"Why not?"

"Because I don't want to be a hand-to-mouth dirt farmer all my life. I don't want to bring children into the world wondering if I can feed them. I have nothing to offer her but a run-down old farm that is only one fifth mine. I think Karin has the right idea about getting away from this place. You stay too long and it begins to get to you, like a sickness."

"But if you love each other..."

"I thought you'd understand, Kath. Of all the people I know, you're the one person I thought would understand."

"I do understand, but I also understand Karin's feelings. I'm not saying either one of you is right. I'm only thinking there could be a compromise somewhere."

"Like what?"

"Maybe you could get married, both of you going wherever your destiny leads you, working for the things you want together."

"And children? Just how do you think we'd manage that with three or four babies trailing after us? Or did you think we could just put a hold on that side of marriage?"

Her face turned red. "I don't know anything about that side of marriage, so I'm not the right person to ask."

He sighed. "I'm sorry, Katherine. I didn't mean to take it out on you."

"I know. And I didn't mean to sound like I didn't understand what you were saying. I was just hoping to give you a little inkling of how a woman feels about things, how they're different from the way a man feels. A woman feels with her heart, and when she meets the man she loves and wants to spend the rest of her life with, it's only natural for her to want everything to be as perfect as possible, and that means having enough money to get by. A woman is a nurturing creature, and when she sees her man bogged down with worry and indecision, it's her natural way to want to offer to help, to feel she's doing her share. When a woman loves, it's her whole existence. But for a man, love is only one slice out of the pie. And when a woman knows she would forsake everything—family, fortune, dreams, hopes, and even her life for the man she loves, it's hard for her to accept the fact that he is trying to fit her in with five other slices of equal size."

"You know an awful lot about love to be a woman who has never been in love."

"Who said I've never been in love?"

"I've never heard you mention anything about it."

She came to her feet. "I've never mentioned anything, true, but that's not the same as never being in love."

"Well, I'll be damned!" he said. "Our little Kath in love? Now, who would've thought it?"

"Not you, Alex. That's for certain."

He stared after her wondering how angry she would be if she knew just how much he did know. He shouldn't have teased her like that, knowing how she felt about him, he thought, watching her open the door and step softly inside. Just before closing the door, she turned and said, "Thanks for your help today. I needed someone to keep me from feeling sorry for myself. I'm glad you came by."

"I am too," he said, feeling that he had

spoken the absolute truth. "And I'm glad we talked."

And Alex was glad, but as the next few weeks passed, he found he was still as restless as he had been, and it wasn't getting any better. He knew that was because of all the pressure that was on him. He and Adrian were almost broke, and now Karin was putting more pressure on him by being seen on occasion with that Beau whatever-his-name-was.

He felt it was time to seek his fortune, for it was obvious he needed something more than he had to hold Karin and keep her happy. He didn't know where he'd find that *something more*, but he knew it wouldn't be found in Limestone County. It was time for him to move on, to seek his fortune. He prayed to God Karin would still be waiting when he found it.

About this time, Adrian was harboring the same thoughts of getting away, but he had even more reasons than being broke. It was killing him to watch his brother and Karin, then to look at Katherine, seeing the pain in her eyes and knowing there was nothing he could do. He loved Katherine, but that street had no outlet. She loved Alex and Alex was his brother. Over and over again, since they weren't much more than children, he had tried to show Katherine how he felt, hoping that she might return those feelings. It never did any good. Katherine never encouraged any more from him than his friendship. He couldn't spend the rest of his life desiring a woman that didn't want him. Leaving seemed the only choice. He never dreamed that when he decided to go, Alex would want to go with him.

But he did.

A few days later, Alex brought a Waco paper home. The next morning he was reading it over a cup of coffee while Adrian was shaving in the kitchen. Suddenly, something caught his attention: an article reprinted from the *Californian*, dated March 15, 1848, that headlined, *GOLD MINE FOUND*. After he read the article to Adrian, it didn't take Adrian long to decide he was heading for California. After all, he had nothing here to hold him. The woman he secretly loved was in love with his brother, and his fool-headed brother was in love with her sister. He couldn't spend the rest of his life in this eternal triangle watching himself long for Katherine, while she longed for his brother and his brother longed for Katherine's sister. A man could go crazy.

Alex and Adrian both knew their money was gone and their hopes along with it. They had needed a break or two. They hadn't gotten it. What they had gotten was a long, dry spell, a herd of cattle that turned up with hoof-and-mouth disease and had to be destroyed, and a well that turned to salt water. Adrian, nursing a wounded heart, was the first to make the decision to go. For a while, it looked like he was going off to the California goldfields alone because Alex was having a hard time making the decision to leave Karin behind—even for a little while.

But when it came time for Adrian to leave, Alex, knowing his brother was right about their prospects of making a go of farming, knew he had to go with him. News that the Mackinnon brothers, so newly back from the Mexican War, were going to California moved quickly across the dry, brittle fields of Limestone County, spreading faster than a sudden outbreak of chicken pox, according to the county's only doctor.

Everywhere folks were likely to gather, the news about the Mackinnon boys was the latest bit of gossip: over a game of horseshoes beneath the spreading oak tree behind the smithy's; among the old war veterans that spent their afternoons whittling in front of the general store, and inside, the younger generation discussed it as they gathered over a game of checkers. The news traveled over the wild grapes that covered most of the fences in the county. It penetrated the thick layers of lather on the men being shaved down at the local barber's and the profusion of flowers and feathers drooping from the hats the ladies were trying on down at the local millinery. It was yelled from the church steeple as the roof was being repaired, and across the broad back of the plow horse Jeremiah Jones was shoeing. It was whispered over pews at church, and between the sheets by the whores down at the Sundance Saloon. But not once during all the gossip did anyone stop to think just why it was that two men who fought so bravely under General Zach Taylor were still being called the Mackinnon boys.

Only when Katherine pointed it out over dinner on their last night there, did the brothers speculate on the strangeness of it, never coming up with a good explanation, figuring they would come back from California in a few years, and find they were still referred to as the Mackinnon boys.

All things considered, people were mighty sad to see the last of the Mackinnons pull out. And no one was any sadder than Katherine Simon. But by the time they were ready to leave, she was thinking it was just as well, for at least she wouldn't have to live with the constant reminder that she wanted something she could never have.

After supper on the evening of their departure, Adrian and Katherine volunteered to do the dishes, giving Karin and Alex time to sit on the porch alone. Katherine watched her sister walk from the room, her arm tucked through Alex's, while she laughed at something he said. Karin had done everything possible, short of threatening to shoot herself, to keep Alex at home, but when nothing worked, she joined the ranks of those wishing them godspeed and good will, although not with much enthusiasm. To have seen her tonight no one would have guessed this same lovely, perfectly groomed young woman had thrown a fit in the barnyard just a few days past because Alex told her he was leaving, and while doing her most dramatic whirl had slipped and fallen in the pig's breakfast, commonly known as the slops.

Watching Katherine, Adrian waited until

Karin and his brother were out of the room. "Karin will survive," he said, "but what about you? How are you faring?"

"I'm doing fine," Katherine said, throwing him a look.

"You can be honest with me. Is it going to be hard on you?"

"Not any harder than it was before." She turned toward him. "You forget that I'm a veteran at this kind of thing by now." Then tossing the dish towel at him, she said, "Now, are you going to help me with the dishes, or stand there flapping your jaws all night?"

"Can we do both?" he asked, joining her at the cabinet where she had a tub filled with soapy water.

"No," she said, "we most certainly cannot. Now dry!" She shoved a cup toward him.

He took it and began drying. "Don't you wonder just what's going on out there?" He nodded in the direction of the front porch.

"No."

"Aren't you just a little curious?"

She turned on him. "Honest to Betsy! Will you hush up! No, I don't wonder what's going on. No, I'm not curious, and just in case you ask, no, I don't want to sneak outside for a peek. Now will you finish drying, or am I going to have to do your work too?"

"As you can see," he said, picking up a plate, "I'm drying my little heart out."

"Good!" she said and flicked a little soapy water on him, shrieking when Adrian growled and gave chase.

While Adrian was chasing Katherine around the kitchen table, Alex and Karin were pursuing a more serious activity, but that turned humorous a few minutes later when they were joined by Katherine and Adrian. "My, that was fast," Karin said.

"That's because we didn't finish," Katherine said. "All Adrian wanted to do was play, so I decided we might as well come on out here. I'll finish the dishes later."

Karin looked at Adrian and laughed. "Why, I swan, Adrian, I do believe you've got a bit of the tease in you."

"I do," he said happily, "at times."

The conversation settled in like an old hen setting on her twentieth batch of eggs, turning as it often did to stories of their childhood and times long past. But after a while the laughter died away and things grew quiet once again. "Well," Katherine said, rising to her feet and leaving Adrian sitting on the porch steps alone, his back to Alex and Karin in the porch swing. "I best be getting those dishes finished."

"What's your hurry?" Adrian asked, swiveling around and looking up at her. "I kinda like sitting on the steps with you. Don't you want to visit a while longer?"

"No, I hate teary good-byes."

"This one isn't teary," he said, coming to his feet and holding open his arms. "Come tell me good-bye."

"It'll be teary if I stay, and I hate good-byes," she said, then flinging her arms around his neck she kissed him on the cheek and said, "Take care of yourself, Adrian."

"I will," he said, but Katherine had already turned away.

"You too," she said, giving Alex a quick peck on the cheek. Alex nodded.

Katherine disappeared inside the house, knowing the only way she was going to avoid crying was to lose herself in the mess in the kitchen, which she did, all the while trying to keep her thoughts of a positive nature. Soon the dishes were washed and dried, the floor swept, the new cloth put on the table. With a satisfied sigh, Katherine looked around the neat kitchen and gave a sigh of approval, her hands going behind her to untie her apron.

"Hello, sweet Katherine."

Katherine jumped, just as she felt warm hands cover over hers to take the apron ties and give them a yank. She turned to see Alex pull it from her waist. She took the apron from him and folded it, placing it on the cabinet. The house was strangely quiet. "I wanted to say good-bye," he said.

"I thought we already had."

He nodded. "We did, but I didn't think it was the right kind of good-bye between friends of such long standing." Katherine stared at him in silence, desperate to commit to memory every dear and beloved feature of his face, the exact way the lamplight gleamed on his dark brown hair that looked so black right now, the light, mesmerizing color of those lazy blue eyes. "I'll miss you," he said softly.

"I'll miss you, too," she said, just as softly.

"Will you?" he asked. "Will you really?"

She looked put out. "What a thing to ask. Of course I will. I'll miss all those pointers I got on fishing, and the help I've had with Clovis. I'll miss mopping those muddy tracks from the kitchen floor and washing all those extra plates at supper."

"I'd like to think you'd miss more than that."

Katherine felt her face heat with embarrassment. Surely to God he didn't know how she felt. She spoke quickly to hide her discomfort at being forced to speak like this when all she wanted to do was fling herself into his strong arms and have him hold her until they were both too weak to stand. "Oh Alex, you will have forgotten me long before you reach California."

"I seriously doubt that," he said. "One never forgets his friends."

"No," she said softly. "One doesn't."

"Well, I guess I'd better be going."

"Yes, I guess you better."

"Damn, but this is harder than I thought," he said, looking away.

"Did you get everything smoothed out between you and Karin?"

"No, not really. She said she wasn't angry anymore over my going, but she wasn't going to make any promises about waiting."

"She didn't mean it."

"I'm not too sure."

"She just hates to see you go. She'll understand better after you leave. Women don't always mean what they say, you know."

"I hope you're right."

"I am."

"I'll write to you," he said, taking her hands in his.

She felt terribly shy. "I'd like that."

He drew her against him, his arms loose around her, indicating his affection. "Would you write me back?"

"If you stay in one place long enough for my letters to catch up with you," she replied.

"I can't promise that," he said, "but I don't want you to forget me."

"I could sooner forget myself," she said.

"So could I," he said, and strangely felt that it was true.

In spite of the surprise upon the lovely face turned toward him, in spite of his awareness that the full, pointed breasts pressing against his chest were curiously disturbing, he had no thought to kiss her. He had never kissed her except in friendship before, and in truth, he did not want to kiss her any other way now. Before Katherine could say anything more, or even begin to guess his intent, his hands came out to clutch her upper arms, pulling her more firmly against him at the same time his mouth descended. He had intended to kiss her on the mouth, but a quick, chaste kiss, nothing more. Yet, Katherine was so completely astounded that the mouth he had always found so perfectly shaped dropped open in astonishment. As his lips touched hers, he realized instantly what had happened and jerked back as if his lips had touched live coals. But as soon as he had pulled back, he groaned, finding that the mouth he had touched moments ago was too sweet, too tempting to stay away from.

Before she could exhale the next breath, his mouth trapped it where it was, his lips moving warmly and firmly over hers, tasting and tempting her with lips that awakened a response in her without speaking a word. She fought a grinding battle to maintain her dignity, the integrity of her soul. No matter that she had for so long used her will to press and squeeze to lifelessness her desire, for her discipline rebelled against its training, and she managed, by what had to be a hairsbreadth, to control herself, in order to remain perfectly still and as unresponsive as one so desperately in love could. But there was too much held back for too long, and suddenly it didn't matter. Her resistance softened and her body melted against him, warm and fluid, molding to his body while his arms held her so powerfully. Concurrently he began to fully realize that this exquisite being he held in his arms was not Karin. Not Karin, but Katherine. Katherine, too much his friend to ever be his lover. Katherine, too foreign to be so well known. Katherine, unwelcome and unknown. For Katherine could never make time cease to beat until it began to surge and swell, bursting like a flood upon his soul. Then his mind reeled and slipped backward, spinning with blinding color until it was consumed by darkness and the brilliance faded like a candle that had gone out. This was not Karin. He did not love this woman. But why was reality so desolate? How could something that had, for the twinkling of an eye, felt so right suddenly transform before his eyes into something so very wrong? He broke the kiss, yet found he was still clinging to the memory like a dying man in a desert crawls toward a mirage he can never reach. He looked down into her face, staring blankly, unable to understand the pain, until he realized dumbly, that he had been slapped.

Katherine reared back. Stunned and hurt and feeling such outrage, she shoved him away from her, her voice quivering, her eyes crystalline with unshed tears. "You had no right," she said, wiping her mouth with the back of her hand, as if by so doing she could remove the insult, the agony of being kissed by the man she loved above everything, knowing how he felt about her sister. It wasn't the kiss. It was the mockery of it. "You mock me," said Katherine, "and I'll hate you forever for doing that."

"Yes," he said sadly, "you probably will." His hand came up, absently rubbing the burning imprint of her hand upon his cheek.

She should be crying now, the tears flowing freely, an anguished sound coming from her throat. But he knew the tears that shimmered in her eyes would remain as they were, controlled and held at bay. She was strange, this sister of the woman he loved, for unlike Karin, she did not share her grief; she preferred to be alone with her pain.

He hated himself at that moment. Stupid, selfish fool! You should have known what this would do to her. And for what? To satisfy your own curiosity? To make yourself feel more of a man in the face of Karin's rejection?

"Just tell me one thing, Alex. Why? Why did you do that?"

He looked at her strangely and shook his head. "I'm not sure," he said, sounding as if he were as amazed at what happened as she. "Honest to God, Kath, I don't know."

"But I do. She won't forgive you for going. She won't give her word that she will wait. And that bites like vinegar, doesn't it?"

"I shouldn't have kissed you," he said. "I know that. All I can say is that I'm..."

"Don't say it," she said sharply. "It isn't the kiss. I could forgive you for that. But you used me, Alex, like a spurned husband would seek the consolation of a whore. And that hurts." She turned away, her back toward him. "I'm not sure I can ever forgive you for that," she said softly. "Only time holds the answer." She heard him as he turned and stumbled away, but she did not see the look on his face, the look of a man who has just awakened from a long, long sleep.

She did not move for quite some time. Alex had kissed her. And it wasn't the kiss of a friend. He had kissed her as a man kisses a woman and she would always have the memory of it to hold private. But how could she hold the kiss separate from the motive that prompted it? She stood in the dim light of the kitchen lamp, feeling strange that things were happening the way they were: no crying, no clinging, no begging him to stay. Nothing but the feeling that all the beauty and life inside her were shrinking. But in spite of that feeling, she knew she would make out all right. Oh, she would constantly be asking herself things about him—what was he doing, how were things going for him—or wondering if he ever thought about her. And there would be times, she knew, when she would even wonder if he was still alive. She felt all thought drain from her mind as she stood silently staring at the door, remembering all the times she had seen his beloved form standing in that same doorway, his arms braced against the jamb, the teasing light in his eyes, that roguish smile upon his face, and she wondered, *Oh, Alex, Alex... Will I ever see you again?*

She knew he was gone the moment she opened her eyes the next morning. She blinked, then looked around the familiar room. Everything was the same; the same faded coverlet lay across her bed, the same chipped basin stood in the corner where she washed her hands, the same oil lamp rested on the table in front of the window, absorbing sunlight and throwing rainbows of color on the opposite wall. She threw back the bedcovers and untangled the length of cotton gown that was twisted around her legs. Walking to the window, she drew back the curtain and looked outside. Like her room, everything there looked the same. The sun still shone in a clear blue sky streaked with a few whisps of clouds as thin and delicate as a bridal veil. Over by the barn, Clovis was gnawing on the new boards of a sturdy pen Alex had constructed. Scattered about the yard, hens were busy clucking and scratching, the morning glories on the fence had opened their blooms. Over by the water trough a goose flapped her wings and trumpeted her welcome to the morning. But inside the run-down house, Katherine Simon stood uncertainly before the window—a young woman standing barefoot in a threadbare cotton gown, a cloud of rich mahogany hair falling down past her waist. Alex was gone, and there was nothing to do but turn her mind to getting over it. But it was hard. Not so much because she missed him as a lover, but that she had had to say goodbye to him as a friend. She rested her forehead against the cool pane of glass. She was viewing everything that was dear and familiar about her, but what was she seeing? Nothing but years of emptiness stretching before her like the silent, weed-pocked tracks of a road no longer used.

CHAPTER
TEN

Time passed like a bird overhead, leaving nothing behind but its shadow. Katherine saw this passing as a time for ripening, for not only growing older, but wiser, for she saw it as a journey into her future, a healing of grief and resentment.

The weather grew cooler and autumn arrived, as silent as the signs of approaching decay. Down by the creek the beaver was waddling from place to place busily cutting down trees with his four orange front teeth, and Katherine didn't mind that because his dams would dot the creek and hold water. Winter came, cold hearted and shaped out of snow. A barn owl with his monkey face took up residence in the barn's highest rafters, and Katherine invited him to eat his fill of mice. Spring, being spring, came unexpectedly, like a promise kept at the end of a long winter day. The pink-nosed mother possum nursed nine hungry babies in the hollow of a rotted-out log and Katherine put away her recipe for possum stew. At last came lavish summer, breeding rosy fruitfulness in winter's bed of frozen decay. In the pasture, snowy egrets followed the cows around, and Katherine gathered their lost plumes to refurbish her old straw hat.

Thoughts of Alex were always with her.

Each evening, when words faded and thoughts came alive, an exhausted Katherine would go to her room and find memories of him waiting, a touch of joy borne on the wings of night. She found it strange how her mind gave sanctuary to the merest trifles, like small fish trapped in a net that let the big ones get away. As darkness closed around her, she hugged his memory close, calling back the soft, warm heat of his kiss, and waited for the grace of sleep that came like the peace of a tree, tranquil and silent.

Thoughts of Alex were always with her.

Letters from Alex and Adrian were slow in coming, the news old by the time the first one arrived. But she looked forward to each one and the things they had to tell. Katherine found it difficult to sit quietly over her sewing, stabbing her needle in and out as she listened to Karin read her letter from Alex when all Katherine wanted to do was to yank those yellowed pages from Karin's hands and savor each word until she knew it by heart. Of course, she had her own letter, for Karin always handed Adrian's missive to her, and while she enjoyed and learned much from all the interesting things Adrian had to say, his thoughts were just that—thoughts—while the words Alex penned were, to her, the very breath of life.

As the months grew into a year, then two, Katherine waited for each of Alex's letters as silently as she waited for his love. She did not share her feelings with anyone, not even Fanny Bright, whom she knew had her own suspicions about where Katherine's heart lay.

Fanny had dropped by two days after the first packet from the brothers arrived. "Come on in, Fanny, and rest your coat," Katherine said and held the door open for her.

"It's mighty nice weather we're having for November, don't you think?"

"It is, and not coming a minute too soon,

if you ask me. Especially after that cold spell last week."

"Ain't it the truth. A real stove hugger, that was." She laughed at something and seeing Katherine's questioning look, said, "You remember that mean old bull that belongs to Festus Freemeyer?"

Katherine nodded. Festus's bull was almost as famous in these parts as Clovis the mule.

"Well, I hear tell he got what was coming to him. The story in town is that he got his tail froze in the watering trough and old Festus had to lop it off."

"That'll lower the value of that bull," said Katherine.

"Law! I hadn't thought of that! That'll kill old Festus, sure enough. He's so tight he crawls under the gate to save the hinges."

"Maybe he's got the right idea. At least he isn't as broke as a busted trace chain."

"Well, sugar is low in the barrel for pert-near everybody in these parts now, but things will pick up. They always do. This is a fine country, and like a good man, you can't keep it down for long." Fanny settled herself back in the chair. "So, what's been happening around the Simon place since I saw you last?"

"We received letters from Alex and Adrian, just two days ago."

Fanny began asking so many questions that Katherine was tempted to get the letters and let Fanny read them for herself. After a few more rounds of questions, she did just that. Fanny looked at Adrian's letter and laid it in her lap. Then she looked at the letter Alex wrote. She handed Alex's letter back to Katherine. "Those words are so small they look like they were written to a midget. You'll have to read this one to me."

December 23, 1849

Dear Karin and Katherine,

The trip out took longer than we expected, but we're in California and are now set up in camp and panning for gold. The journey was long and difficult, but not as difficult as the poor fools going around the Horn had it, and those who chose to sail to Panama and then go overland to the Pacific had it even worse, I hear.

We've tried our luck in a few camps. They all have such fitting names—Dry Diggings, Hell's Delight, and Git-up-and-Git. It didn't take us long to face the realities of grubbing for gold. There isn't much glamour separating gold dust from rock with a shovel and a washpan, or in getting wet in the streams during the day and sleeping on the ground in wet clothes at night. What I thought would be striking it rich should be called misery and high prices. Some weeks we make over a hundred dollars, but that is soon gone because of the high prices for necessities. Molasses sells for a dollar a bottle, vinegar too. Flour is forty cents a pound, pork five dollars.

The life of a miner is different from what I expected. The camps are crowded and overrun with men, the workday is long, backbreaking, and more often than not, unyielding. Our tents, when we have them, are small, drafty. If you're lucky enough to have beds, they are lumpy, hard, and uncomfortable. Luxuries are scarce and lice are plentiful. There isn't much to do in the diggings (that's what we call the mining camps) except work. On Sunday each man has a little time to pursue his own interests, but there isn't much to choose from—having fights, horse races, drinking contests, laundry, Bible reading, or a weekly bath. Our evenings are spent repairing equipment, or on good days, weighing gold. We talk about old times and home a lot, the Simon sisters always a big part of both. We take turns cooking but Adrian, I have to admit, is a better hand at it than I am, but that doesn't make him do it any more often. Our supplies come into camp from Stockton, usually by six-mule teams, but none of the mules I've seen are as ornery as Clovis.

This letter will have to draw to a close. A wagon is about to leave for Stockton, and if I don't send this now, I don't know when I'll have another chance. Adrian and I talked last night. Everything around here has been heavily worked for some time. We are thinking about going farther north and will probably be pulling out soon, so it might be a while before we have a chance to write again.

My regards to Katherine.

Regards. Katherine laid the letter in her lap and felt her eyes burn. After months and months of waiting, all she got was regards.

"What's the matter?" Fanny asked.

"Nothing. I was just remembering a story Adrian told about a funeral he and Alex attended. A hole had been dug to bury a deceased miner, and while the preacher went on and on, the miners kneeling beside the grave were getting bored. They began sifting dirt through their fingers. Someone found some traces of gold and yelled, 'Color!' The deceased was tossed out of the hole and everyone started digging—including the preacher."

Fanny's laughter joined Katherine's, but she wasn't about to be sidetracked. "Is that the end of the letter?"

"No, but the next part reads, "Karin, this is for you."

"Well? Go on! Read it!"

"Oh, Fanny, it's just a few words about how much he misses her, how he hopes she has forgiven him for leaving, and how he thinks of her all the time."

"Thinking of her at all would be more than she thinks of him," said Fanny.

"Honestly, Fanny, how can you say that?"

"It's easy. I just open my mouth and the truth flows out."

"That's not the truth. Karin misses Alex. I know she does."

"Yes, I've noticed how much she misses him every time I see her being squired around in Hiram Garrison's new rig."

Alex and Adrian were deep in the Sierras at a place called Grass Valley by the time their second letters arrived. As they had before, Katherine and Karin sat in the parlor while Katherine read Adrian's letter, then Karin read the letter from Alex.

August 4, 1850

Dear Karin and Katherine,

We're settled in at our new diggings and things look promising. We've built a sluice and that helps us process more gold-bearing dirt than using a pan. It's also easier on our backs. We've been digging more and more dirt out of crevices and rocks and our luck is getting better each day. We weighed 17 ounces the first day, 25 the second, 31 the next. At sixteen dollars an ounce, we'll be rich men if our luck holds. And it has been, for our take has been increasing slowly, and both Adrian and I feel this digging may hold up for a while. We're keeping our find to ourselves, in hopes that this will keep other miners away. But we know the news will leak out somehow. It always does.

The weather is turning cooler now, and we've got to think about building a cabin, but we both hate to take time away from the diggings. If things sound good, they aren't. We are both suffering from terrible bouts of homesickness. What we wouldn't give for a good home-cooked meal, a real bed, and a look at two lovely lasses we left behind.

My regards to Katherine.
Karin, this next part is for you.

Karin's eyes skimmed over the words. Her

face crumpled, tears coming into her eyes. Then, as if she had given herself a good mental shaking, her entire countenance changed. "Enough of that," she said, and stood, wiping the tears from her face. She refolded the letter and placed it in the envelope. She tossed the envelope on the table, her hoop popping against the table as she swept past on her way to the door.

"Aren't you going to keep it?" Katherine asked.

"No."

"Aren't you going to write him back?"

"No."

"Karin! How can you be so cruel."

"I'm not cruel, Katherine. I'm practical." She leveled her eyes on Katherine. "Show me where it says it's wrong to be practical. Just because you lead with your heart doesn't mean I'm always in the wrong to lead with my head. Sometimes, you can have the most absurd values that get you absolutely nothing, or nowhere. As the saying goes, 'Admire a little ship, but put your cargo in a big one.' "

"If we're going to get down to platitudes, why not settle for an ass that carries you, instead of a horse that throws you?"

Karin smiled. "Because I, sweet Katherine, plan on having both: the horse that carries me. So, tell me again why I should write Alex?"

"Because he wrote you," Katherine said flatly.

"I didn't ask him to. In fact, I specifically remember telling him the night he left *not* to write me. As far as I'm concerned it's over." Seeing the way Katherine was looking at her, she said, "I know you think I'm heartless, but I have other fish to fry, and Alex Mackinnon isn't one of them. I told him I wouldn't wait when he left here."

"Alex will come back. I know he will. He said they were getting richer every day."

"Alex always did know just what to say to keep me hanging on. I'm through with waiting. I've almost got enough money saved. It won't be much longer until I can be on my way. Even now, I'm putting my feelers out for work. Mr. Dunlap down at the newspaper is saving his newspapers from Houston and Dallas for me. Whenever the right job turns up, I'm gone. I can't...I *won't* wait around forever for a man to waste his health shoveling dirt in California. I've heard stories in town, Katherine. I know what that kind of life can do to a man. I heard about a woman in Waco whose husband came back after he'd lost everything, including his mind. Now he just sits in a rocking chair talking to himself." She whirled, her skirts swirling around her as she began to pace the floor. "How do I know he'll ever come back? The odds are against it for either one of them. Fools! That's what they are, thinking they'll ever come back rich. I've heard about what's going on out there. Misfits from every continent have poured into California. For every miner that's working to strike it rich, there are two reprobates waiting to take what he's found. The place is crawling with men there who do something besides earn an honest living. Crime and bloodshed are everywhere, and those that don't get killed drink themselves to death, or starve to death. There're disease and murderers and thieves of all sorts out there mingling with the miners. More than one man has struck it rich and turned up missing. I won't waste the best years of my life waiting for a man who might never come back, or one who'll come back a babbling fool!"

"What are you going to do?"

"Exactly what I've been doing," said Karin, her perfectly trimmed nails fluttering about her exquisitely coiffed hair. "I said a long time ago I was going to marry a rich man and I haven't changed my mind one iota."

"There aren't many rich men available, not even in the big cities. By the time they get rich, they're married. You should know that."

"There are always a few prospects that aren't married. And don't forget the widowers," Karin said.

"You're going to count the ones that are old enough to be your father? Is that what you want? Some old man with one foot in the grave? A man who can't give you children?"

"I don't care how old he is, or how many feet he has in the grave—just as long as he lives long enough to put a ring on my finger. *That's* the important thing. As for children, you know I've never been as fond of them as you are." A smile of delight crossed her face. "I'll be your children's rich aunt. I'll come to visit at Christmas and bring a carriageful of presents and invite them to Europe with me in the summer."

"Now, who's being impractical?"

Karin's eyes narrowed. "You'll see! I'll show you! I'll show all of you!"

Katherine watched in silence as her sister swept from the room with a swish of her colorful plaid taffeta skirt. She thought about Karin, wondering why she couldn't have been born such an exquisite looking creature as Karin. Karin, so small and built on voluptuous yet controlled lines, with eyes and hair and skin as fair as an angel's, not to mention her beautiful soft hands and small, dainty feet. Her voice was as musical as the coo of a dove, her movement as graceful as a swan. *While you,* Katherine thought, giving herself a critical eye, *are as plain as a peahen, with a voice about as musical as the squawk of a chicken hawk.*

Any suppositions she had about Alex Mackinnon and herself withered. Katherine wasn't a whiner, but she knew when to quit. The illusions she had long harbored about growing up to marry Alex Mackinnon had died of starvation a long time ago. She just hadn't laid it out for burial. The weight of dragging that dead carcass around behind her was suddenly unbearably heavy. It was time to reconcile herself to the fact that nothing was going to change things between herself and Alex, irregardless of her whimsical dreams. She might as well get on with her struggle to exist—a straight and narrow path that led directly to the grave.

By the next morning, all thoughts and

remembrances of Alex's letter firmly put out of her mind, Katherine saw Karin off to the seamstress shop and set about making something out of nothing, for truly, nothing was what she had to work with.

The past summer had been unbearably long, hot, and dry. The creek was down to a mean little trickle, the fish having long ago been fished out of the little pools that had been so neatly dammed by beavers. And now the pools themselves were no more than muddy hog wallows—if she'd had any hogs to wallow, that is, for in truth, the Simons were about out of livestock.

Katherine had been forced to sell off the last of the pigs, having only one old sow left who was getting too old to breed, a few scrawny chickens, one cow, and of course, Clovis. A late freeze had killed all hopes of fruit on the fruit trees and the garden that had looked so promising in May was withered brown sticks by the end of July. Things didn't look like they were going to get any better, as she pointed out to Fanny one afternoon. Fanny had stopped by, and after listening to Katherine's woes, had asked, "What about pancakes? You've got flour, and chickens and a cow for eggs and milk."

"I've been making pancakes," Katherine wailed. "I've been making them so much we're about out of flour. For the past two weeks I've been making pancakes so thin they only have one side to them."

By the time it had grown cooler and hog-killing weather rolled around, Katherine should have butchered the old sow, but she just couldn't do it. Somehow, that old sow was the last connection she had to better days. Killing her would, in Katherine's eyes, be like throwing in the towel. *As long as that old sow is here,* she told herself, *I'll get by.*

One thing bothered Katherine more than their dire circumstances, and that was being approached for courting. Now, Katherine was no prude, but she wasn't desperate either, not by any means, at least when it came to men. *Better to be alone than in bad company,* was her motto, and she considered the undesirable men around the county as bad company. "Honest to Betsy! Some of these men are so old they creak." Fanny had laughed at that, and Katherine went on to add, "I swear that old Gideon Hamilton smells like mothballs."

Fanny hooted with laughter. "He probably packs it away for the winter."

"Packs what?" asked Katherine.

"Never mind," Fanny said. "Wait until you're married."

"Humph!" said Katherine. "By that time, *I'll* be packed away in mothballs."

Whenever Katherine was asked out by a man, she wasted no time in setting him straight. Being a spinster was fine and dandy, sugar candy, as far as she was concerned. When that decrepit Jacob Atterby asked if she liked ice cream socials, Katherine responded by saying, "Was there any particular reason for your wanting to know?"

When Jacob replied, "I thought I'd ask you to the one next Sunday afternoon," Katherine responded, "Don't."

Karin too was being courted by the inevitable, a man old enough to be her father who was reported to have plenty of money. But unlike Katherine, she didn't send them packing with a few harsh words.

"Who did you say she was seeing?" Fanny asked one morning when she rode into town in the wagon with Katherine.

"Ben Witherspoon."

"Ben Witherspoon! Why, that old fool is older than dirt."

"Yes, but he's got money."

"A lot of good that'll do Karin."

"I'm afraid that may be true." Katherine sighed and yanked the reins, pulling Clovis back from his hasty trot that was rough as all get out, to a smoother, slower-paced walk. "I heard he was a bit frugal."

"Frugal, my eye! He used to pay court to Laura Lavender a few years back, and she said he was so tight he breathed through his nose to keep from wearing out his false teeth."

The last pork butchered had amazingly lasted over three months, and in spite of wondering where their next meal would be coming from, Katherine could have gobbled up the last bite of it like she hadn't tasted pork in years, so happy she was to see the end of it.

"I suppose I can stop selling all the eggs and butter," Katherine said to Karin over the last bit of boiled pork.

"What can you make out of eggs and butter? We don't have a staple in the house."

"I'll think of something."

"I don't know what, except scrambled eggs, and I'm sick of them," Karin said, then stood. "I need to get changed. Ben is coming by at eight."

Katherine cleaned the parlor with care and steeped a pot of tea, having virtually nothing else to offer Ben Witherspoon when he came to call on Karin. But the pains she took went unnoticed; Ben couldn't tolerate tea, "breaks me out in hives," he said. As for the clean parlor, Ben took no notice of that either, his hungry eyes fastening upon Karin like a starved wolf eyeing a chop.

Katherine had grown weary of Ben Witherspoon and rose to excuse herself.

"Got anything to offer besides tea?" Ben inquired.

Katherine debated her answer. Should she lie in order to keep their dire straits a secret? *Why should you? Maybe you should tell him. Maybe he'll offer to give you a few scraps from his overstocked table.* She opted for the truth.

"I see. Well, maybe I can help out a little," Ben said. "I'll bring you gals a little something to tide you over next time I come to call."

"Why, thank you, Ben," Karin said, scooting to the edge of her chair and giving him a bright smile.

Please God, let that be soon, thought Katherine.

"I can't rightly sit back and watch two purty little things like you starve in a pile, now can I? Things have been going good for me and it's only right that I share a few of my blessings with the less fortunate. That new well I dug last year saved the day for me. I've got sacks of dried fruit and my root cellar is full of vegetables. And you know I always butcher a cow as soon as my beef runs low. I've always been a beef man myself. Never could tolerate pork. No sirree! Give me a juicy slab of beef any day over a bowl of greasy boiled pork." Ben stopped to think a spell, his eyes still devouring Karin's small frame. "I'll have to give it some thought—just what I can bring you. I know how you gals have never been ones to raise much beef, so I reckon I could furnish you with a little…"

Mary, Jesus, and Joseph, please don't let it be pork, prayed Katherine. *How I would love to sink my teeth into a nice beef roast! Or even the leg of a nice fat goose!*

"…pork," Ben finished a minute later.

"I can't believe it," Katherine said.

"Now don't be thanking me," Ben said. "I know how this must touch you, but the truth is, I can't bear to see anyone starve, and if I can do something to see it doesn't happen, I'll do it. Lucky for you, it's still cooler weather and pork should keep for quite a spell. I've heard tell that folks who watch themselves can stretch a fat old sow out four, maybe even five months."

Karin groaned.

Katherine couldn't make a sound, so close she was to clapping her hand over her mouth and rushing from the room. The thought of what Karin must be putting herself through to sell herself to this shriveled old man was almost as close to gagging her as the thought of a kitchen full of the sickening smell of steamy boiled pork. Of course she couldn't express her feelings—to do so would have been humiliating to Karin, and Karin had a right to sell her soul to whatever devil she chose.

However, she did not have to stay in this room a minute longer, so she bid her good-byes to Ben Witherspoon and hastily kissed her sister on the cheek, quitting the room as quickly as she could, short of a bolting run.

That winter things were as harsh and hard as the previous summer. Fanny's husband died and the bank foreclosed on the mortgage. Fanny, who wasn't called Bright for nothing, had seen it coming, and shortly after her husband's funeral, had enlisted Katherine's help in moving everything edible to the Simon place, and as much of her farm equipment and livestock as she could get away with and time—since they had to do these things in the dead of night—would allow.

Two weeks after the funeral, Fanny was ordered out of her house, and without giving it a thought, Katherine insisted she move in with them. Karin, who had been stuffing herself on Fanny's staples for two weeks, could hardly voice a complaint.

The rest of that bitter winter passed, and while not exactly plentiful or pleasant, they hadn't starved as they fully expected they would, for truly, the death of Fanny's husband had been, at least for Katherine and Karin, a godsend. And not only because it put food in their mouths, for Fanny not only paid her way, but she lightened the load in two ways: by putting her back to the chores that Katherine had always undertaken by herself, and by her good-natured ways and sense of humor which kept optimism high and spirits light.

Spring came and Fanny and Katherine busied themselves with the breeding of their few animals and the plowing and planting of much-needed crops and a garden. Indeed, things did look promising. At least until the Sunday the minister preached a sermon he called, "The Lord giveth and the Lord taketh away."

Four days later Katherine stood on the back porch and watched as the white billowing clouds began to grow taller and taller, building over the green fields until a dark curtain of rain closed in. As the wind increased, whipping her skirts about her legs and driving the hard, pelting rain against her face, she remembered how for weeks and weeks last summer she had stood in this same spot and watched helplessly as the sun and wind sucked every bit of moisture from the earth, while praying endlessly for rain.

"It must have been an omen," Katherine said later, as she sat at the kitchen table with Fanny and reflected on how the sermon had almost been a warning. In a way it had, for everything that had looked so promising had suddenly been taken away.

For that was the year the summer drought and the bitter winter were followed by spring rains. It rained. And it rained. And it rained. It was the year the saturated skies opened up and beat the earth below with torrential sheets until the creek overflowed its banks and flooded the fields, ruining the crops.

When it was all over, Karin and Katherine and Fanny hitched up their skirts and walked through the knee-deep mud to survey the damage. They had only two cows and both of those were gone. They were found later, miles down the creek, their bodies stiff and bloated with death and the calves they would never have. The chicken coop and all the chickens were missing. The coop was located, caught in a tangle of brush half a mile from where it stood, but no trace of the chickens could be found. The garden was washed away, and the storm cellar was a good foot under water. But that didn't matter much now. The food stored there would be rotted by the time the water soaked in enough for them to get down the steps.

"Well," Karin said, while extracting her heavy boots from the oozing muck, "at least I have my job."

But the following Monday the flood had taken that as well, for a tearful Mary Mahoney confessed the rains had wiped her husband out and he was bent on giving up on farming. "We're going back to Kentucky," she said. "We've lost everything."

"But you still have your shop," Karin said.

"Yes, but no one around has anything. Times have been hard, but they'll be even harder now. The last thing anyone will spend money on is a new dress or hat. I'm sorry, Karin. You had such good ideas. The business had really been showing promise since you came." Seeing the hopeless look on Karin's face, she asked, "What will you do now? I know you and your sister didn't fare any better than the rest of us."

"I don't know," Karin said. "Nothing seems very certain now."

Mary looked at Karin, who looked radiant in crisp yellow dimity, in spite of the gloom that hung over the tiny town like another rain cloud. "I have a distant cousin... you may have heard me speak of her... she lives in Waco."

"Yes, I've heard you mention her," Karin said, her mind on what she was going to do. "She runs a boardinghouse, doesn't she?"

"Yes, ever since her husband died. She's often said she would love to have a shop such as mine, and..." Mary sighed, tears coming into her eyes as she looked around her neat little shop. "As much as I hate to part with everything, Josh says we can't possibly haul it back to Kentucky with us. He's going to drive me over to Waco on Sunday. I'm going to let Georgia have everything for whatever she can afford to give me. If she wants to buy me out, I'll tell her about you. That is, if you'd like."

"Thank you," Karin said. "I'd be mighty beholden to you for that, Mary."

Mary took Karin's hand. "It's the least I can do for you, Karin. You've been a good worker."

And a good customer, Karin was thinking. For the first time she could remember, she was regretting spending so much on clothes. *If I had saved more money, I would have enough to make Mary an offer.* But then it registered on her just what Mary had said. Waco. Dear Lord above! Waco. If Mary's cousin Georgia bought her out and wanted Karin to work for her, and Karin prayed she would, then she would have a job and a place to live in Georgia's boardinghouse, and in Waco. There were men in Waco. Rich men.

Karin was so happy she couldn't wait for her ride home, and set out walking. She wasn't even tired when she reached the house and found Fanny and Katherine encased in mud, as they dug around in the muddy remains of the garden pulling up a few onions, carrots, turnips, and potatoes that had remained buried.

"Mary's husband is wiped out and they're going back to Kentucky. She's selling her business and I've lost my job," Karin said. She picked her way daintily through the mud and went into the house. Katherine and Fanny watched her go, and when she disappeared inside the house, Fanny looked at Katherine, her hands on her hips as she shook her head. "That girl is past strange," she said, before bending over to root out another potato. "If I didn't know better, I'd swear she was happy about the whole thing."

Of course Karin explained everything that night over a bowl of boiled vegetables. "If it works out that I get the job, you and Fanny could come too," she said to Karin. "I'm sure you could find jobs in Waco."

"You talk like Waco is the mecca of the world," Fanny said. "It ain't."

"It's better than staying here and starving to death."

"You're right about that," Katherine said.

"Then you'll come?"

"Let's see if you get the job, first," Katherine said.

Karin got the job. Mary dropped by the farm the following Monday to tell her. After Mary left, Karin hurried to find Fanny and Katherine, who were harnessing Clovis to the wagon. "I've got the job! I've got the job!"

"That's wonderful," Katherine said. "When do you start?"

"Mary said Josh will be moving everything to Waco this week. Georgia, who is Mary's cousin, is making the front room of her boardinghouse into a shop, just until she clears enough to rent a bigger place. She wants me to come a week from Monday to manage the business. I'll get a percentage of the sales and free room and board." Karin kept her distance, because of Clovis. "You're coming, aren't you?"

"I don't think so," Katherine said. "Fanny and I have talked it over..."

"I'm too old to start out at something new.

Farming and housekeeping is all I know."

"You could get a job keeping house for someone in Waco," Karin said.

"With my mouth? Lord girl, I'd be fired in a week. I couldn't work for anyone else. I can't hold my tongue."

Karin looked at Katherine. "Why won't you come?"

"I don't know," she said. "I guess I'm just not ready to call it quits."

"What will it take? We've lost everything!"

"We still have our land."

"Our land," Karin scoffed. "You speak of it as if it were part of the family, when in truth it's nothing but a cold, heartless pile of dirt—dirt I'd just as soon never lay eyes on again. Go ahead. Stay here killing yourself. It's just a matter of time until it's gone too," Karin said. "What will you do then?"

"I don't know," Katherine said.

"Starvation drives one to extremes," Karin said.

"I know," Katherine said.

"God has moved in stranger ways," said Fanny. "He never closes one door that he doesn't open another. Why, just look at you. You're going to Waco, something you've always wanted."

"Something will come along, I'm sure of it," Katherine said.

"Katherine Simon, you're a bigger fool than I am. Nothing is going to come around his godforsaken place but more drudgery and hardship."

"You may be right," Katherine said, "but this is my home and here I'm going to stay. It would be a grievous mistake for me to leave here."

"Well, we all make mistakes," said Karin.

"And you may be falling victim to one right now," Katherine warned.

"Or perhaps you are," Karin said.

CHAPTER ELEVEN

In spite of $1,000.00-a-month rooms and eggs that sold for ten dollars a dozen, Adrian and Alexander Mackinnon were suddenly richer than they ever imagined. Being the most conservative of the Mackinnon brothers, and seeing too many miners lose all they worked so hard to gain, they decided to quit while they were ahead.

"I've been thinking," Adrian said to Alex one afternoon, as he took a break from shoveling dirt into the sluice.

"God help us!" Alex said, giving his brother a side glance and taking a bigger bite out of the dirt with his shovel.

"I'm serious, Alex. I've really got some ideas worth listening to."

"So far, your ideas have landed us in the middle of the Mexican War, sent us traipsing across half the continent to come close to starving to death, and gotten our asses frozen off in California. I pray to God you haven't come up with another idea for a wild goose chase. I've been homesick since the day we came here. I'm more than ready to go home. Almost two years! That's two years too long for any man to spend with a shovel in his hand, especially when he's salted away a fortune in the Sacramento bank."

"And don't forget that it was one of my wild ideas that put that fortune in your hands."

"I'm not forgetting. It's just that I wasn't born with wings on my heels. I've got a wee bit o' the farmer in me, laddie," Alex said, breaking into the Scots brogue that sounded so much like their father, John Mackinnon.

Adrian couldn't help grinning. "And you can't help that any more than I can help having a bit o' the rover in me."

"True." Alex took another swipe at the rich earth.

"Alex?"

"Now what?"

"What if I said I had an idea that would help us double, even triple our money? What would you say to that? Would you still want to go home?"

"What do you have planned this time? Robbing a bank?"

"Alex, I'm serious. What would you say?"

"All right." Alex sighed and stabbed his shovel into the dirt and left it there. Holding his hat, he wiped his forehead with the crook of his arm, then turned to look at Adrian. "I'd be a fool not to consider it, but I'll tell you now, I don't want to spend the rest of my life out here. Texas is our home and farming is in our blood just like it was in Pa's."

"Pa had a bit of the rover in him too—that's where I got it. That's what made him leave Scotland to come to Texas."

"I know, and I haven't minded all this moving around—up to now—no matter how much I prod you about it. But I'm ready to settle down, put out some roots. I know we had no choice. But now things are different. We've got money. Lots of it. I say, the Mackinnons have been homeless vagabonds long enough. I'm ready for a home and family, to..."

"I know, to put down roots." Adrian said it like he'd heard it often enough, and he had.

"Yes, and to do that I have to stop this gallivanting around. I can't do both. You know what they said about the pig that had two owners."

"No, what?"

"He starved to death."

Adrian laughed. "Only you would think of something like that." His face turned serious. "Alex, I want you to listen carefully to what I have to say. You may change your mind about going home straightaway."

Alex looked at the sky. "It's almost quitting time anyway. Why don't we go into Grass Valley and have ourselves a nice, juicy steak?"

Adrian looked at Alex like he'd lost his mind. "Have you forgotten what a steak dinner costs?"

"No, but you seem bent on words and

pestered with a head full of ideas, and I figure if I'm going to have to listen to it, the least I can do is listen with a full stomach."

Over a steak dinner that cost over two hundred dollars, Adrian enlightened Alex on his idea. For the next hour or so, he outlined a plan that would use their newly acquired riches to buy land in California.

"California!" Alex almost choked. "I'm a Texas boy, Adrian, a farmer. What could I grow out here? Gold dust?"

"Hear me out, Alex." Adrian went on to say how the goldfields had filled many a head with dreams of money, realistic or not, and that had meant a continued influx of people, and people needed houses, and houses were built primarily of wood, and wood came from trees, and the land in Northern California, being covered with trees, would be a wise investment.

"Lumbering?" Alex croaked, his throat suddenly dry. "The two of us in the lumbering business? Why, we'd be fools to... no, not fools, we'd be plain *crazy* to put all our money into something we don't know anything about."

"We've done crazier things," said Adrian.

"And damn near lost our asses doing it."

"But this won't risk our lives," said Adrian.

"No, just every penny we've broken our backs for. To risk it would be fool-headed crazy."

"What's so crazy about us getting into the lumbering business, buying land, and building a mill? What's crazy about doubling, even tripling our money?"

"We don't know a damned thing about lumbering, that's what," Alex replied.

"We didn't know anything about mining either," Adrian pointed out.

"That's different."

"Lumbering would be easier than anything we've ever done."

Alex looked at his succulent steak. "I knew this was too good to be true," he said. With a sigh he laid his fork down. "Okay. How do you figure that?"

"We're rich men, Alex. We can afford to hire the best lumbermen available to help us get started, to build our mill."

Alex looked thoughtful—not hooked on the idea but thoughtful. "What if I said I didn't want to do it?"

"First, let me say that I need you, Alex, I need your levelheadedness, your steady hand at the helm when I get my sheets too full of wind."

Alex grinned. "Are you admitting that you're a little impulsive, that you get a bit carried away?"

"I am, but I'm also saying that I'll go on alone with this if you aren't interested, and that would mean we'd have to split our money now, each of us going our separate ways."

"Why? We have what we came for. Hell! We have more than we came for. About a hundred and fifty thousand more. You can overdo everything, Adrian, even lovemaking."

"I know that. And you may have all you want," Adrian said, "but I don't. I want more than money, more than a run-down old farm that will take all I have to give and give chicken feed in return. *No one* gets rich farming, Alex. You and I both know that. You get comfortable, that's all." He put both hands on the table and leaned closer to Alex. "To build the kind of place you're thinking of will take a powerful lot of money. Right now, all you have waiting for you is a piddly little piece of land with a run-down house on it. You need more land, Alex, not just acres, but sections, not to mention breeding stock, equipment..." He looked Alex straight in the eye. "You know what I'm saying, and believe me, our goals aren't so far apart. I want a new life too, one with some security, something I can build for my children so they won't be left with nothing like we were."

And that was true. Adrian's dream was to build a lumbering empire so big that he would have enough money to build a mansion and fill it with the finest things that money could buy, and when he did, he hoped to tell Katherine Simon it had all been for her.

After giving it some thought, Alex pondered a spell upon what Adrian had said. His thoughts ran something like this: So far your roaming has benefitted you more than it's hurt. *I agree, but on the other hand, an ass can roam the world over and still come home an ass.* You have a point there, but on the one hand, you have to lose the worm to catch the fish. *That's right, but on the other hand butter spoils no meat, moderation no cause.* This is true, but on the one hand, to hit the mark you must aim a little above it, and don't forget, love might be sweet, but it tastes best with bread.

Necessity, they say, turns the lion into a fox.

"All right," Alex said. "I've got to be crazy for saying this: When do we trade our shovels for saws?"

Adrian laughed, taking his brother's extended hand in a firm shake. "What made you change your mind?"

"Necessity," said Alex.

"Necessity?" repeated Adrian.

"I'm not saying any more," said Alex with a grin.

"You won't be sorry," Adrian said.

"I'm already sorry," Alex said. "My steak is as cold as a widow-woman's thighs."

Adrian laughed. "You'll have enough money to eat steak three times a day, if that's what you want," he said. "I promise you won't be sorry."

Alex snorted. "As the Bible says: 'Answer a fool according to his folly.'"

"At least you'll be a prosperous fool," Adrian said.

Alex remembered those words a few months later as he crouched, trying to build a fire out of wet cedar shavings in pouring rain. He didn't feel very prosperous. He felt like a fool. He watched Adrian disappear inside a tent, and looked around the small camp—a crude affair that consisted of little more than seven or eight tents, a pit, and a platform where he and Adrian worked an eight-foot whipsaw. A rather pathetic start, he surmised, for two men determined to make their mark in lumber.

But a few months later, after the first shipload of much-needed supplies reached their small camp north of Humboldt Bay, things looked more promising. This was largely due to the arrival of their first logging crew and their foreman, Big John Polly, who brought along his wife to help the cook. The cook was a feisty little import from China lured to California by the gold rush, who, faced with starvation, quit the goldfields for a steady job as a lumber cook.

Big John Polly was a sturdy, awesome fellow, a self-reliant lumberjack with a barrel chest, powerful arms, and a thick neck who had learned his trade in the Talbot mills in his home-town, East Machias, Maine. His wife Molly was even sturdier.

"My God!" Alex said, when he first saw her coming off the ship. "Would you look at that! A man wearing a dress!"

"It's a dress all right, but that ain't no man. That's my wife," Big John said with a laugh as he came toward them and shook hands. He went as far as to admit Molly was "a bit of a full-blown wood nymph," but Alex, who was staring at the biggest woman he had ever seen, slack-jawed and too awed to speak, thought Molly, who weighed a little over two hundred pounds, was more tree trunk than wood nymph. But regardless of what anyone thought, she was a powerful woman who smoked cigars and kept order in the cook tent with torrents of profanity and barrages of well-aimed kindling wood, as often as not aimed at Wong, the cook, during one of their epic arguments. He decided to call her M.P., because a name like Molly Polly was a bit much for anyone.

Alex and Adrian's investment turned out to be a wise one as far as lumbering prospects went. It took a lot of back-breaking work to get their business started and the sawmill built, but it was a money-making endeavor right from the start.

Once their prospering lumber empire was on its way, Alex found his mind occupied more and more with thoughts of Karin, the foremost of these thoughts being that she was a beautiful woman any man would want for a wife. Alex wanted to be that man.

"It's a little premature, don't you think?" Adrian said. "Our house isn't too grand. Do you think she could be happy living there?"

"She'll love it up here."

"Perhaps," Adrian said, "but I think you're rushing things a bit."

"You're entitled to think what you will," Alex said, "but I'm ready to send for Karin and I won't be put off much longer."

Alex was right about that, for it was just a month later that he and Adrian had an argument that was as epic as the ones Wong and M.P. frequently indulged in.

Although Alex and Adrian were older and more mature than they were as young boys growing up in Texas, they had never outgrown their tendency to settle their arguments with fists. One such argument stemmed from a disagreement they had over whether or not they wanted to buy more land farther north, near the Canadian border.

"It's prime land, a good place to build another mill," Adrian said.

"I agree, but we haven't gotten this mill completely finished and on its feet yet. It's too early to think about expansion."

"If we wait any longer, the land may not be available. Too many people are coming up to this neck of the woods with the same ideas we had. I say we buy now."

"I say we wait."

This argument went on for days, until Big John Polly, who was sick of it all, suggested they "sit down and sensibly discuss the matter over a drink like civilized men."

And they did. But the brothers soon found they were unable to settle the matter in a civilized way either. As their arguments always had, this one grew in proportion to the amount of liquor consumed, until a free-for-all erupted. Alex had a slight handicap to begin with because his mind was more concerned with thoughts of Karin than it was on discussing business. Adrian found this distracting preoccupation of his twin's mind infuriating. It wasn't any fun having a discussion with a man whose mind and heart weren't set on arguing. Adrian wanted to discuss another mill. Alex wanted to stare dreamy eyed at the whiskey bottle and talk about Karin Simon. Always more of a peacemaker than Adrian, who was at times a bit hotheaded, Alex responded to Adrian's badgering in his good-natured, humorous way, and this angered Adrian further. Drowning his fury in whiskey and consuming far more than his half of it, Adrian had had enough and as a result, Alex found himself sprawled in the dirt. Adrian had the advantage at first, but soon found himself outstepped, outmaneuvered, outsmarted, and outdone by the less-drunk Alex.

The fight, which lasted over an hour, was finally broken up by M.P. who knocked Adrian out with one pop beside the head with a stick of kindling big enough to fell a grizzly—just about the time Alex was getting the best of him. Alex, bleeding from a dozen wounds, one of which was on his forehead and flowing like a river into his face, couldn't see too well. When Adrian went down, he looked at the large, shadowy form standing over his brother's still body trying to figure out just who had the audacity to break up one of their fights— something that had never happened before. Wiping the blood from his face with his sleeve and squeezing his eyes shut, Alex staggered around for a moment or two, trying to clear his vision. When he opened his eyes, they focused on M.P.'s massive volume, resting on the stick of kindling still in her hand.

"M.P., what in the hell did you do that for?" Alex asked. "I was winning. I didn't need your help."

"Because I'm trying to get some shut-eye, and on top of that, it was time for this nonsense to come to an end before you two fools fought all night."

Alex looked at his brother who was coming to and trying to figure out what hit him. He tried to raise himself to his feet. After three unsuccessful tries, Adrian collapsed like a closed umbrella and sat looking at M.P. "Why didn't you hit him?" he asked.

"Because you were drunk."

"So was he," Adrian said, pointing at Alex.

"You were further along, so you were easier, and since you were about to pass out anyway, I figured it was more fair."

"Fair!" shouted Adrian, staggering to his feet. "If you wanted to be fair, you should have knocked us both out."

"That would've been a fool thing to do. I only needed one of you out to stop the fight."

Alex looked at M.P. He looked at Adrian. They opposed each other like two pieces of granite, and Alex figured they might be here for a spell, so he picked up the bottle of whiskey and started walking off.

"Where do you think you're going?" Adrian called after him.

Without stopping, or even looking back, Alex said, "Adrian, I feel as sore as a boil and I'm going to get drunk."

Alex went to his room. By the time the bottle was finished, he wasn't feeling any pain. In fact, he wasn't feeling much of anything. For a while he sat on his bed thinking about Karin, and reflecting on the past. A vision of Karin rose before him—Karin the way she had looked that day at the creek when he'd spied on her. Karin, wet and naked and the most beautiful thing he had ever seen.

Drunker than a skunk and barely able to stand, Alex staggered around his room, bumping into things that were stationary, and knocking over things that weren't. At last, he made it to his desk and managed to sit down. After much effort and numerous attempts, he located the drawers, opening them one at a time and rummaging through the contents until he had placed paper, ink, pen, and envelope on top of the desk. For a moment or two, he sat staring at the objects that appeared to be swimming before him.

"Who cares," he said. "I could ask Karin to marry me if I was blindfolded."

Alex picked up the pen and dipped it into the bottle of ink before he made a few circular swings over the top of the paper. At last, he located the top of the page and managed to stop there, his pen scratching out two words.

My Dearest

He blinked once or twice and looked at the paper again. *My Dearest.* Dearest what? He laid the pen aside and sat back in the chair, his eyes on the paper until he remembered and a smile crossed his face. He picked the pen up, dipped it again, and wrote in earnest, four sentences.

Can't wait any longer to ask you to marry me. Will arrange passage to San Francisco and meet you there. Please don't disappoint me.

I've come to my senses at last.
Alex

CHAPTER
TWELVE

The cow kicked over the milk bucket.

She had done that three times already. But with iron-willed resolve, Katherine slapped the cow on the rump and righted the bucket. "Try that again and I'll tie your tail in a knot. See if I don't." She began milking again.

Apparently, the threat worked, for Katherine finished milking and carried the bucket into the house. Fanny Bright was stitching down the ragged edge of her best straw hat, the one she wore to church each Sunday. Last Sunday it must have looked particularly appealing to Clovis, for he had taken a couple of chomps at it while Fanny's attention was given to a circle of ladies who were sharing the latest gossip about Mabel Price, who was seen picnicking with Horace Stillwood, who was old enough to be her grandfather.

Katherine put the pail down and looked at Fanny. Dear, blessed Fanny. She shuddered, thinking what might have become of them if it hadn't been for Fanny. She thought about the food they had on the table, the crops that had been replanted, the new cow in the barn, and gave a brief prayer of thanks. God did indeed move in mysterious ways. How else could they explain the apologetic way the mortgage clerk at the bank showed up at their front door with a bank draft in his hand.

"What's this for?" Fanny had asked.

"Ben Witherspoon bought your old place,

lock, stock, and barrel. It brought more than was owed on at the bank, so this is yours." He handed her the draft.

Fanny looked at it. "Well, I declare," she had said. "If this don't beat all."

After that, Fanny had insisted they use the money to replenish their stock and replant the ruined crops. Katherine and Karin felt badly about Fanny using her money for their benefit, but Fanny wouldn't have it any other way. "You gave me a home when I had no place to go," she said. "Besides, I like living here. It's like home." She had laughed then. "It saves me from having to come over here all the time."

Things had flourished after that. They weren't rich, by any stretch of the imagination, but they were comfortable.

Dear, sweet Fanny, Katherine thought again. *God bless her.*

Katherine looked at the ragged edge of Fanny's Sunday-go-to-meetin' hat. "I'm sorry about the hat," she said. "Sometimes I think I'd be better off to shoot that blasted mule."

"Clovis is more important to us than any silly old hat," Fanny replied. Then without looking up, she said, "There's a letter on the mantle."

Katherine's eyes grew wide with delight. "A letter? From California?"

"I reckon it is, seeing as how you don't get letters from anyplace else."

Katherine hurried into the parlor, spying the letter and rushing to where it lay propped against the mantle clock. *Alex.* She recognized the handwriting immediately.

Miss K. Simon, Groesbeck, Texas.

Alex always addressed his letters like this. Katherine guessed he did so in the beginning because he was writing to both of them, with a personal note included for Karin. Gradually the notes to Karin had gotten smaller and smaller, which was understandable, since Karin never wrote to him. Alex had noticed that, saying once or twice: "I guess Karin is still angry, since I haven't heard from her. Ask her to write."

After a while, Alex stopped saying that.

Katherine guessed that was because Karin hadn't written. When Katherine read those parts of the letter where he had asked her to, Karin had said, "Alex and I are finished. You write him."

Katherine did. From that moment on she continued to write him. Faithfully. Often, she sent five or six letters to his one or two, and in time, Katherine had grown to feel she had become a much bigger part of his life. In his last letter, Alex had gone so far as to say, "Katherine, the land here is like something you've never seen. I wish you could see it. I know you'd love it as much as I do."

Katherine knew she would too.

She had carried that letter around for days, reading and rereading it, enchanted with the knowledge that Alex had not only thought of her, but had thought of her in terms of the land, something he loved as much as she did. *He's coming to his senses at last,* she heard herself saying. *I was always better suited to him than Karin was.* And Katherine believed that with all her heart. There was one other thing she believed with all her heart and had never mentioned to a living soul. Karin was much better suited to Adrian than she ever was to Alex, and vice versa.

Katherine looked at the letter again. It was the first one that had come since Karin had moved to Waco. For a brief minute she pondered whether she should open it now, or wait for Karin. *After all, it's Karin that Alex loves.*

The changes Katherine had seen in Alex's letters, the way he mentioned her name more and more in reference to one thing or the other, made Katherine wonder if maybe—just maybe Alex's love for Karin had cooled a bit. Karin's affections for Alex certainly had. Katherine doubted Karin would ever be interested in hearing what Alex had to say, because Karin could take one look at that letter and leave it on the mantle without a flicker of curiosity, and Karin was a *very* curious person. Then again, why would she be curious about a letter from Alex? She was knee-deep in courtship with Will Burnett, who was reported to be richer than Ben Gump—whoever Ben Gump was.

In the end, Katherine decided to wait. Karin was coming next week, and she could tell her about the letter, then announce her intention to read all future letters whenever they came, instead of waiting for Karin.

Karin came the next week. It was the sunniest of Sundays the afternoon Will Burnett drove a brand, spanking new black rig into the front yard and helped Karin down from the shiniest red leather seats anybody had a right to see. Karin made what Fanny termed "a benevolent trip," making the jaunt from Waco to the Simon place to see them every so often, since Fanny and Katherine had no way to get to Waco, save a rickety wagon drawn by an ornery old mule.

Katherine and Fanny took an immediate liking to Will. Fanny amazed them all when after Sunday dinner she asked Will if he would mind taking a look-see at Clovis who was acting a little colicky.

"There isn't anything wrong with that mule that a good board up beside the head wouldn't cure, or a shot between the eyes," Karin said while pulling on her spotless white gloves. "Honestly, I don't know why you two fret over him so."

"We *fret* primarily because neither me nor Katherine has an itching to pull a plow," Fanny answered as she walked from the room.

Karin watched Will amble out behind her, then turned to Katherine. "I don't know how you put up with that mouth of hers. She's got more gall than a government mule and she's as opinionated as they come, not to mention that tongue of hers. Louder than a bell clapper."

"Every tree bears some fruit," Katherine said. "Besides, I like Fanny; I like having her here. She's a lot of company to me and we get on well. Don't forget either, that if it hadn't been for Fanny, we wouldn't even have a farm."

"I know she's a kind and generous soul. I'm simply saying *I* couldn't put up with her underfoot for five minutes. I don't know why you won't come to Waco and live with me. I could get you a room in the boardinghouse and a job."

"I can't picture myself living in one little room. I'd go crazy. And who would look after things around here?"

"Fanny could."

"Yes, she could, but I probably won't ever ask her. I've lived here all my life. Why should I change? I'm happy here."

"Katherine, you're being foolish. Will is a very prominent man with influential friends. Wealthy friends. Wealthy, *men* friends."

Katherine caught herself in the nick of time. She had been about to say she didn't want another man, only Alex. "Maybe I am foolish, but I prefer to stay here. I guess it's a doggone shame we can't all be like you. Unfortunately, some of us are too soon old and too late smart."

Karin's look softened and her hand came out to touch Katherine's shoulder. "I'm sorry. It seems I always have good intentions when I come, and then when I get here, all I do is find fault with you and the way you live."

"You just need to realize I'm not you, Karin. I don't see things through your eyes."

"I should know that by now," she said, smiling. "You're just like Ma when it comes to stubborn independence." She reached into her drawstring reticule. "At least let me leave you a little money."

"You don't need to, really. We're getting on fine since Fanny got that money from the bank."

Karin dropped the coins back into her reticule with a *clink* and drew the strings together, looping them over her arm. "You'll let me know if you need anything?"

"I will."

Karin folded her hands together. "Well, I guess I'll locate Will."

Katherine followed her through the parlor, seeing the letter on the mantle. "Oh, wait a minute! I almost forgot to tell you about the letter that came." Katherine hurried to the fireplace, taking Alex's letter down from the mantel.

"You haven't read it yet?"

"No. I was waiting until you came."

Karin threw her hands up. "Lord preserve us! Why, for heaven's sakes? You know Alex and I are finished. You're the one who's been writing him. Why didn't you read it before now?"

Katherine didn't say anything. "You've got the patience of Job, you know that? Sometimes that smiling, inexhaustible patience drives me mad. I couldn't let a letter sit five minutes without opening it."

"You would if it was from Alex."

"Yes, I suppose you're right. I would." Then giving Katherine a look that was a little put out, she said, "Aren't you going to open it?"

Katherine slapped the envelope against her palm a time or two, thinking. "Yes," she said, "I guess I am." With a smile, she hurried to the sofa and sat down. She studied the envelope, then turned it over, suddenly feeling the strangest attachment for everything about her—all the things she had always loved—things Karin hated with a passion. The white frame house with its story and a half, now gray and weathered and needing paint, the surrounding yard, trampled hard and washed with winding gullies when it rained, the dilapidated fence covered with fragrant woodbine. Beyond, where the farmyard began to slope down toward the creek, the fields in between now green with a stand of corn, and down near the creek a small sorghum patch. But strangest of all was the feeling that this was all slipping away from her, and soon the things that had meant so much to her and her mother before her would be beyond her sight.

Katherine opened the letter with the strangest conviction that something monumental was about to happen. She shifted in her chair, holding the letter up to the lamp to have better light, her eyes skimming over the words. "Oh, God! Oh, my God!" she gasped. The letter fell to her lap and her hands flew to her astonished face.

"What's wrong? Has something happened?" Karin crossed the room, taking a seat beside Katherine and picking up the letter from where it had fallen.

My Dearest Katherine,
    Can't wait any longer to ask you to marry me.
Will arrange passage to San Francisco and
meet you there. Please don't disappoint me.

                    I've come to my senses at last.
                Alex

Katherine, her face paper-white turned
toward Karin. "There must be some mistake."

Karin stared at the letter. She wanted to
scream. She had thought herself over Alex, that
much was true, but seeing her sister's name—
seeing the offer of marriage—she felt angry and
jealous that Katherine had managed to do
what she had been unable to do.

Katherine had Alex.

Alex had a great deal of money.

Her anger wasn't born so much over the loss
of Alex. She had already given up on him, and
now she had feelings for Will, deep feelings.
Her anger wasn't over the fact that Alex had
money. Ben was wealthy beyond her wildest
imaginings, and unlike Alex, he had the social
position, the prestige of old, accepted family.
He was the stable hand of maturity and security that she had always needed. He treated
her like a queen. Alex would never do that. It
wasn't in him to put a woman on a pedestal.
He would want a woman to work right along
beside him, someone to share with and be his
partner. With Will, things were different.
Nothing was too good for her. Karin liked being
loved when it had an element of worship to it.

Karin didn't really know why she was angry. Just the shock of it, she guessed. She looked at Katherine's anxious face, knowing that behind all that innocence, she had wormed her way into Alex's affections. She remembered the way Katherine had paled and said, "There must be some mistake." Karin wanted to break something. "Oh, I think not," she said. "I think you've been very busy since Alex has been gone, writing to him with the faithfulness of an old hound, pouring your heart out to a man eaten up with loneliness. Well, you always wanted him. Now you've got him."

The shock of Karin's words held Katherine speechless for a moment. "No," she whispered. "That's not the way it was at all. I never said anything in those letters that could be taken as personal. I only told him what was going on around Limestone County. I thought he'd like to hear about the news from home."

Karin saw her sister's face twisted with pain and remembered how careful Katherine had always been to hide her feelings for Alex. She couldn't help the fact that she loved him, no more than Karin could help loving Will. She felt the anger slipping away. She knew her feelings for Alex had passed a long time ago. She had no reason to be angry with Katherine. She knew that as well as she knew her sister. Katherine would have never stooped to undermine things between herself and Alex, if she had thought there was anything there to undermine. She had told Katherine herself that things were over between them. Why shouldn't

Katherine believe it? It was true. Katherine was welcome to Alexander Mackinnon with her blessings. If she had her way about things, she would be married to Will before a body could say, *scat!*

"I know you didn't do anything. I don't know what got into me. I was just jealous, I guess, sort of like, I don't want him, but I don't want anyone else to have him. That's a foolish way to be, I admit. I know you've always loved Alex. Longer than me, I think. You're better suited to him than I ever could be."

"I'm not."

"Oh, yes you are. The two of you will have a grand time making mudpies in all that land you love so much." Karin shuddered and made a face. "I prefer tea parties." She came to Katherine, giving her a hug. "Marry Alex. It's what you've always wanted. Remember how Mama always said opportunity didn't knock twice."

"But Alex always loved you."

"Even Alex can come to his senses. I guess he began to see through your letters that you were the right one for him. Alex—even Alex with money wasn't the right man for me. Now that I've met Will, I see that."

Karin kissed her quickly, then turned, walking through the door.

"Karin..." Katherine called after her. "Are you sure?"

"Of course I'm sure. Do what you've always advised me to do," Karin called over her shoulder. "Follow your heart."

"But what if Alex is still in love with you?"

"Then it'll be up to you to convince him he isn't. You've always been a scrapper, Katherine. I have full faith in your ability." With a swish of lavender taffeta, Karin was gone, the musical notes of her trilling laugh passing over Katherine like bubbles of happiness.

CHAPTER THIRTEEN

Karin.

Her name had been in his mind like a song he couldn't stop humming, coming to Alex with the habitual ease of breathing. *Karin. At long last. Karin.*

Beneath the hazy sunlight of overcast skies, Alex and Adrian stood side by side at the water's edge, watching the hull of the tall-masted ship wend its way silently through the cold gray waters of San Francisco Bay, its canvas sheets dropping to bare the skeleton of its triple masts; a great hulking carcass stripped to the bone.

It had been a cold journey by ship all the way down from Humboldt Bay, and it seemed even colder when they reached San Francisco, because of the penetrating wind that had suddenly come up, blowing across open water. Alex turned up the collar of his greatcoat and stuffed his hands into his pockets, feeling the bite of wind on his face as he glanced around the docks where everything looked dark and inhospitable, as if it were covered with black frost.

"It's been a long time," Alex whispered. "A long, drawn-out wait."

Adrian was standing next to Alex, but the keening cry of a gull overhead drowned his brother's words and he didn't catch what he said. "What?"

"Nothing. I was just thinking out loud," Alex said.

Adrian looked at Alex, wondering at the almost melancholy cast to his appearance. "What were you thinking?"

"I was thinking I've been waiting a long time for my woman," Alex said.

"Well, old man, cheer up. You're not the first man to wait a long time for a woman," Adrian said. "Jacob waited seven years to marry Rachel..."

"And was tricked into marrying her sister..."

"And had to work seven more years to get Rachel," Adrian finished, then laughed. "See? Compared to fourteen years, your wait doesn't seem so long."

"But Jacob got two wives out of the deal," Alex said.

Up went Adrian's brows. "Is that what you want? Two wives?"

Alex laughed, the melancholy that gripped him suddenly gone. "Hardly. It's too much trouble just getting one."

It seemed an eternity before the ship, *Leah*, came around and drew even with the dock, her wood wet and glistening darkly. The harbor was crammed full of ships, their bare masts like so many charred lucifers with heads pointed toward heaven from whence they had been cast.

Alex closed his eyes and listened to the sounds of a ship coming to sudden life as the *Leah*'s crew made ready to dock. He opened his eyes, able to make out the captain standing on the quarterdeck, seeing only a big face and a prominent hawk nose.

He saw two women come up on deck, one of them too rotund to be Karin, while the trimmer one was almost hidden behind the immense form that stood beside her like a great gray iceberg. His eyes strained to see more of the smaller woman—although he was looking straight at her, he could not see any detail of her face—no more than a shadow beneath her green bonnet. The rest of her was blurred too, a vague patch of green and gold, yet she looked warm and comfortable, and although he could not see the direction her eyes were cast, he felt they were upon him.

Karin. Deep within his pockets, his hands clenched as he fought the fierce, wild eagerness that tore at his heart. It was all he could do to keep from running down the dock like some wild, mad animal, shoving and trampling all those who stood between him and his beloved.

The *Leah* drew closer, coming to dock against the wharf like a great groaning whale, her decks alive with the excitement of passengers pushing forward, crowding the crew who lashed the *Leah* to her berth. Alex watched several men secure the plank, his body suddenly too warm beneath his coat, his palms damp with sweat. The passengers surged forward, spilling down the gangway, and Alex lost sight of her, the woman in gold and green.

And then he saw her, coming toward the gangplank, her feet on it now, moving toward the wharf, coming closer, the smiling face beneath the green bonnet no longer a shadowy blur.

"My God! It's Katherine!" Adrian whispered.

Cold as a piece of granite, Alex felt his heart crack, then shatter. He looked away. He could not look until he was once again master of himself.

The cold drizzle fell all about them and the sickening smell of wet jute, fish, and damp gull feathers rose like steam in his nostrils. He felt himself weave on his feet as Adrian's words rolled over and over, endless waves throwing themselves upon a lonely beach. *It's Katherine...It's Katherine...It's Katherine...*

Alex felt his world encase itself in silence, broken only by the thud of the ship bumping against the wharf, the soft lap, lap, lap of the water pushing against her hull, as if it was trying to push the *Leah* away. *Leah.* The name had sudden meaning. *Leah,* sister of Rachel. *Leah,* whom Jacob was tricked into marrying after working seven long years for his Rachel.

Across the water, the sound of voices danced

around his ears, teasing and whispering, their words too faint to comprehend above the words still ringing in his head. *It's Katherine... It's Katherine...It's Katherine.*

The sound of Adrian's dry laugh was what brought him back. "They're up to their old tricks," Adrian was saying. "Katherine must have come with Karin, and they're trying to pull a fast one on us."

The world seemed to pull away from him, and Alex felt as if he were a million miles away, looking down upon this moment with dazed detachment. "No," he said at last. "It's no trick. It's Leah."

"Leah?" Adrian's head whipped around to stare at Alex. "You aren't making sen..." His words died in his throat. "Leah," he said, looking at his brother with a sickening sense of shock. "Leah," he repeated, seeing Alex's face blanch, the muscle knot in his clenched jaw. "Not Rachel."

But Alex didn't hear. Something had been tugging at his mind since the night he and Adrian fought, the night he wrote that fateful letter. A knot twisted inside his stomach. An agonized expression froze the features of his face. He would never understand how he had done it, but it was enough that he knew that he had. He had written to the woman he loved. He had asked her to marry him. But he had written her sister's name instead.

The keening shriek he heard was not that of a gull, but the anguished cry of his sorrow as Adrian's hands whipped out to clutch the collar of his greatcoat, jerking him against a face twisted with rage. "You bloody bastard," Adrian said. "What have you done?"

Dead inside, his senses numbed, Alex looked at his brother for as long as a minute with his expression sealed. "I've asked for the wrong sister, I'm afraid."

Another anguished cry. Alex felt himself released and shoved backward, Adrian's look saying he found the sight of him as repugnant as his touch. But his brother's eyes still burned into him as fierce as coals, his words coming sharp and precise as pistol fire. "She will be off that ship in a few minutes. What are you going to do?"

"Do?" Alex said. "I have only one choice."

"You're exactly right. One choice and one choice only," Adrian said through clenched teeth. "You're going to marry her, you bastard."

Marry her? Alex frowned. *Marry Katherine?* That wasn't the one choice he was thinking about. He had always liked Katherine of course, but enough to marry her? Impossible. Out of the question. The whole idea was unthinkable. It was Karin he loved, not Katherine. He would simply have to tell her the truth about what happened. Katherine was an understanding sort, and she had always been his friend. She would understand. She had to. For the only thing to do, in Alex's mind, was be man enough to tell the truth and admit the mistake was his, telling Katherine as gently as possible.

Alex glanced at Adrian, to tell him his thoughts, but Adrian shot him a silencing look. Adrian looked mad enough to kill. Alex was baffled. He had expected Adrian to help, or at least understand. "I can't marry Katherine, Adrian. You of all people should understand that."

Adrian's face was a cold, hard mask. "Why not? You've already committed yourself. You don't have any choice now."

"I can't marry someone I don't love."

"You should have thought about that before you wrote that letter when you were too drunk to stand." Adrian finished his reply with a strong left to Alex's jaw that almost leveled him as Adrian said, "You sorry, drunken bastard! I ought to kill you!" And he did his best to try, until a large, burly stranger pulled them apart.

"Here now, let's have none of that," the stranger said. He was a well-dressed, giant of a man with mutton chops. As soon as he pulled them apart, he stepped between them. When Adrian lunged at Alex again, the man collared him, giving him a good shake as he said, "Try it again and I'll toss you in the drink. You want to fight, you take it away from here. My wife is on that ship, and terrified of coming to a place as uncivilized as this. I'll not have the likes of you undoing all the convincing I've been doing for months."

By that time, Adrian's rage was slowly being replaced by common sense. He didn't want Katherine to see them like this. Besides, if Alex didn't see things his way, he could always do this later.

Stunned at the intensity of Adrian's anger, Alex wiped the blood from his mouth. "What are you acting like this for? It was a mistake, that's all. An honest mistake."

Adrian was feeling enough rage to kill Alex at that moment. For a brief moment he considered telling Alex that he would take her for his own wife, when the thought froze like ice stabbing into his heart. Katherine had come out here to marry Alex, the man of her heart. She couldn't—wouldn't—settle for him any more than he could turn his affections to Karin. His eyes rested on his beloved Katherine as she drew closer. Seeing the smile, the light in her eyes, the look of complete and utter satisfaction and sublime joy on Katherine's face was more than he could take. Without a doubt Adrian knew with a painful twist to his stomach that she would never look at him like that, that she would never, ever love him like she loved his brother. There was only one thing left for him to do.

His face twisted with pain and anger, his voice bitter and cold, Adrian spoke carefully, saying each word with the deadly intent he felt. "If you ever tell her, if you ever let her know, I'll kill you," Adrian said. "If you ever so much as make her regret becoming your wife, I'll make your life a living hell." He straightened Alex's greatcoat, taking the handkerchief from his hand and tucking it in his pocket. "Take care brother, or you'll come to wish you had never been born."

"Adrian, listen..."

"No! You listen. You aren't going to back out of this now. It's too late for that." He grabbed Alex's face, twisting it to look in the direction of the ship. "Look at her, damn you! Take a good, long look at her face! What do you see? Joy? Happiness? Elation? She's in love with you, you poor stupid bastard. She's always been in love with you."

But Alex turned his head away, refusing to look at Katherine. "It isn't anything she can't get over."

"She won't have to now. When you wrote that letter, damn you, you gave her the answer to her lifelong dream." *And in doing so you shattered mine.* "You better watch yourself from here on out brother. For what you've done, I could easily kill you without blinking an eye."

"Adrian, listen to me. How can you expect me to marry someone I don't love?"

"It's too late to be asking that question now, brother." Adrian grabbed Alex by the shoulders and jerked him around in time to see Katherine coming toward them, her face radiant. "Tell me, can you hurt her like that? Can you tell her you made a mistake? Do you have any idea what it would do to her?"

Alex opened his mouth, but the words never came out. He looked at Katherine, the familiar face, the lively step he remembered so well. Katherine, laughing, happy Katherine. Always his adoring friend. But she was like a stranger to him now, a beautiful woman he was seeing for the first time.

He remembered the time she had come downstairs wearing Karin's dress, and how pathetic she had looked, the back misbuttoned, the sash dragging, and how Karin had embarrassed her until she ran up the stairs crying. His heart had gone out to her that day. "You shouldn't embarrass her like that," he had said.

"Heaven knows why you're so eager to champion her cause," Karin had replied. "She's always making a fool of herself in front of you and we both know the reason why. She'd give her eyeteeth to have you for a beau."

And there were other memories too: the time she fell while watching from the tree; the rope burns she got climbing to spy on them in the hayloft.

He recalled the day in the pasture when he found her crying over the dead fawn, and the way she had looked at him and cried. And after that, the vision of her standing on the porch the first time he saw her after the war, and the way she had looked at him in welcome. They came back in a flood, the day he found her hoeing the garden; the afternoon he taught her to use blood bait to catch more fish; the day Clovis tore down all the laundry; her catching him with Karin down by the creek. But most of all he remembered leaving for the goldfields, the memory of Katherine's kiss burning like a brand upon his lips.

Memories weren't reason enough to marry. He opened his mouth to tell Adrian that, when suddenly she was there, in front of him, and his eyes locked with hers. The breath drained out of him, the words he was about to speak withering in his throat. It was so clear to him now, he marveled at how he had never seen just how deep her feelings for him ran—the love, warm, tender, and unmistakable that was shining in the depths of her eyes, the same look he had seen a million times before, only then he had been too blind and insensitive to see.

Katherine stopped in front of him and looked into his face, so deathly pale, that she wondered if he had been ill. He was still incredibly handsome, but he looked much older than she had expected him to, and drawn, as if he had recently experienced some deep emotional sadness. But this was Alex, the man she had loved since she was a child, the only man she would ever love, the man she thought she would never have, the man who granted her the dream of a lifetime, along with the sun, stars, and the moon.

"Katherine," he said, taking her gently in his arms and kissing her lightly on the forehead before he released her.

She smiled up at him, thinking this wasn't the welcome that she had expected, but they had the rest of their lives together, and there would be time enough for that. She greeted Adrian with a kiss on his cheek, thinking he was looking as pale and strained as Alex, but she didn't have much time to reflect upon that, for Adrian announced he had some business with the captain of the *Mermaid*, and that he would tell him they would be ready to set sail soon.

Later that afternoon the *Mermaid* headed north, toward Humboldt Bay, pitching and wallowing in an angry sea, balking like a sullen mule every inch of the way. It was raining now, with such violence that nothing could be seen farther than five feet away. His clothes were soaked, if not from the rain, from the deluge of spray sweeping the deck, but Alex could not make himself go below. Not yet.

Katherine was below. The thought terrified him. *Dear God! What can I say to her?*

She was in a small cabin, but she was dry and as happy as she could ever remember being. She was sitting on the small bunk thinking about the way Alex had greeted her with a kiss more suited for an aging grandmother than the woman he was about to marry. Moments later, his expression empty and without meaning, he had looked into her upturned face for a full minute before he said, "Welcome to San Francisco. How was your trip?" And that was it! *Strange creatures, men. You spend your life knowing one only to wake up one morning and find you don't know him at all.*

CHAPTER
FOURTEEN

As quickly as it had come, the rain had stopped. Seeing Alex make his way up to the deck, Adrian followed him.

"I want to talk to you," Adrian said.

Alex scowled and stepped behind some crates stacked on deck. Adrian was itching for an argument and he wanted to be out of earshot of the deckhands. Adrian was staring at him, and Alex said, "Did you want to talk, or stare holes through me?"

"If I thought staring holes would let some of that stubbornness out, I'd give it a try." Alex shrugged and Adrian decided to be more direct. "What are you going to do about Katherine?"

"Careful, brother, you're about to scald your tongue in someone else's broth."

"Isn't that what brothers are for?"

"You're meddling because of Katherine, not because you're my brother."

"I'm meddling because I think you're in love with her." He shook his head. "Unfortunately, you're too stupid to realize it."

"Like hell!"

"You can't tell me that you aren't a little interested in her," Adrian said, "that you don't find her appealing."

"I find a steak dinner appealing, but I sure as hell don't jump up to propose marriage!"

In response, Adrian exaggerated the lift of his brows and looked at him as if he had just dribbled food all over his shirtfront. It was a look Adrian used now and then—with ease and results. It was a look that drove Alex wild. "You aren't being sensible, Alex. That isn't like you."

Alex felt his eyes bulge with anger. "You're not either!" he shouted, knowing he was losing control and unable to do anything about it. He hated it whenever Adrian shifted positions with him like this. Here Adrian was sounding mild-tempered and controlled, when anyone that knew them at all knew Adrian was the hothead of the two.

" 'You're not either?' Now *that's* a powerful statement." Adrian's laugh was mocking—a mocking laugh being another effective tool Adrian used at will. Alex found he wasn't any more immune to this laugh now than he had been at fourteen, when he busted Adrian's nose for that same offense. "Why should I be sensible, brother? I've never been known as the sensible twin. That honor has always been bestowed upon you," Adrian said in the softest, most controlled tones. "Although there are times I question why."

These controlled tones sent Alex into a red rage. Whenever Adrian chose to speak this way, straining to speak with dignity and using quiet repose, Alex always felt like a deer who was run to the ground by a cougar. Like that deer, Alex felt winded and unable to run anymore.

His brother's statement had been a disquieting one. Alex stood motionless, letting

Adrian's words soak in a bit, feeling on the one hand the slightest pinch of truth to what he had said, yet on the other hand never having wanted to punch his brother out half as badly as he did this very moment.

For a long while he didn't reply. Adrian saw the weary look, the dregs of struggle still upon his face, but that didn't keep him from asking, "It's a bit of a teaser, isn't it?"

"A bit."

"You're either interested, or you aren't. It's that simple," Adrian said.

"Speaking of *powerful* sentences. There isn't *anything* simple about Katherine and you know it." He spoke naturally, as if the words came without being forced. "There's no need to bring out the heavy artillery," he added, a trapped look on his face. "I don't think you have any idea what you're asking of me."

How typical of Alex, Adrian thought, *to be down, but still struggling.* He was like a grizzly that kept on coming at you, even after you had pumped three rounds of lead into him. Some people never knew when to give up and call it quits. Alex was one of those. His refusal to yield, to call truce made Adrian edgy. Adrian was close to losing his control, and that was something he couldn't do around Alex because Alex would use it like a second wind to close in for the kill. Like that grizzly one thought dead, he might rise up the moment you nudged him with your gun barrel, and strike the fatal blow. He strove to keep the conversation on target, to keep the upper hand. This was critical. He had to use Alex's emotional confusion to its utmost. "Why can't you admit it? Why is it so hard to admit you're interested?"

"Admit it?" Alex repeated as if he were musing over the words. He shook his head. "You say it like that's all I have to do. Admit it and everything will be smelling like roses. Maybe I'm still in shock. Maybe this has all been more than I can handle. I'm not going to solve a damn thing by admitting I'm interested in her. If anything, it complicates things more."

"You think so?"

Alex showed signs of irritation. "Is that all you want, then? My confession? If it is, that's easily enough given. All right. I'm interested in her," Alex replied. "Does that satisfy you? We've been friends since we were children. Why wouldn't I be?"

Adrian crossed his arms over his chest. "I don't know. You tell me. And while you're at it, tell me why it is that the way you look at her isn't the look of a friend. Katherine has always been more than that to you. You're a complete fool to have never realized it before."

Alex rounded on him. "And you, of course did. Tell me, *brother,* just why it is that you never mentioned this before now? Surely *you* knew it all along, since you've always been in love with her yourself."

Adrian opened his mouth to speak, but nothing came out. Alex was right. It had never occurred to him before now that Alex's feelings for Katherine ran deeper than either of them realized. He wondered why it had suddenly come to light now. To give himself time to consider, he addressed Alex's other statement, the one concerning his own feelings for Katherine. That Adrian had always cared for Katherine was immaterial, since Alex and everyone else had always known he was sweet on her. "We aren't talking about my feelings here. I'm not the one that lured her out here with rainbow-colored hopes," he said. As for Alex's other comment—why hadn't he realized before now that Alex had deeper feelings than friendship for Katherine? And what caused that knowledge to surface now? The answer came swiftly.

Alex's reaction.

Of course that was it. Adrian knew the depth of Alex's feelings, because of the way Alex reacted. Adrian knew his brother well. There was a part of Alex that was mystically a part of him because of their being twins, and that meant there were some things about Alex that Adrian understood, when there was no logical or reasonable reason why. He simply understood. Adrian knew Alex was much more easygoing than he was, but Alex was more stubborn. Even when backed into a corner, he would fight to the death for something he believed in. *If* Alex felt strongly against Katherine, if he abhorred her, if he had no interest, no inclinations toward her at all, no one could force him to marry her, come hell or high water. He looked at Alex. He had balked at the idea for sure, and he was still kicking, but that wasn't the same as a point-blank refusal. Adrian knew as certain as he knew his own name that Alex would have busted his face the first time he mentioned marriage to Katherine—*if* he had found the idea as unpalatable as he let on. No, the idea wasn't wholly unsavory to Alex; he just hadn't had time to adjust to such an unexplored idea.

"So, you think I have deeper feelings for Katherine than friendship?" Alex said. "Maybe I do. I've always known you did, but me?" He laughed, but there wasn't a damn thing funny going on here. "Hell! Maybe we're both in love with her. Now, wouldn't that be a hoot? It runs in some families, you know, and I'm feeling a bit tetched right now. How about you?" He looked at Adrian, seeing the serious expression. Alex sighed and shoved his hands in his back pockets, palms facing outwards. "What are you trying to do, Adrian? Soften the blow? Stir up more trouble by trying to convince me I'm in love with her so I won't feel the slightest bit of remorse if I marry her?"

"Oh, you'll marry her. Rest assured of that. I'll see to it."

Alex's features tightened. His fists clenched. The muscles of his neck bulged. He knew what Adrian said was true; he knew that Adrian would keep on and keep on until he hit upon the one thing, the one reason for this marriage that Alex could not deny. He was going down, and in his anger, he reached out to deliver one more blow. "And will you see to it that I find her as fucksome as you do?"

He never saw Adrian's fist, but he sure as hell felt it. Out of nowhere it came, swift and hard, slamming against his jaw with all the force of a thunderbolt, knocking Alex's head backward, and the rest of his body along with it. It could be said here that it knocked a little sense into him as well. Two seconds later Alex sat in a crumpled heap rubbing his aching jaw. He looked at Adrian a bit sheepishly, unable to remember a time when he looked as angry as he did now. Ordinarily Alex would have lit into him for all he was worth, but he was a fair man. He knew he had delivered a low blow, and he knew he deserved what he'd gotten. "I'm sorry. I shouldn't have said that. We both know I like Katherine. I admire her. I care about what happens to her. She's pretty enough and woman enough that I could easily make love to her. But it wouldn't be out of love. Bastard that I am, I couldn't see myself doing that to her. She deserves more than that—more than me. She's a decent woman, and she's always been an honest sort. It pains me to think what she'd be getting here… a husband that was in love with her sister." He paused and looked thoughtful. "I don't love her in a husbandly way. If that's what you're thinking, you're imagining things."

"Am I? Am I imagining that you know the minute she steps onto the deck, or the minute she goes below? Do you know how many times I've caught you watching her, or how I've noticed the way your hands clench into fists every time some other male on this ship stops to talk with her? She has come up on deck three times, and three times you have sent her below. Why? Because you're jealous?"

"What are you doing? Conducting some sort of survey? Stop reading false interpretations into things. I know the minute Wong goes to the kitchen to start breakfast, but I'm not in love with him. I used to clench my fists anytime someone tried to ride my horse, but it wasn't out of love." He threw his head back and closed his eyes as if he were already tired. "You're a lousy matchmaker, and you don't know shit about love. Maybe that's why you're out behind the shed when it comes to knowing what's going on here."

Adrian shrugged. "I may know more than you think. And no, I'm not conducting surveys. I'm merely pointing out that you, my self-righteous brother, are nothing more than a hypocrite."

Alex shrugged. "Think what you want. You always do, no matter what I say."

"An attribute I share with my twin, only he's more stubborn and less subtle than I am."

Alex shrugged again.

"You'll have to marry her, Alex. She'll be ruined if you don't," Adrian said.

Alex, his dark head bent, was still sitting on the deck, only now his arms rested on his updrawn knees. Adrian had just delivered the deciding blow, just as he knew he would do eventually. He felt tired, drained. This had all been inevitable, and he had somehow known that from the beginning, from the moment he had seen it was Katherine walking off that ship. He lifted his head slowly, the breath he released coming out of his mouth like a vapor. "Another broadside," he said, turning his face into the wind which was steadily increasing.

Adrian offered his hand, pulling Alex to his feet. Alex looked up as the windlass began to spin, the ropes groaning as the ship rose and plunged with each successive wave. Alex was looking too, aware of the dizzy pitch of the ship, finding it nearly overpowering to think at a moment like this. Too much attention had been given to Katherine. What about him? What about Karin? Right now he was so sick at heart over the loss of Karin that he couldn't think straight. Couldn't Adrian see that? But Adrian only repeated his last statement. "If you're honest, you'll have to admit I'm right. You have to marry her, Alex. You know I'm right in saying she'll be ruined if you don't."

Adrian was right. In his heart Alex knew that. But he had lost so much today and he felt so damned, so trapped. He might be forced to marry Katherine, but he sure didn't have to lower his head and be led like a blind man. He spread his feet farther apart to brace himself for the next wave. "Ruined is a bit severe, don't you think?"

"No, I don't think it's severe at all. She has traveled halfway around the continent to marry a man who proposed to her..."

"Now wait a minute," Alex interrupted,

"I didn't propose to Katherine, not intentionally. You know that."

"In this instance, intentions don't count—only what's written on paper. In the eyes of the law, you proposed. Now, can you imagine what it would do to her, what it would be like if she had to go back home now? She would be ruined and humiliated and it would be all your fault. Can you do that? Can you stand there and look me in the face and tell me you can do that to Katherine?"

Alex didn't say anything.

Adrian's voice became more demanding. "Answer me, damn you! Can you?"

Alex stared across the bow of the ship seeing nothing but gray water and gray skies. He was thinking what strange tricks the mind plays upon a person. Here he was at a crucial point, making a decision he would have to live with for the rest of his life, a decision that not only affected his life but that of Karin, Katherine, and in some ways, he supposed, Adrian as well. And what came into his mind? Here he was, needing sharp mental acuity for a major decision and for some odd reason he was remembering a time years ago when he had come upon Katherine working in the flower beds that ran in a complete circle around her home.

She had been on her knees, her hands in the rich, black soil, breaking apart the bulbs and tubers to thin them out and replant—cannas, lilies, and gladiolas scattered all about her, a small bucket nearby. He had stopped, watching her separate a long earthworm from a clod of dirt and drop it into the bucket, covering it with a little soil. He had asked her what she was doing, "planting bulbs or harvesting worms?" Katherine had jerked her head around to look at him, her hands caked with dirt, her eyes alive and oh, so warm. She looked up and saw him standing just a few feet from her, her eyes telling him how happy she was to see him. "If I could only grow flowers as big as these worms," she said. "Alex, do come have a look at them." Something about his expression must have made her self-conscious, for she lifted her hand and took a swipe at a trailing curl on her forehead that had escaped her bonnet. Her face was damp and her hand left a smear of mud. She was totally unaware of the seductiveness of the way she moved, the soft, sultry expression in her eyes. Funny thing. He hadn't been aware either. Until now. *This is how people go crazy.*

"Are you listening, Alex?" Adrian asked.

"Yes."

"Well, can you do that to her?"

He shook his head, feeling the creeping sadness that had threatened since San Francisco slowly consume him. "No," he said, "I can't."

"Then you agree you can't cry off?"

"I don't know."

"You don't know...a fine answer. Evasive as hell." He threw up his arms. "That's what

Katherine deserves, more beating around the bush!"

"It's an honest answer, Adrian. I really don't know. I don't know what I'm doing in a mess like this. I don't know what I'm going to do about it." Alex sighed, his hand coming up to massage the tight muscles at the back of his neck, then tenderly touching his sore jaw. "You didn't have to hit me so hard."

"Yes, I did. I wanted to knock some sense into you. Now, tell me if you agree you can't cry off?"

"I suppose you're right—at least the way things look now—I can't cry off, until I think of something else. I'm sure in time..."

Adrian slammed his fist against the railing. "Dammit! Time is something you don't have. You're already running on borrowed time as it is. You should have married her in San Francisco, but it's too late now to worry about that. At the moment, your only option is to have the captain marry you before we reach Humboldt Bay."

"Hell's bells, Adrian! What are you trying to do to me?"

"I'm trying to make you see things as they are, Alex, in black and white. Katherine is a beautiful woman. She can't live in a logging camp with a rough, woman-hungry bunch of men in an unmarried state. We both know what would happen to her if she tried. And you can't send her back. There are no other choices. You'll have to go through with the marriage, and you've got to do it now. There's no one to perform the marriage in camp." Adrian sighed, shoving his hands deep into his pockets and looking very much his brother's twin at that moment. "You've always been a fair man, Alex. I know, in the end, you'll do what's right."

What is right. What is right. What is right?

A deadly calm settled over Alex. Adrian was right. In his heart he knew it. He would have to marry her. He didn't love Katherine. He didn't want to marry her. But he had always liked her. She had always been a friend. He didn't want to hurt her. When Adrian had joined him a few minutes ago, Alex had been standing at the bow of the ship searching his mind for a way to escape the lifetime of bondage that was being forced upon him. He had gone so far as to consider putting the marriage off under the pretext of getting to know each other better, then making life so miserable for her she wouldn't want to marry him, wouldn't want to do anything except return to Texas.

You will do what is right. He hadn't counted on the rightness of what Adrian was saying, or the way his troubled mind agreed. He was responsible. He couldn't argue with that. He was the only one who could set things right. He had forgotten for a time that Katherine had been a vital part of his life since childhood. A man couldn't be a man and turn his back on things like that. And he could never be happy knowing he had. *You will do what is right.*

Yes, he thought. *I will.*

His eyes were drawn toward the helm where Katherine had just come on deck. She stood talking to the captain, the wind in her hair, the sparkle of the sea in her eyes, the enthusiasm of a young girl in her expressions as they talked. She had come to California to be his wife because he had written a letter asking her to. With one slip of the pen he had ruined any chance she might have of finding another husband or living a life free of humiliation and disregard if he turned his back on her and sent her home.

Seeing he was looking at her, Katherine smiled radiantly and waved. It was the face of a child on Christmas morning, or a woman who looks at her newborn for the first time; a face alive with belief in magic. He did his best to look her over with critical disregard, but all he felt was deep affection. He couldn't humiliate her by sending her back in shame. He couldn't crush her spirit by telling her the awful truth. The hard knot of matrimony that would join them forever tightened around his neck. The burden of the secret he would have to keep from her grew heavy and demanding. He had many regrets in his life, but this was the biggest regret of all. And what stung the most was the helplessness he felt. *The goddamn helplessness.* It was the first time he could ever remember his life slipping out of his control. *And I can't do anything but stand here like a fool and watch it go.*

Adrian was about to say something else

when Alex cut him off with a wave of his hand. "We've talked this thing to death. There's nothing more to say. I'll speak to the captain," he said roughly and turned away.

Speaking to the captain is precisely what Katherine was doing, or more correctly, the captain was speaking to her. "The best thing about rain," Captain Steptoe was saying, "is that you get a rainbow when it's all over." He looked down at the rapturous face turned up toward his. "You do like rainbows, don't you—and believe in the pot o' gold?"

"I suppose, although I've seen plenty of rainbows and nary a pot of gold," Katherine answered. "Besides, what's always interested me more is what's on the other side."

"Well now, I've n'er given that a thought," he said, turning away for a moment to give a dressing down to a seaman who had broken forth with a volley of nautical oaths from the rigging overhead. Katherine, who heard it all quite clearly, clamped her hands over her mouth so as not to appear unladylike and laugh, for the oaths, colorful as they were, weren't really embarrassing because of the way the seaman seemed to squawk and flap in the rigging like an awkward parrot about to lose his footing.

When Alex joined them he was solemn and spoke softly. "May I borrow my intended for a minute, Captain?"

"If you promise not to take her too far away."

Alex nodded, taking Katherine by the arm

and walking her across the deck. "I doubt you're enjoying this trip after already being so long at sea," he said to her.

Katherine smiled up at him. "I'm enjoying it—only because I know it's the last leg of it, for in truth, I am nigh sick of ships and even sicker of ship food."

He laughed. "It won't be much longer," he said, pausing near a deserted section of railing and leaning over it to look out across the water.

Katherine stood beside him, adoring this closeness, this chance to be with him at last. A stiff silence stretched between them and she took advantage of it. She wasn't foolish enough to think everything was rose tinted and lined with gilt between them. Alex had loved Karin. But in his wisdom he had proposed to her. She said, *in his wisdom,* simply because she believed it was true. Whatever the reason that prompted him to write for her, there was no doubt in her mind that it had been the right thing to do. She looked at the dear features of his strong profile and thought, *You may not love me completely now, but you will, Alex. I have enough love to sustain us until you do. You will love me. You will! I'll become your wife soon, and there's never been anything you did that was more right. I was always the mate God intended for you. Perhaps that's where all my frustration came from—because I always knew it, and you didn't.*

"I must apologize," he said, and Katherine jumped a country mile.

He smiled. "Is an apology from me so

unheard of that it would send you overboard?"

She returned the smile. "No, you startled me, that's all."

He looked down into the small, oval face that looked at him with such trust and knew he couldn't hurt her with the truth. For a moment he had been about to tell her just that. The truth. He had, in fact, been staring at the water, as if it were a dark, gray slate where he had written all the reasons why she would hate being married to him—only he hadn't counted on her looking at him like that, with the huge trusting eyes of a child, or a favorite childhood pet. How could he savagely kick out at that?

As he stared down at the sweet, adoring face, he tried to think of all the things he had in common with her, anything to soften the jolt of what he was about to do. God only knew many marriages had started with less. At least she wasn't some stranger he'd never laid eyes on, and the Lord be praised, she wasn't homely. He had always been able to talk to her, to tease and test her wit. Only now, the time he wanted most to unburden his heart to her, he could not. God, he felt as though he was saddled with so much. There were so many secrets between them, secrets that would shatter her if she ever found out—and while the secrets were enough to drag him down, it was the strain of knowing, being terrified he might let something slip, that he might unknowingly reveal the truth, or score a direct hit in a moment of anger, that caused him the most concern. Secrets were such ugly things, like slavery. Once you knew a secret, you were its captive instead of the other way around. Tension coiled like a deadly snake within his belly and he felt as if he could do nothing except wait—wait for the moment it would strike.

"What were you going to apologize for, Alex? Surely not the weather. I promise I don't hold you responsible." She looked about her. "At least it stopped raining."

His mind raced. What could he tell her? What could he apologize for, now that he had decided to keep the truth from her? "A little slipup," he said at last, "nothing more. We should have been married in San Francisco. There isn't anyone at camp who can perform a marriage."

The light faded from her eyes and her voice faltered as she spoke. "We... then we won't be married. Is that what you're saying?"

He felt the lightning flash of temptation prodding him to say what she feared was true, that they could not be married. He began walking along the ship's railing, tucking her arm through his, but not looking at her. He had been silent for several minutes before he finally said, "What I meant to say is that we'll be married by the captain, here, on this ship."

Married to Alex, at last!

She almost accepted his proposal.

If she had been any other kind of woman, she would have. But Katherine was an honest sort, and the question that had been nagging in the back of her mind gave her no peace. She had tried dismissing it, tried putting it off until after they were married, she even tried ignoring it, hoping it would go away. It never did. Like gathering storm clouds, it grew and grew, picking up more moisture until it swelled, dark and thunderous, threatening to burst. Just as they reached her cabin door, it did just that. It burst. The moment it did, Katherine knew she had to ask that awful question. As Alex reached in front of her to open the door, she placed her hand lightly upon his sleeve.

"Alex, why did you write for me?"

He sucked in his breath and closed his eyes, willing the dryness in his throat away. So much rested upon his answer. Two lives were at stake here, his and hers. He opened his eyes and looked into hers. They were filled with hope. Hope, for Katherine was always like a cat; it had nine lives. In her eyes lay the disappointment of eight others. He felt the weight of it. *Dear God! The desire to tell the truth, the guilt if I do.*

"Because it was time I took a wife." *Let it be, Katherine.*

But she couldn't. *Let it be, Katherine.* "Why me and not Karin?"

The hope was still there, shining as brightly in her eyes as before. He remembered an old musket his father had over the fireplace. On its stock were engraved the words: "Hope is a great falsifier of truth." "Because it was meant to be, Katherine." Desperate to ease the tension, to put her mind at rest, to stop all these painful questions and get on with this mockery, he forced a smile and as much light-heartedness as he could muster and said, "Because I knew *you* would come."

Starbursts of delight shimmered in her eyes. Her laugh was musical and light as she shoved him playfully. "Oh you! You're mean to say that. Why do you think Karin wouldn't come?"

Her playfulness brought back the old teasing closeness he had always felt around her, and that made it so easy to slip into the mood with her, like a boat drawn along by the current. "Because she wasn't speaking to me," he said, "and you were."

She accepted that answer because it was true. Karin wasn't speaking to him, hadn't been writing to him the entire time he was gone. His honesty surprised her. It also thrilled her. *He's trying,* she told herself. *I can do no less.* Katherine was so full of joy, she felt she must have floated through the doorway. Once inside, she turned to look at Alex and said, "You aren't sorry, are you Alex?"

Go on, man. This is your last chance. You better take it. "No," he said, and turned away. He heard the door close behind him. He felt like a spider that spun himself into his own silken cocoon. He was trapped and the helplessness of it ate at him like a canker.

They were married the next morning.

But it wasn't the wedding she had always imagined she would have. In fact, it wasn't the wedding she imagined anyone would have.

They repeated their vows the next morning in the captain's quarters which smelled of fish oil and stale wine. It was raining again, and that meant the portholes were closed, the smoke from the lamps mingling with the other unpleasant smells to a choking degree. Five people were gathered there, waiting for the bride, two of them being Alex and Adrian; the other three the captain, his first mate, and the cook, who served as witness.

At that moment Katherine was looking at herself in the mirror. Remembering the saying, she recited, "Married in blue, you'll always be true." And today was what? Friday? What was the saying there? "Monday for wealth, Tuesday for health, Wednesday best day of all, Thursday for losses, Friday for crosses..." A bad omen. *But it could have been worse, Katherine. At least this isn't Thursday.* She turned away from the mirror. Stepping outside, she pulled her cloak over her head to keep her bridal bonnet dry. *Happy is the bride the sun shines upon,* the superstition went.

It was raining.

Rain, according to the saying means there will be tears ahead. Another bad omen.

She walked slowly toward the captain's cabin, another old saying coming to her. *A bride weeps on her wedding day, or tears will fall later.* She pulled her bridal handkerchief from beneath her cuff, for already there were tears in her eyes. It wasn't hard to cry, for although she would, in a few moments time, be married to the man of her heart as well as the man of her dreams, she felt a heaviness inside that she could not shake.

Alex stood beside Adrian as he watched Katherine pause in the doorway in her makeshift wedding finery, his eyes dropping immediately to the pitiful bunch of artificial petunias clutched in her hand. *She's always loved flowers. She should have real flowers.* But then he remembered this whole marriage was a sham, a fake, so why not have fake flowers as well?

Her cheeks were rosy from the brisk cold, her hair rich and glossy and beautifully arranged. Alex was tempted to just let his gaze rest there. But he didn't, for something drew his attention away, allowing him to take notice of the rest of her. Katherine's wedding dress was blue.

She was wearing what he recognized as her Sunday-best blue linen, but something new had been added. Before, the dress had been collarless and cuffless, the rings from previous hemmings all too obvious. A white collar, delicately embroidered, was a new addition, as well as the white cuffs. Three tiny black velvet bows were new as well—tied beneath the collar, going down the front of the bodice—three black velvet bows that matched three rows of black velvet ribbon banding the skirt and hiding the telltale signs of how much she had grown.

Seeing her thus, it struck Alex powerfully and he was immediately overcome with shame. Here he was, one of the richest men in California and his bride was wearing an old blue dress he had seen a million times before. It was considered bad luck for the bride to make her own wedding gown. Shame ate at him. Not for Katherine, for there was nothing shameful about her, or the way she walked proudly into the cabin, her face so radiant it seemed to transform her. No, the shame was for himself and his callous disregard of what should have been obvious. He cursed softly under his breath at allowing her to set foot on this ship without buying her the finest clothes to be found on any sailing vessel in port. He should have taken her to the hotel and given her time to rest. He remembered her comment about ship's food and another arrow of shame shot into him. He hadn't even given her a decent meal before yanking her off one ship and shoving her into the bowels of another one. And regretfully, following that thought was the reminder of the hot bath and shave he had treated himself to before going to meet her ship, and just how long it had probably been since she had enjoyed such, after being on a ship for all those months it had taken to come here. At that moment, Alex wasn't feeling very proud of his treatment of her.

As if sensing the same, Adrian picked that moment to lean toward him and whisper, "She looks more dignified and more lovely than I've ever seen her." Alex simply nodded. He couldn't speak for the choking remorse lodged in his throat. Katherine deserved more than she was getting. *I'll make it up to her.*

Katherine hung her cape on a peg and came

to stand beside Alex, knowing her best drab dress was damp and smelled of mildew. Her cream woolen shawl she had tried to mend as best she could, but that was rather difficult, because some rat had stolen into her trunk and eaten a hole in it big enough for a cannonball to pass through. About the only consolation she got was vowing to kill every rat she came across. If Katherine had been a woman of more fragile emotion she would have cried a second time.

But she was dry-eyed as she stood at his side before the captain, scanning the room with her eyes, trying to imagine herself standing just like she was, only inside the small church back in Limestone County and wearing the loveliest gown of white, carrying a bouquet of real flowers, surrounded by those she had known and loved all of her life. But reality was much too real for such imaginings to come to life. She looked at the captain, the first mate, the cook, then at Adrian, and finally, Alex. They were all strangers to her—stiff, polite, formal strangers.

Not really aware she had been here long enough to give her consent to the captain's questions, her body recoiled in shock when the captain pronounced them man and wife.

"You may kiss the bride," said Captain Steptoe.

It was a pale, startled face that looked up as Alex took her shoulders in his hands with a steadying grip and brushed her surprised mouth with cold lips.

His lips weren't the only thing cold.

At least cold is how Katherine chose later to describe her bed on her wedding night. Well, either cold or her second choice: empty. In truth, it was both empty and cold, she decided, thinking back upon the way he judiciously walked her to her cabin, declined her invitation to come in, gave her a kiss she could only call perfunctory, and departed with all the precision and feeling of a Swiss clock.

And so, Katherine, who was married in alien surroundings in a world foreign to her, found herself sitting in her cabin, thinking it queer that the only thing familiar to her was the bouquet she still clutched in her hand—the one she had fashioned herself out of the horribly crushed petunias of her old straw hat. While removing the petunias she had had a flashing glimpse of Fanny Bright, as she had been that day she mended the ragged edges of her straw hat, the one Clovis took a chomp out of after church.

And then they came in a rush—thoughts of home and Clovis—Clovis, with his long, satiny ears pricked forward at the scolding she had given him, bits of Fanny's hat still protruding from his mouth in a way that made them look like whiskers. And that thought gave way to another—the recollection of Clovis as a baby—an adorable collection of legs and ears, fuzzy as a bear cub. The attachment had been instant and she had felt a specialness for him from the moment he first looked at her with his soft brown eyes. Feeling her own eyes fill with tears, she thought it almost funny, the things that could bring a normally strong, self-determined woman like herself to tears. It wasn't the hardship of her grueling journey. It wasn't the separation from home, friends, and family. It wasn't even the indifference Alex had greeted her with. No, the one thing that brought the tears coming one after the other was something she admitted to herself as being totally ridiculous: a mule.

One does not lose control over a mule, Katherine. Normal people don't form such attachments to animals.

But no matter how she chastised herself, she couldn't forget the day she had left and the way Clovis had run along the fence that ran beside the road as far as he could, watching as she and Fanny rode past, heading for town in the wagon. When he reached the end of the pasture and found his way blocked by another intersecting fence, he stood with his ears hanging forlornly and brayed his heart out, the sound of it ringing in her ears in such a way that the sound of it haunted her long after they were too far away to really hear.

Adrian picked that particular moment to knock on her cabin door. "Katherine?"

"Go away," she said, bringing the back of her hand up to wipe her face.

"Katherine? Are you all right?"

She gave her face another swipe. "Can't you hear? I said *go away!*"

The door opened and Adrian came into

the room. Seeing her distress, he crossed the room and took the chair beside her. "Sweet Katherine, what's wrong?"

"Nothing," she said, taking a halfhearted swipe at her eyes. "I'm just a little homesick, that's all."

"Well, that's to be expected," he said in jovial tones. "Everyone gets homesick now and then." He laughed and said, "Even Alex." He had meant that as a joke of course, but Katherine did not smile. "Try to relax, Katherine," he said, giving her hand a fond pat. "It only means you're just like any other ordinary person."

She sprang to her feet. "That's just it!" she exclaimed. "I'm not ordinary. I'm not ordinary at all."

"Katherine, you could look the world over and not find one person who hasn't at some time in their life suffered bouts of homesickness. We all miss the home and family we left behind."

She cast a skeptical eye in his direction, her hands coming up to clamp, sugar-bowl fashion, upon her hips. "But I lay you odds I'm the only person in the world who has ever missed a *mule*!"

Sudden understanding flickered in his eyes. "Ahhhh, Clovis," he said with a fond smile. Leaning his head back in his folded hands against the chair, he closed his eyes for a moment, then opened them and chuckled. "Well, I can't say I would ever feel homesick over a mule, but I know Clovis wasn't just any old mule." He smiled at her, the fondness in his eyes warm and glowing. "Yes, I suppose I can see how you would feel that way."

"If you can see that, you're as crazy as I am."

He laughed. "That's probably the most truthful thing you've said today, but like you, I know Clovis isn't just any ordinary mule."

"No, he isn't," she said. She turned toward him with a smile so radiant, he thought for a moment the rain had stopped and a shaft of sunlight had lost its way and blundered into the room. "Thank you, Adrian," she said softly, coming to drop a kiss on his forehead. "Thank you so much. You don't know how much it means... how much it helps, just knowing you understand."

"That's me," he said, rising to his feet. "Always destined to be a man of great understanding, if not great love."

She lifted her eyes and resisted the urge to touch him again, knowing that if she did, he might not be able to accept it in the vein it was offered—one of friendship. "For now, that's true perhaps, but it won't be true always. Love will come your way, Adrian. I know it will. And knowing you, and how obstinate you are, you'll probably fight it every step of the way. But in the end, you'll know it for what it is—real—and when you do, you'll experience something far greater and more powerful than anything you have ever felt before."

Another knock broke the silence.

"Who is it?" Katherine asked, as Adrian moved to open the door.

"Alex," a voice said as Adrian opened the door.

"My, isn't this cozy. I come to see my bride and who do I find? My brother." He looked over Adrian's shoulder, locating Katherine, then said to Adrian, "What are you doing in here?"

"Cheering her up."

Alex looked at Katherine, seeing the obvious signs that she had been crying. "It doesn't look like you've been doing a very good job of it. What's wrong?"

Adrian shook his head. "Only my brother could ask a question like that."

"What is that supposed to mean?"

"It means it should be obvious to you what's wrong here, Alex."

"Well, it isn't, so why don't you enlighten me?"

"Look at her. What do you see?"

"I see Katherine," Alex said, then seeing the exasperation on Adrian's face, he added, "what do you see?"

That did it. Adrian threw his head back in a hopeless gesture. "I don't think you would understand if I drew you a picture."

Alex stiffened in resentment. "I'm not that thick-witted."

Adrian merely raised his brows and said, "Oh? Can you prove it?"

Alex scowled. He wasn't having such a good day either. He felt his anger rising as he lashed out at his brother. "Just what in the hell is going on here? I find you in my wife's room…on our wedding night…and you light into *me*. It should be the other way around, don't you think?"

"You know, I found myself thinking the same thing. *You* should be the one in here with your bride on your wedding night." Adrian looked at Katherine, who was standing beside the chair clutching the petunias against her breast. He didn't want to air this in front of her, so he shook his head and turned away, but Alex caught him by the shoulder and shoved him around. "I asked you a question," Alex said.

"Why don't you listen to what you just said. *Your wife's room…your wedding night.* Don't you find it just a little odd that I didn't find you in here with Katherine when I knocked?"

Alex looked quickly at Katherine, then grabbing Adrian by the arm, he said gruffly, "Come with me. This isn't the place to talk."

"Thank the Lord for small favors," Adrian said dryly. "At least some part of your brain's functioning."

They went into Alex's cabin and closed the door. Adrian went into the room, but Alex leaned against the door and crossed his arms. "Okay, talk," he said.

Adrian had been about to point out a few things to Alex, but decided this wasn't the time. It was too early for Alex to understand Katherine's feelings or to understand his own feelings for that matter. But he had to say something. He decided to keep it short. "I saw you take Katherine to her room and leave her. That was a bad move, Alex."

"So you made another bad move and moved in?"

"I went there knowing how she would be feeling, hoping to cheer her up, to give her some comfort."

"I'll just bet you did. What *sort* of comfort did you have in mind?"

"The same kind I've always given her. The understanding of a friend."

"You've always wanted more from Katherine than friendship and don't try to deny it."

"I won't. Problem was, Katherine never wanted more from me."

"I've known her as long as you have. How come you know so much more about her than I do?"

"I wasn't blinded and dazzled by Karin like you were, although I never understood your fascination with her. Katherine is ten times the woman Karin is, or ever will be, but it will be a long time before you realize that, if you realize it at all."

"Leave Karin out of this."

"She was never right for you, Alex. Never. Can you picture Karin here right now? Can you see her in a place as rough as a logging camp? She'd be miserable more than five miles from a dress shop."

"I could buy her all the dresses she'd ever want, or anything else, for that matter."

"Yes, you could, and she'd be thrilled. But

is that what you want? A woman you have to buy to keep?"

"Karin isn't like that."

"Isn't she? Do you think she would have set foot on this ship without buying half of San Francisco? Do you think she would have worn an old, refurbished dress to her wedding, or carried a pathetic bouquet borrowed from a hat that should have been thrown away years ago? I'll tell you something. I envy the hell out of you; no, not just for Katherine, but for the obvious favor God must hold for you. You say that writing Katherine's name in that letter was a mistake, but I tell you now... *That* was no mistake. God, fortunately, has more sense than you." He shook his head. "I envy you, and yet I pity you."

"Pity? Why?"

"Because you've been so busy all your life, running after a rabbit that you didn't notice the buck standing in the trees."

Adrian walked to the door and Alex stepped away. "What do you think I should do?" Alex said to his brother's back.

Adrian sighed and rubbed his forehead before turning to look Alex straight in the eye. "Think," he said. "Just think, and be guided by what's in your heart, not what's in your pants." He opened the door and stepped out into the corridor, closing it with a click behind him. Alex stared blindly at the closed door, wondering at Adrian's words. *Be guided by what's in your heart,* he had said. But that was the problem. He knew that when he searched his heart, he would find only Karin.

With a softly uttered oath, Alex went to his bunk and sat down, intending to remove his boots, when the picture of Katherine's white face rose before him. He wasn't being very fair to leave her in her room alone. But what could he do? *She's your wife.* So, what does that mean? *Make love to her.* The idea had a certain amount of appeal, true, but he couldn't. Not now. Not yet. Not for all the wrong reasons.

A few minutes later he knocked on Katherine's door, pushing it open when she didn't answer. His bride was sitting on her bunk, absently plucking at the bridal bouquet of wax petunias in her hand. She looked up when he entered, her expression turning dark and thunderous. "Doesn't anyone around here respect privacy?"

"I knocked, but you didn't answer."

"Did it ever occur to you that maybe, just maybe I didn't want to be bothered?"

"No. Why would you feel that way?" His amused glance dropped to the flowers in her hand. "Are you having too much fun twiddling your petunias?"

"What else would I twiddle?" she said in a long-suffering voice.

He grinned at that one. "I'd be happy to make a suggestion."

She wasn't in a teasing mood. "I *meant* this cabin isn't big enough to cuss a cat." Remembering the way he had dumped her in this cabin earlier and realizing he was probably here solely because Adrian had talked him into it, she felt her mood go sour. "Don't start on me," she said. "I'm not in the mood for sermons right now. I'd rather have a shot of whiskey than a sermon."

He laughed, reminded how Katherine's anger always had an element of humor in it—at least as far as he was concerned. "Are you in the habit of taking a nip now and then?"

"No, but I may start."

"Well then, mind if I join you?"

"I don't have any whiskey."

"I do."

"Where are you going?"

"I'll be right back."

And he was, a moment later. He came through the doorway, a bottle of whiskey in his right hand, two glasses in his left. He kicked the door shut behind him and walked toward her, putting the bottle and glasses on the table.

Katherine eyed the bottle. She never dreamed Alex would take her seriously. What should she do now? *Talk him out of it, or your goose is cooked. You've never had a drink in your life.* Her eyes left the bottle and centered on Alex. "I didn't mean I intended to start right now."

"There's no time like the present," he said, taking a seat.

"I was just getting ready for bed."

"You were?" His eyes went to her clothing.

"I was just fixing to unbutton myself when you knocked."

He folded his arms behind his head. "Go ahead. Don't let me stop you. I'm your husband, remember?"

"I remember, but I was wondering if you did?"

"I remembered."

"If you remember, why were you avoiding me? Why was I left alone on my wedding night?"

He saw the tears trembling like ice crystals on the tips of her lashes. He felt like a heel. He was a heel. He moved to the bunk to sit beside her, taking her in his arms, not as a lover, but as a friend. "Katherine, look at me." His voice was low and soft as velvet.

Katherine tried not to appear too eager to do so. When her gaze was fixed on his, he said, "You're upset with me because I left you here alone. I want you to understand why I did. You may not believe this, Katherine, but I did it for you."

"Well, don't!" she snapped. "I don't know who would tell you that I prefer to spend my wedding night alone, but it isn't true. I would...rather..." Her voice slowed to a mere trickle, fading to horrified silence.

"You would rather what?"

Katherine couldn't have said the words if he'd choked them from her. Unable to answer him, she simply looked down, which wasn't such a good place to look. Seeing that mysterious part of a man at such close range was—well, the answer to that swelled like fast-rising dough in the back of her throat. She jerked her head to look at the wall to her left. It was a blank wall, but she feigned interest.

Alex wanted to laugh. If she wanted to remind him of all the reasons why he had always found her so charming, she was doing a bang-up job. Katherine, he knew, didn't have more than an inkling of what went on between a man and a woman, but she was ready to find out. He wasn't in the best frame of mind to give a tender, young virgin her first lesson in love, and since this tender, young virgin was also his wife, he didn't want to bungle the job. He didn't want to open that can of worms, so he decided a half-truth would be best. A half-truth and a few kisses would be the safest way to ease her apprehensions without forcing him to make love before his mind caught up to his body, which was having no difficulty deciding what it wanted to do.

Taking her face in his hands, Alex said, "We've been friends for a long time, Katherine, but friends aren't the same thing as lovers. It's natural for a woman to be a bit shy the first time or two, even with a man she is used to being around. Since we haven't been around each other for a long time, I thought the right thing to do was to give you time to relax, to put your mind at ease."

Katherine didn't feel it was her mind that needed easing.

"Would you like me to hold you?"

The violent nodding of her head thumped against his chin. He smiled and eased her more fully against him. "Better?"

"Ever so much better," she said with a slow sigh. Her voice sounded lazy and relaxed, as if in a near-slumber, but there was nothing lazy or relaxed going on inside her—and nothing, absolutely nothing was anywhere near a slumber. To the contrary, everything was full alert, all body parts humming and churning and sizzling like a firebrand. Over and over her mind repeated the same little chant: *Alex is holding me. Alex is holding me. Oh, thrill! Oh, joy! Alex is holding me.*

"What are you thinking?"

She looked up and gave him a smile whose sweetness made something melt inside him. "Nothing."

She seemed suddenly very vulnerable to him, alone and isolated in a marriage she had traveled halfway around the world for. He felt a little better about what he had done, about taking her to wife, now that some of the shock and anger had had a chance to wear off. If one of them had to suffer heartache, better him than her. He wasn't a man to hurt others, and even if he were, Katherine would have been the last person in the world he would have been able to wound. Even as he tried to imagine how it would go for them, what their life together would be like, the insanity of what he was trying to do, what he was trying to pull off, robbed him of the joy.

He discovered something else as well. Katherine made more of an impression on him than he thought. He could feel the warm penetrating heat of her, the moist caress of her breathing, the fresh fragrance of innocence—all of it blending together in a rich harmony that was Katherine. Without thinking, without even being conscious of it, he lowered his head and began nuzzling the soft place below her ear. He heard her breath suck in and hold, only to exit in a heated rush when his hands came up to caress her neck and shoulders, easing the tension he could feel there.

"What are you doing?" she whispered.

"Helping you relax."

"It won't work," she said. "Everything is frozen in fright."

"Do I frighten you?"

"The old Alex doesn't. *This* Alex does—a little."

"I'm the same Alex I've always been."

"Oh, no you're not. You're not the same at all. The old Alex was my friend. This new one is my..."

"Lover," he finished for her, and turned her head up to his. "I think we can do something about that frozen fright," he said.

"What? What are you going to do? Will it hurt? Are you going to do it now?"

"Katherine, will you shut up and kiss me?"

She was trying to think of a way to answer that, short of throwing her arms around him and forcing him back on the bed, kissing him until his ears whistled, but before she got very far, he took the desire to think away. How could she when he was busy dotting her brow with tiny kisses, pressing them carefully against her closed eyes? She was about to ask him if he was finished, when his mouth pressed over hers with the faintest pressure. The hands holding her back rubbed back and forth with such lazy, sensual ease that she thought he must have done a great deal of this sort of thing. Strangely enough, that thought pleased her.

"I'm glad you've made love to other women," she said matter of factly, and obviously without thinking, for the moment the words were out, she buried her head against his chest in mortification.

His laughter hammered against her sensitive nerves like a pelting of arrows. "Now, *that* is something I never expected to hear my wife say. Would it be asking too much to ask you why?"

I would rather not say, she thought hastily. She remained silent, hoping he would think she had dozed off.

"Katherine?" He nudged her. "You've got my curiosity aroused." *As well as a few other things.* "You might as well put my mind at ease. Tell me why?"

"Because I think it's of prime importance that *one* of us knows what they're about, and you don't exactly learn that sort of thing in books. Do you?"

"No, it's not the sort of thing one would find in most books."

"Most books? You mean it's in some?"

"So I've heard." He paused, gazing down into her upturned face, mesmerized by those huge, luminous eyes of hers, and he felt another little part of him open to her. Looking into her eyes was like looking through glass, for there was nothing there that troubled him, that made him wonder about her. She was as pure and innocent as they came, and it showed in the clarity of her eyes. He had a feeling her heart was just as pure. "Do you know," he murmured softly, "that a look like that can seduce a man? What an enchanting creature you are."

"Oh Alex, I think you are the most beautiful man I've ever known, inside and out. I've loved you for so long, I can't imagine what it would be like not to."

His mouth closed over hers in a kiss that went longer, deeper, and was more urgent than the first one. His breath came rapidly, mingling with hers, and his mouth opened fuller, encouraging hers to follow. She did, feeling his hands press her closer. This man was so dear to her, the joy of it sang in the brightest of notes, humming and singing through her blood until her skin tingled from the effect of it.

It was much the same for Alex. Desire for her came in a swift, heated surge, racking his body with jolt after jolt until he knew he would either have to stop now, or take her.

Alex drew back, staring down into the liquid, drugged eyes, unable to believe he had come as close to making love to her as he had.

Love-smitten and dizzy with the intensity of her love, Katherine felt his heart hammering beneath her hands that were splayed across his chest. Her eyes rested on that soft, sensual mouth of his, amazed that it had drawn as much feeling and response from her. Slowly her eyes made their way upward, until she was looking into a pair of deep blue ones. It didn't take an experienced woman to know Alex desired her, that he wanted to make love to her, but she didn't want it this way. She wasn't so foolish as to think he had forgotten her sister completely. Alex was a man, a normal man. He could make love to her or any woman right now, and never think anything more about it. But that wasn't what Katherine wanted. When Alex made love to her—and he would—it would be for all the right reasons.

"I think I'll have that drink now," she said shakily.

"Make that two," Alex said, holding up two fingers. They both laughed. It was the break they needed.

Alex was every bit as shaky as Katherine, a fact she noted proudly as he reached for the bottle. "A good, stiff drink before bed is a great relaxer."

Katherine leaned lazily back. "Funny you mentioned that word. I was just thinking how I've never felt so relaxed in my life. Must be something soothing about the sea. Why, I'm so relaxed, I'm limp as noodles. I don't think I can move."

"Ahhh! Then a drink is what you need.

Quite fortifying, a drink is." He pulled the cork and poured the two glasses full, picking up one of them and taking a healthy gulp. "Yes-sir, I always say a man should have a good, stiff drink. There's nothing like it to erect his fortifications."

"Erect his what?" she asked, shooting straight up. Her voice a little higher and more shaky, she said, "Never mind." Then she frowned. "Alex, are we talking about the same thing here?"

"God, I hope so," he said, and began to laugh, feeling the impulse to go to her and take her in his arms and hold her against him once again. But then the memory of a time long past began to crystallize in his mind and he remembered the night he had told her good-bye, the night he kissed her in the kitchen.

He had never really forgotten that kiss, but somehow over the passing of time it had blended in with the memory of Karin. How could the memory of the woman he loved become confused with one he liked only as a friend? But he hadn't kissed her as a friend that night before he left, and the way she kissed him back wasn't exactly the kiss of a friend either. The corners of his mouth lifted as he remembered how he'd gotten his face slapped for the effort, but there wasn't anything humorous in remembering how he had thought for months afterward that it had been worth every painful moment of it. He dismissed the thought and the memory from his mind, but then he looked at her, his eyes going to her perfectly shaped mouth and he found himself wondering what it would be like to kiss her now.

And then he was putting the drink down and coming to stand beside her, his hands on her shoulders. She looked up into his face, her eyes wide as it came closer, then closing when his lips lightly brushed hers. He drew back, gazing into her upturned face, feeling desire sting with fresh insistence. *You're building a fire on thin ice, man. You kissed her once, a long time ago, and got your face slapped for the mockery of it because she knew you didn't love her. You still don't. So, don't mock her again by making love to her now.*

"I'm sorry, Katherine. I shouldn't have done that. I'm not trying to force you."

She looked at him, her eyes opened wide, the sound of her long indrawn breath touching him like a soft stroke. "What made you think I thought you were?" she asked.

His face took on a sleepy, dazed look. "I'm not sure. I had a reason a moment ago."

She felt the heat of the moment reach out and touch her, spreading, softening, pricking her numbed senses. In all ways he touched her, overwhelmed her, and left her disturbed. She wasn't sure what she would do and the insanity of it left her open, vulnerable, and completely irresistible. She looked into his eyes and gave him a smile, not a smile meant to seduce, or to placate, but one so genuine that it shot straight through him.

He saw how alone she was, isolated in her

confusion, not knowing what was in his mind. And how could she? He did not know himself. He had no awareness, save the feeling that he was experiencing the same ease and sense of satisfaction he had always felt around her, warming and filling, like an aged wine one has drunk before. She must have felt it too, for suddenly she leaned her head forward, resting her forehead against his chest and asked in a breathless way, "Alex, what would you have done if I had asked you to kiss me again?"

"I would have kissed you, and kept on kissing you until you asked me to stop."

"Then kiss me, Alex. Please."

With a low, anguished groan, he tipped her head back and pressed his mouth over hers. She had thought herself ready, but she was unprepared for the softness of his lips or for the depth of feeling that swept to the center of her. His lips touched the curve of one cheek, then the other. They were on her throat now, touching everywhere, blindly and without direction, leaving a trail of fire. Her breath caught in her throat and she felt herself slipping into another world where nothing was anchored and all she could do was float.

His breathing was more rapid now, as was hers, the two of them mingling as his mouth searched for hers, finding it with a groan as his arms came around her, moving her to fit so perfectly against him until she felt herself floating again and clutched him to keep from drifting away.

"Katherine," he whispered, kissing her

mouth again and again, slow and deliberate this time.

And then it was over.

He pulled back, pushing her away at the same time, his breathing ragged, his expression confused. He looked at her, seeing the bewildered look and knowing it was as impossible for her to put her feelings into words as it was for him. He hadn't planned for things to go this far and the only explanation he could find was that for a moment he had forgotten who she was, the real woman replaced with the overlay of the one in his mind. But as he made his apology once again and moved away, opening the door and closing it behind him, he couldn't understand why the memory of Karin came to him so sharp and vivid and familiar, yet when he reached for it to draw it closer, it wasn't Karin's face he saw, but that of her sister Katherine.

CHAPTER FIFTEEN

The times Katherine spent on deck were few, as most of their journey was a time of wailing winds and overcast skies, when the mists lay low and the sun was rarely seen. She spent most of her time in her cabin reading, which must have been quite a bit, since she had time to finish Wordsworth and Boswell's *Life of Samuel Johnson*.

All in all, the trip had been a stormy one,

the weather going from cloudy to rain and back to cloudy. The clouds had given way to rain again the day they were to reach Humboldt Bay and after that the logging outpost Alex, Adrian, and now Katherine would call home. Alex had spent most of the morning with her, walking her around the deck for exercise, answering her questions about the new life that awaited her. They had lunch with Captain Steptoe and Adrian. Shortly after lunch, he vanished. She hadn't seen him since. It seemed as though he had disappeared altogether. *From a ship in the middle of the ocean?* She felt like she had married a ghost.

This type of reflection was a big part of her afternoon, whether from lack of anything better to do or due to the scarcity of appearances from her husband, she wasn't sure. Perhaps it was both. Her past lay behind her now, like a discarded ribbon, shiny in places, wrinkled in others, stretching straight, then curved, and as she looked back upon it, she saw the memory of it growing thinner and thinner, as if she were staring down a road to the horizon.

Thinking about the past can play odd tricks upon the fancy, and Katherine found herself wondering what she would be doing at this moment had the letter from Alex never arrived. She found herself stretched out upon her narrow bunk in a tranquil stupor as the rain battered and lashed at the sea, and the sea, in its anger to get even, thrashed and pounded back at the small ship. How like life it was, that the innocent are often the victim of another's wrong.

She knew there was never any returning to the past, no matter how close it was to her. But reasoning did not prevent the same thoughts from stirring again, awakening that sense of dread, of something not being quite right. And then she would think of the letter and the question that came often. *Why me and not Karin?*

Let sleeping dogs lie, Katherine. Don't be digging this up again. Alex told you why. Be satisfied with that.

But could she be?

At that point she turned her thoughts away. She had everything she had ever wanted, yet the joy of it was like a cold, sculptured thing, beautiful but lifeless like a mask. How she wished Fanny were here to talk to. But she had asked Fanny the same question and Fanny had said to not question the workings of fate. Besides, Fanny was another part of the past that was gone to her. She had been through much in her life, but now she seemed to be at the crossroads, a moment of distress and trial where a premonition of tragedy was difficult to shake. *You aren't the first person this has happened to. We all have our own little devils that torment us until we face them down.* But no matter how hard she tried, the sense of dread would return. When would she be able to face her own torment? Would she emerge finer and stronger, tempered and happily secure, once it was over? Or would she live with heartache and regret, the question unanswered for the rest of her life?

Often she would call herself nine kinds of a fool for rushing into marriage this way, before she put her mind at rest. Was she wrong to love him so much that she was willing to live with her devils, never knowing, rather than risk not having him at all? She had talked to no one about this ever, save Fanny. A smile curled across her face like the happy curve of a cat's tail. *Dear Fanny. How I must have driven her to distraction with my questions, my doubts.* Her mind spun backwards, to the day before she left for San Francisco.

"For a woman who has just been given something she has waited half her life for, you don't seem as happy as I would have thought," Fanny said, catching Katherine coming out of the henhouse with a basket of eggs on her arm. Fanny fell into step beside her. "What's wrong?"

"I've been thinking."

Fanny raised her arms, pleading heavenward. "Lord help us. The last time you did any thinking I found you trying to fry boiled eggs."

"I didn't realize they were boiled."

"Because you lose touch when you're thinking. I've never seen anyone think like you do. Lord, you go into a coma." Her tone turned serious. "So, you were thinking? What about?" She took the basket as Katherine opened the gate.

"Why do you think Alex asked me to marry him and not Karin?"

"Don't question the workings of fate. As the

saying goes, 'A wise man turns chance into good fortune.' Besides, not all questions *need* to be answered. Now I ask you, what difference does it make *why* Alex asked you? There could be a hundred reasons, there could be none. He asked you. *That's* what's important here. Not why. Don't question the workings of fate." She shook her head as Katherine took the basket back from her. "You know, people are such fools when it comes to love. Here you are driving yourself to distraction with a question that, put to Alex... well, he probably couldn't answer it himself."

"Wouldn't you wonder... if you were me, I mean?"

"Not any more than I would question God's wisdom. He made mosquitoes, but I've never asked him why."

Katherine laughed. "That's a poor parallel."

"Not really. You think about it. God made mosquitoes, pesky little devils that they are. What's important is that they're here and we have to learn to live with them, best we can. That doesn't change one whit whether we know why God made them or not."

Now, Katherine was a patient woman—to a point. But enough was enough. And in her book she had had enough. She had spent the earlier part of the afternoon in her cabin, thinking. She made a surprising discovery; she, who had imagined all her life what it would be like to be married to Alex, had missed the boat with her imaginings. She gave a small angry snort. Marriage to Alex wasn't what she imagined at all, in fact *marriage* in general wasn't what she imagined. She gave another snort—this one of disgust, directed toward herself. *All right. So, your husband isn't being too attentive. At least you* have *a husband. After all, you knew it was Karin he had always loved. Just because he asked you to come doesn't necessarily mean he's forgotten all about Karin.*

That sounded reasonable.

Remember the time you saw the most beautiful pair of ice-blue satin slippers? Katherine nodded. *Do you remember what your mother said when you said you wanted them?* Katherine nodded. *She said those slippers were lovely to look at, but not very practical. And then? She convinced me we should buy those ugly brown shoes that buttoned halfway up my leg.*

Katherine shuddered, remembering the incident in vivid color, and remembered too, her disappointment over not getting the lovely blue satin slippers. To this day she had not forgotten those slippers; or the tiny clusters of sparkling crystals on the toes; or the way she had been talked out of them. She also remembered how she felt. She felt wronged. She felt angry and cheated, ready to kick the first person she saw. Whenever she wore those ugly, brown shoes she did her best to scuff them, going out of her way to stomp through mud puddles and kick rocks. She took all her anger out on those shoes, when it hadn't been the shoes' fault at all.

Those ice-blue satin slippers are like Karin is

to Alex. He chose you, because you were sturdy and strong like those—Katherine stopped right here, determined not to allow herself to be compared to those ugly, brown, high-top shoes. *That's just Karin's luck*— she *gets to be the dainty, ice-blue satin slippers. I get to be the clumsy boots.*

Funny thing, minds are, they don't always do as they're told, so Katherine went on thinking. *Alex was wise and chose the brown high-tops, but like you, he hasn't forgotten those blue satin slippers, no matter how impractical they were. Now, you can get back at him by being a pair of stiff, uncomfortable brown shoes that rub blisters on his heel and pinch his toe, or you can be of the softest leather, durable and weather-resistant; something to make his job easier and give him comfort.*

Well? What's it going to be?

I'm thinking.

She was thinking about Alex and the way he had looked this morning when they had strolled the decks. She didn't remember much of the conversation, because she was seeing how the color of the sea matched his eyes, and the way the wind ruffled his hair. Several times she had caught him staring out across the water. "What are you thinking?" she had asked.

"Nothing," was his reply.

Karin, she thought.

Funny, but whenever she thought he might be thinking of Karin, Katherine didn't get mad, she didn't feel angry. She felt... tenacious.

Karin might have Alex's thoughts. *But I've got Alex.* She wasn't about to give him up either. This was one prize she intended to keep. He was the summation of a hundred million dreams; everything she had ever wanted in a man: warm, kind, thoughtful, funny, gentle, strong when he had to be, a lover of the land.

Katherine thought about the way she had come to him. The hand of Providence was in all of this, she knew that much. God had given this wonderful man to her, and the devil was already trying to take him away. He was hers. And by golly, she meant to keep him. *Hell hath no fury...* as the saying goes.

Thinking helped for a while. Before long Katherine was feeling restless, and she wanted to see Alex. When she found Adrian on deck after being chased up there by Captain Steptoe during one of their blessed but infrequent lulls in the rain, she made her way toward him. Alex was nowhere in sight.

Adrian was sitting on a coil of rope, one leg stretched out before him, the other bent, his hand holding a whetstone balanced over his knee, a knife in his other hand. "Didn't you just sharpen that knife the other day?" she asked.

"That was my knife. This one belongs to Alex."

She looked around. The deck was deserted except for the first mate at the helm and a few seamen scattered about. Even Captain Steptoe had vanished. "Where is Alex?"

"Alex?" He shrugged. "He's around here someplace."

"Thank you," she said. "That was most informative." She watched him rub the knife's blade against the whetstone in rapid, circular strokes. "Adrian, why did Alex ask me to marry him?"

Adrian's head snapped up, his hand frozen in place. He studied her face for a moment before answering with a sort of helpless wrath. "Don't you think you should ask Alex?"

"I did."

"What did he say?"

"He said he married me because he wanted a wife."

"Then believe him."

"But..."

"Katherine, scripture says I'm my brother's keeper. I am not privy to his thoughts. Do you think Alex tells me everything that goes through his mind?"

"No, but couldn't you take a guess?"

"I could."

After a moment of silence, she said, "But you won't. Is that it?"

"Look," Adrian said, laying the knife and whetstone to one side and rising to his feet, "a guess would be no more than that—a guess. Guesses and suppositions are all gray. Reality is the green of the grass, the sky's blueness, the red in your hair. You're sitting on a rainbow, Katherine. Enjoy it. Don't rob yourself of the moment by wondering how you got there."

"But wouldn't you wonder?"

"No. If the woman I loved married me I

would count my blessings and spend the rest of my life making sure she never regretted it, not making myself miserable to the point that she did. When you keep on asking questions you can't avoid the answers. Tread carefully, sweet Katherine, or you may discover more than you wish. Don't unearth a burial ground digging for a potato."

She sighed, propping her elbows on the railing. "You think I should just forget it then?"

Adrian laughed. "Jumping Jehoshaphat! If I didn't know better I'd swear you were too dumb to ride a horse and chew tobacco at the same time. Of course that's that I've been saying."

She smiled at him, feeling just a little foolish. "I don't chew tobacco," she said, "but I notice you still do."

He tapped her on the nose. "And I'm not about to quit, so don't get technical. You know what I mean."

She did, of course, and when she opened her mouth to speak, he placed his finger over her lips. "Katherine, Katherine, what a tempting sprite you are. If you weren't a married woman..."

"Oh, posh!" she said, giving him a whack on the arm. "I don't kiss men who chew tobacco."

"Maybe I'll quit, then."

"Too late for that," she said, laughing.

"Too late," he said softly. "The story of my life."

"Adrian, do you think Alex…"

He laughed and placed his fingers over her mouth to silence her. "You're a nosy, talkative lass, I'll say that much."

"I just can't help wondering."

"Wondering is okay, as long as you don't overdo it. When you do, it's like laying bricks over the road to happiness." He paused and placed his hands on Katherine's arms, turning her toward him. "Keep making yourself miserable with all this wondering and you'll make him miserable as well."

"I'd have to see him to do that. He hasn't exactly been my shadow for the past two days."

"Small wonder."

She stared at him, her eyes wide with apprehension. "What do you mean by that?"

"You haven't exactly made yourself into a person one would want to shadow. I can't blame him for not wanting to be around you."

"What have I done?"

"Nothing."

She could see the teasing light in his eyes and she gave him a shove. "Stop teasing and give me an answer."

"I did, truthfully. You haven't done much of anything, and that's the problem." He laughed. "Katherine, if I've ever seen a face that had a steady forecast of rain, it's been yours."

"How can you say that, Adrian?"

"How? Katherine, you've been as gloomy as the devil."

"Maybe that's because I am."

"You may be, but you don't have to *look* that way."

"I don't...do I?"

"I'm afraid you do. I'm not one to give advice, but if I were you I'd try to stand out like a ray of sunshine against all these gray clouds and rain, not do my damnest to blend in with them." She looked like she didn't follow what he was saying. "That dress," he said. "It's worse than drab."

Now she looked miffed. He could almost see her drawing her feelers in. "I don't have anything to wear but my old gloomy dresses."

"That's because you're too busy being miserable to notice what's going on around you. You have more choice than you think, you just haven't bothered to look."

"A lot of good that would do. All I'd see around here is more indifference and more rain."

He sighed. "I said I wasn't going to get myself involved in this." He looked heavenward. "Isn't that what I said? And now look at me. Jumping in with both feet, I am." He took her by the arm. "Come with me. I want to show you something. And then, by God, I'm staying out of this."

He led her to her cabin and once they were inside, he went to the wall of drawers and louvered cabinets, opening several of them. Katherine's mouth dropped open in astonishment. Inside two of the cabinets hung several dresses—six to be exact. Another cabinet held a blue wool cape and matching bonnet. The drawers were filled with all manner of things a woman would need: undergarments, stockings, mittens, a fan or two, a drawstring pouch, handkerchiefs, toilet water, a hand mirror, milled soap, talcum powder. She closed the last drawer and turned toward Adrian in wonder. "Alex?"

"Who else?"

"Where did he get these things?"

"Captain Steptoe. He has several crates of clothing he's taking back east."

"When?" she asked. "When did he do this?"

"Is that important?"

"Yes. It is."

"Yesterday, after your marriage."

"Oh, Adrian, I'm so ashamed. When he came back last night, I didn't know."

He laughed. "Cheer up. You've got the rest of your life to tell Alex. Better yet, why not show him?" He went to the door and paused, giving her a wink. "Keep your hook baited."

The door closed and all Katherine could do was stand there and wonder. The uncomfortable unknown stretched before her, yawning like a giant mouth eating its way toward her. But one thing Katherine had was resilience. She might get pushed, or even knocked down, but she had enough pluck to bounce back. So far she had suffered a temporary setback, nothing more. She would see to that.

A knock interrupted her thoughts. *Alex!* She flew to the door and jerked it open. Disappointment was instantaneous. Captain

Steptoe stood on the other side. "I wanted to let you know Humboldt Bay has been sighted. We should be docking in less than an hour."

She didn't have a minute to waste. Forty-five minutes later, she had changed into a bright green challis with red and gold braid twisted and looped over her shoulders, shiny brass buttons trimming the front. The rest of her new clothing had all been packed and two seamen had come for it less than ten minutes ago. She stood before the small mirror, anxious to see her hurried results. She wanted to look as *colorful* as possible in her new dress when Alex came for her.

And she did. But it wasn't Alex who came for her. It was Captain Steptoe. He walked her up to the deck and she had her first glimpse of Humboldt Bay. It began to sprinkle and Captain Steptoe excused himself for a moment. Katherine hadn't been standing on deck for long when he returned. She had opened her umbrella, keeping little more than her head and shoulders dry. In spite of Captain Steptoe's offer to take her below until it eased up a bit, she refused, having already vowed to never put another foot in that miserable cabin for as long as she lived. She wasn't really angry at Captain Steptoe, or even his fine ship for that matter, but she was disappointed and hurt that Alex had sent Captain Steptoe instead of coming for her himself.

"Well, at least wear this," Captain Steptoe said at last, putting a long waterproof coat over her shoulders.

"I can't take your coat," she said.

"I've got another one."

Katherine didn't say anything else. She didn't wish to be rude to Captain Steptoe, but she needed some time alone to get control of what was going on inside her. No matter how many times she told herself she was going to be cheerful, she found it harder and harder as time passed and Alex never appeared. At last, she couldn't stand it any longer. "Are we waiting for Alex?"

Captain Steptoe cleared his throat. "Ahem! No… that is, we are waiting for the boat to come back."

"From where?"

"Shore. Alex and a few of the men went ahead to make everything ready."

"Oh, I see," she said, but she really didn't.

As she had always been able to do, Katherine pulled herself out of her downward turn and forced large doses of optimism down her throat. She wasn't going to let one more tiny setback spoil the beauty of her marriage to the man she had loved all her life. As she had been told often enough, it was an answer to a life-long prayer and nothing should be allowed to steal the joy of it.

At last the boat returned and Katherine was rowed to shore. She saw him standing with a group of men on the dock ahead. She knew it was Alex, even though the dim gray light gave little color to him or the tall towering trees which seemed to melt together behind him into complete darkness. By the time the boat reached the dock and Alex came to lift her to dry land, the wind was coming through the tops of the trees with a low, moaning sound that sounded like the sea.

Katherine looked about her at the dismal surroundings. *It's a wild, dreary place, gloomy enough to give a body the shudders,* she thought, in spite of all the wonderful things Alex had told her when she had asked him about her new home.

"You'll learn to love it. It's beautiful country, and as far as business is concerned, it's perfect. The forests are so dense you can't ride through on a horse, but there's a flat point of land near a river that was just what we needed for our mill, and it's close enough to deep water that we can load our timber on to ships for transport. The hills slope right down to the water, so the logs are easier to get down, and everywhere you look the land is covered with trees— Douglas fir, redwood, hemlock, Sitka spruce, cedar—all towering overhead a hundred feet and more, the redwoods going over three hundred. Some of the cones are over two feet long and five inches across. I swear, you've never seen anything like it."

And of course she hadn't.

After Alex's enthusiastic description, she had expected to see something spectacular, a paradise where everything was new and fresh and green, the air crisp and smelling as fragrant as a Christmas tree. But that wasn't the sight that greeted her. The logging camp was a crude assembly of ugly cabins sitting on soil that had been scraped bare of all vegetation, then littered with piles of scattered bark, tree limbs and dotted with smoldering piles of sawdust whose smoke clung low to the ground, burning her eyes and taking her breath away. In a way that was good. She buried her face in her muff and coughed. At least she could use the smoke as an excuse for a face that looked half crumpled and close to crying.

"Watch your step," Alex said, coming up beside her and taking her arm. Katherine looked down in just enough time to sidestep the biggest cow pattie she had ever seen. Her eyes flew up to Alex. "Oxen," was all he said before he guided her away.

She fell into step beside him, sensing the change in him toward her and feeling the tension of it stretch dangerously close to snapping. When they reached the house he helped her step onto the porch. When she turned to look back at him, he said, "Well, what do you think?"

He was talking about her surroundings and she knew that as well as he, but her thoughts weren't going in that direction any more than his were and she knew that too. They were both standing on the porch now, looking at each other in a way neither of them had dared since San Francisco. Unaware of their surroundings they took in the changes the years had made in each other, wondering what the other one was thinking. In Katherine's eyes were memories and feelings she realized she should have kept hidden, for she felt that was the reason Alex broke the contact and stepped back, holding himself stiff and erect, looking at her in a completely detached way, putting more distance between them than had existed before. *This should be the happiest moment of my life.*

But it wasn't.

Here she was, on the receiving end of indifference from a man she had known all her life, a man who had asked her to marry him, and she was in love enough, and hopeful enough, to think they needed more time to reacquaint themselves. She wasn't going to let her questions and misgivings come between them. He had been in love with her sister for years and this was the first time the two of them were together in any capacity other than friends. It didn't bother her that he had been in love with Karin. She had always known she was better suited to Alex than Karin was.

She reminded herself once again of what Adrian and Fanny had said: Why wasn't important. The important thing was that he had married her. Katherine looked at him intently, fighting the feeling of dejection that had hovered about her since her arrival. *Think of something happy.* The memory of the way he had kissed her the day he left for California, and again on their wedding night came clear as crystal into her mind. She saw the distance between them written on his face. Her first inclination was to run inside and slam the door and leave him standing there with his distance. But then she looked deeper, and she saw the emotions she had overlooked before, the confusion, the uncertainty. She felt sympathy for him. He was probably as uncomfortable as she was. "I know you must think me terribly callous for not having said something earlier, but I do thank you Alex." Her voice softened. "The clothes are beautiful and far lovelier than anything I ever dreamed of owning—much too lovely to be worn in a lumbering camp."

"They are fitting for my wife. I expect you to look the part."

Hold your temper. Don't let him goad you. Remember you catch more flies with honey than with vinegar. She took a fortifying breath, swallowed, and gave her best imitation of a smile. But when she spoke, the only good thing she could say was, "Then I shall do my best not to disappoint you."

"Thank you," he said. Alex was no fool. He could tell by the look on her face that his harshness had hurt her, and in turn, her hurt affected him. He didn't want to hurt Katherine. She was innocent in all of this. *But Adrian sure as hell isn't!*

Alex couldn't remember when he had been so angry as he was when Adrian sauntered up to him on deck early that afternoon and told him, "I've taken the liberty of selecting a few things for Katherine from Captain Steptoe's stores."

"What kind of things?"

"Clothes...underthings, the usual."

Alex let fly with a right that sent Adrian reeling backwards. Holding his aching jaw, Adrian said, "What was that for?"

"I took the liberty of thanking you." He grabbed Adrian by the collar and hauled him up against him. "Stay away from my wife. Understand? If there's any giving around here, I'll do it."

"I didn't let on that they were from me. Katherine thinks you..."

Alex hit him again.

"What in the hell's gotten into you, Alex? I tried to tell you she thinks they're from you."

"But they're not, are they? Don't do my thinking for me, Adrian. Katherine is my wife, not yours. I'll handle it my way."

Alex had been furious all afternoon, partly because Adrian had way overstepped his bounds; partly because he hadn't thought of it first. Little did it matter that he was still too shocked and angry from this marriage to think clearly. Adrian had acted rashly, and he had overreacted, but it was Katherine who had suffered, because Alex had been too angry to go to her, and leaving her alone all afternoon wasn't wise. Even he knew that much. Katherine was smart. She would wonder why. If she asked him, what could he say? He had answered her with one lie. He didn't want to make it two.

He looked down at Katherine's sweet face. She smiled and her entire being seemed to light up from within. She was trying. He could do no less. He smiled back.

The smoke from the sawmill hovered over the camp like a low cloud, choking and burning the back of her throat. The air was stagnant with the smell of smoke, the lubricants used to thin pitch, drying wool clothes, and the steamy aroma of boiled beef and potatoes coming from the cookhouse. Katherine sighed and looked about her, seeing nothing but a motley cluster of gaping men, a few thin dogs, a cluster of tiny cabins, a bunkhouse, and a pigpen. She wanted to cry. For a minute she just stood there amid the tools and trappings of the lumberman's trade, her arms hanging loosely at her sides, her green eyes burning from smoke and the threat of tears. *Here we are standing like two complete idiots grinning at each other.*

Alex, make love to me.

Sweet Katherine, if you knew what was in my mind right now, you'd be horrified. I want to pick you up in my arms and carry you inside and peel all those layers from you and see what lies beneath.

She watched him swing down off the porch. "Alex?"

He paused, turning to look at her.

"Is… is this where I'm going to stay?" She saw the muscle work in his jaw.

"For the time being, until the roads are cleared of logs and we can get up to the house. This infernal rain has slowed everything down. If things aren't cleared by supper, I'll take you up to the house on horseback, but you may have to wait until tomorrow for your trunks." He looked over his shoulder toward the wagon. "Some of the men will be bringing your trunks up here for now. You can show them where you want them. Supper is in the cookhouse at six." Knowing he was being harsh again, he tried to soften things a bit by saying, "I wish I had time to show you around, but that will have to wait. I've been gone too long and this is a very critical time for us. I'll see you as soon as I can."

He was still standing there looking at her when Katherine glanced toward the cookhouse, suddenly aware that the small motley group of men had grown to at least fifty and every one of them was staring at her. "Are there any women about?" she asked, her throat suddenly dry.

"Only one," Alex said. "You'll meet her at supper." He tipped his hat and turned away, just as a commotion erupted in the cookhouse.

Katherine's gaze drifted in that direction, lured by the sound of something metal being banged, followed by the sudden, high-pitched chatter of someone on the run. The door to the cookhouse slammed open and a small man dressed in baggy black clothing and a funny little hat shot out, a long black braid down his back, the tiniest black slippers on his feet. "Molly P. crazy! Wong not work here! Molly P. crazy!" he said, repeating it over and over as he dodged chunks of wood being tossed at him by someone inside the cookhouse.

Alex laughed. "It seems you won't have to

wait till supper to meet the other woman in camp after all," Alex said.

"Who is she?" Katherine asked, looking around. Another piece of wood sailed out the door. *What is she?*

"She's the cook's assistant. She's the one chunking the kindling."

"I gathered that," Katherine said as she squinted in the direction of the cookhouse, trying to see into the dark interior. Suddenly someone stepped out holding a squawking chicken by the feet. Katherine's first thought was, *Trees aren't the only things of enormous size around here.* If that was a woman holding that chicken, she was the biggest woman Katherine had ever seen.

"Come on," Alex said, coming her way and taking her arm. "I'll take you over to meet M.P."

"Let me freshen up a bit. My hair is wet."

Alex looked her over. "You look fine to me, and your hair will dry. It's stopped raining. Come on." He took her by the arm and led her toward the woman, who loomed larger with each step they took. As they reached the bottom of the steps, Alex said, "M.P., I want you to meet Katherine, my...wife."

M.P. wore a very pink dress which clashed horribly with her red cheeks but went rather nicely with her pink hair—and it did look pink, although Katherine supposed it could be called a light, pinkish red. Still, pink seemed the better description. As for the rest of her—the dress reminded Katherine of something a madam would wear. It was a bit fussy for a cookhouse and the neck was lined with jet fringe that trembled when she talked—and Katherine could understand that. She felt a bit like trembling herself. The woman was an ominous as thunder.

"Bless my soul! *This* is your intended? She's not at all what I expected a man like you would pick out." The sharp black eyes narrowed in scrutiny. "She's a scrawny little piece of goods, wouldn't you say? A bit too tall and thin?"

"She probably won't look so tall once she's eaten your cooking for a while and feathers out some," Alex said—too good-naturedly in Katherine's opinion.

"She'll have to feather out a great deal," answered M.P. "And I'm not sure you'll have much when she does. But we'll see. There's nothing like crisp mountain air to whet a body's appetite."

"Obviously there isn't," Katherine said, giving M.P. the same scrutinizing once-over the woman had given her. "You must have been here for some time."

Alex looked like he was about to choke, then muffling a cough, he turned his head away.

Initially Katherine felt the desire to shrink away from this woman's piercing look, but she had seen women of this ilk before. They came on strong as a gust of wind, just to test the lay of the land. If Katherine backed off in fright, this woman would make life miserable for her. On the other hand… Katherine was determined to hold her ground. If this was to be a battle of wills, she might as well win herself a spot in this camp right now, or this woman would take over. The thought of turning to Alex or even Adrian for support in the future never entered her mind. She had been taking care of herself for quite some time now and after the hardships she had endured, what was one woman, even if she was as big as a mountain? She was quite accustomed by now to fighting her own battles. Of course, that didn't mean she wasn't a tad uncomfortable.

The chicken, who by this time must have been as uncomfortable as Katherine, began to stir up a fuss. Without any inkling that she was going to, the woman suddenly grabbed the chicken with her other hand and with a quick twist, yanked the head off. The head went one way, the chicken in the other. Katherine watched the headless chicken run in circles, flapping and slinging blood everywhere before falling on its side and lying still after a few stiff jerks.

Katherine's eyes flew to the woman. She had never seen anyone wring the neck off of a chicken that fast. M.P. must have been at least six feet tall, and over two hundred pounds if Katherine knew anything at all about size. Her eyes were a deep, polished brown that looked almost black, her hair a washed-out strawberry blond color that looked as if it had spent the past year and a half in a crimping iron, for all Katherine could think was it looked like it had been fried. Maybe it had. Maybe that's why it looked pink. While

Katherine was taking all of this in, the woman pulled out a cigar and bit the end off of it, then offered it to her. "Smoke?"

"No," Katherine said. "No, thank you."

The woman shook her head. "It's a shame you don't. Right soothing on the nerves. If you change your mind, you let me know, you hear?"

"I'll see that you're the first to know," Katherine said.

Molly Polly lit the cigar, releasing a gray coil of smoke that curled slowly upward. "Hold out your hand," she said to Katherine.

"Why? So you can lop it off like you did that chicken's neck?" *Or use it to put your cigar out?*

Molly laughed, then turned to Alex. "She's scrawny, but she's got a sense of humor. She might make it." Then to Katherine she said, "You afraid to hold out your hand?"

Katherine held her hand out, watching as Molly blew six perfect smoke rings that encircled her arm like a bracelet. Molly laughed, giving Alex a poke in the ribs. "Brave little thing, ain't she?"

Katherine thought she might faint. Instead, she drew herself up, standing tall and straight and stiff. "I'm stronger than I look," she said before Alex had a chance to respond. "And I don't take too kindly to being talked about or poor-mouthed in my presence."

Molly Polly slapped her leg. "Raised on firebread and sassy too!" she said, then laughed. She gave Katherine a contemplative look. "Well, bless me, Alex! It appears you got yourself one that plows a straight furrow and goes to the end of the row, though I'd have never guessed it by looking at her." She narrowed her eyes at Katherine. "You ever been in a fight, gal?"

"No. I always heard it was the still sow that got the slops."

Molly threw back her head and laughed. She slapped Alex a healthy one across his back. "Seems she's up to snuff," she said, "in spite of her size." To Katherine she said, "Don't you worry none, I'll put some meat on those bones."

Katherine was about to respond to that, but Molly caught sight of Wong and yelled for him to "Come get this here chicken," then she turned back to Katherine. "I've got to get back to my rat killing before that fool cooks that chicken with the feathers on." As she turned away, she gave Katherine one last glance and said over her shoulder, "If you ever need anybody to push you in the creek, you just let me know. Hear?"

Katherine smiled. "I hear."

"Now that's interesting," Alex said, moving to stand beside Katherine as they both watched Molly fall into step beside Wong.

"What is?" Katherine asked.

"You're the first person she's taken a liking to."

"That was a liking?" asked Katherine.

Alex threw back his head and laughed and Katherine lost herself for a moment in the joy of it. *Oh Alex, you are so very, very dear.* A minute or two later, she turned to follow him down the steps, but when she reached the last one, Alex swept her up into his arms. "What are you doing?" she asked.

"I would think that would be obvious. I'm carrying you."

"I know that, but why? I walked over here."

He grinned and lowered his head close to her as he whispered, "Maybe I just wanted to hold you, and with all these people about it's the only way I could think of." He tossed her up a bit to get a better hold on her and she squealed. He grunted. "If you'd relax, it would make this job easier."

"If it's such a taxing job, you can put me down."

"I could," he said, "but I won't." Seeing she was about to say something else, he said, "Katherine, for once in your stubborn life, will you close that sweet mouth of yours and just lay back and flow with the current."

"Oh," said Katherine, her body going slack. She closed her eyes and dropped her head back. A moment later she opened one eye and looked up at him. "Am I flowing enough?"

"I don't know about you, but I sure as hell am," he said, crossing the distance to the other porch. He stood her on her feet, but kept her in his arms. Katherine glanced up at him. His eyes were on her. The expression on his face resembled that of a man who'd just been handed a smoking package and didn't know if he should stay and open it, or throw it as far as he could. Their eyes still locked, he said, "Make yourself comfortable. As soon as the road clears I'll come back for you."

"All right."

"Do you want me to take you inside?"

"Do you want to?"

He grinned. "Come on," he said, releasing all but her arm which he held on to.

The room was small and neat, but the smell was past intolerable, almost painful. Katherine clamped her hands over her nose. "What's wrong?" he asked.

She lifted her hands just enough to speak. "I can't stay in here."

"Why not?"

"The smell! Alex, it's awful. Has something died?"

He sniffed the air and laughed. "No. This is the foreman's cabin. They all smell this way."

"The foremen or the cabins?"

"Both."

"Why?"

"Lumbermen don't bathe too often."

"It doesn't smell like they bathe at all."

"Oh, they bathe, just not with any kind of frequency."

"How often is that?"

"Once or twice."

"A month?"

"A year."

Katherine thought she was going to be sick. "Please," she croaked, "Take me outside. I can't stay in here. I'll be sick."

"Katherine, it may start raining again."

"Alex, I'm serious. I am going to be sick. I prefer the rain. Really I do. At least *it's* clean."

He picked her up again and carried her outside. When she was in fresh smoky air she inhaled deeply. "You can put me down now. I'm all right."

"I'll carry you," he said, and walked around a team of oxen hitched to three enormous logs. He carried her to the edge of the trees and stood her on a carpet of pine needles and dried leaves. "If it rains, there's a tent you can stay in." Seeing the way she looked at the tent, he laughed and said, "It's open at both ends so it's well ventilated."

"Thank you," she said, their eyes locking again.

"You're welcome," he said.

"So are you."

"Katherine..."

In the silence that followed, neither of them seemed to be able to move. It was the same feeling she had felt around him so many times before, and she wished they were someplace private.

He turned to look back across the logging camp until the silence was almost unbearable, then he exhaled, removing his hat and raking his fingers through his hair. He slapped the hat against his leg a time or two, then put it back on his head. Then he looked back at her with the unspoken yearning pulling tighter between them.

He looked like he didn't know what to do

or say, and she understood that, for she felt the same. As long as they had been on the ship and he had avoided her, she had been too hurt and angry, or too busy thinking, to think much about what would happen once they reached Humboldt Bay. But they were here now, and in a few hours or less he would come for her, to take her to her new home. It would be dark by then, and when it was dark, people went to bed. She had often dreamed of lying beside Alex in a bed, but the reality of it had lost its dreamlike state. *I love you, Alex.* She felt herself drawn toward him, so much she swayed on her feet. His arm shot out to steady her.

"There are times when I think I'm going to enjoy being married to you," he said in that same husky voice she remembered so well. She had been about to ask him just when those times were when she realized this must be one of them and any further thought vanished from her mind. His hands came out to turn her face upward. As he kissed her, his hands went beneath her cloak, pulling her tight against him. Her arms started around him when he pulled back. "Right now I'm wondering if this is the same woman I kissed in a kitchen a few years ago in Texas."

"She's the same one," she said.

"She doesn't kiss like it," he said. "*That* kiss was different."

"You remember that?"

"Oh, I remember. A man doesn't forget something like that."

Even when he's in love with her sister? she almost said, but the look on his face was pleasant and the teasing light in his eyes was one she remembered so well. "And how was it different?"

He grinned. "The words escape me," he said, his lips moving against her cheek. "But I can show you." She felt his mouth brush hers, warm, beguiling, inviting, and she groaned, leaning into him, her arms going around his neck. "That's more like I remembered it," he whispered against her open mouth as his hand upon her back rubbed with lazy ease. And then, as quickly as it had come, it was over, and she felt a shattering emptiness when he pulled away. He studied her face for a moment, his eyes a darker blue now, their feeling closed to her. He stepped back and looked around him like he didn't know which direction to take.

"I better get going," he said. "It'll be dark soon and I've got a lot to do." He started off, going not more than two or three steps, then turning. "You'll be okay?" he asked.

"I'll be fine."

Alex stared dumbly at her. What was she doing to him? A week ago he was in love with her sister. And then she shows up. And what did he do? *I married her, for God's sake.* Why? *If I knew the answer to that, I wouldn't have to work for a living.* And if that wasn't enough, you had to start kissing her. *That was her fault. She shouldn't look at a man like that if she didn't want to be kissed.* And you, old man, shouldn't kiss a woman like that when you claim you don't care for her. He began to feel angry at her for what she was doing to him. Nothing was as it seemed anymore. There had always been a sort of special bond between them, a long-lasting friendship, nothing more. But now that bond was stretched, forced to encompass more. From the moment he saw her coming off that ship in San Francisco he had felt strange, like she had some hold over him. And perhaps she had. Otherwise, he would have sent her packing. Why hadn't he? *It sure as hell wasn't because of that puny threat of Adrian's,* he said to himself, knowing it was the truth. It irritated the dickens out of him to think she was in control. Yet he didn't seem to be able to just toss her back like a fish he didn't want.

He remembered the many times he had done just that with Karin, simply walked away and left her stewing and fuming, making demands that he laughed at. But with Katherine it was different. It wasn't easy staying away from her on the ship. He told himself it was because she was a beautiful woman and it had been too damn long since he'd had a woman—even an ugly one. But he knew that wasn't the reason. He might not love her, but he desired her. The other reason would come later.

"If you need anything, just send one of the men for me." He didn't give her a chance to respond, but turned quickly away.

Katherine looked through the dim mist that swirled around his retreating back. "Dear God," she prayed, "you've given me the answer to my prayers, and I'm mighty beholden and terribly grateful. But if it's not asking too much, could you show me, now that you've given it to me, just what I'm supposed to do with it?"

CHAPTER SIXTEEN

He came for her at dusk.

She did not notice him at first, for she had been standing outside the tent since the rain had stopped, watching the sun set like an orange rind, the fiery twilight kindling the jagged peaks of the mountains and crowning the treetops with fire.

"It's beautiful, isn't it?" he said, coming to stand beside her.

"I've never seen anything like it. It's more than beautiful. It's like a jewel that no one has ever seen; a jewel that has lain untouched for millions of years. I feel so alone, like I'm the only person in all its vastness." She glanced at him to see if he was making any sense of what she was saying. Seeing his face, she knew he did. "I can't help wondering what it's like up there, far over the hills to the jagged peaks beyond." She turned to him. "What's over there?"

He laughed. "More mountains."

"Which ones? The Sierras?"

"They're closer to Sacramento."

"Then what do we call our mountains?"

Our mountains. He didn't answer right away. "The Klamath Mountains and the Salmon, farther over you'll run into the Cascades."

"Are they covered with snow?"

"The higher peaks are year around. The rest get snow only during the winter."

"I suppose we'll be seeing some of that soon."

"Not here, but farther up."

"I'd like to go up there, to see it when it snows." She looked hesitant, almost shy, and he was suddenly aware of how their marriage had changed things between them. There was a stiffness, a formality between them that had not existed before. That made him miss the easy comfort and camaraderie they had once. He realized then that she was speaking. "You know how little we get back home," she was saying. "Every five years or so."

"You won't have to wait that long anymore. A few hours ride will put you in all the snow you could ever want."

She turned away and walked back toward the tent. "Can we get up to the house now?"

"The roads are still blocked, so we'll have to go by horseback." He stepped inside the tent to see if her trunk had come. Seeing it had, he pulled the saddlebags from where they lay across his shoulder and handed them to her. "You'll have to pack anything you'll be needing in here. There's not much room. I'm sorry, but it's the best I can do. Tomorrow we should be able to get those logs cleared and get the wagons with our supplies and your trunks up to the house."

She took the saddlebags and moved to her trunk. With quiet efficiency she removed a few things she would be needing: her brush, a gown, a simple skirt and blouse, underthings. She closed the bags and he took them, tossing them over his shoulder once more. Taking her arm, he walked her down the slope toward the camp, where Adrian waited with two horses. When they reached the horses, Adrian dismounted. "I'll help her up as soon as you're mounted," he said.

Alex nodded, and Katherine watched him swing into the saddle as she had seen him do a hundred times, but this time seemed so different. The goldfields and lumbering had been good for him, for his body was more muscular, more mature now, the body of a man. She thought what fine legs he had when Adrian's hands came around her waist and he lifted her up to sit in front of Alex. Her breath caught when she felt his arms come around her, pulling her back to rest against his chest. "It's a bit awkward, I know," he said, but Katherine was thinking it was wonderful. His chest was warm and smooth and hard. She smiled and closed her eyes, inhaling deeply. He even smelled like Alex. *Smelled like Alex? Of course he smells like Alex, you dolt! Who else would he smell like? Sometimes you amaze me, Katherine. You really do.*

"All set?" he asked, his words stirring in her hair.

There was an awkward moment when she felt his breath warm on her cheek, felt his arms tighten around her, and her heart leaped into her throat. "Yes."

"I don't suppose I need to tell a farm girl like you to hold on."

"I've seen how you ride, Alexander Mackinnon. I'd be a pure fool not to hang on for all I'm worth."

He laughed and Adrian said, "That's one drawback to marrying a woman that's known you all your life. There isn't much you can surprise her with."

"I'm sure I can find something she hasn't seen," Alex said.

"I'm sure you can too," Adrian said, laughing. "*If* you put your mind to it."

"My thoughts lay in another direction entirely," said Alex.

Katherine missed the point and then, from the way her face seemed to flame with heat, she was glad it was too dark to see it.

They rode through the trees for some time before the lights from the house glimmered up ahead. When they reached the clearing in front of the house, it was too dark to tell much, except it looked like three or four log cabins stacked together to make one big one, a long, sweeping porch tacked on the front. "Well, this is it," Alex said, bringing one leg over and dropping to the ground. His arms came up and she slid down into them.

She felt his body stiffen at the moment of contact, but he released her and moved quickly away the minute he heard Adrian approach. By the time Adrian was beside them, Alex had turned to the saddlebags. "Take her on inside while I get these."

She had enough time to take in the main room before Alex arrived. It was much larger than she had first thought, at least thirty feet long. The furniture was made from logs and covered with brightly patterned Indian blankets. Three enormous fur rugs almost covered the floor. She wasn't sure what animal the fur was from, but whatever it was, it was big. The fireplace was large enough to stand up in, made of stone and taking up one entire wall. Someone had been expecting them, for a good fire was going and the room was warm and filled with a delicious aroma that reminded her how hungry she was.

"Well, what do you think?" Adrian asked.

"It's much nicer than I expected...and larger."

"You'll have a much larger one in a couple of years," Alex said, coming into the room and closing the door behind him. He looked at Katherine standing small and uncertain in the large room. "Would you like time to yourself before dinner?"

"What I'd really like is time to myself *after* dinner," she said. "I'm starved."

Alex laughed. "And it isn't ship food."

"Thank God," she said. "Where's the kitchen?"

"Through here." She followed him into the kitchen, seeing another large room, surprisingly well stocked and neat for two bachelors. "Wong gets the credit," he said.

She moved to the stove and lifted the lid off the pot. "Did he cook this as well?"

"It had to be Wong or M.P., since they're the only two that cook around here."

She leaned over the pot, stirring it and inhaling deeply. "Hmmmm, beef stew. It smells wonderful."

"I think it's grizzly."

"Grizzly?" she repeated. "As in bear?"

He nodded. "Um-hmm."

"You have grizzlys around here?"

He nodded again.

"Close?"

"Close enough." He laughed, his hand coming out to ruffle her hair. "About as close as you can imagine. You just walked over two of them when you came in... of course they were dead. You'll be eating another one in a few minutes. They're not quite as plentiful as cattle, and a damn sight harder to bring to the supper table, but you'll soon find we eat a lot of fish and a lot of grizzly, as well as deer up here."

"I'm hungry enough to eat anything that doesn't eat me first," she said, looking around, opening a door or two. "Where are the dishes?"

"In that cupboard."

She removed her cloak and hung it on a peg by the back door, exchanging it for an apron and tying it around her waist. Alex had never seen her in a dress as lovely and finely made as this before, and never had he seen her in such vivid color. The white apron brought out the intense richness of the deep green color of her dress, the bow at the back made for a man to undo. Her cheeks were rosy. When she glanced up, Alex was looking at her, a strange light in his eyes. "You wore one of the dresses," he said. "The color is good on you."

"Of course I wore one. If you only knew how long it's been since I had a new dress you wouldn't dare wonder if I'd wear them or not. But I'll warn you now, you may get sick of seeing me in them. It'll be hard to get me back into my old clothes after this."

Remembering the worn fabric, the drab colors, and seeing how lovely she now looked, he said, "If I never saw you in them again, it would be too soon."

She laughed, and it struck him how different her response was compared to what Karin's would have been. Katherine laughed. Karin would have been furious and in tears by now. "You'll be seeing my old clothes soon enough," she said. "I'm not about to ruin my beautiful new clothes with housework. But I promise I'll be wearing one of my new ones each evening when you come home from work."

Something about her words caught him like a fist in the gut, and he felt the impact of it so strongly, his breath felt trapped. There was something about the way she said, *each evening when you come home from work* that leveled him. It made him feel a part of her, made him feel as if they belonged together, like he had been coming home to her for a long time.

He watched his new wife busy herself in the

kitchen, and felt a man's satisfaction in seeing her happy. He had to hand it to her. She had everything a man could want in a wife: beauty, strong confidence, humor, intelligence, quick wit, devotion, loyalty—the list went on and on. What man in his right mind wouldn't give his eyeteeth to be married to a woman like that?

But Alex wasn't in his right mind. True, Katherine was a good-natured, agreeable woman who smiled with her heart, and he was fond of her. True, she had always been a part of his life; someone he found it restful to be around, and comforting to talk to. He wasn't foolish enough to think this was love, but it was peace, and there was something strong and reliable and comforting at least, about that. It wasn't Katherine's fault that he had dug his own pit and fallen in. She didn't deserve to pay for his mistakes. He didn't love her. He had no way of knowing if he ever would. But he was attracted to her.

And even that made him angry. He didn't want to be attracted to a woman he was forced to marry. He wanted to stay angry, as if by staying angry, he could prove the depth of his love for Karin. And that's where the problem lay. Deep, deep within the very soul of him, Alex was afraid.

He sat there with a blank, absorbed expression on his face, like a person losing his mind, a person who heard and saw things no one else could. He felt like he was two people. On the outside, he was a strong, determined man who worshipped Karin with a strange form of craving idolatry, a man who knew there was really nothing left between them. He hadn't lost Karin when he wrote that letter. He had let her go a long time ago. They had never been lovers. She had never fired a spark of passion within him with just a look from across the room. For years they had continued to call themselves in love, when, in reality, they had grown so completely out of touch. And like a man who fears impotence, Alex had continued with his declaration of love long after it ceased to exist.

On the inside, Alex was a different man, a man who found Katherine fascinating, as if the essence of some exotic perfume had intoxicated him. Katherine was like the woods, where the soft, moist darkness hid the vastness of life, the secrets of curling mosses and fragile, unfolding buds—a sort of quiet, hidden existence, a world separate unto itself; a world one tends to overlook.

There had been a sort of freedom in loving Karin, a sort of mysterious stillness that allowed a man to be private and withdrawn, for the serpent that held him to her was lust— lust that was kept alive by Karin's refusal to have sex. It was simple, really: He wanted. Karin didn't. She said she loved him, loved everything about him. And maybe that was true. Except for sex. This denial kept him clinging to her, but it wasn't love.

Katherine glanced at him and smiled. The smile he gave her back was forced. She was his wife now, and with that came the feeling that he could no longer be private and withdrawn, that he had been connected to a world that wouldn't allow him to be either. Loving a woman like Katherine would strip a man down to the bedrock, where he lay naked and vulnerable, in order to build and refine, layer by layer. It was like the difference between having sex with a woman and leaving, and having sex with one and staying with her, putting your arms around her and wrapping your legs around her and feeling the peace. Katherine was the latter, and yet Katherine was also the kind of woman a man could sleep with and be chaste with as easily as he could give in to the yearning for sex.

But those things didn't make him any less angry. Deep in his heart, Alex knew he probably wouldn't have been content with a woman like Karin, but he refused to acknowledge that now. He deserved a chance to test that belief, to make that decision for himself, and it had been denied. It was also highly possible that Karin wouldn't have come even if he had written her name. It was also possible that Karin wouldn't have come, even if he had told Katherine the truth and sent her back. But he deserved to find out for himself. But those discoveries, those choices had been taken from him.

Taken away by Adrian.

The initial anger and shock had worn off, only to give way to a deeper layer of resentment. Now that he had cooled down a bit, Alex knew he would have done the right thing by Katherine, that he would have reasoned all this out by himself and married her, in the end. Once again, he was denied the chance by Adrian. It was Adrian who rushed in to champion Katherine's cause; Adrian who could now boast of forcing Alex to marry. Adrian, of all people! Adrian, who had never forced Alex to do a damn thing he didn't want to do. Alex felt betrayed and trapped, unable to be his own man. And that made him strike out at moments he least expected, moments he had no influence over. He felt like a smoldering volcano. He had no knowledge of or say about the moment it would erupt.

For days Alex had lived with this kind of tension and strain, feeling it more intensely at certain times than others. He was feeling it intensely now, and that made him sullen and angry. He looked at his brother sitting across the table, knowing Adrian was whetting his *meddling* knives, readying himself to poke and prod him into taking Katherine to bed, so he could claim the credit for even that. He looked at Katherine, feeling sorry for her, but unable to do anything about his feelings of resentment. He knew she had no role in this showdown between brothers, but she would feel the consequences, nevertheless.

The distance between them grew even wider during the meal. Often the only sound in the room was the click and scrape of spoons against soup bowls, the occasional shuffle of feet beneath the table, feet that were restless and anxious to be on their way.

Adrian made several attempts at conversation, but after a few fruitless attempts, he too, stopped trying. Katherine ate as they did, in silence, but mentally, she was taking it all in. Alex never looked at her, eating his soup in a methodical way, as if he had been doing it this way for years. As she sat there brooding, she couldn't help wondering what he was thinking about. It occurred to her that this wasn't exactly as she had pictured their first meal together in their home. She had visualized a romantic dinner for just the two of them—giving little notice to what they ate. A candlelight dinner shared by two people in love. She had missed it all the way around. There were three of them, not two. There were no candles. And if there were two people in love, it must be Alex and Adrian, for she had never felt more excluded from anyone in her entire life.

Katherine finished first, having found the sudden discomforting strain between herself and Alex had taken her appetite. She took one last bite and laid her spoon down. Alex was silently watching her, as he had been doing throughout the meal. "I thought you said you were starving," he said.

"I was."

"You've given a pretty poor showing for it."

She made a lamentable attempt to laugh. "I think I'm more exhausted than I thought. Right now all I can think about is spending the night in a bed that doesn't toss me out when the weather gets bad."

He laid his napkin down and stood, coming around to her side of the table. "I'll show you to your room, then."

"Please," she said, rising, "finish your meal. I can..."

"*Someone* has to show you where you'll be sleeping."

Not us, she thought, *but where you'll be sleeping.* "Of course. I hadn't thought of that." She glanced at Adrian, who was now standing, apology written all over his face. "Good night, Adrian."

Seeing her discomfort, Adrian tossed down his napkin. "Why don't you finish your meal, Alex? I'm through. I'll show Katherine up."

Alex froze, a white-hot fury seeping into him. Turning his head slowly to look at Adrian, he said in the coldest tone, "She isn't your wife, Adrian. The duty is mine."

"Oh, for heaven's sake!" Katherine snapped, having about all of this she was going to take. "If it's such a *duty*, just tell me where the blasted room is and I'll find it by myself, or better yet," she turned and stomped out of the room, finishing her sentence on the way, "I'll find some other place to stay." The door banged behind her. She wasted no time moving to the table where Alex had placed the saddlebags. Picking them up, she heard Alex call after her, just as she reached the front door.

"Katherine!"

She whirled around to face him, her hand still holding the door open, her eyes brilliant with anger. "You might as well save your breath, Alex. I am spitting mad and when I get this way it's impossible to reason with me. I'll talk to you tomorrow when I've had a chance to cool off." She turned through the door, pulling it shut behind her. She had barely reached the first step when the door opened and Alex's shadow stretched dark and ominous in front of her.

"If you spend the night outside you may cool off more than you intended. It can get down to forty or so at night this time of year."

"Fine," she said, and whirled around and stomped back into the house. Alex stood just inside the door watching her. She marched to the closest, and smallest, grizzly rug, grabbed it by one paw, and dragged it behind her and through the front door.

"What are you going to do with that?"

"I'm going to use it. You did say it might get down to forty, didn't you." Katherine didn't break stride as she started away from the house, the grizzly rug bringing up the rear, thumping along in the darkness, the saddlebag slung over one shoulder as Alex had done, but her shoulders being much narrower than his, it kept sliding off. She kept pushing it back, determined not to stop.

By this time, Adrian had come to stand in the doorway, a big grin splitting his face. He crossed his arms and leaned against the door. Alex turned a helpless look over his shoulder at him. Adrian shrugged. "As you said, she's your wife."

Alex was torn between flattening his brother

and going after his wife. He sighed and started after her. "And here I always thought she was so sweet and docile," he mumbled under his breath.

Adrian heard it, though, and said, "Katherine? Docile?" The mocking sound of Adrian's laughter followed him.

A more stubborn woman Alex had never seen. He started after her, feeling admiration for her on the one hand, an overpowering desire to throttle her on the other. "Katherine, for the love of God, will you slow down?"

"I will not!"

"Okay. Will you at least be sensible?"

"I doubt it. You can't even be civil! Why should I be sensible?" she called over her shoulder. The grizzly rug caught on something and Katherine muttered something unlady-like under her breath and came back to free it. Then she was off again.

He caught up to her just where the road took a bend after leaving the clearing in front of the house, or rather he caught up to the grizzly rug, which was just as well, for the moment he stepped on it, it jerked Katherine back and she stepped on a round stone that turned under her weight, throwing her off balance and she came tumbling backwards.

Seeing her sprawled on her back, Alex laughed softly and followed her down, catching her arms before she could roll over and get up. "That's the way I like my women," he said softly, "flat on their back."

"Oh, do be quiet," she said hotly. "From what

I've seen, you wouldn't know what to do if you did have one flat on her back!" She saw the twinkle of humor in his eyes and wanted to bash his head in. This man had been worse than an ass to her and she had taken all she was going to. Furthermore, she had already decided she wasn't about to give in so easily. "I've changed my mind. *You* wouldn't know what to do if you had one flat on her back and buck naked!"

He laughed. "I ought to prove to you, here and now, just how wrong you are."

She struggled to free herself. "Let me up, you big oaf! You don't need to prove anything to me...*you've* proven far too much already." She bucked beneath him. "Let...me...up!"

"Will you be still and talk this thing out if I do?"

She nodded.

"That won't do, Katherine. I'm on to your tricks. If you want me to release you, you'll have to say so."

"I'll talk," she ground out like it pained her, and knowing her as well as he did, he knew it did just that. Katherine was a proud woman. She didn't like to be bested. By anyone. He released her and Katherine rolled to her feet, but she didn't stop there. She started off down the road again, dragging the saddle bag and the grizzly rug behind.

"Katherine!" he called after her. "You gave me your word."

"I had my fingers crossed!" she called back to him.

Remembering how many times they had used that out as children, he shouted, "You're a grown woman! That doesn't count anymore, and you damn well know it!"

"I said I would talk, and I will. But *not* right now."

He followed her. The road was getting darker now. She was just a few yards in front of him when they heard something rustle the trees, a twig snapping. Katherine stopped, listening. Hearing nothing more, she started up again. Alex was no more than four feet behind her now. "Katherine, I'm going back to the house. If you want to continue, I think it only fair to warn you that it's very likely there are grizzlys about. We see signs of their coming into camp all the time."

"You're just telling me that to scare me."

"Am I?" Another twig snapped, closer this time. Katherine stopped. Alex would have laughed if he hadn't suspected it would send her stomping down the hill. "Katherine, I'm sorry if I did or said anything to hurt you."

"If?"

"Look, this isn't any easier for me than it is for you."

She kept on going.

"Will you listen to me?"

She dropped the rug and saddlebags and clamped her hands over her ears.

He came up behind her and grabbed one of her hands, pulling it down. "I don't have a gun with me, Katherine. If we run into a grizzly, we don't stand much of a chance." She stopped. They started back toward the house.

She began to walk faster, pulling ahead of him and saying over her shoulder, "I'm still not in the mood to talk to you."

"All right. It can wait."

"And I'm still upset."

Alex stopped and picked up the saddlebag and the grizzly rug. "I understand."

"No, you don't. I think you've been terribly unfair."

"I think you're probably right."

"You haven't been exactly kind to me."

"No, I haven't."

She stopped, and shot him a hostile look. "Then why are we having this disagreement, if you agree with everything I've said?"

Alex started to speak when they heard something moving in the brush again. "Oh, never mind," she said, starting toward the house again. "We can talk about this later. I never did like to discuss things in the dark anyway."

He noticed her walk was much faster now, for he had to speed up a little himself to stay up with her. Alex felt a curl of pleasure and he didn't understand why. He should be furious with her. Perhaps it was because he had never seen Katherine like this. She had always been so levelheaded, so sensible, so even tempered. Now she was acting just like a woman.

They reached the clearing, the light coming through the opened door, making it much easier to see. Adrian was sitting on the front steps. He didn't say anything, and he didn't have much time to, for at that moment, whatever it was that had been following them through the brush burst out into the clearing with a howl. Katherine jumped a mile and would've taken off like a blue streak if Alex hadn't grabbed her. "Katherine," he said calmly. "It's all right. It's only a dog. See?" He turned her and she saw a large hound loping toward them, hitting the porch and Adrian with such force he almost knocked him over.

"Well, Jeremiah," Adrian said, giving him a few wrestling moves and a final pat. "What are you doing out this time of night?"

Jeremiah left Adrian and trotted over to Alex. Katherine stood to one side, eyeing him speculatively. Alex gave him a pat. "Jeremiah is what you might call the camp dog. He usually sleeps in the bunkhouse."

"He smells like it," she said, still unwilling to be placated. Katherine was giving Jeremiah the eye. "I think you knew it was a dog all along," she said. "You just wanted to scare me." Turning to Adrian, she said, "Would you mind showing me to my room? I've had about all of this nonsense I want for tonight."

Adrian looked from Katherine to Alex. "Take her on up," Alex said. "I need to get Jeremiah fastened up before he gets into trouble."

"Alex?"

"What?"

Adrian had a rather helpless expression on

his face. "Ah…That is…Oh, hell, Alex. Where do you want me to put her?"

"In the spare room," Katherine answered before he had a chance to answer. "Where else?"

Adrian looked pleadingly at Alex. "You heard her," Alex said. He tossed the saddlebag to Adrian and turned away, calling Jeremiah to follow him.

"Alex?" Adrian called after him. Alex stopped.

"What is it?"

"I'll take Jeremiah," Adrian said, coming up beside him and handing him the saddlebag. "You show Katherine upstairs."

"I wish someone would show me before you wear that saddlebag out passing it back and forth." Leaving the porch and stepping into the house, she said, "Why don't *both* of you put Jeremiah up and *stay with him*. I'll find my own place to sleep." She slammed the door and crossed the room to the table and picking up a lamp, she started up the stairs. She opened the first door and saw a hat hanging on a peg and a pair of boots standing beside the door. She shut that one and opened another, seeing a desk scattered with papers, a coat draped over the back of the chair. She shut that door and opened the next one. It looked unoccupied, but she saw another door. Opening it, she saw it led to the bedroom next door. She slammed the door and left that room, walking past the next two rooms to the last room at the end of the hall.

It was the largest bedroom she had seen, and

at the corner it had windows on two walls. "This will do," she said, and stepped into the room. She moved to the bed and placed the lamp on the table beside it and sat down, bouncing up and down a few times. It was fairly soft and didn't squeak. She could do worse. Still sitting on the bed, she looked around the room. The floor was unfinished and bare of any rugs, but it was clean and the smell reminded her of the woods back home. It was sparsely furnished: a wardrobe, a washstand, a straight-backed chair angled in the corner. *Put some curtains over the windows, exchange that straight chair for a rocker, throw a few rugs on the floor, a counterpane on the bed... I could be comfortable here.*

You could be more comfortable in the room with Alex.

She kicked the door shut with one foot. It occurred to her just how tired she really was. Wearily she stood and crossed the room to the washstand. The china pitcher was thankfully half full. A bar of soap, used but still big enough to do the job, lay in the soap dish. She picked up the towel and sniffed. It smelled clean. *At this point, I don't even care.*

She removed her clothes—leaving her chemise and bloomers on—and hung them on the pegs in the wardrobe. After she washed, she realized her nightgown and brush were in Alex's saddlebags, but she would have to make do. She let her hair down and combed through it with her fingers, then she began braiding it in one long braid down her back. She pulled the ribbon from her chemise and used it to tie the braid. She had almost reached the bed when someone knocked on the door. She made a dive for the bed, threw back the covers and leaped in, jerking the covers up to her neck. "Who is it?"

"It's me. Alex."

"What do you want?"

She could hear him sigh through the door. "Do I have to want something to knock at your door?"

"You'd look pretty stupid going around knocking on doors for no reason at all."

"I brought your things."

"Just put them beside the door. I'll get them in the morning."

"Katherine, I want to talk to you."

"Well, I don't want to talk to you." She flopped over.

"If you're still angry about tonight, you shouldn't be. You should be overcome with gratitude that I didn't let you freeze your rosy little bottom sleeping outside."

How could she have known this man all her life only to find she had married a stranger? How did he know if her bottom was rosy or not? And what had he said? Overcome with gratitude—the very sound of those words brought chills to her spine.

He saw the light under her door grow dim and disappear. His fists clenched, he silently wished her to perdition, then started away. A second later he stopped. He and Katherine were married, regardless of the reason, regardless of how they felt about each other. He couldn't spend the rest of his life like this. He was going to have to get control and it might as well be now.

The door opened and Alex stepped into the room, a square of pale light flooding around him. Katherine shot straight up. "Do you always barge in on people? Don't you have *any* manners at all?"

"I wasn't aware I had to wait for an invitation. You *are* my wife."

"A fact you remember and forget as it suits you."

"It suits me now to remember," he said, his eyes on her.

Katherine leaned over and turned the lamp up enough to see his face. He was staring at her so intently that for a moment Katherine was mesmerized, seeing nothing but a tall man leaning negligently against the door frame. But then it occurred to her that whatever the man was looking at, he was devouring it with his eyes. She looked down, following the direction of his stare. He was looking at her. She was jerked from her absorption by that sobering fact. To be caught in her chemise was bad enough, but to be caught with a gap at the top where it opened was even worse. She remembered pulling the ribbon out to tie her braid. Then she remembered she had better cover herself.

And she did, jerking the covers up to her chin. But the memory of what he had seen was burned upon his mind. He had always thought Katherine a beautiful woman, but tonight she was incredibly so. *I'm so starved for feminine company a dress on a broom would look good.* But that was no broom he'd looked at. It was all warm, vital woman. He could never remember seeing so little of a woman's breasts and having it affect him as it had, for in truth, very little of the skin between her breasts had been exposed. But it was enough to make him want to see more. "Katherine," he said, stepping into the room and closing the door.

She was immediately aware of the change in him, the heavy-lidded eyes, the husky speech, and although she wasn't experienced, she wasn't a fool either. She felt her eyes burn, the tears she tried so desperately to hold back slipping down her face. She loved this man. She wanted more than anything to have him take her in his arms and make love to her. But she wanted it because he loved her, not because he had seen something that aroused him.

It took him a minute to overcome the desire he was feeling and for it to register that she was crying. "Katherine?"

He was standing beside her now.

She turned her face away. "Go away, Alex. Just leave me alone."

"What's wrong."

"Nothing...everything. I think I'm too tired to be sensible right now."

"I'll leave your things."

"Thank you."

"I'll see you at breakfast."

"Fine."

"Do you need anything?"

"Just a little sleep."

"Well, good night."

"Good night, Alex."

Then it dawned on him that he was being dismissed, and Alex didn't like to be dismissed. "Really Katherine, that was remarkable. I congratulate you."

She sat up in bed. "Alex, what are you talking about?"

"Where did you learn to be such a tease? That was clever of you, you know. Draw the ribbon from your chemise, flaunt just enough bosom to entice a man, then flood him with tears until his guts are twisted with desire and remorse, and then turn a cold shoulder on him."

She just sat there looking at him. He saw she was confused, insulted, angry, but she didn't say anything.

"I find it interesting. Tell me where you learned to do that."

"Only if you tell me where you learned to be so hateful and cruel."

"I see this conversation is going nowhere," he said. "I will see you in the morning."

"*Not* if I see you first." She flopped over again and pulled the covers over her head.

The door shut. The room was dark and quiet. Katherine was exhausted. Everything was perfect for sleeping. But she couldn't sleep. This day had been too much. Alex had been too much. She began to cry.

When Katherine did anything, she did it with complete and utter devotion, and crying was no exception. Giving her misery her undivided attention, she didn't hear the door open, didn't hear her husband cross the room and pull back the blankets on her bed. But she felt the weight of his body as he lay next to her, felt the comforting heat of him as he took her in his arms and rolled her against him, cradling her head against his chest. "Go ahead and cry," he said softly.

What a stupid thing for a man to say, she thought. *Here I am crying my heart out, and what does he say? Go ahead and cry! It's hopeless. Absolutely hopeless.*

She took two swipes at her eyes. "I'm all right. You can leave now."

"Do you really want me to go?"

"Why would I want you to stay? You're an ogre, Alex, an uncaring, unfeeling ogre."

"You're right, but even ogres need love."

"Then go find another ogre and leave me alone."

He laughed, burying his face in the hollow between her shoulder and neck, where the skin was soft, fragrant and oh, so warm. "Katherine," he said softly, the sound of it low and vibrating like a kitten's purr.

Her heart thudding in her breast, she turned toward him. "I am tired, Alex. Will you please leave me alone?"

"No," he said. "I can't. I'm going to bother you, Katherine, and keep on bothering you until you scream from the exquisite agony of it. I'm going to bother you, like you bother me, like you bothered me all these years when I didn't understand why."

"You were too stupid, that's why."

"I'm not stupid now."

"It's too late now."

"Why?"

"Because I *know*, Alex. I know it isn't me you want. I don't know how you came to write that letter, or why you wrote my name, but I know you don't want me."

"You're wrong," he said, taking her hand and placing it on that part of him which was huge and hard, "I do want you."

Surprise and shock held her mesmerized for a moment, then she squeezed her eyes shut, as if she could blot out the reality of his presence, of the words he had uttered. Before she could speak or respond in any way, his mouth found hers. His kiss was warm and demanding, and when she tried to resist, his arms tightened like tightly drawn cords around her. He kissed her for a long, long time. Katherine discovered there are kisses and then there are kisses.

She forgot for a moment the humiliation and pain she had felt a moment ago, forgot the reasons she had for being angry at this man. For a time, she forgot, melting against him, into him, her breasts crushed against him, an ache curling, low and hot, deep in her belly.

She had only been kissed once in her life, and that was the time Alex had kissed her before leaving for California. But that kiss had been nothing like this one. Lost in the knowledge that no one, not even Alex had kissed her like this before, Katherine moaned at the feeling of pleasure she felt when his hand slipped inside her chemise to cup her breast, his thumb bringing her to the point of readiness. His kiss was more urgent now, his breathing harder and more ragged. A moment later, Alex drew back. "Let me get my clothes off," he said between nibbling kisses. "I want you, Katherine. I want you so much, I can't wait any longer."

That had a sobering effect upon Katherine. While she had vowed to make Alex love her, vowed to show him she was the right woman for him, it had never occurred to her he might want to make love to her for any other reason than love. Perhaps this was because she loved him so dearly and desired him so much, she naturally thought the two of them—love and desire—went together. Confused, and wanting him for all the right reasons, she pulled back and said, "I won't make love with you, Alex. Not like this."

It took a minute for that to soak in, but when it did, it hit like a pan of cold water. "What? What do you mean, you won't make love with me? What in the hell do you think you're doing right now?"

"Throwing you out of my bed," she said, giving him a hard shove. Alex, who was precariously close to the edge to begin with, toppled over, hitting the floor with a thud.

A second later, a face with a furious expression popped up. "Are you crazy?" he asked.

"I must be," she said, sitting up, "for thinking this is what marriage is all about."

"Marriage!" he said. "This isn't a marriage!"

"You are absolutely right. It isn't, and it won't ever be like this."

"Like what?"

"Married people don't have separate rooms."

"You're the one that made that decision!" he shouted.

"And it was a wise one," she said. "Keep your voice down."

"It is down! Hell! Why shouldn't it be down? Everything else is."

"Good night, Alex."

"Katherine, what is this all about?"

"I told you. I won't make love with you like this."

"Not ever?"

"I didn't say that."

"Do you have any idea when?"

"When I decide to move into your room."

"It will take me a fast five minutes to accomplish that," he said, coming up off the floor.

"I said, *when I decide to move,* Alex, not when *you* decide."

"What difference does it make who decides, as long as one of us does?"

"Only you could ask something that stupid," she said. "I'm beginning to think you don't know anything about women."

"Hell! I'm beginning to agree with you."

"At least we agree on something," she said.

The next morning, Adrian was sitting at the table in the kitchen, shoveling it in, when Alex walked in. Wong was shuffling around the stove, cooking and talking to himself, as he always did. Alex paused just inside the room and looked around. "Where's Katherine?"

"She hasn't come down yet," Adrian said.

Alex sat down and Wong brought him a stack of pancakes. "Maybe she'll be down in a minute," he said.

"Maybe," was all Adrian said.

By the time Alex finished eating, Adrian was on his third cup of coffee. Alex looked at his brother's cup. Adrian never had more than two. It was obvious he was hanging around for something. "Don't you have work to do?" Alex said.

"Don't you?" was Adrian's reply.

"I'm going to have a cup of coffee."

"So am I."

"You never have more than two."

"Today I'm having four. Is that a problem for you?"

"No." Alex looked at his timepiece. It was almost seven. It would be lunchtime soon. Where was she? He had another cup of coffee. So did Adrian. "Have they cleared the logs out of the road yet?"

"I don't know."

Alex scowled. "Well, don't you think you

should check to see if they've at least started on it?"

"No, but you go ahead if you want to."

Damnation! Wasn't there any way to get him out of the kitchen? Maybe he should forget about Katherine. Let her sulk in her room. He looked at Adrian. Adrian smiled. *You're enjoying this.* "Wong!" Alex shouted. "Bring me another cup."

"Me too, Wong."

The brothers sat in silence as Wong gave them a strange look and brought the coffeepot. When he returned it to the stove, Alex couldn't stand it any longer. "Wong, run upstairs and see what ails my wife. Tell her breakfast is getting cold."

Wong left.

He was back in a few minutes. "Well?" Alex said. "What did she say?"

"Missy say she doesn't feel like eating breakfast this morning."

"Why not? What's wrong with her?"

Wong shrugged. "Wong no ask."

"Well, go back and ask her what ails her," Alex said.

Wong shot from the room. A few minutes later he was back. "Missy say she is overcome with gratitude."

It was the second time in as many days that the sound of his brother's laughter followed him away from the house. *Overcome with gratitude?* Those words had a strangely familiar ring to them. But that only irritated Alex further. *I'm not going to put up with much more of this, Katherine.*

CHAPTER
SEVENTEEN

A week passed and things hadn't changed much. Katherine was still sleeping in her own room and Alex was still mumbling, "I'm not going to put up with much more of this, Katherine."

It might have surprised the two of them to know that after a week of disagreements, there was one thing they actually did agree on. Katherine, like Alex, didn't think she could put up with much more of it either.

The weather had taken a turn for the better, being uncommonly warm and clear for November. Taking advantage of the lucky change, Katherine gathered up the things that needed washing and followed Wong, who carried her basket of laundry down to the cookhouse, where two large tubs designated as laundry tubs stood on the back porch. Molly (Katherine absolutely refused to call a woman by her initials) was just finishing a little laundry of her own.

Over the past week Katherine had become quite fond of Molly, looking to the older woman for friendship, guidance, counseling, and help in adapting to a whole new way of life. But it hadn't been easy. There were times that Katherine wondered how their friendship would ever get on solid ground. Molly wasn't the easiest person in the world to get to know.

The first time Katherine had paid her a visit, Molly was in the cookhouse cutting steaks as big as a blacksmith's apron for supper. Katherine opened the conversation with, "I need a bit of feminine advice."

To which Molly replied, "Well, it looks like you came to the right place, since the only other female in camp is Fatima."

"Who is Fatima?"

Whack! went the meat cleaver and Katherine jumped a country mile. "An ass."

That gave Katherine a start. "You mean literally?"

Whack! Katherine jumped again, but Molly went on talking. "I couldn't say about that, seeing as how I don't exactly recollect what literally means."

"What I mean is..." *Whack!* "are you saying Fatima..." *Whack!* "is really an..."

"Ass," Molly supplied. *Whack!*

"With long ears?" *Whack!*

"And four legs," *Whack!* "and a fondness for braying," *Whack!* "like some people I know." *Whack! Whack! Whack!* Katherine didn't jump this time, but she did blink three times, noticing each time she opened her eyes how the fat on the underside of Molly's arms swung to and fro like the dewlap on a cow. Katherine wanted to look beneath her own arms, but Molly still held the meat cleaver and she decided she could wait. After a few more whacks Molly put the meat cleaver down and Katherine felt relief down to her toes.

"So, what bit of feminine advice did you need? Don't tell me you two lovebirds have started flying at each other."

"No," Katherine said solemnly. "We're not that far along. We haven't even made it to lovebirds yet."

"Sounds like you're about as compatible as a cat and a dog."

"We don't really fight, it's just that we seem so far apart. We're like two strangers that have the same last name."

"Sometimes it takes a while for married folk to settle in to the idea they've become one. I spent the first twenty years of our marriage trying to convince Big John that two halves made a whole."

"Did he ever understand?"

"He can't do fractions."

Katherine laughed. In spite of their slow beginning, their conversation soon grew warm enough that they could be called friends, although no one in camp would have ever believed Molly capable of such.

Rube Dexter, one of the bull whackers—Katherine still blinked when she heard that word—said Molly was "too mean and too big and talks to herself too much to be anybody's friend."

But Molly simply said listening to herself was "better than listening to that maddening malarkey of that Mandarin magpie."

It took Katherine a minute to figure out just who the Mandarin magpie was, and she was immediately relieved that Molly's term for her was nothing more than "that too-thin talkative Texan."

But Molly was taking her into her confidence more each day and after a week or so she confessed to Katherine that she talked to her-self because she liked polite company and interesting conversation, and she was the only one in camp, capable of both. "Until you arrived, of course."

Molly did talk a lot. Wong said her tongue moved faster than the logs she chunked at him, but Katherine enjoyed her brand of humor and the things she had to say. So it was a pleasant surprise to Katherine to find Molly on the back porch of the cookhouse finishing up her laundry that day.

The minute they saw Molly on the cookhouse porch Wong started acting fidgety, like he always did around Molly. It didn't take Molly a minute to send him packing when she said, "Fetch me a hunk of wood from that woodpile, would you, Katherine?"

"Boss need Wong. Wong better go, fast. Boss get mad."

Katherine watched him go as fast as his bandy legs would carry him. She couldn't help laughing, for Wong *was* rather like a magpie, hopping across the yard, maddening malarkey pouring out so fast it sounded like two people talking. "He's a good sort," Katherine said, trying to say something kind.

"I don't know how you can say that. He can't whisper, he can't tiptoe, he won't look you in the eye, and you can't understand a blessed thing he says. And he's got more teeth than a falling saw. Every time he smiles I expect to hear someone shout, *Timber!*"

"Oh Molly!"

"I know I don't have any room to be talking. I've got a face that looks like it was rained on before it got dried, but I wouldn't trust him for a minute. His brains are too close to the ground."

"His brains... What?"

"Don't tell me you haven't noticed how short he is."

Katherine laughed, but she stood up straighter after that. "What's a falling saw?"

"The crosscut used by the faller, and before you ask me what a faller is, they're the ones who fell the trees. But don't you ever go calling one of them a feller."

"I won't. Thanks for telling me." *Faller, not feller,* she reminded herself. She sighed.

"You've got a lot to learn. Somebody's got to teach it to you."

"I'm glad it's you," Katherine said.

Molly laughed. "You don't have much choice, do you. It's either me or Fatima."

"I already know how to bray, thank you, so Fatima couldn't teach me a thing. I have a mule at home." The reminder of Clovis sent a wave of homesickness over her.

Molly wrung out the last shirt and tossed it in her basket before turning to help Katherine put her things to soak. "I'll help you carry your basket to the bushes," Katherine said.

"It's heavy."

"I'm strong."

"I'm going up the hill a ways."

"I'll make it."

"You're getting a mite sassy."

"I've had a good teacher."

"You'll do."

"So will you."

They both laughed, then each of them grabbed a handle of the basket. "Two halves make a whole, right?" Molly said and Katherine agreed. Halfway up the hill they stopped and began spreading Molly's wash on the wild berry bushes that grew in the clearing there.

The locket Molly always wore around her neck caught on a low branch as she leaned over. "I'll be a son of a b"—Molly glanced at Katherine—"bucking saw," she finished. Katherine laughed, reaching for the locket which had sprung open. The faces of a young man and woman smiled up at her. Katherine looked at it for a moment. "Who is this?"

"Me and that big oaf I'm married to," Molly replied, taking the locket from Katherine and snapping it shut before dropping it inside her shirt. They hung out the rest of Molly's laundry and then Katherine went back to the cookhouse to wash out the things she had left to soak.

Katherine realized with something akin to outrage that the kind of life Molly had followed her husband into had laid its hand so harshly upon a face and body that had, at one time, been quite lithe and fair. For days afterward, everytime she saw Molly, she couldn't help remembering the beautiful young woman she had once been.

Her face had been dried and wrinkled by the sun, her hands roughened and knotted by hard work. The body, which had looked as delicate as a china cup in the tiny painting was sturdy and muscled from heavy use. Her dark auburn hair had thinned and lightened to a rosy red-pink, and her teeth weren't as straight as they once were. Spending her life around a bunch of rough-talking men had made her language as tough as her hide. But her eyes were as sharp and bright and alive as they had ever been, and inside their shining depths lay the secret to living life to its fullest.

Katherine finished her laundry and carried it back to the house to hang out. As she walked, she wished it was as easy to win Alex's friendship as it had been Molly's, which hadn't been easy at all.

Since she had come to the logging camp Katherine hardly saw Alex except at mealtime. He was a hard worker, as was Adrian, and it was easy to see why the two of them were so successful since coming to California.

In time, Katherine and Alex established a kind of routine which they kept by unspoken agreement. Alex kissed her on the cheek when he came down for breakfast each morning and when he came home at night. He carried anything heavy for her, relayed bits of information and the latest news that came by ship from San Francisco. He complimented her on her appearance. He laughed when she had something funny to say. Many was the time she found him looking her way. Once or twice he had gone so far as to kiss her.

But she hadn't moved into his room.

Katherine made it a point to learn her way around camp, learning the names of most of the men, asking question after question so she could learn as much as she could about her husband's work. She served the meals on time. She kept his clothes clean, and his house too. She kept her complaining to a minimum and reminded herself daily to be gracious and charming no matter how much she wanted to bring the churn down over his thick head. She was a determined woman, determined to show Alex she was the woman for him. If she couldn't be the wife Alex wanted, she would be the one he needed.

But Alex, it seemed, didn't need anyone, least of all her.

I might as well be a redwood. No, that's not right. If I were a redwood, he'd notice me.

For Alex, having Katherine around left him confused and frustrated. While her presence here constantly reminded him of the mistake he had made, he couldn't help noticing how much his life had changed, and for the better, since he had married her. He had to give Katherine credit for the many ways she had it over Karin. Alex wasn't fool enough to think Karin would have adapted to this lumbering lifestyle as rapidly or as easily as Katherine had. Even the lumberjacks were easier to deal with since Katherine had made such an effort to call them by name and learn so much about what they did.

Day after day, he watched his wife perform acts of love for him, watched her seduce him in a hundred ways—until he was ready to toss her over his shoulder and carry her upstairs to *anybody's* room and make love to her.

He had just decided to tell her he was through with all this nonsense and that he wanted her in his room and in his bed, when he and Adrian had to go to San Francisco. "I can't take you with me, Katherine."

"I understand."

"No, I don't think you do. It isn't because I wouldn't like to, but this ship is a logging ship, built to carry lumber. Adrian and I will bunk in with the crew. There isn't a place for a woman."

He left, promising to be back as soon as he could, no more than a week, he thought. She had walked him down to the dock to see him off, and Alex, seeing the men standing around like they expected something, realized they were waiting for him to kiss her. Alex's face filled with indecision. Inside, deep within his heart he knew he wanted to take Katherine in his arms and kiss her like he had never kissed her before. What force prevented him from doing it? Over the past weeks he had admitted to himself time and time again that marriage to her wouldn't be half as bad as he made it out to be. She had so many good qualities. In fact the only thing he could find wrong with her at all was that she wasn't Karin. And even then, admitting that, he knew in all ways she was probably better. *What's wrong with me? Why can't I forget Karin and get on with my life? Why can't*

I love my wife? He wanted to. And he had tried.

Only yesterday he had been returning from the higher elevations and spotted Katherine talking to one of the new hands, a young Swede that had hired on for the loneliest job of all, a windfall bucker.

Her gleaming auburn hair caught his eye as she left the cookhouse with a big ledger of some sort under her arm. The young Swede was walking toward her.

"Hello," she said.

The Swede stopped, looking her over a couple of times like he'd never seen the likes of her before and wanted to see a whole lot more in the future. "You're Mrs. Mackinnon, aren't you?"

"Yes, I am. I thought I had met everyone here, but it looks like I missed you."

"I'm new. Just arrived yesterday. I'm Emil Erikson." He offered his hand and Katherine juggled with the ledger for a moment before he laughed and said, "Looks like we'll have to shake later."

"I'm afraid so. My hands seem to be full."

"You keeping records?"

She laughed. "Hardly. I don't know enough about lumbering to hold a polite conversation. And I'm afraid record keeping is far beyond my reach."

Erikson laughed. "We all started out that way. It doesn't take long to learn."

"It must not. You aren't old enough to have spent much time in the business."

"I'm twenty-one." He glanced down at the ledger again.

"They're just notes. I talk to everyone around here that doesn't see me coming first and high-tails it." She laughed. "Once I have them cornered and at my mercy, I begin asking questions until they volunteer to go out with another logging crew just to get away from me."

"I can't imagine anyone wanting to get away from you. You could ask me all the questions you like."

Katherine cautioned herself. Friendliness was all right up to a point, but then it some-times shifted to interest. She tried to cut things off before they reached that point. She shifted the ledger and started walking, hoping Emil would be on his way.

"I'm a windfall bucker. Do you have any notes about that?"

Katherine started to say she did, and thought, *What if he begins to ask questions? You could make an enemy quite easily. Take it slow, Katherine.* "No, I don't believe I do."

She watched his pride puff out his chest. The next minute he was giving her a full-blown lec-ture on what the windfall bucker did. In spite of his youthful tendency to brag a bit, she couldn't help liking the tall blond giant. "You know what a windfall is, don't you?"

"A tree that blows down in a storm," she said.

"And has to be cut apart so it can be hauled away so the loggers can get to the trees they've chosen to cut."

"You do that all by yourself?"

"And with the worst saws in the camp. For some unknown reason windfallers end up with what's left in the buckers' saw rack after everyone else has had his pick." He laughed. "Here I am complaining already, but if I'm going to complain at all, I have to do it now. Tomorrow I'll be too tired. I'll be leaving with the bull of the woods in the morning."

"Big John Polly," she said. "Have you met him yet?"

"Oh yes. And *Big* Molly too!" Katherine laughed. "I was just on my way over to pick up my supplies," he said. "Big John will be taking me up early tomorrow. I hope I can find my way back when I'm done."

"Katherine!" Alex said so loud that Katherine jumped, dropping her ledger. Walking toward them, Alex said, "You're needed at the house."

"At the house?" she asked. Her face flushed, she stammered and said, "I was just learning about windfall bucking from Mr. Erikson."

"Whatever you want to know, you can ask me." Alex arrogantly walked between Katherine and Emil, taking Katherine by the arm. Then turning to Emil, he said, "If you don't want me to take a ten-pound sledgehammer to you, I suggest you get on with what you were doing before you detained my wife."

Emil picked up Katherine's ledger and handed it back to her.

"Thank you," she said.

"You're welcome," Emil replied.

"*You* are on borrowed time," Alex said, glaring at Emil.

Emil grinned. "I heard you hadn't been married very long," he said, then turned, whistling as he walked away.

"Arrogant foreigner," Alex said.

"Arrogance seems to go with the business," Katherine said and walked away.

Alex caught up with her. "I don't want you talking to him anymore."

Katherine walked faster. "Just him, or does that go for any of the men?"

"Any of them that act like he does."

"He wasn't doing anything."

"He was standing too close and acting too friendly."

"So what do you want me to do next time someone says something to me? Bolt and run?"

"I expect you to act like a lady. *A married lady*."

She gave him a cold look. "Sometimes you have the mentality of a stupid sheep, you know that?"

"What is that supposed to mean?"

"It means I *barely* qualify to be called married at all, and that is *only* because we had a marriage ceremony. We certainly haven't had any of the other *things* that go along with marriage," she said.

"I know one *thing* I've been trying like hell to give you for over a week," he said. "If you aren't getting what you want, Katherine, it isn't my fault."

"No?"

"No. *You're* the one who's refused to share my room."

"Well, *you're* the one who's too pigheaded to understand why."

Alex opened his mouth to speak, but Big John walked up and asked Alex if he had a minute and Katherine took advantage of that to hurry up to the house. When she arrived it didn't take her long to find there was no one there. Coming back down the stairs after her fruitless search, she was steaming. "So, I'm needed at the house, am I? Might I just ask *who* was needing me?" she said quite loudly, since there was no one there.

"I'm the one that wanted you here," Alex said, coming into the room from the kitchen.

Katherine noticed he said *wanted*, not *needed*. "Well, you have me. Now what was so important that you had to embarrass me like that?"

Alex looked a mite remorseful as he crossed the room to her. "Look, I'm not trying to embarrass you or make life miserable for you. You don't understand what it's like for these men, how long it's been since they've even seen a woman."

"So I'm to confine myself to the house so they can't *see* me, is that it?"

"No," he said, then paused, his expression becoming lighter, a gleam appearing in his eye. "You can go out... on occasion."

"Thank you. And what occasion might that be?"

"After it's dark." He couldn't help laughing at the expression on Katherine's face.

"That isn't funny, Alex."

"I don't know," he said. "There were parts of it..."

"Oh, do be quiet!" she said and started up the stairs again. Alex caught her and swept her into his arms and Katherine was so startled her mouth dropped open.

It was one of the few times she couldn't think of a thing to say.

He put her on her feet when he reached the top, backing her across the floor and pinning her against the wall. "What did you call me?"

"I didn't call you anything."

"Yes you did. Outside. You said I had the mentality of a..."

"Stupid sheep."

"I thought all sheep were stupid."

"They are. But the stupid ones are even stupider."

Alex wasn't even going to attempt to understand that one. "Katherine, what am I going to do with you?"

"Send me back, I suppose."

The image of that stabbed like a pain in the heart of him. *Never,* he thought. *Never.* He looked at her adorable face, thinking he could never part with her. But he couldn't find the words to say that yet. *In time,* he thought. *In time, I'll tell her.* He laughed softly to hide what he was feeling and pulled her close against his chest. He hadn't wanted to marry her, and now he didn't want to send her back. *What's going on here?* he asked himself, wondering if he could be falling in love with her so easily. *No,* he told himself. *She's a lot of company and you enjoy her, but that isn't love. She's brought joy and laughter into your life, but that isn't love. She makes you look forward to seeing her and listening to what she has to say, but that isn't love.*

Being forced into this marriage still didn't sit too well with him, but he didn't blame her. He looked into her upturned face. "I can't send you back. It's too late for that, I'm afraid." His lips touched the top of her head, then he was looking at her, the blue of his gaze like a clear summer sky. "There's always been something about you, something that has always made it difficult for me to stay away from you."

Why should you? Why can't you give in, Alex? I know you want to. I know you love me. I know it.

He drew her closer with the slightest urging of one hand and nuzzled her neck. Then his lips were at the side of her face. He was all soft breath and warm, living man. His lips touched her brow in a slow circular motion before going down over her small perfect nose. He kissed her once. Twice. Then he sighed, drawing her even closer as he brought his mouth down on hers. His grip was hard, determined, but gentle. It was the sort of kiss that drew one out and left her with an aching, unexplored need. Cool and dry and in complete control, his searching mouth taught her the way to kiss a man. The belated scorch of passion burned away her pique and she melted, warm, and infinitely lovely in his arms. He drew back, looking down at her upturned face. Her eyes were closed, the lovely dark lashes outlined against milk-white skin; her cheekbones were delicately defined and curved gently down to her lips which were full and slightly parted, glossy now from his kiss. As he studied her, her lashes fluttered and her eyes opened, green eyes as deep and languid as pools he could drown himself in.

"Why can't I stay angry at you?" he asked gently.

"Because I'm so adorable," she said with a laugh.

"Wrong," he said. "Try again."

"Because you don't have any reason to be angry at me at all."

That was uncomfortably close to the truth. He laughed, then looked at her for a moment before he cupped her chin in his. "Do you always see to the heart of things? How'd you get so wise?" His thumb began making slow, lazy circles around her mouth.

"I'm not wise. If I were I wouldn't..." She saw he was going to kiss her and she tried to turn her head away, but he caught it firmly with a kiss. This time he let her feel some of the heat he was feeling. His hands came up to hold her face as he drew his lips back and forth across hers before dropping lower to the soft curve of her throat. Her breath drew in sharply, catching in her throat. "Ahhh, Katherine, I never knew you could taste so sweet." He caught her mouth again, his fingers tracing the contours of her ears, his breath coming soft as a whisper.

He had kissed her before, but those times he had done it simply because the occasion presented itself, or because he desired her in a moment of weakness. But this time it was different. This time he kissed her for none of the those reasons. This time he kissed her because he wanted her levelheadedness, her ability to heal, her sweet nature, her understanding smile. He wanted her ability to make him forget, to see her as something strong and secure and right in his life. He wanted things to be back the way they were between them before he married her, when she was a friend most dear, the one person in the world he could talk to and feel she understood.

"Alex," she said softly, her huge eyes shining in the dim light. "Don't do this if you aren't ready. Don't tease me and then push me away."

"If I'm not ready for what?"

"To know me as your wife."

To know me as your wife. To know her as Abraham knew Sarah. *Abraham knew Sarah and she conceived.*

Alex released her and slowly turned his head away. The sound of her running to her room and the door slamming ended long before he reached the bottom of the stairs.

But that had all happened yesterday, and now someone was shouting, "Come on old man! Kiss her so we can get underway." The men began to cheer as Alex took her in his arms.

"Give her a good pucker."

"Give her one that'll last a week!"

411

"Give her one for me!"

Alex laughed and kissed her, thoroughly, giving her all of those things.

"We said week, Mackinnon, not a month."

The laughter almost drowned out Alex's last words. "Take care, Katherine. I'll be back in a week I hope."

"I'll miss you, Alex."

"I'll..." He glanced at the ship. "I'll be back before you know it."

Alex had been gone two weeks and two days the day it happened.

Katherine had wandered up to the higher elevations and was sitting on a redwood stump, sketching a squirrel and daydreaming about Alex. There was no one about to disturb the quiet beauty of the trees towering around her, or even the squirrel's preoccupation with an owl he was scolding for occupying a branch of his tree. The light slanted through the branches in extended shafts, splotching the forest floor with color. Everything around her seemed fresh from creation.

Occasionally sounds from the loggers would invade her solitude, but as the wind rose the sounds grew steady and stronger until the thwacking of axes and the rasping of saws seemed to be moving closer.

She had been sketching for almost an hour when the silence was broken by a distant shout and a bursting crack followed by the crash of a tree that struck with such force the earth beneath her trembled. Then she heard a cry, and another and another until she sprang to her feet, the sketch falling to the forest floor. There was an urgency and the sound of panic in those voices, a sound far different from any she had heard before. Without thinking she started off in the direction of the cries and shouts, running and stumbling as the sharp branches ripped at her clothing and hair, often stabbing into her flesh with a flash of pain, but something urged her on.

Breathless, her legs rubbery from the long uphill run, she reached the clearing littered with stumps and loosened limbs called widow-makers. *Widow-makers.* Her heart pounded painfully in her chest, her eyes searching and finding the logging crew gathered around a felled tree across from her. She ran up to the group of men. One of them she knew only as Halfpint stopped her. "You don't want to go up there, Miz Mackinnon. It ain't gonna be a pretty sight."

"What..." She fought for breath. "What happened?"

"One of the fallers didn't get clear and he was carried down the hill with the tree."

"How bad is he hurt?"

"Don't know yet. We ain't got to him."

Katherine lifted her skirts and started down the hill. "Maybe there is something I can do." She reached the group of men who were cutting and chopping away the branches of the huge redwood.

"Where is he?" she asked.

Jumbo Shay was standing beside her. "He's

caught beneath those branches. They're trying to get to him, but it's gonna take a while to cut through everything."

"Isn't there any other way to get to him?"

"Not unless you ain't big as a minute and can crawl through."

Katherine didn't hesitate. "I'm not very big. Maybe I can."

"There wouldn't be much you could do, Miz Mackinnon. Not until we cleared everything away so as to get him out."

"That man may be dying. He shouldn't have to die all alone."

"He may already be dead."

"Then I can tell the men they don't need to risk another life by being in a hurry."

She stepped across the debris, coming closer to the tree, seeing where the men were working. Jumbo followed her. "Miz Mackinnon thinks she can crawl through to get to Birkham."

The men moved away, letting Katherine through. When she had gone as far as she could without crawling, she looked at the small space between the splintered branches. "I'll have to remove my skirt," she said, her hand going to her waist.

Jumbo's voice boomed. "All right you slobbering fools, I want every one of you to turn around and face the other way. Any man that looks will wish he hadn't."

To a man they turned around and Katherine slipped her skirts off, peeling down to her drawers. She didn't think about how it must look, or give any thought to being embarrassed. There were more urgent things filling her mind. She crawled through the small opening. It was tight, branches and leaves cluttering her way, scratching her skin, but she inched her way through, crawling over any obstacles. Jumbo called out to her. "Can you see him yet?"

"No." But a moment later she shouted, "Yes! I see him. ...Oh God! He's bleeding badly."

"Is he breathing? Can you tell?"

His face was turned away from her, but the arm that was bleeding so bad was within her reach. She placed her fingers over his wrist, picking up the faint pulse. "He's alive." She looked at his other arm. "I think his arm is almost severed." She had never seen so much blood, or had any idea how sickening sweet it smelled. She had to stop the bleeding. *Think, Katherine. Damn! I wish I had my petticoat.* But she did have the ribbon in her chemise. She worked her way around so she could support herself without any weight on her arms, then she unbuttoned her blouse, finding the ribbon and pulling it through. She remembered another time she had pulled her chemise ribbon out, a time when Alex had been nearby. But Alex was far away from her now.

Hearing the sounds of the men working to clear the way, she moved back to where Birkham's arm lay twisted in the dirt, using her hand to feel, since the light was too dim and there was too much blood to see the wound. She found the cut, just above the elbow and her stomach heaved in revolt. A shower of dust fell around her. She prayed the men were getting closer. Her hand felt the wound. There wasn't more than two or three inches of flesh still connecting the two pieces of his arm. For a moment she thought she might be sick. She felt higher, above the cut, then slipped the ribbon around his arm and drew it tight.

Her arm ached from the position she had to maintain in order to keep the ribbon tight. It seemed like years before she heard a crack overhead, then the scrape of brush and a flood of light washed over her. "We can get him now, Miz Mackinnon." It was Jumbo's voice. Close. Comforting. She heard another crack. She could see his worn calked boots. Then she felt the warmth of his body as he moved next to her.

"Let me get at him," he said.

"You need to hold this," she whispered, her voice too dry to do more. "Hold it tight to stop the bleeding."

Jumbo angled around and took the ribbon. "Okay Jake, help her up."

She was lifted to her feet so fast she felt dizzy, then a strong pair of arms came around her as Jake lifted her, his strong legs climbing over the debris until he had her free. Halfpint met them, throwing her skirts around her.

"I'll need help pulling him free," Jumbo called and the men moved away, giving Katherine time to step into her clothes.

When the men carried Birkham free,

Katherine went down the hill toward the camp with them. "Bring him to the house. It's closer and we have a big table in the kitchen. Send someone for Molly."

Molly was waiting in the kitchen when they arrived, a kettle of water boiling, a stack of clean cloth waiting. They stretched Birkham out on the table and Molly chased most of the men out as they set to work. They did what they could for him, but Katherine feared it was the wounds they couldn't see that were the worst. Blood seeped from his mouth and nose. There was even a little in his ears. His breathing sounded like a rattle. It had been dark for some time when they had done all they could for him. "It's up to the Good Lord now," Molly said.

Katherine looked at her, then at Jumbo. "You've done all you can. I'll stay with him."

"You're plumb tuckered out, Miz Mackinnon," Jumbo said.

"Let me stay with him," said Molly.

"I'll send Wong if I need you," Katherine replied. "You've got to be in the cookhouse at four. Your rest is more important."

Katherine pulled a chair beside the table and sat there, her elbows propped on the table, her chin resting in her palms as she watched Birkham's face for any signs of change. Dear God! He was so young. Not more than eighteen or twenty. Too young to be away from home. Too young to die.

Molly and Jumbo came at five. Katherine was still awake, standing over Birkham, putting more blankets over him. "He's so cold," she said.

Molly came closer and put her hand on Birkham's forehead, then her head against his chest. She looked at Jumbo and shook her head.

"Nooooo," Katherine wailed, dropping the blanket, her arms clutched around her middle. "He's too young to die. He hasn't even had a chance to live yet."

Molly's arms came around her. "I know, but it happens that way sometime. I lost both my boys not more than a year apart. They weren't much older than him. It's a hard life. You learn to live with it."

Katherine stared dry-eyed at the young boy stretched out on her kitchen table. "I won't ever get used to this," she said. "Not ever."

"Maybe not, but you'll learn to get over it," Molly said. "Time will see to that. You come on up to your room with me and let Jumbo get some of the men to help him move Birkham."

Molly put Katherine to bed, drew the covers under her chin, and tiptoed to the door. "Molly?"

She turned back to Katherine. "What?"

"How... how did your sons die?"

A flash of pain crossed Molly's face. "Peter— he was the youngest." She stopped and looked at the ceiling as if there she would find the words. "There's a jack called a Boker that's used to move large logs. When the lock slips, the levers reverse and the handle spins backward powered by the weight of the log. Many men have had their arms broken when that has happened, but my Peter was hit in the head. He died instantly. Hiram was two years older than Peter. He was killed a few months later when he didn't get clear of a tree, like Birkham. Only Hiram was dead before they carried him down the mountain. His back was broken."

"Oh Molly, I'm so sorry."

"I know," she said softly. "I know. It was a long time ago, but sometimes, when I let myself think on it, it still hurts."

Katherine slept until the next morning. She bathed, feeling rested, but the heaviness of Birkham's death still weighed upon her. She had no hunger, but her body felt weak and she knew she needed food. When she reached the kitchen, Wong came rushing in the door. "Boss back. Wong see. Wong tell Missy. Missy come?"

Katherine smiled. "Thank you, Wong. Missy come."

Her bandy-legged Mandarin friend was bursting with pleasure, proudly holding the door open for her. The warm weather they had enjoyed was gone, and it was apparent that November had been reminded of what it was about and was settling in. The sun was shining, but a thin veil of gray clouds stole most of its shine. Katherine returned for her cloak, then hurried down the road toward the camp, Wong running ahead and pointing the way, then running back to her, much like a faithful dog.

She saw Alex and Adrian immediately, surrounded by a large number of the men. She knew they were telling them about Birkham, but she had no idea how Alex would feel about what she had done. Right now, he looked grave and solemn, and that, for her, was not a good sign. But then one of the men looked up, and nudged one of his friends. Katherine's heart froze, her step faltered. *Dear God, they don't blame me for Birkham's death, do they?*

Hearing the men whisper, Alex looked up and their eyes locked. His gaze was so direct, so penetrating, she was stunned. And then the strangest thing happened. Jumbo pulled his hat off and held it between his hands in front of him, and if it were some sort of signal, the other men began to do the same. Once their hats were removed, they began to move back, opening the circle they had formed around Alex and Adrian. A hush came over them as, down to a man, they bowed their heads as if they were standing before a shrine. Katherine didn't know what to make of it.

But Alex knew.

They said Katherine had appeared shortly after the accident, that she had worked so hard to save Birkham until they could free him, and once they had, she had insisted he be brought to the house and she had stayed over him throughout the night. They had said she had their gratitude. But there was a feeling here, among these rough, uneducated men, a feeling that went much deeper than mere gratitude. There was regard and a respect for her now that her gender could not claim. It was one thing to receive their thanks, but when timber beasts such as these rugged, raw-boned men with more than their share of rough edges and a blistering vocabulary joined for a unified show of devotion it meant something more had happened than what had been relayed to him. He saw the way his wife gave each man present a tentative look and how they answered with a look of fierce protectiveness. It was something Alex had never seen before, something that humbled a man and brought him to his knees.

For him, it was a magical moment when the brooding clouds parted and the sun came out. The men, sensitive to the moment, began to move away and Alex looked at Katherine and knew his time to resist her had come to an end. He saw she was looking at him like she didn't know if she would be welcomed or sent on her way. "Hello Katherine."

She nodded. "Alex... Adrian," she said, "welcome home."

"The men tell me we all owe you a debt of gratitude," Alex said.

Her face looked sad and drawn, making her seem older than she was. "Birkham died," she said in a raw, aching way. "I couldn't help him. You owe me nothing."

"I've got to go over some things with Big John," Adrian said. "I'll be up at the house later," He studied Katherine for a moment, seeing her lovely face drained of all color. "Do you feel all right, Katherine?"

"I'm fine."

To Alex he said, "She's pale as a ghost, Alex. Why don't you take her home?"

But Alex had already slipped his arm around

her and the two of them started up the hill. A thin little breeze stirred the stillness and the scent of her reached him. It was fresh and sweet and warm, and very, very feminine. It was a smell that penetrated like hundreds of silver drops spilling into his blood, rushing to the tips of his fingers and gushing wildly into his head.

Adrian stood in the center of the camp, watching as they climbed the hill and made the curve that would soon block them from sight. But Katherine and Alex never turned around to see if he was still there. And even after they had gone, he remained in the same spot, feeling an aching void, an emptiness, and a sense of terrible loss. Katherine had never been his, he reminded himself. She had never loved him. But the pain wasn't from that. It was in knowing that she never would.

CHAPTER
EIGHTEEN

"Are you hungry?" Katherine asked.

"Starved. My stomach thinks my throat's been cut." Alex opened the front door and followed her into the house. "You remember what ship's food is like."

"I'd rather not. I'm trying to forget."

He laughed. "Let me know if you succeed."

"I will. Why don't you go wash up. I'll see what I can do about scaring up some breakfast for you."

A few minutes later Alex, wearing a clean shirt, his hair combed, came into the kitchen. Katherine handed him a steaming cup of coffee. "Take a load off your feet," she said. "It won't be long."

Alex cupped the coffee with both hands, his elbows resting on the table. It was pleasant here in the kitchen since she had come. The sun shone through the window and the big calico cat that usually bunked down by the cookhouse was sunning herself on the outside ledge. While he drank his coffee, Katherine busied herself at the cupboard, making an occasional comment to herself like she always did when she was preoccupied. She was quick-footed and as energetic with this as everything else she did. He had never noticed before how Katherine was as proper here, in the kitchen, as she was anyplace else, wanting everything to be done in a neat, orderly fashion with as much decorum as possible.

"You might as well stop begging. I'm not going to give you a bite until breakfast is over."

Alex looked up to see who Katherine was talking to. The calico cat was standing now, watching Katherine through the window. "How long has this been going on?"

"You mean with the cat?"

He nodded. "She seems to have taken up residence here while I was gone."

"I suppose she has. I made the mistake of feeding her one afternoon. She's been here ever since."

"She'll probably stay, too, as long as you keep feeding her."

"I hope so. I like her. It's nice to have animals about. That's one of the things I miss..." She caught herself, snatching a quick look at him then looking away.

It hadn't occurred to him before now that Katherine might miss anything about the home and life she'd left behind, but once the thought crossed his mind, he chastised himself once again for being an unfeeling brute. Of course she would miss things she had been around all her life. He suffered bouts of homesickness didn't he? "What else do you miss?"

Her hands were still busy, her words flowing with her movement as naturally as two rivers coming together. "Just farm life in general, I guess. You know, things like that big old barn with its corncrib and hayloft; my garden, the early morning chores." She looked wistfully at the ceiling for a moment, then went back to work. "I'd be putting up pumpkins and winter squash right now, and watching Clovis and the milk cow put on winter fat. The cornfield would be drenched in sunlight and yellow as a little girl's hair. The hay would all be cured and the hayloft filled, the rest stacked in the fields. And the creek..." Her voice broke. "I suppose it would be running full after the fall rains. What I'm trying to say is, I miss the familiarity, the sense of belonging, of knowing the names of all the plants and trees, the wildlife, the history of the land around me." Her hands had been busy kneading biscuit dough, but they were still now. She gazed out the window, as if the sight that greeted her wasn't the towering barrier of redwoods, but the gentle rolling hills of Limestone County. "This land," she was saying, "it's quite awesome to a farm girl like me. There's so much to learn. And I'm not sure where to start."

He stood, the scraping of the chair forlorn, like the distant cry of a coyote. Katherine turned her head to watch him as he walked to the stove and picked up the big enamel pot and poured himself another cup. "I'd say you've made a pretty good start already. You haven't been here two months, yet you've gained the respect of every lumberjack around here. And you know a lot more about lumbering in that time than I would've thought you could pick up in a year."

As they stood there, separated by the distance of that great kitchen, he with his coffee cup, she with her hands covered with biscuit dough, the silence seemed to close upon them. Katherine looked at him, thinking he was the only thing familiar about this foreign place, and yet, in a way, he was a stranger too. For the briefest moment another little wave of homesickness came over her. Her eyes misted and she sniffed a time or two. But she reproached herself for giving in to a moment of weakness. She thought of the times when she was a young girl with pigtails that hung below her waist, and how she would sit in the schoolroom, her feet crossed and tucked beneath her bench, her head resting in her hands as she stared at the side of Alexander Mackinnon's face, the girlish giddiness that swept over her when he turned and, catching her look, gave her a wink. And, like a woman, she remembered the pain of knowing she had lost him to her sister, and how God in his infinite grace and wisdom had given this wonderful man back to her. Not his affections, for she wasn't fool enough to think she had won that part of him yet. *In due time, Katherine. All in due time.* She felt the moment of retrospection and weakness pass, for there was within her a lust for adventure and a conquering spirit, patiently suppressed during her years of hard work on the farm; a lust for adventure and a conquering spirit that perfectly matched that of the man God had chosen to be her mate. God had given her the opportunity. What she did with it was up to her. She could hear her mother say, *God gives us the milk, Katherine. He doesn't furnish the pail.*

She gave the dough another punch or two, then picked up the tin, cutting nice fat circles in the thick dough. Moving to the oven, she removed the pan, seeing the fat had melted. She dipped the biscuits in the fat, first one side then the other, then shoved the pan into the oven and shut the door.

While the biscuits baked, she sliced two rounds of ham and put them on to fry. When the ham was done, she made redeye gravy, scrambled six eggs, and gave the grits simmering at the back of the stove another stir. By that time the biscuits were a golden brown and she buttered them liberally, then filled a plate fit for a lumberjack and carried it to the table. "Eat it while it's hot," she said to him before turning away to clean up the mess.

She cleaned up the kitchen, but it was only an excuse to watch him eat. Lord, there was something satisfying about that that made her feel as full and happy as if she'd been on a two-day fast and just eaten her first big meal. But soon the kitchen was tidy, and Alex had eaten his fill. "Well," he said, coming to his feet and picking his hat up off the table where he'd placed it when they came in. "I guess I'd better get to work before this kind of treatment begins to feel too good and the men start accusing me of getting soft."

She looked at the hard-muscled body and said, "That's something no one could ever accuse you of, Alex Mackinnon."

He had made it as far as the door, then turned. "Oh, I don't know," he drawled, "I've been known to show my soft side from time to time."

Once again they were separated by the length of the kitchen, brought together by the look in their eyes as if they both knew what was happening here, both felt a little awkward and shy. The calico meowed and arched her back, rubbing it along the window. Alex smiled and said, "Looks like she's ready for that bite you promised her."

"She's always ready."

"A good trait for a woman to have," he said, then slipped through the door.

She watched him leave, his words hammering like an echo in the back of her head. "I've been known to show my soft side from time to time."

There had been a time in the past, when their friendship was like a strong link between them and Katherine would have laughed and said something like, "Only when you want something."

But this wasn't the past and she didn't feel like laughing. As far as she was concerned, Alex never wanted anything—at least not from her. She went to the table and picked up his coffee cup, holding it in her hands and staring at the spot where he had placed his lips. She clutched the cup in both hands savoring the closeness of something still warm from his touch, then she pressed it to her chest as if to ease the bittersweet pain that lodged there. *Oh, Alex. Alex. Alex. Alex.* She closed her eyes and dropped her head down, the cup still pressed against her.

The back door rattled and she opened her eyes at the exact moment Alex stepped inside. "Alex..." She lowered the cup, her composure slipping into place. "Did you forget something?"

"No... yes." He looked like a man who had been imprisoned for years and had just been released. For several minutes he stood there not knowing if he should speak or retreat. Finally he said, "I had breakfast on the ship. I just wanted you to know that."

"I know," Katherine replied softly.

He looked like he was searching for words and she felt his discomfort so intensely she wished she could help him. She had seen this same confused expression on his face so many times when he and Karin had quarreled and he had come to her to talk things over, telling her how he wished Karin had her ease of understanding, her gentle compassion. She felt as if he wanted more than just her understanding, her compassion, wanted it, but didn't know how to go about getting it. How many times had she seen a newborn calf that seemed overwhelmed with the prospect of coming to its feet that first time, and how many times had she given it a nudge or two to get everything rolling?

"Was there anything else?" she asked.

He seemed so relieved for the question that she almost laughed. "Yes," he said, almost leaping with the response. "I'm going up to the higher elevations to scout for the areas where we'll be doing our next cutting. It won't be much of an outing, but if you'd like to come..."

Happiness lit her face. "Oh, Alex, I'd love it. I've been dying to see what it looks like on the other side of the mountain."

He laughed. "It looks pretty much like this side, I'm afraid." He looked at her, his eyes going over her from head to foot. "It'll be colder up there, you'll have to dress warmly, and we'll be going by horseback."

"I'll find something to wear," she said, thinking how happy she would be if he wore exactly what he had on; the tight buff breeches and blue muslin shirt that pulled the color of his eyes from his tan face. His thumbs were hooked in his belt loops.

They stood there, this new awareness of each other suspended between them. She had wanted this for so long, wanted him to notice her, to think about her, to include her in his life. Before, he seemed so distant it didn't really matter what she did or said, but now things were different and she felt the pressure of it mounting.

He watched her looking so white and still in her dark green dress with the white collar and cuffs, her hair tied back like a young girl's with a green satin bow. He saw how her eyes widened and she moistened her lips as she stared at him with some sort of expression he could only liken to wonder, as if he were undergoing some sort of transformation right before her very eyes.

Their eyes met. Awareness of each other hovered over them, Katherine neither feeling ashamed nor looking away, for she felt no shame over the way she felt for him. She had loved him too long and too well to undergo simpering schoolgirl shyness now. He must have felt the same way. "I've always wondered what you would look like with your hair down," he said. "Take it down, Katherine. Now."

Her hands went up to the bow in her hair, giving it a yank, the emerald satin ribbon trailing over her shoulder as she lowered her hands and released it, letting it flutter to the ground. The heavy mahogany strands of hair fell about her face, a deep wave arched over her cheek. She did not move. She dared not breathe, as he took first one step, and then another and another, each step well directed and deliberate, until he was standing before her. For a long time he stood looking down at her in the same hungry way she was looking at him, drinking in every feature of a face he knew so well, yet didn't know at all. After a long look he lazily lifted one hand and brought it up to the side of her face, threading his fingers through the heavy weight of her hair and dragging them through it, bringing its incredible length forward and over her shoulder, his knuckles grazing her breast. "You always did have such beautiful hair."

Beneath the warmth of his knuckles, her chest rose and fell with each increasing breath. "It feels like heavy satin," he said, "and smooth as silk." His eyes dropping to where his knuckles rested still. "There too, I would imagine."

He leaned forward, his lips grazing her forehead. "Time," he said softly, "never seems to be on my side." His mouth moved lower, in no apparent hurry to rush the scattered kisses that led eventually to her mouth.

"I could be trite and say we had the rest of our lives," she said between kisses.

"You shouldn't be saying things in the middle of the kitchen, in the middle of the day that give a man ideas," he said.

"Mackinnon," she said dreamily, "if I

thought it would give you ideas, I'd serve you nothing but tipsy cake."

"You get a humorous streak at the damndest times," he said nuzzling the softest, sweet-smelling place just below her ear.

"It was necessity, not choice," she said, pulling away from him and turning toward the back door. "In case you couldn't hear, someone is knocking at the door." She opened it and in popped Wong, a load of wood in his arms.

As Wong gave them a look and crossed the room to the wood box, Alex joined Katherine at the door. "Can you be ready to leave in an hour?"

She nodded, watching him step outside. "I'll be ready," she said, but he had already closed the door.

True to his word, he came for her in an hour. She had dressed warmly, layering her clothing, bringing her old cape along for the colder weather of the higher altitudes. She followed him outside where the horses were tied. He helped her mount, then rode ahead to speak to Adrian, who was standing outside the bunkhouse talking to Halfpint. A moment later, Halfpint stepped off the porch, walking away from them. She waved to Adrian as Alex turned his horse back toward her. Adrian waved back, giving her a warm smile and sticking his thumb up in the air, like he was giving her the go ahead. She nodded and laughed, feeling the brisk air and warm sunshine, thinking she couldn't remember ever being so happy.

Alex caught up to her and for the first half hour she rode beside him, listening to him talk about his life since he'd left Texas: the goldfields, the lumbering industry, his desire to return to Texas one day.

"I had no idea you wanted to go back," she said. Already she felt the knot of dread tightening in her stomach. Home. She thought of it often. She missed it of course. But home meant something different to her now than it did before. Home was where Karin was. She didn't want to think about going home until she felt secure with Alex's feelings for her.

"I never intended to spend the rest of my life up here. Adrian always figured I'd change my mind, but I don't think so. There's no point in making that decision now. I've got plenty of time. It'll take a lot of money to buy the kind of land I want, to build the kind of future I've always dreamed of. Right now it's a dream. Nothing more." He kicked his horse and turned up a steep embankment.

She followed him, her horse falling behind his because the trees were thicker now, the terrain rougher, making it necessary to go single file. "Well, like you said, it's a ways off," she said.

He didn't get to say anything else because his horse began acting up. Katherine reined in, giving him plenty of room to bring the mare under control, which judging from the looks of things, might be some time. Finally, Alex had taken all he was going to take from this cranky old mare, and he whopped her a good one up beside the head. "Stubborn Old Bitch," he said.

"Alex! How awful of you to call her that."

"Why shouldn't I? Old Bitch is her name."

"I'm afraid to ask the name of mine."

One wallop must have been enough, because Old Bitch was behaving herself now. When she had settled down, Alex shifted in the saddle enough to look back at the horse she was on. "I think that's the one they call One Speed."

"One Speed?"

"Slow," he said.

"Good," Katherine said. "It can't be slow enough for me."

He reached the top and pulled up, watching her as she pulled up beside him. "What about you? How do you feel about going back home?"

"I've always felt I could be happy anywhere," she said.

"You could see yourself going back then?"

She tried to smile. "I suppose I can see myself going wherever you go."

It was almost like her words surprised him, as if he had forgotten that one glaring fact: they were married. "Of course," he said. "Well, come on. We've got some rough riding ahead, but it's beautiful country—like nothing you've ever seen."

He was right on both counts. By the time he reached a high ridge and pulled up, dismounting and coming to help her down, she felt as if she had been riding a mountain goat instead of a horse. She was glad for his assistance when she dismounted. If it hadn't been for Alex's strong arms, she would have fallen the moment her feet touched the ground.

When her legs steadied, he led her along a trail deeply cushioned by fallen hemlock needles. The trail ran along a cliff edge and when they reached a grove of statuesque pines they stopped. Katherine stood a few feet from the edge of the cliff, looking down at the foothill slopes robed in redwoods and firs they had ridden across. "This must be how Moses felt," she said, "when he first glimpsed the promised land." She inhaled deeply. "Up here the air is sharp and fresh and clear. You can't smell the sawdust and the sea. It's hard to imagine it's been here forever. Everything seems so new. So untouched."

"Look over there. It seems we're being watched."

She stood beside him for a time watching a tawny colored squirrel, his tail arched over his back like a jaunty feather in a lady's hat. The squirrel watched them for a minute, then apparently bored, he stood on his hind legs, nibbling at something he held in his front paws.

They left the horses tied and walked along the trail. Often Katherine would run ahead to examine a tiny mountain stream, or a stone overgrown with moss. "Oh, Alex, look!" She'd stop and point at something she found and he'd stop and look in the direction she was pointing to see a deer or a wolf running across the slopes below. Other times she'd drop down and exclaim, "Look at this? Have you ever seen anything like it?" He'd come up behind her and she'd turn, her face angled up to see his, her hands cupping a pinecone, or the branch of a strange plant she'd never seen. Once she'd come running back to him, grabbing his hand and pulling him up the trail with her. "It's a bear! It's a bear! I've never seen a real one, but I know it's a bear."

He laughed. "Yes, it's a bear, and I'm mighty glad we've got that ravine and river between us and it. It's a grizzly."

"But it's beautiful. Look at it! It's standing on its hind legs."

"It's picked up our scent."

"It must be six feet tall... or more."

"More," he said.

As he watched her run from discovery to discovery with the awe and enthusiasm of a child, he found himself enchanted with her.

His reflection was broken when Katherine found a miniature forest of hemlock seedlings nursed and nurtured in the rotting log of a tree toppled by age, disease, or perhaps just cold, hard weather. And then her attention was drawn away by a spider's dew-dappled web that looked somewhat bedraggled. "I suppose the weather has already gotten cold enough up here for the spiders to have laid their eggs and died."

"And it's going to be getting colder for us too." He glanced at the sky. "It'll be getting dark in a few hours. We'd better start back down."

She walked to the edge of the trail and

looked out one last time. Below, everything spread out like autumn's green and gold tapestry, aloof and distant from human intrusion. She hugged her arms around her waist, lifting her face into the first sharp stirring of wind. "This is what I needed to see," she said softly. "This, more than anything helps me understand what I'm doing here." He came to stand beside her but she didn't look at him. "I would love to go there sometime, to see what it's like just over that big mountain there. But just seeing it makes me understand just how lucky we really are. Do you realize how few people have ever looked at anything so beautiful?"

He didn't answer because he knew she didn't expect him to. The view was spectacular with the afternoon mist already cloaking the distant peaks. But his eyes were drawn from nature's beauty to one of human form. From his place beside her he watched her lose herself in the wonder of what she was seeing, and in a way, he was doing the same, for his thoughts were spinning backwards to a lazy summer afternoon on the banks of Tehuacana Creek when he'd taught her to fish with blood bait.

He shook his head, wondering why he reflected on times they had spent together in the past. "We'd better be going," he said, hating as much as she to break the magic of the time they had shared.

She turned away, pulling her cloak around her. "I would love to come back up here in the spring, just to see it when everything is brand new."

"Maybe we could sneak away for a few days."

"Oh, could we, Alex? Could we?" Her voice was high and trilled and he couldn't help smiling at the face turned up to his. Without thinking, his hand came up and he touched her nose with his finger. "I think we could." Then he grinned. "We might find a nice river and I could teach you how to fish."

"And we could cook them over an open fire. I've heard that fish cooked over a campfire is some of the best eating around."

He laughed, finding he was enjoying her immensely. "It's not as glamorous as it sounds. You get burned fingers and cinders in your eyes, and your hair smells like smoke."

"I wouldn't care," she said.

And somehow he felt she really wouldn't.

They walked back down the trail toward the horses. "Do you think Old Bitch will be rested enough to give you trouble when we get back?"

The sound of his laughter rocked out across the mountaintops, and as she had always done, she thought it was the most beautiful sound she had ever heard. She stopped, her cheeks rosier than they had been a moment ago, her hands going to her hips as she glared at him. "You told me that was her name."

"It is."

"Then what's so funny?"

"Its just that I never expected you to belt

it out like that." He stepped closer, his hands coming out to take her arms. "There are times when I find you utterly adorable. You know that?"

"Is this one of those times?"

"Yes," he said. "I believe it must be because I'm having a hard time convincing myself that we need to hurry down this mountain."

"Why?"

"Because I keep wondering what it would be like to kiss you," he said quietly, "just kiss you and keep on kissing you and see where that led."

She wasn't sure how to take his teasing, for he had caught her off guard with that one. She tried to laugh, but did it weakly. "You'd find that rather shocking, I'm afraid. My lips are cold."

He drew her closer. "We could warm them up a little." He lowered his head, his lips brushing lightly across hers, his breath and the pattern of his lips warming her with their imprint. She was looking at him in much the same manner she had gazed out at the view only minutes before, a sort of wide-eyed look of wonder, her mouth slightly parted.

"Let's try that again."

An incredibly sweet sensation washed over her and she felt herself lean against him just as he kissed her. At first the touch of his lips was no more than the brush of a butterfly wing. He kissed her slowly, his mouth learning the shape and texture of her own, his breath learning to pace itself to her own. Slowly and with infinite patience he kissed her until she pulled back and placed her chilled fingers over his lips. "I think they're warm now," she said.

"But we can make them warmer." His body tensed, his arms tightening to draw her hard against him, the pressure of his chest like a warm caress against her breasts. "You feel so good," he said against her hair. "Maybe we can wait a while to go back down."

"I don't think that would be a good idea, Alex. I think we'd better go right now."

"Why? Aren't you enjoying yourself?"

"I was."

"I see," he said stiffly. "What's the matter? Can't you stand for me to get close to you?"

"It's not you I mind getting close, Alex. But I think that's a bear."

He pulled back, seeing her eyes were locked on something behind him and he whirled around, putting her behind him.

A dark shape was coming down the trail, still too far away to tell what it was exactly. "I think you may be right. Come on."

He grabbed her hand and hurried down the trail, pulling her with him. After a few minutes, they paused and turned, looking back up the trail. It was obvious it was a bear now, for it stood on its hind legs, its head in the air.

"It's picked up our scent," she said.

"Yes."

"It's not as big as the other bear."

"This one is a black bear, but they're not much fun to tangle with either."

The bear was still standing on its hind legs sniffing the air when they turned and hurried on down the trail. When they reached the horses, Alex helped Katherine mount. "You go on ahead."

Katherine urged One Speed forward, praying Old Bitch would behave herself, or at least wait until they had put more distance between themselves and the bear before she decided to misbehave. A moment later she heard Alex coming up behind her. "You can slow down now."

Katherine turned and looked at him. "I am slowed down. That's the only gait this horse knows."

He grinned, kicking Old Bitch to ease around her. "She'll probably move a little faster if she's following and not in the lead. We stayed longer than we should have. It may be dark before we get back."

"Can you find your way in the dark?"

"The horses can. We'll just give them their head."

Alex had been right. It was dark when they reached the logging camp. Adrian was just sitting down to dinner when they came in. "Glad you're back," he said. "I hate eating alone."

"Go ahead and eat," Alex said. "We need to clean up."

"That's all right. I don't mind waiting," said Adrian, smiling slowly when Alex shot him a hard look.

Katherine said, "Wong, I think I'll have dinner in my room. And put some water on to heat, will you? I've been dreaming of a nice hot bath for the past two hours."

Alex sat down at the table and watched her go, a frown on his face.

A wide grin split Adrian's face. "Well, here I thought it was just me you reserved those looks for, but I see it isn't. Did you have a nice outing, brother?"

"Adrian," Alex said harshly, "sometimes you don't know when to shut up." He rested his forehead in his palms, his elbows braced on the table.

Shut up. Adrian knew that was what Alex wanted him to do, but he also knew how much his brother needed a good shove now and then, just to get him off dead center. He sat in the chair across from Alex and waited him out, not speaking until Alex looked up. When Alex raised his head, Adrian went on speaking to Alex as he often did after dinner, bringing up the same topics of discussion they covered almost daily: about constructing a skid road to enable them to move more logs faster and from greater distances, or if it was a good idea to buy another gang saw, inefficient though they might be. Yet, even in discussing their routine subjects, Alex's mind seemed to switch around.

"Well? What do you think? Should we go for it?"

"Go for what?"

"Constructing a skid road... Alex, aren't you paying attention to anything I'm saying?"

"I'm listening."

"You may be listening, but your mind isn't on skid roads and gang saws, or even lumbering, for that matter."

"How would you know?"

"Because you haven't had a worthwhile idea since we went to San Francisco."

Alex slammed his hands down against the table so hard the lid on the sugar bowl rattled. "All right! So I haven't had a decent idea since San Francisco. So I don't have my mind on business. So what are you going to do about it? Give me another ultimatum? Don't think you can get away with threatening me as easily as you did before. I did what you wanted. I married her. Now, you can stay the hell out of my business."

With a rage that matched his brother's, Adrian said, "And what have you decided to do? Let her sit here for the rest of her life wondering why you married her if you never intended to make her your wife? Do you realize you spend more time talking to Wong than you do to her? Is it your plan to ignore her until she does what any normal woman would do and takes a lover?"

"And we both know who that would be, don't we?" Alex said.

"That's it, Alex. You continue to elude the problem by throwing obstacles in the road. Is that what you want to do? Discuss my sins? Katherine is your wife. Why don't we talk about yours? Why haven't you taken her to bed?"

A chill penetrated the room that had nothing

to do with the weather. When Alex spoke at last, each word was isolated and frozen, thrown with the sharpness of an icicle. "That is none of your business."

"You're a fool. The real tragedy in this situation isn't the fact that you married a woman you didn't love. It's in your refusal to love the woman you married."

"You think it's easy, don't you? All I have to do is say I love her, and it happens."

"It doesn't happen because you won't let it. Don't examine your feelings too closely, or you may find you care more for her than you thought. And now that I've gone this far, I might as well go one step more and tell you the reason Katherine is still here isn't because she's too big a fool to see what you're doing, it's because you keep her waiting by giving her little insignificant doses of hope. You don't want to be married to her, but you care enough to keep her tied to you. You can't go on like this anymore, Alex. It's time to fish, or cut bait."

"You don't know what in the hell you're talking about."

"Don't I?" Adrian leaned back in his chair. "You don't want her to leave because you want her. Even when you were lusting after Karin in Texas, I saw it. Back then, you covered a lot with a blanket called friendship. Now you don't even bother to do that. Every time you look at her your body stiffens harder than a railroad spike. You've got it bad, like a sickness. You look at her with enough heat in your eyes it's a wonder you don't turn to ash. But she's Karin's sister and not Karin, and somehow you can't forgive her for that, no matter how much you really might care. You could have at least taken her to bed *once* after you married her, except it was more important to punish her than it was to see if there might be some feeling there. So many times I've called you a bastard. But I see I was wrong. You're worse than a bastard. A bastard would have at least consummated the marriage before he let it grow cold."

"A bastard would have told her the truth and never married her in the first place. It's time you remembered something. The reason we have a problem here, dear brother, is because you intervened and tried to play God."

Adrian looked suddenly tired. "You don't know how many times I've told myself that. And if I could undo it, I would." He stood, pushing his chair in. "I guess there's only one thing to do."

"And what is that."

"I'll tell her the truth. I'll tell her it's all my fault. I'll take her to San Francisco and get her a lawyer so she can get the marriage annulled. And then I'll put her on a ship and send her back to Texas."

Alex was around the table so fast, Adrian didn't even see him move. His hand uncoiled like a striking snake to grab Adrian's shirt and shove him back against the wall. "*If* and when Katherine is told the truth, it will be me that does the telling. Don't think I don't see through your righteous offer. Katherine is *my* wife. I mean to keep it that way."

Adrian began to laugh, his arm coming around Alex's neck as he wrestled him playfully across the room. "Damn me for a fool, Alex. I thought you'd never see the light and say so."

"I ought to beat you raw as a piece of liver."

They scuffled for a minute or two, then Adrian said, "I'm too tired for any more of this. Let's go have a drink."

"You go ahead. I'll join you in a minute."

"Where are you going?"

"I've got to put the horses up."

"You aren't going off to sulk, are you?"

"I'm a little old for that, don't you think?"

Up went Adrian's hands in surrender. "Please don't make me answer that."

"Get out of here," Alex said, picking up a biscuit and throwing it at him.

Adrian darted through the door into the great room just as the biscuit passed him.

Upstairs, Katherine had just finished her meal and bath. Once she was out of the tub, she realized just how cold her room was. She would have to go downstairs and sit in front of the fire to dry her hair, but that didn't bother her. The thought of sitting on one of the thick rugs and brushing her hair dry in front of a crackling fire sounded like the perfect way to end a perfect day. She wrapped a towel around her head, then put on her gown and wrapper.

The great room was empty when she went down, and she had no more than settled herself—none too comfortably, since she'd been on a horse all day—on the rug in front of the fire when Adrian walked in. He went to a long table that stood along the wall and poured two drinks out of the decanter. Crossing the room, he offered one to her.

"No thank you."

"Take it. It'll warm you and relax your muscles. I imagine you're going to be pretty sore tomorrow."

"I'm already sore," she said, taking the drink. "What is it?"

"Brandy." He smiled at the face she made when she sniffed it. "Go ahead. Take a sip. It'll cure what ails you."

"It smells like it could remove paint."

"We save the cheaper stuff for that," he said, moving to the chair across from her and sitting down, his legs stretched out in front of him.

Katherine took a sip, coughed for a spell and announced she was off liquor for good. "It tastes terrible."

But Adrian merely laughed and told her to sip a little more. "After a few sips it'll start tasting pretty good. Before long, you'll feel like it's been years since you've ever seen a horse."

She eyed the contents of the glass skeptically.

"Katherine, you've known me for a long time, haven't you?"

"Why are you asking me that? Weren't you there?"

He laughed. "Will you stop yapping and drink your brandy?" He sighed. "Trust me."

"Those two words have gotten more women in trouble."

"Would you stop being so obstinate and drink it? Even for someone as mild mannered as me, it's a little trying at times to further the knowledge of someone who's squirming like a worm in hot ashes."

"I was thinking about having a cup of hot tea."

"I've already told you once. Will you listen to what I'm saying this time? Take a few more sips. It gets better with each one."

She picked up the glass and downed the contents.

"Jumping Jehoshaphat! I said *sip it*." He shook his head, going for the decanter. "I can see I've got my work cut out for me." He filled the glass again. "Now, let's try this again. Pick the glass up Katherine, and take a *sip*."

She took a sip, just to placate him, hoping he'd tire of his lessons and go on to something else. She put the glass down and unwound the towel from her head and began drying the ends briskly. "I've never seen your hair down or wet. It's longer than I imagined."

"It's too long. I need to cut it off some."

"I like it the way it is," Alex said, walking up behind them. Katherine dipped her head to look at him from beneath her arm. He didn't look at her. But he did look at Adrian. "Comfortable?" he asked, looking at Adrian.

"Remarkably so," Adrian replied.

"Is that brandy?" Alex asked.

"There's more on the side table," Adrian replied. "Want me to pour you a glass?"

"I'll get it myself." He looked at the glass sitting next to Katherine.

"She hasn't got the hang of it yet," Adrian said.

Alex didn't say anything, he just stood there looking at the glass, then turned away.

He poured himself a glass and returned to the fire, taking a chair to one side and a little behind Adrian. Katherine watched him take a sip of brandy. His hair was damp and he had on fresh clothes. She wondered if he had taken a bath. Alex took another sip of brandy and Katherine followed suit. Then she turned back to drying her hair.

The fire snapped, sending a shower of sparks up the chimney. Katherine shifted her position, sitting on one side, her legs curled back behind her. Once the excess moisture was out of her hair, she removed the towel and began brushing it, leaning her head forward and brushing the hair over her head.

A moment later she got up. "Where are you going?" Alex asked. "Why don't you stay down here for a while longer?"

"I'm going to the kitchen to put on some water for tea. Can I get you anything?"

Alex shook his head. She looked at Adrian. "Nothing for me, thanks."

They watched her leave. "Her hair is the color of hot coals," Adrian said and Alex shot him a smoldering look. But that didn't deter

Adrian. "But it's got much more life and fire in it than mere coals. It's easy to see why a woman's hair has been called her crowning glory."

"That's enough," Alex said.

The cast-iron undertones of those two words would have been enough to send an ordinary person into concern for his safety, but Adrian, who was used to such chilling words from his brother, simply laughed. "So, the stress of the situation is finally wearing even your thick hide thin in places. I must hand it to you though. I never thought you'd last this long, especially knowing you've cared for her a lot longer than you've apparently realized." Adrian leaned forward in his chair and fixed his eyes on his brother. "You *have* realized that by now, haven't you."

"Adrian, I'm warning you."

Adrian leaned back and brought the tips of his fingers together. "Yes, I hear, but you know how your threats have always terrified me into doing exactly what you ask."

The room grew silent save the occasional snap and sputter of the fire. Katherine came back into the room. As she approached the fireplace, she could feel the silence stretch uncomfortably. She glanced at Alex and found him contemplative, his gaze a bit melancholy as he stared steadily at the flames leaping behind her. She sat down and looked at Adrian, curious at the cat-that-ate-the-cream expression on his face. *What is going on here?*

Feeling a bit uneasy, she looked away and

gave her attention to her hair, but she soon found her calm interrupted by the feeling she was being watched. Stealing a second look at Alex, she observed him for a moment, realizing that his brooding gaze wasn't directed at the flames leaping behind her at all. He was, in fact, staring directly at her.

Alex made no effort to conceal the blatant gaze that raked over her to a breathtaking degree. She was aware of each and every part of her body he touched with his eyes, feeling it as acutely as if it had been the palm of his hand. From her head to her feet, he looked her over, stopping at all the points in between. The possession she saw in his eyes was almost physical. Her body grew warm, her breathing coming strong and slow.

Katherine had picked up the brush, but she wasn't using it. She looked back at him, the brush gripped tightly in her hand, and still suspended in midair. Her surprised mouth was slightly parted, and in her mesmerized gaze was an expression of wondering reverence tinged with apprehension. Not being in on what had been happening between Alex and Adrian, Katherine found Alex's expression difficult to understand, but Adrian, apparently, was having no problem. He came to his feet and stood there for a moment looking first at his brother, and then at his brother's wife. There was an oddly shrewd smile in his eyes. "I know the Bible says it's better to marry than to burn," he said, walking quietly from the room. "I had no idea you could do both."

CHAPTER
NINETEEN

Katherine felt Adrian's departure had signaled a change in things between herself and Alex, the beginning of...Something was all she could think to call it. *Something, but what?*

The disturbing intentness of Alex's gaze compelled Katherine to look away. She ran the brush slowly through her hair a couple of times, brushing with more vigor when she heard him rise and come toward her. He stopped next to her, his boots brushing against her leg. The indrawn breath was a natural reflex to such a rash display as actually allowing his boot to touch her leg. But she did not look up.

Her body jerked at the thud of a log tossed into the fire, the hungry leap of flames and responsive shower of sparks. The silence, the strain was a painful thing that pulled at the very heart of her, making each breath she drew enter her lungs like a sharp slicing blow with a knife. She waited, drawing the brush through heir hair with deliberate slowness, waiting, waiting. *Do something, say something,* her mind screamed. *Don't keep me waiting like this.*

She listened to the scrape of his boots as he turned and walked back to his chair. Frustrated, she picked up the rhythm with the brush until it matched the reckless pounding of her heart.

She had never thought of tension as a palpable thing. Hoping to ease the strain that pulled at both of them, Katherine said, "I shall never forget the things I saw today. I don't know how to thank you."

Immediately she felt the heat of his gaze. "Don't you?" The sound of something as basic as the brush of fabric as he crossed his legs grated on her nerves. She felt like screaming. "I think you misjudge yourself," he said, his voice low and throbbing. "I think you know very well how to thank me."

Somewhere above them a door closed, but neither of them acknowledged the distraction. She wondered at her own expression when she saw the normally relaxed features of Alex's face were hard and drawn in cynical appraisal.

Stop looking at me like that.

Stop denying what we're about.

"It's getting late," she said.

He glanced at his watch. "It's half past nine."

He took a sip of brandy, swirling the amber liquid in the glass before putting it down. *You're seeing the man where you once saw the boy,* she thought. *You're seeing a husband where you once saw a friend. Is that what frightens you, Katherine?* She laid the brush aside and for lack of anything else to do, she began plaiting her hair.

"I like your hair that way. Leave it down... at least for tonight."

At least for tonight. Her heart leaped at the thought of it. Dryness clawed at her throat. She drew her knees up to her chest, hoping to ease the wildness of a heart pounding so fast it felt close to exploding from her chest. Unable to take the tension, the strain any longer, she sprang to her feet. "This is ridiculous!"

"I agree. Especially when there is one thing we could do that would put us both at ease."

Her nostrils flared with understanding. "You are enjoying this, aren't you?"

The fire behind her was hot. But the look in his eyes was hotter. "Not half as much as I could," he said.

"I'm going to bed," she said angrily.

He let her words ride until she gathered up her towel and brush and started away. "Katherine."

She was no more than a foot from him when he spoke her name. She paused and looked at him, anger still in her voice. "What?"

"Come here."

"I'm not your horse."

He chuckled. "I know that. If you were, I'd take you for a ride you'd never forget." Then he added, "I may anyway."

"Try it," she said, backing away and clenching the hairbrush like it was a weapon, "and you'll be sorry."

He was on his feet now, taking one step for each of hers, but his were bigger. "Will you stop this?" she said, seeing how he was gaining on her. "This isn't the way it's supposed to be done!"

He almost choked on that one. "Are you an expert then?" He went on smoothly, "Assuming we're both talking about the same thing, why don't you enlighten me? Just how is *it* supposed to be done?"

"Don't you know?"

He laughed. "It's been a long time and my memory seems to have failed me. Why don't you give me a hint."

She eyed him for a moment. "Oh, never mind. Why should we stick to convention when absolutely *nothing* about this marriage is conventional. Sometimes I don't know if I'm married or not!"

"Why is that?"

"Because I don't *feel* married." She was feeling good and frustrated now.

"Katherine, come here."

"Why?"

"Because I want you to."

"I know that, Alex. But why do you want me to?"

"Do you want me to be specific?"

She nodded. *Tell me you love me, Alex. Tell me now.*

"Because I want to make love to you." He saw the sudden flare of disappointment across her lovely features and understood the cause of it. "I want you to feel married, Katherine."

"Well, I don't, and if the past is any indication, I probably won't. And on top of that, the way you're going about everything..." she said angrily, "it just isn't done this way! You don't tease a person until their brain is addled." She remembered how he had said,

Because I want to make love to you, and she got mad all over again. "*And* you don't schedule it by appointment!"

A slow, reluctant smile tugged at those sensual lips of his, and he shook his head. "What would you have me do? Send you to your room to put on a matronly gown and lie stiffly in the bed, agonizing over the brutalities your husband will soon commit against your body?" He stepped closer, close enough to reach out and touch her, his hands coming out to take the towel and brush from her and drop them to the floor. Katherine's heart began to hammer in expectation. His hand came up to her face, his finger lightly tracing the curve of her jaw. "Is that what you want, sweet Katherine? Would you prefer to go to your room now and wait? *That's* the way it's *conventionally* done, then when I come to you, you'll be stiff and scared and dry as a bone. And that will give me the opportunity to show you that your husband is the animal all the ladies at church assured you he would be. But I'll stick to convention, keeping the room dark so I won't ease your fears by allowing you to see how much I desired you, or so I won't see if the way I've imagined you is the way you really look. I'd be sure to not raise your gown any higher than necessary, or touch you, or hold you, or kiss you, or do any of the things I wanted to do. I wouldn't want to show you my feelings and ease what was to come." His hand was behind her neck now, his other hand against the flat of her back. He pulled her against him, his lips brushing her mouth as he spoke. "Oh, I could do these things according to convention, all right. I could *assert my conjugal rights* as impersonally as a stallion mounts a mare. But I won't do that Katherine, because I'd leave you bleeding and hurt and vowing to never submit to such savagery again." His hand was rubbing her back, the warmth of it penetrating her stiffness like liniment, the steady current of his breath brushing her face like assurance. "I'll apologize now, if making you my wife isn't all you hoped it would be. I can't make you any promises that it won't hurt. And I can't promise it'll be what you've been led to expect. But I will promise you this, I won't leave your bed, Katherine, until I've heard you beg for more."

He swept her into his arms and carried her up the stairs. Her mind hammered with indecision. She had made the statement that she wouldn't make love with him until she shared his room, something she did not do. Not a woman to back off her word, no matter how much she wanted Alex, she did some quick thinking. With a soft, feminine sigh, she put her arms around his neck and whispered, "I've decided to move into your room now."

The sound of his laughter bounded up the stairs ahead of them. Katherine was both thrilled and mortified; thrilled that the moment she had dreamed of for so long was about to become a reality, mortified at the thought that she might be too much of a burden, that he might be winded by her weight. Her weight?

There's something wrong with a woman that thinks about something like her weight at a moment like this. Get your mind on what's happening here, Katherine. I'd rather not, came a weak little voice inside her head.

As it turned out, Katherine didn't have to remind herself of a thing. The moment he set her on her feet beside the bed, Alex took care of everything. His hands were at her throat now, his thumbs tilting her head up so he could see her face. She saw so much in those eyes, desire, of course, and a feeling he was asking something of her. But what?

"Are you afraid?" he asked.

She released a long-held breath. "No, relieved."

"Relieved?" His eyes never left her face. "You shouldn't be feeling relieved now, Katherine." Then his voice went soft and throaty. He trailed a finger down the length of her throat. "That comes later."

She drew a sudden quick breath, conscious of the wild beating of her heart prompted by the smoldering look of need in his eyes. "Well, I'm sorry if I've jumped the gun on you, but you asked me and I'm telling you, I'm relieved. And you would be too, if you'd been waiting for this moment as long as I have."

He threw back his head and laughed. Then he looked at her with humor, warm and infinite, in his eyes. He had never seen her more adorable than she was at this moment, or more desirable. She felt the vibrations of his laughter. She had never heard a more beautiful sound. He drew her closer, his words fluttering the hair around her face. "Do you know what happens now?"

"Of course I do. I grew up on a farm, remember. I've watched animals..."

"Dear Lord! I don't know which is worse... ignorance, or the barnyard kind of knowledge." His hands tightened on her arms. "Listen to me Katherine, try to forget everything you think you know. No matter what you've observed, it isn't like that between a man and a woman. I'm not going to attack you from behind."

He had thought his words would embarrass her, or even bring a flare of anger, but her reaction surprised him. She smiled up at him, then dropped her head against his chest, the sound of her laughter bubbling up and washing over him like a free-flowing spring. "I don't know if I'm relieved or disappointed."

He dropped his head against hers, the sound of his rocking laughter muffled in the thickness of her hair. This was a side of her he never knew existed. He knew, of course, that Katherine had a sense of humor, but to exhibit it at a time like this considering she had never been intimate with a man. It was both unexpected and rare. Here was a woman that could match him stroke for stroke, word for word. For an instant he held her so tightly she thought her bones would crack. Then he was whispering inaudible things laced with the groaning of her name just before he smothered her with a kiss that was warm, hard, and demanding.

Katherine was in awe as much as she was in love. Here she was, married at last to the man of her dreams, being held in his arms and wanting him as much as he wanted her. Grateful and frustrated that he had shown such kindness, such patience, she pulled her mouth away far enough to say, "Alex, are you going to make love to me now?"

"Yes Katherine, I am."

"At last," she said with a satisfied sigh. Her smile hovered like a luxuriant haze, only to vanish with a soft, shuddering gasp as his hands came up to loosen the tie on her wrapper, sending it to the floor. A moment later her gown followed.

If anyone had ever told her she would be standing bare as a scraped carrot in front of a man and he fully clothed, she would have thought the least reaction she could have expected from herself would be to dive into the bed and bury herself under the covers. So it was as much a surprise to her as it was to him when she looked at him and said, "I love you, Alex."

"I know," he said. "I guess in a way, I've always known." His eyes traveled the length of her. His mouth went dry. Even in the dimness he could see she was small and delicate with a waist his hands would go around, yet her hips were wide enough to receive a man, her breasts full and generous and perfectly formed. And her legs were long and slender, yet strong enough to hold a man. "I knew you would be beautiful," he said.

He let his gaze move back to her face as his hands came up to lift the heavy length of her hair over her shoulders to fall like a curtain over her breasts. The warmth of his mouth found the most sensitive spot of her neck and she curled against him, fragile as a flower. He kissed her, not with a wild urgency, but with a slow-burning heat that seemed to grow hotter and hotter. While he seduced her with his mouth, his hands eased across her back, following the indentation of her spine to spread firmly across her hips. Then he was away from her, his hands coming up to the buttons of his shirt.

"No," she said, her hands coming up to push his aside. "Let me."

Delight sang through his veins, and he marveled at the open honesty of her. She lifted her eyes to his as her fingers nimbly slipped the buttons through, one by one, until she reached the waistband of his pants. Tugging, she freed his shirt, pushing it back from his shoulders and down his arms. When she reached for his pants, he pulled back, hopping first on one foot to remove his boot, and then on the other. "Now," he said, dropping the last boot to the floor, "where were we? Here?" he asked, drawing her to him and kissing her until she swayed against him.

A moment later he felt her hands on his chest, tentative at first, then growing bolder, slipping downward to stop at the button at his waist. Her movement was less confident and not as smoothly executed as it had been with his shirt, but she finished the job, pushing his pants down over his hips until he took over and pulled them from his body. When he was finished and as naked as she, she did as he had done, looking him over slowly from head to foot. "Oh Alex, you're the one who's beautiful."

He took her hand, drawing her with him to the bed where he threw back the covers. To ease the awkwardness of the moment he sat down, his hands holding hers, drawing her down with him as he lay back, until she was lying beside him. He held her close and kissed her slowly until he felt her relax, his hand showing her he knew all her secret places and knew them better than she.

Such wonderful things, hands. She had never imagined ten fingers could do so much, could evoke such a range of emotion. His lips buried in her hair, she held her breath when his fingertips delighted with weightless strokes the trembling skin of her throat and breasts. Suddenly his kiss was dissolving the living part of her and his wants became her wants, his needs, hers. Untutored and innocent, her hands were guided by a desire to please and be pleased, as something inexplicable guided her hands. Here arms enfolded him, one palm pressing with slow, easy movement the contours of his back, the other exploring the strength of his neck, then twisting into his hair as she strained to intensify their closeness and feel more acutely the pleasure of his beloved weight pressing her down. Never had she felt such desperation to feel so many things at once, to be all things, do all things, and to understand, at last, the mystery of love in its completeness.

And then it began to build, a spiraling heat that knew no end, filling her body, drawing upon the feel of his hands, the rasp of his harsh breathing against her ear. "Please Alex..."

Alex felt his body tense. Had he been moving too fast for her? Was she frightened? *Dear God, please don't let her be one of those.* His mind exploded with the thought of spending the rest of his life with a cold, passionless wife. His heart in his mouth, he whispered against the softness of her throat, "What, love? Tell me, Kath."

"Touch me," she whispered. "Touch me and keep on touching me."

Starbursts of delight sang through the tensely held muscles of his body and he felt himself relax in delight. "Where, sweetheart? Where does it give you pleasure? Here?" He touched her breasts with his mouth, delighting her, but she wanted more, much more. "Tell me, love."

"In all the places, Alex. The unravished places."

Her words were like music penetrating his soul and his body flowed outward in a rhapsody of enchantment. "My precious wife," he said and softly bit her neck.

He found the unravished places she was talking about, much to her delight, and with a queer sort of obedience, the desirous hand began touching her, first in the ravished places—her face, her neck, her breasts—touching her with a familiar assurance that was infinite and wily, beguiling her with both pleasure and promise. Yet the assurance was always there, the soft-spreading assurance that flamed within the center of her.

She lay perfectly still, hearing nothing but the tempestuous mating of breath mingling with breath, the sound of her own heart pounding in her ears. The softness of his words, the gentle touch of his hands whispered against her body as his hands came down to touch her, preparing the way. With a quiver of pleasure, she opened to him, and he touched the heat of her, sweeping her along in a drowsy, aching warmth of a drugged kind of sleep that unfolded like a flower into a world intense and powerful, bursting with vivid color.

And then he rolled, coming up to brace himself on one knee before he spread the way and eased his body between hers. How to describe it? It was like nothing she had ever known, the exquisite feel of warm, hungry flesh pressed against warm, hungry flesh. This man was her husband and she loved him with all her heart. And the rightness of it pleased her. She closed her eyes to savor the feel of it, opening them and looking deep into his eyes the moment she felt him between her legs. As he arched his body and entered her with one sure, swift stroke, her breath caught, then rode away on the current of her next words.

"There was never anything more right than this," she said. "Never."

For a moment he was still, swollen and quivering inside her. As he began to move, he kept hearing those words, understanding their meaning, knowing what she had said was true. There was a rightness to what had passed between them, a rightness that went far beyond the act of coupling. He fought the feeling, but his thoughts grew farther and farther apart. His body the authority now, he drifted on a rising swell that moved in a slow, helpless rhythm. He lured her from the sweet sleep, awaking her with a strange ripple of pleasure. One after another—rippling, rippling—the constant overlapping of gentle waves, then running and running, faster now, coming closer and closer together until they melted together into points of exquisite brilliance—intense, so intense until she convulsed with a wildness unknown to her, drawing him deeper into her, urging him on with untamed cries until she felt herself filled with him—and it came, a warm, liquid heat, that crested, then burst with all the force of the Pacific where it crashed against the craggy rocks of Humboldt Bay.

For a shattering of an instant, she knew, she knew! She knew the mystery, the spiraling awareness of what it felt like to be born. *Too beautiful, too beautiful!* her mind screamed out, trying to hold onto the moment, to stop the ebbing away of all the loveliness. She clung with a deeper tenderness to the man now bound to her forever, taking into her hand the beauty of his wilting penis, touching it as tenderly as she would a babe, understanding now its frailty, knowing for all time the power of its thrust. She began to cry softly.

"Angel-love, sweet Katherine, what's wrong? Have I hurt you?"

"It's too beautiful... too beautiful," she cried softly. "How can anything be too beautiful to hold onto?" He kissed her tears and said nothing, only rolled to his side, taking her with him, tucking her head against his chest, the curve of his throat cradling the top of her head, and she knew nothing but peace, exquisite peace.

Some time later, Katherine stretched like a cat awaking from a long nap in the sun, warm and satisfied, opening her eyes to a world of blinding color. Nothing would ever be the same for her.

"Hello," he said, the words vibrating against her ear like a hum coming from deep in his chest.

She lowered her voice a decibel or two and said in deep rumbling tones, "Hello yourself."

He smiled, kissing her forehead. "Tell me what you're thinking."

He felt her smile tickle the hairs of his chest. "I was thinking I'm glad that's over."

He pulled back and looked down at her, his face concerned, serious. "Was it that bad, that painful for you?"

"It was sort of like, Ouch! That felt wonderful!"

The bed rocked with his laughter. His arms came around her tightly and he hugged her to him. "You're unbelievable. You know that?"

"No, I'm honest."

"That's what I said, you're unbelievable. Your honesty is not only refreshing, it's unheard of. Now, tell me what you meant when you said you were glad that was over."

"I meant, I'm glad all this fuss about chastity and virginity is over. And I must say, I have been led down a merry, primrose path that led absolutely nowhere." She rolled away, coming up on her elbows, her face slightly above his. He had seen that look before. She was wound up tighter than an eight-day clock and ready to talk. He might as well settle in. He folded his arms behind his head and readied himself.

"Where, in heaven's name," she asked, "did all those bits of information I've had spoon-fed to me all these years come from?"

"What kind of facts?"

"Groundless ones," she said. "You know, silly things that women are always told about purity and holding themselves back for marriage. The way it was all presented, I expected something quite transforming... nothing short of a miracle...something like the parting of the Red Sea."

"Hmmm," he said with a laugh. "There could be a striking similarity there." He was laughing harder now. "You know, that adds a new dimension to an old story. I'm afraid

I'll never be able to listen to a sermon about the parting of the Red Sea without giving it a whole new perspective."

She smiled, looking down at him with such love in her eyes, a feeling of ripeness filling her and giving her absolute peace. She reached up and smoothed his hair, tucking the strands back in place, giving special attention to a cowlick that had a mind of its own. Then she traced the shape of his brows, his nose, his mouth. So hungry to learn everything about him, every little secret of his body, every detail. He closed his eyes, giving her license to roam at will, and she did.

When she sighed and rested her chin on her arms that were folded across his chest, he opened his eyes, content to simply look at her. She had unbelievable eyes, and Lord! what hair—past her waist, it was fragrant, silky, cool to the touch and now, wrapped around his body like a cocoon. Suddenly it struck him. She had a lovely face, a shapely body, and the most delightful openness and honesty he had ever seen assembled in one woman. Yet as far as he knew, there had never been a man in her life, at least no one serious. He found himself pleased as much as curious. "How come you never married?"

"Because I wasn't willing to settle for half a loaf."

"That kind of thinking is a bit risky, isn't it? You could have ended up with no loaf, like a leaf that waits too long to drop and finds itself frozen on the vine."

" 'If Winter comes, can Spring be far behind?' "

"Am I supposed to have heard that before?"

She nodded.

"Who said it? You?"

She laughed. "Apparently I remember the year we studied Shelley better than you do."

"You were always better than me at that sort of thing."

She trailed her fingers through the hair on his chest. "We break even then. There are some things you're better at."

He gave her a sideways glance. "Such as?"

She stretched like a cat again, then rubbed her nose against his.

"Keep doing that and you won't get any sleep tonight."

"Some things are worth losing sleep over," she said. " 'I have perfumed my bed with myrrh, aloes, and cinnamon. Come, let us take our fill of love until the morning.' "

"Did we learn that in school, too?"

"Nope, church," she said, tapping him on the nose with her index finger. "Proverbs."

"I was never good at quotes. Why don't we pick something I'm good at?"

"Okay."

"Your pick," he said.

She trailed a slow finger across his chest. "You want me to tell you or show you?"

He grinned. "Show me."

And she did.

Afterward, he held her close to him for a long time, until she rubbed her nose sleepily against him and said in a groggy little way that was seductive as all get out, "Alex, if I beg for more, could we save it for tomorrow?"

She was still asleep the next morning when he awoke. He dressed then came to stand beside the bed, content just to look at her relaxed features, so tranquil and golden, framed in a square of early morning sunlight. He had walked among the stars with her last night. He wondered if it could ever again be that good, and saw no reason why it wouldn't. As he turned away, the sun passed behind a cloud, absorbing the room's light, filling it with grayness and shadow.

Over the weeks that followed, Katherine never knew such happiness. Was there ever anything so wonderful as to go to sleep at night, wrapped in the solid warmth of someone you loved? Not unless it was waking up each morning and looking down at the raw beauty of a man when he sleeps, the warmth of the sun making his skin look all warm and buttery. He was like two pieces of warm toast she wanted to crawl between.

The coming together of their marriage had worked wonders around the camp as much as it had between them. Alex's newfound energy, his cheerful spirits were like a whirlwind of energy that soon had the men singing as they worked, and Alex swore it was the reason why Molly Polly chunked fewer pieces of wood at Wong.

Every morning Alex arose before dawn and

dressed quietly, kissing her cheek before he went downstairs. Wong always had breakfast ready and he ate with Adrian before he saw to the day's business with all the enthusiasm of a child with a new toy. He made rounds, talking to each of the men, discussing their problems, their needs, then he went over the accounts with Adrian, turning in his orders for supplies. He visited the logging sites, putting on his own calked boots and picking up a wood mallet to drive wedges into saw cuts to spread them apart and keep the saw blades free. Other times he put climbing irons over his boots and climbed to lofty heights to work with the toppers. And at night, when he came home, Katherine would sit down at the table with Alex and Adrian, listening to Alex as he asked about her day and told her about his. Because of his newfound enthusiasm, his willingness to share his life, words like pickaroon and springboard and cant hook and peavy head became a living, breathing language to her, while loggers' jobs and lingo like undercut, deacon seat, peeler, bindle, and tin pants became tools she used expertly to converse with the men, understanding the jobs they risked their lives to perform daily.

Alex felt changes in himself. He saw changes in her. Daily, he heard the effects of both in the songs, the jokes, the high morale of the lumberjacks who preferred to call themselves timber beasts. Never had Alex been so pleased with his life, so comfortable. Never had he felt so guilty.

Katherine was everything he could hope for in a wife, and more than once he saw the wisdom in his decision to marry her. Katherine complemented him. She brought out the man in him and soothed the beast. He thought of her eagerness as a foil for his steady plodding. She brought to his retiring ways, life, beauty, and vitality. She was enthusiastic and responsive, with a sort of breathless wonder, and she was to him like a cold drink from a free-flowing well on a hot summer day. Maybe she wasn't the woman he had always fancied himself in love with, but he was comfortable with her. And he had married her. That's where the guilt came from. It ate at him sometimes, and he wondered if he would ever be able to deal with it, short of confession—something he could never do. He could never tell Katherine the truth, that he had married her because of a mistake, because Adrian threatened and forced him to see what it would have done to her if he had not. Even when he had the chance to tell her the truth, the day she had asked him on the ship, he had let the opportunity for cleansing his soul slip away. She had asked for the truth. He had fed her lies—not blatant lies, but covert ones—little half-truths. Was it as he claimed, to protect her? Or was it to protect himself? It was hard to live with, this constant fear of carrying truth in a glass, spilling it while trying not to.

There were times while he was thinking about the many ways Katherine pleased him when thoughts of Karin would creep forth. He had as much difficulty bringing thoughts of Karin here, as he had picturing her as his wife. It was like forcing his foot into a shoe that was too small.

He remembered Karin as smart, ambitious, and at times selfish. Her nature was slightly rebellious and she was confident in her judgment. She didn't particularly need him, for she was too independent and daring, with an attitude of self-sufficiency. There had been a time he appreciated those qualities in her, appreciated them because he knew she wouldn't be the kind of woman to demand much of him—as long as he had the money to keep her in the style she fancied herself entitled to.

But with the passage of time, and probably influenced by his marriage to Katherine, he realized that what he had first called independence was nothing more than her refusal to be influenced by those she had no desire to be influenced by, and what he had called confidence was more a blustery attitude; what seemed daring was a form of obsessive competitiveness, which he understood well, since Adrian had that same quality. That wasn't to say he suddenly found fault in Karin, for realizing she lacked some of Katherine's admirable qualities didn't diminish the qualities in her that had so seduced him in the past. Karin, he realized, was no longer his, simply because she never had been. At one time he felt she belonged to him, but now he saw that was because no one else had come along to attract her attention. Using Katherine as a gauge to go by, he knew there had been little emotional depth in his relationship with Karin—knew as well that his feelings for her had ebbed long before he wrote that letter. There had been much conflict with Karin, and he wondered if the intense emotional quality coming from that conflict had for years masked itself as love, for he believed now that he had never loved Karin in the true sense. What he had felt lay somewhere between worship and adoration. To him Karin had been as fine as porcelain, a fragile ornament to be treasured. He had been spellbound by her, held for years in a border zone, caught between the boundaries of illusion and reality. The stamp of Karin in his mind was the epitome, the ideal of womanhood he had formed in his impressionable years when the visual qualities outshone those of a deeper nature. He could remember watching Karin sitting on her front steps when he was sixteen. She was brushing her long, golden hair, her face as perfect in form and color as the face of a bisque doll. He had stared at her in awe as she caught her polished curls back into a blue satin ribbon and tied it into a perfect bow. When he thought of Karin, he thought of beauty and perfection, something he now saw as shallow and one-sided. He could remember so many of the things he had adored in her: the dainty way she tossed her curls, the soft sound of her voice, the sweet, floral scent of her, the flawless perfection of her appearance. But there was no warmth, no life in these mirror images that flashed before him, no feeling of intoxication when he saw the doll-like image of her.

It was Katherine that intoxicated him now. Katherine was like the earth he loved—rich in what she offered, enduring, consistent, self-sufficient, and capable of returning something for everything he invested.

Often he would let himself go, enjoying his new life with her, the humor, the love, and understanding Katherine surrounded him with. The times he seemed to be happiest were times of inner turmoil, times when guilt began to eat at him and wear him down—guilt and the knowledge that he still held something back, that he had not given Katherine as much as she gave him. His insides would twist at the memory of her face the many times she told him she loved him, only to hear him say, "I know," when he knew the words she wanted to hear. Guilt, self-anger and feelings of inadequacy would temper his joy and he would turn sullen and reproachful, criticizing Katherine for her mother-hen ways, accusing her of smothering him and robbing him of his will.

These were the times he took anger at himself out on her. These were the times he made it a point to wipe his feet on the new rug she hooked that lay on the inside of the kitchen door, rather than the old one on the back porch, to only half-clean his shoes so that they left tracks on her spotless floor. Her lips tight and clamped together, she would clean up the mess, never saying a word, angering him more than any pot shattered over his head ever could. Other times he would make love to her until she cried from the joy of it, only to disappear for three or four days for a visit to one of the logging camps farther inland. And in between, there were always the times that he would get a bottle of brandy or whiskey and sit in front of the fire, staring at it in his brooding way, drinking more than he should.

Then he would go slowly up the stairs, knowing he had been wrong to betray Katherine in this way, knowing he couldn't blame her for what had gone wrong in his life. His guilt would eat at him and he would go to her, seeking her forgiveness, knowing she was lying in her bed upstairs, always tender and willing and warm. Somehow, he made it through each day and night, wondering each time he did, how long it would be before he was either claimed by complete and total peace or ruled completely by insanity.

CHAPTER TWENTY

Jumbo brought her a kitten. It was a scrawny little piece of fluff that she named Banjo.

"Oh, how precious!" she said, taking the tiny thing from his big calloused hands and holding it up so she could see the small owlish face that was mostly huge yellow-gray eyes. "Hello there. Where did you come from? Did you fall out of a tree?"

Jumbo laughed. "It's one of Clara's kittens. She had them about six weeks ago."

"Clara?"

"That motley colored cat that I've seen sleeping on your kitchen window."

"Oh, the calico. I had no idea she had kittens."

"Eight of them. Had them in a box right behind my banjo." He looked at the kitten. "I... well, that is, this one seemed to be the prettiest one and...aw heck, Miz Mackinnon. I ain't very good at this sort of thing. I don't know what I was thinking...bringing this kitten over here like this. If you'll just hand it over, I'll take it back. I'd appreciate it if you wouldn't tell Mr. Mackinnon. You know, word might get out that I'm a little soft and that..."

"I won't say a word about the kitten, Jumbo. If anyone asks, I'll say I saw them and asked you if I could have one. But, you can't have the kitten back. I've already named her Banjo." Then she laughed. "It is a her, isn't it?"

His face turned red. "I didn't think to check."

"Well, it doesn't really matter. Banjo is a good neutral name."

She glanced around the room. "I think I'll keep Banjo here in the kitchen where it's warm. I'll get Wong to help me find a box for her to sleep in."

Jumbo was a big, brawny fellow, as tall as a fir and bigger around than a redwood. He had on so many layers of clothes he looked even larger. It touched Katherine's heart to know someone as big as he was had such a gentle heart. Never would she forget the way he had looked when she opened the door, his hat in one hand, the tiny kitten dwarfed against his body in the other one. "Well," he said, shifting his weight from one foot to the other, "I guess I better be going. You're sure you want the kitten? It won't be no bother if you don't."

"Don't you dare try to take Banjo from me now," she said with a smile. She put the kitten on the rug, then moved to the table and a huge chocolate cake she had baked only this morning. She picked up a knife and cut a large slice that she wrapped in brown paper and handed to him.

"Oh, no ma'am. I couldn't take that."

"Of course you can. My feelings will be hurt if you don't."

He looked at her. He looked at the cake. Then he reached out his hand as Katherine handed it to him. "I like that name," he said. "Banjo. It's got a nice ring to it." He started for the door, then checked himself. "Oh, I almost forgot. I brought a letter for you." He reached into his big shirt pocket and pulled out a wrinkled, folded letter.

Katherine took the letter, recognizing Karin's handwriting. "Thank you, Jumbo."

He thanked her for the cake and went outside. After she closed the door, Katherine opened the letter and scanned it quickly. Karin was concerned about their farm. The neighbor man they had hired to help Fanny had moved. "Men are still scarce in these parts," she wrote, "and I've been unable to find help. It's too much for Fanny to run alone, and I'm not sure what we should do. If I don't hear from you soon, telling me otherwise, I think I'll put the place up for sale. Old Mr. Ledbetter has contacted me a time or two about buying it."

Katherine didn't want to sell her home place. Not for any reason. She knew someone could be found to help Fanny. All it would take was a trip to Dallas or Ft. Worth, maybe even an ad in the newspaper, but Katherine couldn't depend on Karin to do it. She decided to write Fanny, asking her to place an ad, and then send another letter to Karin telling her she didn't want to sell.

The kitten tucked in her arm, Katherine went searching for Wong. She found him in the great room, stacking wood next to the fireplace. She showed him the kitten, telling him they needed to find a box. "Boss no likey kitten," he said, shaking his head solemnly. "He make Missy give it back. Boss no likey."

"Boss no havey any say about it," she said. "Boss lady keepie kitten." Wong grinned at her, his black tooth giving the impression that it was missing. "Okay, boss lady. You keepie kitten. Wong find box. Boss no likie. Wong not stay in house when boss get mad."

"That's fair enough." *We may both be out of the house if boss no likie.* "Now find me a box." It didn't take him long to find one. They decided to put it in the kitchen next to the stove where it was warm. Katherine carried Banjo, Wong dogtrotting behind her with the box.

About that time, Alex came crashing through the kitchen door, barging into the room like some great lumbering grizzly. Katherine eyed the muddy tracks across her floor. "Alex, couldn't you clean your feet outside so you don't make tracks all over my clean floor?"

"Don't start on me, Katherine."

"I'm not starting on you. I asked a simple question that could be answered with a simple reply."

Alex didn't say any more, for he had spotted the box on the floor. "What in the hell is that?"

Katherine picked Banjo up, stroking its head. "It's a kitten, Alex. What does it look like?"

"More trouble!" he said. "We don't need it."

"We don't need your snarling, either, but we seem to be getting it." Wong moved behind her. "Did we get up on the wrong side of the bed this morning, Alex?"

He took the kitten from her and thrust it around her, into Wong's face. "Get rid of this."

"Okay, boss." Wong took the kitten.

"Give me the kitten, Wong. I'm keeping it in the kitchen."

Wong held the kitten toward her as Alex spoke.

"Put it outside."

"Put it in the box."

By this time Wong was looking a bit confused. "Boss say put kitten outside. Boss lady say put kitten in box. Wong no can do both. If Wong put kitten outside, boss lady be unhappy with Wong. If Wong put kitten in box, boss unhappy with Wong. Wong no please both. Wong no try. Wong put kitten on floor, then Wong leave." He did what he said he would do, putting the kitten on the floor. Katherine watched his long black pigtail swing to and fro as Wong hurried his dogtrot along and headed for the back door.

Once he was gone, Katherine picked the kitten up and put it in the box. When she turned back, Alex was gone.

The next time she saw him was at dinner. Alex seemed to be his old self. He even went so far as to laugh at a few of the kitten's antics. After dinner, when they moved into the great room and she served Alex and Adrian thick slices of chocolate cake and steaming cups of coffee, Alex was warm and considerate. After they finished, Katherine carried the cups and plates back into the kitchen and after she cleaned them, she went upstairs. She lay in bed, waiting for the sound of Alex coming down the hallway, the sound of his hand opening the door. But he never came. It was the first time since she had moved into his room that Alex didn't come to bed.

The next morning she went to see Molly, driven by the need to have a woman to talk to.

Molly was in the cookhouse, going after a mountain of potatoes with a knife bigger than a meat cleaver.

"Hello, Molly," she said with a glum tone, coming into the kitchen and sitting on a stool.

"Well, what brings you out in the cold?"

"I just felt like having some feminine company."

"Let me get these potatoes on to boil, then I'll fix us a hot cup of coffee." Katherine sat on the stool, watching Molly go after those potatoes until she had them all neatly quartered and dumped in a pot. Then she poured two cups of coffee from a pot so large she had to pick it up with both hands. She carried the cups to a small table with two chairs and motioned for Katherine to join her.

"So, you're getting tired of just having menfolk to talk to?"

"I can't talk to them about this."

"Uh-oh! This sounds serious."

"To me it is."

"Hold that thought. I'll be right back." Molly went to another table that held a dozen or so sugar bowls. Picking one up she carried it back to the table. Katherine watched her ladle sugar into her cup. She had never seen anyone put six spoons of sugar in a cup of coffee before. A minute later she took a sip of her coffee and saw why.

"Pass the sugar," she said, making a face.

Molly laughed, sliding the sugar bowl toward her. "So, what do you want to talk about?"

"My marriage."

"What's wrong with it?"

"Alex and I aren't getting along."

"When did this start?"

"When I came to San Francisco."

Molly's eyebrows rose, but she didn't say anything at first. She simply sat there, adding another spoonful of sugar to her coffee and stirring it. "What went wrong?"

"I'm not sure. He just never acted like he was very glad to see me. We married aboard the ship on the way up, but he didn't take me to his bed."

"He was probably waiting until you reached home."

"He didn't take me to bed then either."

"Oh, dear."

"That's what I thought."

"And he still hasn't?"

"Well, he has, but..."

Molly let out a whistle. "Is he still coming to your bed?"

"He has been, but he didn't come to bed at all last night."

"I must say I'm surprised. Alex doesn't strike me as the kind of man that isn't interested in that sort of thing. How were things between you when he left for California?"

"We were good friends."

"Good friends? You mean he asked you to marry him when you'd only been good friends?"

"Yes."

"Why didn't you ever become..." She paused a moment, then said, "better friends?"

"Because Alex was in love with my sister."

Molly looked dumbfounded. "He was in love with your sister when he left?"

"Yes."

"And how long was he gone?"

"A couple of years."

"So two years later he writes for you to come to California and get married?"

"Yes."

"Didn't you think that was a little strange?"

"Yes and no."

"Good answer."

"You see, I've always known Alex and I were better suited than he and Karin ever were. And there were so many times before he left that we... he..."

"Felt an attraction for one another."

"Yes. In fact, the night he left, Karin was upset. She said she wouldn't wait for him. After he left her, he came into the kitchen and we talked. He kissed me in a way he had never kissed me before. He asked me to write him."

"Did you?"

"Yes, but Karin never did."

"And the next thing you knew, he wrote you to come to California to be married."

"Yes."

"What did you think? Didn't you wonder why he didn't ask for your sister?"

"A little, but I kept remembering the way he kissed me the night he left. I thought after my writing to him, he had decided I was the right choice. And then there were the letters themselves. At first they included a personal note for Karin, but gradually he stopped these. He began writing to me only, telling me how much I would love the country, or how he would love to show me this or that."

"Let me ask you something. Did you ever ask Alex why? I mean, why he asked you to marry him?"

"Yes." Katherine thought back to that day on the ship when she had asked Alex.

Alex, why did you write for me?

Because it was time I took a wife.

Why me and not Karin?

Because it was meant to be, Katherine. Because I knew you would come.

She told Molly.

"Do you love him?"

"Oh, yes. With all my heart."

"But you aren't sure of his feelings."

"No, I'm not."

"Have you told him you love him?"

"Yes."

"Has he said the same to you?"

"No, not yet."

"You're talking to the wrong person, Katherine. Alex is the one you need to talk to. You two have some serious things to talk out."

"I know, but I'm almost afraid of what I might find out. Sometimes he acts so indifferent that I don't think he loves me at all."

"Honey, they *all* do that." Molly patted her head. "Don't you go doubting his feelings for one minute. I've seen the way he looks at you."

"I don't think those kind of looks are

prompted by the heart," she said woefully. "The source is much farther down."

Molly laughed. "You talk to him. You'll feel so much better when you have these things all worked out."

Katherine stood. "Thank you for talking to me, Molly. I don't know what I would do if you weren't here."

"You'd make do," she said. "Just like I've done all these years." Molly came to her feet, with considerably more effort than Katherine had used. "You think about what I've said. You'll know when the time is right."

Katherine nodded, then turned and walked slowly out of the kitchen into the great dining hall of the cookhouse. It was strangely quiet and deserted, such a far cry from the times she had seen it full of hungry, enthusiastic men.

She took her time walking up the hill, mulling over the things Molly had said. When she reached their house, it was as quiet and deserted as the cookhouse. She went to the kitchen. The kitten, Banjo, was out of his box. Katherine looked around the kitchen, calling him, deciding after a while that he must be in another part of the house. For almost an hour she looked for him, checking all the rooms downstairs, then going upstairs to check the bedrooms, and finally the attic.

As a last resort, she checked Alex's study, finding the door ajar. She went inside and looked around. The room smelled like leather and Alex, with a faint hint of Adrian's chewing tobacco. Wondering where that infernal kitten could be, she began searching, laughing to herself when she found Banjo curled up in the leather chair behind his desk. Picking him up, she gave him a scolding and remembered the letter from Karin. She had planned on writing Karin and Fanny when she went upstairs, but now that she was here in Alex's study she might as well write it now. Holding Banjo in one hand, she pulled out the chair with the other and sat down, putting Banjo in her lap. She stared at the desktop, seeing a pen and inkwell, a blotter, scattered notes and stacks of paper, all of which were written on. *Alex is bound to have some stationery.* She pulled out the center drawer, finding more papers and no stationery. Two drawers later, she found what she was looking for. Katherine took about half an inch of stationary off the top of the stack, then began rummaging around for envelopes. Finding them in the next drawer, she took two off the stack, noticing just as she closed the drawer that the next envelope was addressed. She shut the drawer and picked up the pen, dipping it in the well, when it occurred to her that an addressed envelope had no business being in with the unused ones. She opened the drawer again, taking out the envelope, feeling a letter inside and thinking it was one Alex must have mixed in with the unused envelopes by mistake and therefore did not mail. She was about to prop it against the clock, so Alex would notice it, when she saw the name of the addressee: *Miss Karin Simon.*

With trembling hands, she opened the letter

Alex had written—and never finished—in a moment of anger, the day they had arrived at the camp from San Francisco. Her heart plummeted.

"Dear Karin,

I know you must have been shocked and hurt when I wrote asking Katherine to come to California." Katherine felt a tremendous relief. Obviously, Alex had started this letter to explain his feelings and reasons for asking her to marry him instead of Karin. She read on. "I don't know how to explain the mistake. Adrian and I fought, and I wrote the letter to you. I was drunk, and somehow wrote Katherine's name, though God knows how or why. I didn't realize the mistake until she arrived, and by then it was too late. I had to marry her. I had no choice. I don't think I can ever..."

The letter ended there, but even if it hadn't, Katherine knew there could have been no more words to pierce her any more cruelly than those she had already read. Four things in the letter jumped out at her: Alex had written for Karin when he was drunk and wrote her name by mistake. He didn't realize what he had done until she arrived. He felt forced into marriage, though he didn't say why. And he didn't think he could ever... What? *Forgive Katherine? Forget his love for Karin?*

For some time, she simply sat there looking at the letter, as if by the passage of time, the words, the reality would fade away. The letter was written by Alex—she would recognize that broad, sweeping hand anywhere. The letter was written in grief, after their marriage. *Somehow I wrote Katherine's name, though God knows how or why.* The words stabbed at her. He hadn't wanted to marry her at all—had never intended to marry her. It was all a mistake. But the worst realization of all was knowing that Alex had lied to her, even after she had asked him. Her mind at first refused to believe it, then the agony of certainty closed in. Katherine put the letter on the desk, then put the kitten on the floor. On trembling, uncertain legs, she stood, the back of her hand coming up to her mouth so she could bite back the scream. Her world shattering and crumbling about her, she could only feel the agony of knowing the lie, the shattering humility of knowing the truth. She wanted to destroy and be destroyed. Within her, her essence, her very being seemed to explode into tiny fragments that fell slowly to the floor and lay as a tarnished reminder of her shame. Everything went blank after that.

She didn't remember biting the back of her hand until it bled, and then, when the pain of it registered, the long, agonized scream that tore from her throat. There was no recollection of wadding the letter and throwing it, of her arm sweeping out to clear the desktop with one sweep, sending everything smashing and floating to the floor, or the lamp that shattered the window.

"Katherine, my God!" Adrian shouted as he tore into the room. "What's happened?" He saw the blood on her hand and her dress, saw too, the room in shambles, the broken window, the ravaged look on her face. She was wild and uncontrollable, and the only thing he could do was wrap his arms around her and throw her to the floor, screaming for Wong.

It took both of them to hold her down until the thrashing subsided.

Uncertain, they forced a few sips of whiskey down her throat, hoping that would relax her. Wong bathed her hand and wrapped it in clean linen before Adrian sent him to find Alex. After Wong left, Adrian sat beside her on the sofa, stroking her forehead, trying to soothe her with words. When she had calmed and the frenzy had passed, he asked her again. "What happened?"

"The letter," she whispered. "I found it."

Adrian saw her eyes move to the desk. Leaving her for a minute, he easily located the crumpled letter in the papers that littered the floor. He read the letter.

His heart pounded and he felt sick. He didn't know what to say. "It isn't as bad as it sounds. Alex loves…"

"Don't add lying to the list of violations," she said. "Please save me the indignity of that."

"Katherine, at least give Alex a chance to explain…."

"And what about you, Adrian? What was your part in all of this? Were you part of the choice Alex didn't have?"

"I only did what I thought best. We thought

the best thing to do was for Alex to go on with the marriage."

"We," she said hatefully. "How nice. Just the two of you, planning my life with deceit and lies. I guess it never occurred to either of you to ask me what I thought?" She struggled to sit up, slapping his hands away when he tried to help her. "I don't want your help. You've *helped* enough."

A flash of guilt came and went across his face and Katherine felt no sympathy. She came to her feet. "Katherine, wait a minute. You're in no condition to walk. Stay here until Alex comes."

"No, I can't. I don't want to see Alex...or you. I just want to be alone for a while." She made her way to the door and paused. "I'm not sure if I'll ever be able to forgive either of you for this," she said. She turned away and picked up her skirts, walking out the door.

Adrian picked up the tiny kitten and held it toward her. "Don't you want the kitten?"

"No," she said coldly. "Alex never wanted it. Put it outside. Put us *both* outside."

"Katherine, listen to me. I know how you must feel about what's happened...about Alex, about me."

"No, you don't. You can't possibly know how I feel. Not even your worst imaginings would come close."

"Katherine, at least..."

She slammed the door before he could finish.

She went outside without bothering to collect her cape. It was cold outside, but she didn't care. She wanted to be cold. She wanted to feel something. She wanted to feel anything besides this deathlike numbness. She walked away from the house, away from camp, going up the hill in the opposite direction, knowing she couldn't get her thoughts clear until she was as far away as possible. She had no idea how far she walked, or how long she had been gone. But the sun was dropping low in the sky and the shadows stretched long and thin down the hill behind her.

When she began to think more clearly, she realized she was a long way from the house, and it would soon be dark. She turned around, looked back down the trail and with a sigh decided she couldn't do anything about it now. She only knew she couldn't stay here in this camp any longer, couldn't carry on this charade of a marriage to a man who did not want her, had never wanted her. Whatever happened would have to wait until tomorrow.

Alex was running up the steps when he met Adrian coming out of the house. Adrian explained what happened, explained too, that he couldn't find Katherine anywhere. "You stay here, in case she comes back," Alex said. "I'll go after her." He grabbed his rifle and left the house in a lope. If this had to happen, why couldn't it have happened a little later in the year, after the bears had gone into hibernation? *Dear God, there were so many dangers out there. Katherine. Katherine.* He knew she hadn't taken the road toward camp, or he would have met her. He started off in the opposite direction, praying as he went.

Not long after she turned back, she paused, hearing the snapping of dried brush and sticks coming from her left. She thought it was probably the camp dog following her, when a massive, battle-scarred bear burst into view, crashing through the brush. The moment it saw her, it stopped. It was too close for her to stand any chance if she ran, close enough that she could see the dished face, the turned up nose, the humped shoulder, and she knew instinctively it was a male grizzly.

The grizzly was close enough that she could smell its strange, musky scent, a smell that swept over her in dizzying waves. Strange, how the mind works. Here she was, frozen in place, looking at the fiercest animal to be found in the whole of North America and the only thing that flashed into her mind was the scientific name for the grizzly Alex had told her: *Ursus horribilis*. The next moment it reared up on its hind legs and she saw the powerful long claws, heard the savage growls that made her blood run cold.

The last thing she remembered was someone shouting her name and being told not to run, but when the bear charged, it was instinct, not common sense that sent her running down the trail.

Running for her life now, she knew the bear was too close, that she would never make it. A deadening growl, a stabbing pain to her shoulder. Then she was falling, hitting the ground and rolling, the pain in her shoulder excruciating, the sound of someone calling her name the last thing she remembered before rolling over and over and over, plunging into a black void.

Adrian was sitting in the great room staring at the fire, stroking Banjo's fur and drinking a brandy when he heard the shots. He sprang to his feet and ran for his rifle. As he headed for the front door, he heard the dogs barking outside. Something about their bark was urgent and he was already expecting the worst when he heard Alex shout, "For the love of God, someone open the door."

Adrian opened the door, seeing Alex stagger toward him, Katherine's bloody, inert body draped in his arms. "Grizzly," he said. "Get Molly."

Adrian took off like a pistol shot, his shouts clearing the cookhouse long before he reached it. By the time he brought Molly to the house, Alex had Katherine stretched out, face down, on the kitchen table. He was holding a towel pressed to her shoulder. Blood was every-where.

Alex looked up the minute they walked in and a bolt of terror shot straight to Adrian's gut. He had never seen Alex with such a look of fear stretched painfully across his pale face. He had never seen so much blood, soaking into her clothes, the towel, and drip-ping onto the floor. For over two hours they did what they could do to clean the wounds and staunch the bleeding. Molly was the first to realize their methods were far too primitive to save Katherine. "We've got to get her to San Francisco. She'll never make it. If she survives the wound, the infection and fever that follows will kill her."

"We'll take one of the ships waiting for lumber, one that hasn't been loaded. With the winds behind us and no load, we should be able to cut our time in half," Alex said.

As the men fashioned a bed between two poles to carry her on, Molly went upstairs to pack some of Katherine's things. Half an hour later she carried them on board ship. She stood beside Katherine's pale stillness and used her palm to smooth the frown from the brow of one so lovely and so young. She remained there, looking at Katherine's face until Adrian and Alex said it was time to get under way. She turned and walked to the door, pausing to take one last look. She wasn't sure why she stopped to look. Perhaps it was because she had the feeling she would never see Katherine again.

CHAPTER
TWENTY-ONE

"Damn! That's what I was afraid of," Alex said.

Adrian had been resting his head on the table in the small ship's cabin. Hearing Alex's words he looked up to see Alex leaning over Katherine, his hand on her head.

"She's burning up with fever," Alex said.

Adrian stood, coming over to stand beside Alex. "That's what we were hoping against. Thank God we'll be in San Francisco in a few hours."

"With a fever like this, every minute is precious."

"I know," Adrian said. "We'll take turns with her, keeping her covered with wet cloths."

"I think wet blankets would be better. We can use two, exchanging them as soon as the one in use becomes warm," Alex said.

Adrian put his hand to her head. "As hot as she is, it won't take long."

"Then we'll both stay with her and we'll use more blankets if necessary. She isn't going to die if I have to harness her and dip her in the ocean."

Adrian nodded and thrust his hands deep into his pockets. The two of them stood side by side, staring down at Katherine, feeling useless against the fever that heated her without mercy.

"Hurts," she whispered weakly. "Head hurts." She fought for consciousness, but the disabling chills and throbbing head that accompanied the fever had too great a hold. Soon the effort became too much for her and she drifted off to sleep.

But before long she was robbed of even her sleep, when visions of the bear left her paralyzed and crying. The bear was behind her now, close enough that she could feel the heat of his breath. She writhed in the bunk, trying to free herself as she felt the sharp claws dig into her upper arm and shoulder.

Alex covered her with another cool, wet blanket, tucking the sides around her, then picking her up and sitting on the bunk, holding her in his arms. He felt the shock that ran through her, heard the sharp, indrawn breath that preceded the struggle. He held her for a long time, long after she had worn herself out and ceased to struggle. When he finally did stand up and lower her back to the bunk, it was to remove the warm blanket and replace it with another, cooler one Adrian handed him.

Alex watched her flinch, her lids fluttering when the cold blanket touched her fiery skin. He never took his eyes from her as its coolness began to absorb the heat and she began to drift away.

She didn't regain consciousness, even when she was carried from the ship and loaded into the back of a wagon for the short trip to the doctor.

Alex didn't want to leave her, but the doctor refused to treat her unless he and Adrian both got some sleep and a decent meal before they returned. Adrian was grateful the clever brown eyes of the doctor had correctly taken in the signs of their devotion as well as their exhaustion. He knew as well as the doctor that neither of them would be of any help to her until they rested. But for Alex, it was a cruel command, one he heeded reluctantly. "Leave? Why? So he can stuff her wound with wood ashes and cobwebs?"

"Get him out of here," the doctor said.

Adrian gave him a pleading look. Alex looked at Katherine, hot and dry, her face flushed with fever. "Send word if she gets any worse," he said.

The doctor nodded. "Tell my wife where you'll be. I'll send word. In the meantime, get some rest. She may need you when she wakes."

If she wakes, Alex thought, feeling as if his life was flowing backward.

Once they had eaten and slept, Alex was tense with the need to get to the doctor's office. "We can't go like this, Alex. We both need a bath and a shave, and clean clothes. It wouldn't help Katherine to wake up and see us looking like this."

Once again, Alex gave in. Grudgingly.

Hearing returned to her first.

She tried to listen to the voices, but each word slipped away from her as soon as she heard it. All around her she was conscious of softly muted sound. When she tried to open her eyes, all she could see was a background of great darkness splashed with mosaics of abstract shapes and vivid colors. The red came, like a wave sluicing across the beach, washing away all of the color. Then she slept.

The voices were gone when consciousness returned to her, but as it had the time before, the chore of waking to full awareness proved too much for her and she slept once more. The third time, she heard a voice she did not recognize. "Feel how cool she is. The fever is down."

"Thank God."

Alex.

The next voice she recognized was Adrian's. "Will it go back up?"

"No," the doctor said. "The worst is over. Her fever has broken. She's out of the woods."

The weights on her eyes were so heavy and she felt so very weak. The voices began to fade and she felt herself drifting.

The early morning light touched her closed lids and she frowned, mumbling for someone to "take the light away."

Her eyes were still heavy, but the weights were gone. The first thing she saw was Alex sitting beside her bed, badly needing a shave and his eyes red-rimmed. Gradually, as the room came into focus, she saw Adrian standing behind Alex, and a strange man with a kind face standing to Adrian's side.

"Welcome back," the strange man said. "I'm Dr. Glover. I imagine you're feeling like you've been hit by a locomotive."

"I feel like the back end of hard times," she said crossly, slapping at the doctor's hand when it came out to touch her forehead. "I'm thirsty. Why are you staring at me like you've never seen me before? How did I get here? And where is here?"

Dr. Glover laughed. "Crotchety as they come," he said. "A good sign."

Alex never knew he could float while his feet were planted firmly on the floor. He could never remember feeling so happy or so relieved. He could never remember crying since his parents died, but he knew the wetness on his face could only be called tears. Taking one look at him, Katherine said, "Was I dying?"

She had never realized she had been dangerously close to dying, but there was no reason to keep that fact from her now. After listening to Alex and Adrian she understood their relief, but the tears on Alex's face confused her. She remembered only one time when he had cried.

San Francisco was cold and wet this time of year, the days often gloomy and dim, making it easy for Katherine to sleep. When she was awake Alex was always there, ready to poke her mouth full of food that was cooked to perfection, or to entertain her with stories, or read to her from the latest newspapers taken from arriving ships. In truth, she wanted for nothing, not cheerful company, excellent food, entertainment of various forms.

Only one thing came close to stealing the joy from having Alex with her like this and that was knowing his tenderness and cheerful attitude had been prompted not out of love, but guilt. She never asked him about the letter. It didn't matter now. He knew. That was enough.

She tried not to think about that fateful day. As Alex read to her she looked out the window. The weather was cold and cloudy. Inhospitable. How she longed to see the sun. Thoughts along those lines always made her think of home. As always, when she reached that point, she directed her thoughts elsewhere.

Pronounced "fit as a fiddle," but still "too weak to dance," by Dr. Glover, Katherine left the tiny room in the doctor's office for a more spacious one at the hotel Alex and Adrian had been staying in. Shortly after moving to the hotel, the weather turned cooperative, and although still cold, the sun was shining and the sky was unusually clear. Katherine knew her body was mending, but her heart seemed as wounded as ever.

For several days she spent long hours lying on her bed or taking short walks, her mind always occupied with thoughts of leaving. But she would always think that plenty of marriages—good marriages—began with a lot less than she and Alex had. But then she remembered those marriages hadn't been founded on lies and deceit.

Katherine lay on her bed thinking. Once she had made up her mind to go, she decided to go out with a bang. She might have come to California in shame, meekly coming off that ship, not knowing she wasn't welcome. But she didn't have to leave that way.

She decided to send Alex a note explaining she couldn't join him for dinner. Tonight she was going to make an entrance into the hotel dining room that would far surpass Cleopatra's entrance into Rome. Or her own entrance into San Francisco a few months ago. She went to the desk and composed a short note of regret to Alex, saying she was still feeling too exhausted to take dinner in the dining room, and asking him to please go on down without her. She informed him that she had already ordered a light dinner to be delivered to her room.

She didn't order dinner, but she did order a bath. After a leisurely soak that left her room smelling like roses and her skin pink as a newborn, she spent an hour arranging her hair. With trembling fingers she buttoned the row of tiny buttons on her shimmering green velvet dress, the color as green as the finest Brazilian emeralds. Never had she spent so much time getting dressed. She smiled to herself thinking she had never known anyone that spent this much time. Not even Karin.

When she finished dressing, she looked at herself in the mirror. *Oh, mama, if only you could see me.* Somehow, she had a feeling her mother could. She looked at herself one last time before starting off. The dress was spectacular. She would wager there wasn't another one like it anywhere near San Francisco. At a time when women wore dresses with full skirts and a magnitude of petticoats and necklines that plunged dangerously low, Katherine knew one thing. In this dress, she would definitely stand out.

She checked the time. Half past nine. She had purposefully waited long enough for Alex and Adrian to have finished eating. Knowing Alex, she was certain her rejection this afternoon had stung, and he would probably nurse his wounds over a few glasses of brandy. At least she was hoping he would be.

She didn't want him drunk. She didn't want him at all.

From the moment she entered the dining room and paused at the top of the stairs long enough to locate Alex and Adrian, finding Adrian sitting alone at the table, she knew something was wrong. The moment Adrian looked up and saw her, a sickening expression of hopelessness and dread so plain upon his face, she was positive.

Adrian, along with every other man in the room watched the gorgeous mahogany-haired goddess in green velvet descend the stairs. While most men were envying the man she was coming to meet, Adrian was feeling immensely sorry for him. For Adrian knew exactly who Katherine had dressed for and what it meant. A knot of sickening dread gripped his stomach. He didn't know what to do. He was afraid to look in Alex's direction, afraid Katherine's eyes might follow his. The only thing he could think of was to go to her, to somehow get her out of here before she saw him, or to support her once she did. Adrian downed the last of his brandy thinking, *You're going to need it*. As he rose and hurried up the steps toward her, he couldn't help thinking it was poor Katherine that was going to need it worse than he.

He caught up to her at the first landing. She smiled and held out one gloved hand. "I'm glad you stood up. I would have never found you if you hadn't." She glanced behind him. "Where is Alex?"

Adrian took her arm, turning her away, intending to walk her back up the stairs.

"Come with me, Katherine. I'll explain everything."

She pulled back. "Adrian, whatever is the matter with you. Explain what? Why are you acting so secretive? Where is Alex?" She tried looking around him, but Adrian blocked her view.

"My brother hasn't been himself lately, Katherine. I want you to remember that. And I want you to remember something else. Alex is in love with you."

"All right. I'll remember. Now will you get out of the way?"

"Katherine, please. Come upstairs with me."

"Adrian, people are staring. Why should I go upstairs? And for the last time, where is Alex?"

"He was a little upset all through dinner and he drank more than he should have. He was hurting. He wasn't thinking straight. That's the only reason he was lured to her table. The only reason. It doesn't mean anything."

"You aren't making any sense, Adrian," she said, some of his words beginning to soak in and take effect. "Lured to what table?" she asked, feeling her heart pound with a sense of dread.

"A woman we shared a coach with the other day. Her name is Victoria something or other. She invited Alex to her table for a drink. Her husband is looking for lumber for European markets."

An icy chill swept through her. This was going to be even better than she had hoped. "And he accepted, of course. I wonder why she didn't invite you as well, seeing as how the company is half yours."

Katherine didn't hear Adrian's response. Her head was spinning to keep up with all the blood her heart was pumping into it. Her knees went weak. She had no doubt the woman was beautiful and had more in mind than a drink at her table. Only a few hours ago he had wanted her. It didn't take him long to find a substitute. One more reinforcement that she had made the right decision.

Adrian jerked her arm. "Come on Katherine. Please."

Katherine tugged at her arm, and Adrian eased his hold, while still maintaining it, if only lightly. She stepped around him and started down the stairs.

Alex looked up from contemplating the lush expanse of white bosom so enticingly displayed across the table from him, his attention drawn away from Victoria's numerous endowments to see what had caused the subtle change in the room. A woman like none he had ever seen was standing at the first landing of the stairs, and Adrian was standing beside her. *Adrian?* About that time the woman stepped away from Adrian and into Alex's full view. *My God! Katherine!*

But Katherine as he had never seen her. Alex swallowed, his hand clenching the brandy glass, knowing his expression must look as stunned as he felt. *Katherine?* He could see it was her. But he couldn't believe it.

As she began to descend the stairs, he was immediately reminded that he wasn't the only man in the room stunned by her beauty. And that dress! He had never in all his born days seen anything like it. It looked like it had been sewn to her body. It was all the things it shouldn't be to turn a man's head. It was straight, and tight, and long sleeved and high necked and not one inch of skin showed anywhere, save her face and hands, yet it was seductive as hell. And the woman that was in the dress that was as seductive as hell was his wife. *His wife!* And every man in the room had the same thoughts he did. *Son-of-a-bitch!* The glass in his hand shattered. He never noticed.

He watched Adrian come down the stairs after her and escort her to their table. He saw her beautiful eyes, saw the pride, the hurt. If she had slapped his face, he wouldn't have felt so guilty. But in her dignity, her grace, her bearing that said she was every inch a lady, she exerted much more power than any screaming, slapping shrew would have.

Why did he always think of Karin at a time like this? And why did he think of Karin at all when he knew damn well it wasn't Karin he desired at this moment, but Katherine. He had a sudden understanding of the kind of feeling that prompted men to marry one woman and take another for a mistress. Yet, strange as it was, when he thought of it in those terms, he found himself unable to decide if he wanted Katherine for his wife or for his mistress. Somehow, he kept thinking she fit the role of both, while he had trouble casting Karin in either role. Why was that?

Because you love your wife. He prayed he hadn't come to this realization too late.

He came to his feet. The thought made him stagger. He looked at Katherine, knowing their future happiness depended on his handling of things between them from this moment forward. The realization that he was in love with his wife was too new, too fragile to be dealt with now. He needed time to think things through, time to acquaint himself with his newfound feelings, time to adjust to what he had just realized, time to understand just how long he had been in love with Katherine without really knowing it.

Alex excused himself. "Tell your husband if he's interested to contact me or Adrian."

Victoria's face fell. "Surely you don't have to go now. Your brother looks old enough to entertain himself," she said with a pout.

"Oh, he can entertain himself, all right. But *not* with my wife. If you'll excuse me."

As Alex walked toward Katherine he felt a lightness in his step that he hadn't felt in years. *My God! Katherine! Imagine that! I'm in love with Katherine!*

"He's coming over here," Adrian said.

Katherine looked up, feeling her throat burn. "I can't do this," she wailed. "I thought I could, but I can't. I'm not up to this yet."

But even as she spoke, Katherine knew it was already too late to make a graceful exit. Alex was weaving his way through the tables, coming toward them like he was in a hurry. A smile was on his face, but the look in his eye was guilty, guilty, guilty. A moment later he pulled out his chair and sat down. Katherine swallowed back the shame that sucked her throat dry and lifted her head proudly, thinking that if she couldn't leave, she was at least glad she was seated. Her legs were trembling and her heart pounded furiously in her chest.

"My lovely Katherine, you look beautiful in that dress."

"I'm glad you like it, but then, why shouldn't you? You paid for it." She surprised herself with how relaxed she felt, how calm. She was actually enjoying this. *I'm going to get him for every miserable tear I've ever cried over him.*

"I'm glad you came down. I didn't think you would," Alex said.

"So I noticed," she said, looking straight at him. He looked away.

"I'll get a waiter so you can order," Adrian said, raising his hand and signaling a nearby waiter.

"Don't bother," Katherine said, "I didn't come down to eat. I just wanted to get out around people for a little while."

"Why don't you try something. A little soup? Some poached fish?" Adrian suggested.

"I'm not hungry in the least," she said in carefully controlled tones, using enough firmness to back up the message of indifference.

Knowing how stubborn Katherine was, and recognizing she was locked into a bout of it right now, Alex changed the subject. "Do you feel up to a little stroll? We could walk over to Portsmouth Square."

"I think the stairs will prove to be about all the exercise I can take for tonight. I don't seem to have the strength I had before."

Suddenly she was angrier than she could ever remember being. How dare he flaunt his obvious attraction to another woman right here in the hotel where they were staying! How callous could he be to casually leave the woman's table and come immediately to hers and expect her to go on being his adoring wife as if she didn't have an ounce of brains or the ability to see any farther than the end of her nose? What crust! What insolence! What a bastard!

From the corner of her eye she saw Adrian push his chair back, and she knew immediately that he wasn't just getting comfortable. He was leaving. Leaving her here with Alex. The thought was terrifying. She didn't trust Alex. Worse, she didn't trust herself around Alex.

"Excuse me," she said, springing to her feet. "I think I overestimated my strength tonight. I find I am exhausted. Please don't get up. I can find my way to my room."

"Stay a minute longer," Alex said in a soft voice. "I want to talk to you...just for a minute or two. I promise I won't keep you overly long."

The glance Adrian threw Alex was a conspirator's glance if she'd ever seen one. Then Adrian said, "I'm going to put some figures together to give Mrs. Talbot to show to her husband. The prospect of opening up European markets is something we can't afford to pass up."

No, of course not. Not even if my husband has to sleep with Talbot's wife to cinch the deal.

Adrian nodded at Alex and blew Katherine a kiss before turning away. But all Katherine could think of was that she had been abandoned and trapped.

"Don't be angry with Adrian. He's..."

"I'm not angry with Adrian. Strangely enough, I'm not even angry with you. I just don't care anymore."

Alex winced. He knew what Katherine had been through, and he knew it had been his fault. But that was behind them now. He had something more important to tell her, something she had waited a long time to hear him say. "You care," he said, "because you're not the kind of woman to ever stop caring, no matter what."

"And you *know* all about women, don't you?" Her laugh was forced and cynical. "I don't know why that surprises me."

"Listen, love, I know what's going through your mind right now. I understand you better than you think I do."

"You couldn't understand me too well, or else you wouldn't have put me through all the things you did."

"I know that now. And I'm sorry for what's happened, for the things I've done. But it's not too late, Katherine."

"But it is," she said, her voice shaking. She wrestled for control, vowing she wouldn't crumble before him, that he would never see just how deep the hurt went.

"No, it isn't. We've got too much to work for."

"We have nothing! We never did, save friendship. And now, we don't even have that."

"What about love?"

"*Love?*" she said with contempt. "You never loved me."

"But I do now," he said softly.

"Liar!" she said, springing to her feet, not even caring that her voice had been high pitched and loud, drawing every eye in the silent room.

He remained calmly seated. "Whether you choose to believe it or not, it's the truth."

"Truth!" she said. "Truth is something you tell when it serves you and withhold when it doesn't."

"Katherine, don't go, don't..."

She turned away and he grabbed her arm. "Take your hands off me," she said. He didn't, so she picked up his glass and threw it in his face. He released her and sprang to his feet. A unified gasp went up around the room. While Alex wiped his clothes and sputtered, she gave him her retreating back.

Furious, Alex followed her. She reached her room just ahead of him and slammed the door in his face.

He banged on the door, shouting her name. "Katherine? Open this door, dammit!"

"When you grow hair on your eyeballs!"

"You heard me, open this damn door, or I'll kick it in."

"Go ahead. I'll request another room. This hotel has four hundred rooms, Alex. You can't kick all the doors in."

"I damn well can try."

"Good night, Alex."

"Goddammit! I'm warning you!"

"Thank you."

"Katherine, why won't you open this door?"

The door opened. A crumpled piece of paper came sailing through, hitting him in the face, then falling to the floor. The door slammed again. Alex sighed and ran his fingers through his wet hair. He bent down and picked up the crumpled piece of paper.

It was the note he had written to Karin.

He put the note in his pocket and turned slowly away. He was thinking how much he had to make up for. He had told her he loved her, but she didn't believe him. He had to tell her again, and soon. He had to make her believe him this time. *Tomorrow,* he told himself. *Tomorrow, or the day after. Whenever she cools down.* He glanced back at her door. He would give her time to rest. Then he would tell her. She couldn't stay mad at him forever. There would be another opportunity, another time.

But time was the one thing Alex did not have.

The next morning she walked with Adrian along a winding street that went up one hill and down the other. Adrian was busily explaining the performance of a long-anticipated saw that would increase their production by twenty thousand feet of wood per day, when Katherine was suddenly aware of how she wished it were Adrian she had fallen in love with, Adrian she had married.

As they walked back to the hotel, they crossed Portsmouth Square, where the infamous gambling houses like Bella Union and El Dorado were located. An iron fence with lampposts circled the square, protecting the newly planted trees, for the streets were crowded with horses, parked wagons, and buggies. Gambling, Adrian remarked to Katherine, was a favorite pastime with men in these parts.

"That must include Alex," she said, and Adrian followed the direction of Katherine's look to see Alex walk out of the El Dorado as they crossed the street in front of the Verandah Drug Store. He didn't see them, but turned up the street, walking toward the hotel. Katherine tried to keep her mind on other things, not wanting to give over to despair, so she began taking in the sights of the city around her. Something about it was strange now. San Francisco didn't seem quite as glamorous or exciting as it had a few short months ago when she had arrived.

Walking briskly up the street they passed one

gaming house after another, some with exotic names like Mazourka, Varsouvienne, La Souciedad, Alhambra, while others had names as plain as potato peelings—Parker House, Denison's Exchange, Fontine House.

The doors to one gaming house opened and a Chinese man was shoved into the street. Anticipating her question, Adrian said, "Most of the houses don't like the Celestials—that's what they call the Chinese—playing in them. They've got their own gaming houses over on Sacramento and Dupont streets. They have their own games, one of which is called *fan-tan*, and before you ask," he said, laughing, "I don't have even a glimmer of an idea how it's played. That can be a question you save for Wong."

A quick look down the east side of Dupont Street affirmed what Adrian said. Chinese men were everywhere, all neatly dressed in baggy black trousers and tops, white socks, black slippers, hats, and long, long braids. They were cleaner and better behaved than the miners and lumberjacks that were welcomed in the Portsmouth Square houses. There were some things that Katherine did not understand. This was one of them.

Adrian was enjoying this time alone with her. For so long he had been worried about her health that it was a pleasure to see her cheeks rosy from exercise, her eyes bright with excitement. Her clothes were dreadfully loose, but her eyes were as green as seawater and her hair as bright as a new penny. He had a feeling more changes in Katherine lay beneath the surface. He knew she would speak of them when the time was right for her and no amount of coaxing and prodding would move her to do so any sooner than that.

They stepped out into the shaded street, a cooler breeze blowing up from the water. Katherine shivered and drew her cape higher over her shoulders. A few days out of bed had not prepared her for the enormous drain of energy that came with a walk down San Francisco streets. Her steps slower now, Katherine felt the strain on her body. It made no difference now, but her heart thudded when she looked up the street, seeing Alex just ahead of them, his head towering over the shorter men about him. She wished she could go back to the days before she found the letter in his desk, to the days before she knew the secret and shame of what lay inside.

Her heart ached for him the same way it always had, but her mind offered no hope. Like a wise old grandmother, her head counseled a heart as young and green as a schoolgirl's. She felt the stabbing barrenness of a womb that would never bear a child, the emptiness of breasts that would never suckle. Her heart grieved for the children she had known so well; children whose names she knew as well as her own—Caleb and Jude, Caroline and Juliana.

Adrian and Katherine caught up with Alex in front of the hotel. As Adrian called out to him and Alex turned, Katherine realized that

515

her failure to make peace with her loss of Alex was draining her of energy and stamina she could not afford. She would have to leave him, leave San Francisco, and soon. A peace flowed through her. Not the peace that comes with getting the desire of one's heart, but a peace that comes with making a decision.

Alex did not remove his gaze from her as they approached, but it was a look she could not read. She felt cold and stiff and a thousand years old, and it occurred to her suddenly how much she wanted to get away from San Francisco and Alex and everything she associated with the pain in her life. A year ago she had left her home and traveled hundreds of miles to become this man's wife, an answer to a life-long dream. She had taken his name, but not his heart. Strangely, none of it seemed to matter anymore. Perhaps that's what growing old was, just a gradual easing into comfort, where you sought peace and ease above all else.

She stood frozen, waiting for the conversation between Alex and Adrian to end. Alex had met a man in the El Dorado to talk over the purchase of five more teams of Ayrshire oxen. Alex felt Ayrshires were the prime choice, while Adrian favored Durhams. But Alex convinced him that the Ayrshires being offered were valuable beasts—five pair of leaders for $300.00 a pair.

She found herself looking at Alex, seeing him in a different light. She loved him. But she could live without him. She felt suddenly free, as if some great weight had been taken from her shoulders. She found she was suddenly tired of trying to be everything to him. She had spent half of her life carrying the burden of unrequited love, giving so little time to herself. She found herself growing anxious to see the green fields of Limestone County, to count the spring calves and see the new additions to the family of beavers down at the creek. She wanted to feel the steamy warmth of Clovis's sleek coat as she brushed it when the hired hand brought him in after a hard day's plowing. She wanted to know the joy of watching a chick peck its way out of its shell and step out into a strange new world. She wanted to pull the weeds on her family's graves and to pick peaches until her back ached. She wanted to wake up each morning and say, "Katherine, what do *you* want to do today?"

And by golly, she was going to. As Fanny Bright always said, "Men aren't the cake, they're just the icing; they aren't the whole rooster, just the crow."

Pleading exhaustion, she left Alex and Adrian in the lobby. Once she was in her room, Katherine leaned back against the door, feeling the tears flow freely down her cheeks. She had to get away from here now. For a moment she considered how weak she felt and wondered if she should wait a few more days. *No.* Then she wondered if she should confide in Adrian? *No. He's as guilty in all of this as Alex. Neither one of them can be trusted. If you want anything done right, Katherine, take care of it yourself.* She had lived this long without having anyone to rely on. She didn't need to start acting helpless now. *Change what you can change and make the most of what you can't.* Wasn't that what her mother always said?

Smart people, mothers were.

"This is the last time I'm doing this," she said, packing the clothes she had purchased since coming to San Francisco. Remembering the lovely clothes as well as a few of her treasured belongings from home that she would be leaving behind at the camp at Humboldt Bay, she put a few more clothes into the valise and said, "If this keeps up I'll have clothes strung from one side of the United States to the other." She was still complaining when she sat down to fan herself after wrestling the lid closed.

After her irritation had settled somewhat, she dumped her reticule out and counted her money. Counting the money Alex had given her to buy some more clothes, she had three hundred dollars. Hopefully she could get some kind of accommodations on a ship heading for Texas. If not, she'd go as far as the money would take her, for she still intended to leave San Francisco. But she would make the arrangements herself.

Cervantes may have said, "Heaven's help is better than early rising," but as for her, Katherine decided to try both. That night she prayed her heart out, earnestly seeking God's guidance and help, and come the next morning, she was up before daybreak.

One thing about luck, she discovered, is that

it's always changing. Take yesterday, for instance. She wouldn't have given a plugged nickel for her luck then, but today? Well, today was a different matter. Today her luck had definitely changed, and for the better, for wasn't that Captain Steptoe's ship five spaces down on the list and scheduled to sail today?

Captain Steptoe was as surprised to see Katherine as she was to find his ship in port. "Well, bless my bones, if it isn't Mrs. Mackinnon. How's married life?"

"Let's just say that if it was something I ate, I'd be retching right now."

Captain Steptoe had never been known to show surprise at anything he saw or heard, and yet, here he was raising his bushy brows a good inch at Katherine's remark, his mouth curving into a good-natured smile. "Here now," he said, taking her arm and walking her on board, "it can't be as bad as all that. Why don't we have a cup of tea in my cabin and talk things over."

"The only thing I want to talk over is buying passage on your ship."

"Where are you headed for?" he asked.

"Where are you going?" she replied.

"New Orleans."

"That'll do," she said.

CHAPTER
TWENTY-TWO

Clarabelle Dudley and Jemima Tidwell were both in Draper's Dry Goods when the hack from

Waco pulled up in front of the Groesbeck Hotel. Clarabelle, who was dressed up like a country bride, stood with a bolt of blue calico in her arms. When she heard the hack, she hurried to the front window, calling for Jemima to "Come over here and get an eyeful of this!" which Jemima did with a burst of fervor.

"Well, I do declare! Will you look at that!" Jemima said. "What do you suppose *she's* doing back here?"

"Come back home is what it looks like to me," Clarabelle said, giving Jemima a sly look, "but the question is, why? Didn't that Mackinnon boy marry her?"

"Maybe he *wouldn't* marry her." Jemima crowded closer to the window, trying to push the bolt of blue calico aside so she could get a better look. "Does she look in a family way?"

"No. Not as yet, anyway. But I always say, time will tell."

"Yes, you always do," Jemima agreed, "and you're always right." Jemima took another look. "Do you suppose she'll tell anybody what she's doing back?"

"It would be a frosty Friday before she'd do that, I'd wager." Clarabelle looked at Jemima in a smug way. "But we could form a little welcoming committee and mosey on over there."

"Do you think we should?" Jemima asked, her eyes widening.

"Don't thump a free watermelon. That's opportunity knocking over there. Of course we should go."

The blue calico promptly laid aside, the two ladies departed the dry goods store and marched, single file, across the porch. But about the time they stepped into the street, Carter Mayberry pulled up beside the hack and offered the object of their attention a ride to Council Springs.

That drew the two women up short. With fallen faces they watched Carter and Old Mr. Fogelberg load Katherine's bags into Carter's wagon, then help her into the wagon.

"Well, flip my garter if that don't beat all!" Clarabelle said, her hands clamped on her hips as she watched their opportunity ride out of sight. "She always did have the luck of a Baptist—always up to something but you never could catch her at it."

"Well, I'll swan!" said Jemima, following Clarabelle's lead and clamping her hands on her hips and doing her best to look exasperated.

"Come on," Clarabelle said. "Standing here in the middle of the street like two fools is about as useless as a bug arguing with a chicken."

While the two women made their way back to the dry goods store, Katherine was talking to Carter Mayberry.

"There's something about coming home," she said as they drove from Groesbeck toward Council Springs and the Simon place. "To know it again after a long absence... how to explain?" she said with a sigh. Then, shaking her head, her hands clasped together and resting on her knees. "There's nothing quite like it."

"I've only been away from home once and that was for the war," Carter said. "When it was over, I was so dadblasted happy to be home again—and in one piece—that I swore then I'd never leave again 'til they carried me out in a pine box."

Katherine looked at Carter. Folks in town said he was so thin he had to stand twice to cast a shadow. He did look pretty thin, even to her, his long body folded in the seat in what she could only describe as a comfortable slouch, the reins riding easy in his slack hands, his neck thrust forward as if he were trying to get a whiff of what was being cooked for supper. She thought how fortunate it was for her that Carter had spied her getting off the hack from Waco and offered her a ride. "I'm much obliged to you, Carter, for the ride. I don't know what I would've done if you hadn't come along when you did."

"Heck, Miz Katherine, it ain't out of my way none to come this way. Glad to be of help." Carter slapped the broad back of his mule and the mule kicked, then went back to his same leisurely pace. Katherine closed her eyes for a moment and tipped her head back, enjoying the warm sun on her face, listening to the steady clip, clip, clip of the mule that seemed perfectly spaced between the rhythmic creak of the back wheel. How she had missed this place. She opened her eyes just as Carter put a quid of tobacco in his mouth, which meant what little conversation they had heretofore enjoyed was now over. Seeing Carter chew that tobacco—well, it reminded her of Adrian. She closed her eyes again, remembering the day she asked Adrian why he had taken up that nasty habit. "Why not?" was the only answer he gave.

Still curious, Katherine had gone one step farther and said, "I never took you for one to take up the habit." Then glancing at him covertly, she added, "I can't picture you being happy chewing tobacco for the rest of your life."

"I don't plan on chewing it forever. I'm just waiting for some pretty little thing to come along and ask me, kinda sweetlike, to stop."

They bounced along the long stretch of country road in silence, Carter chewing and taking an occasional spit, and Katherine drinking in every inch of the countryside, like she was committing it to memory.

She thought of herself in comparison with her mother at her age, picturing her standing at the kitchen stove with two young babies playing on the floor behind her. Katherine guessed she would have to resign herself to the fact that she would be the dried-up type, more spinster than married woman.

She made herself stop thinking about that. She was young and healthy and had a passel of things to be thankful for and she would probably live to a ripe old age. *Lord willing and the creek don't rise.* Besides, it was a glorious day and she was home. Everything would fall into place after that.

She was home. Every leaf seemed a bit greener, every breath of air a bit fresher than it had been before. Home. A place to come to. Home. A place that never turned you away. She clasped her hands together in excitement, watching the countryside she knew so well pass like so many turned pages in an oft-read book. She closed her eyes, knowing by heart every mile of the way—every turn in the road, every gate, every watering trough, every barn and pond. More than once she found herself looking back, to the day she had left here, thinking she would never return.

They rattled on down the road, past Mrs. Knight's ruffled drawers drying in the warm spring breeze, past the dead hackberry overgrown with woodbine that dangled fragrant as lilac water over the curve in the road. Then came the old Hempstead place, with Granny Hempstead in her usual spot, rocking on the front porch while she cracked the tough pods of last year's okra to free the seeds for planting this season. And then they bounced past the McFarlane place, and even from where she sat, Katherine could see it must have been a good year, for Mrs. McFarlane had brand new white ruffle curtains fluttering in her kitchen windows. When they passed the Webster place, little Tommy Webster was leading a parade of five of the Websters younger than him, each of them waving a Texas flag as they marched. Much to Tommy's irritation, they broke ranks to run to the fence and wave, and Katherine waved back. But the minute they topped a rise and her home's chimney came into view, something warm and rich as chocolate flooded her soul.

Carter must have sensed it was a moment special to her, for he pulled the mule up and sat a spell while she took everything in. "Coming home sure is nice," she said.

"Yep. My ma always said home was the one place you could go to where they had to take you in." He slapped the mule and they went on down the road.

The house still looked the same, shabby and in need of paint, but it was infinitely more dear to her now. And surrounding it were the yellow-green fields, brushed with the faintest haze of lavender-blue as the bluebonnets were beginning to bloom. There was the curving road, the staggering sweep of stately pecans, the overgrown garden needing the attention of a plow, the fences that always needed mending, the old sow wallowing in the mud with a passel of new piglets squealing at her side. And further over was Clovis, standing beside a hackberry crowded with mistletoe, his ears splayed to each side, his eyes half-closed as he soaked up the warm sun beating against his thick black hide, and on the fence behind him sat the peacock with his tailfeathers drooping into the nurse pen where the calves chewed the ends until they were ragged and bare.

They came to the place where the road cut

off to the Simon place. "I'll get out here," she told Carter.

"Don't you want me to take you on up to the house?"

"No, I want to walk. It's only a short piece."

"What about your belongings?"

"We'll drop them here. I'll come back for them with the wagon later."

"Tell you what, you go on and get out and I'll drive your belongings on up to the house. That'll save you having to hitch up the wagon." He gave her a teasing smile. "Who knows? You may have forgotten how to hitch up a mule by now."

"Who knows?" she repeated with a laugh. "I might have."

She watched Carter mosey on up the road, biding his time, in no hurry to get to the house and unload her things. A few minutes later she waved to him as he passed by. "Good to have you home again, Miz Katherine."

"Why, thank you, Carter. It's nice to be back. It really is."

And that was the gospel if she'd ever heard it.

She walked into the barnyard, seeing the wagon drawn up in front of the barn, blocking one of the double doors. Sacks of seed and mash were stacked in the back. Over near the woodpile was a new mound of wood shavings. The sight pleased her for it meant Fanny Bright was still here, looking after the place, and from the looks of things, she had either found another hired hand, or was keeping up with things on her own. Turning toward the house, Katherine had just walked through the back gate when the back door opened, and with a shriek of laughter, Fanny Bright hurled herself down the steps and came hurrying toward her. "If you aren't a sight for sore eyes," she said. "What are you doing back so soon? Where's Alex?"

"I've left him."

That drew Fanny up short. "You mean as in for good?" Katherine nodded. "Bless my soul, Katherine! You didn't!"

Again, Katherine nodded. "I did. It's over between us, Fanny."

"Hold on, now. How can it be over when it hasn't even had enough time to get started?" She gave Katherine one of those suspicious, *sideways* looks of hers. "Something ain't right here," she said. "I smell a rat in the woodpile." Narrowing her eyes, she looked long and hard at Katherine, seeing the brightness in her eyes. If she had ever seen a body that looked like they were fixing to swell up and bawl, it was Katherine. "Now, don't you go measuring that snake before it's stretched out dead," she said, her arm going around Katherine in a consoling manner. "You come on in the house now, and tell ole Fanny all about it. What's done ain't done until you say it's done."

"This time I think it's done, Fanny—plumb tuckered out, give out and done in, as the old man said."

"I thought the old man said, fizzled, farted, and fell?"

Even that didn't make her laugh. "Must have been a different old man," was all Katherine said, and she said it so morosely that Fanny laughed. Her little gal might be down, but she wasn't done in, no matter if she was feeling lower than a snake's belly right now.

Fanny opened the door and followed her in. "Well, we all get too soon old and too late smart, but don't you be forgetting the man who sits on a red hot stove will rise again."

"And the stove is going to get hotter when everyone starts asking questions."

And ask they did. Over the next few weeks, Katherine felt she had explained her reasons to half of the curious folks in Limestone County. She found herself praying the other half would hear it through the grapevine—or any other way besides from her. It hurt too much to talk about it, and she knew as long as she talked about it she wouldn't forget. "I just don't understand," she said to Fanny one afternoon. "Why hasn't word gotten around to everyone by now? Surely I can't be that interesting."

"I think that old busybody Clarabelle Dudley might have something to do with that," Fanny said. "From what I hear, she and Jemima Tidwell aren't content to let sleeping dogs lie."

"Clarabelle isn't a bad sort. She's just bored."

"Oh yes, that Clarabelle Dudley is a fine, fine woman. Why, she can bear another's misfortune like a true Christian."

Katherine laughed. "Not even Clarabelle can

talk about this forever. She'll wear out sooner or later."

"I 'spect so. But you know how some things move slower than coal tar running uphill backwards. Folks tend to talk a thing to death, waiting for something better to come along."

Katherine figured Fanny was right, and decided to put her mind to reacquainting herself with her home, getting her mind on farming again, and losing herself in her work. Her first discovery was that Fanny had done a good job of taking care of things while she had been gone. She hadn't as yet found a permanent hired hand, but she had found one that wasn't. "Old Festus Maxwell has been helping me out some, in exchange for a few meals. 'Course he and that old mule of his are both so old, they only have one speed."

"I'll place an ad or two," Katherine said. "If that doesn't work, I may have to go to Dallas or Ft. Worth. Has Karin looked for anyone in Waco? That's much closer."

According to Fanny, Karin was so busy with Will Burnett that she didn't have time to be bothered with the farm. "You handle it as you see fit, Fanny," is what Karin had said.

"But she did give me a large sum of money. Together with the money you sent from California, and what I had left from the sale of my place—well, we could be calling ourselves prosperous right now—if we were prone to pat ourselves on the back."

It was early spring and there was enough work to be done for five men. Katherine had been taught at an early age to depend upon herself, to do what needed to be done and to make the most of what one had. To keep her mind off Alex, Katherine worked hard from sunup to sundown, running a sod cutter over the soil, harrowing it, then seeding—doing too many tasks a woman had no business doing, and Fanny told her so. "We've always been able to trade off work with some of the neighboring men for those jobs. There's no need to kill yourself."

At first, self-pity and grief were so keen she could think of nothing but backbreaking work as a form of punishment, a self-fashioned hair shirt she could wear at will. As the days passed, one behind the other, little stretches of peace and security began to fill the void and the pain gradually gave way to a sense of loss.

Katherine hired a man from Corsicana to help with the farm and things settled in nicely. She had been back at the old Simon place a good month before Karin got word and hurried over from Waco to inspect the changes and find out, straight from the horse's mouth, what it was, exactly, that brought her sister back to Texas.

Katherine felt her newfound sense of peace and security flag a bit when Karin arrived, marching into the house amid a flouncing of lavender ruffles and announcing that her sister "was a bigger fool than she had ever in her wildest imaginings imagined."

"Thank you, Karin, and it's nice to see you again, too."

Karin rushed over and took Katherine in her arms. "Oh, Katherine, I didn't mean it to sound that way," said Karin, looking shamefaced for a moment. "Of course I'm glad to see you." Practicality taking over, she added, "You're my sister, aren't you?"

"Last time I heard, I was."

Karin laughed. "I see you haven't lost your sense of humor, so it can't be all bad. Now, do be serious Katherine. You know I have your best interest at heart. I want what is best for you...honestly, Katherine, I just don't understand why you came back"—she paused and pulled off her white gloves—"without Alex I mean."

Karin had been pacing the floor in the parlor, passing back and forth in front of the cheval mirror, when she suddenly took notice of herself and paused dramatically to wet her finger and smooth it over her eyebrow, then wet it again, going at the other one. She turned her head this way and that, fluttering her lashes a time or two and moistened her lips. Eventually, she looked satisfied with herself. "You know I heard some women talking the other day, and I don't mean to imply anything at all, but one of the women just happened to mention the daughter of a friend of hers that had, only a few months before, mind you, up and run off with a hurdy-gurdy player and then come home p-r-e-g-n-a-n-t."

There was a lengthy pause. The sisters stared at each other in the mirror. "You aren't going to have a baby, are you?"

"No, and even if I was, I wouldn't be coming home in shame. You seem to forget I *was* married, Karin."

"Well of course you were," Karin said, looking at Katherine intently, "but people around here don't know that for certain, and you know how they like to talk. But of course if you aren't, *you know what,* they won't have anything to talk about, will they?" She giggled happily. "Isn't it strange how things work out? You were always the one who never had a beau. Just think...if you hadn't married Alex, I wouldn't be here now helping you through this time of trial." Giving Katherine a vague look, Karin's expression was one of amazement. "What a surprise this is!" she said. "And here I always thought you were so much more intelligent than me."

"It only shows when she's doing sensible things...like matching socks," Fanny said, coming into the room with a feather duster, going after the table and mirror next to Karin, stirring up a cloud of dust that drove Karin to the front porch in a coughing fit.

That night Karin came into Katherine's room. Katherine was sitting in the chair next to the window trying to thread a needle in the poor light. Karin insisted that she put the needle and thread away so they could talk. Katherine told her about the mistake Alex made, beginning by saying, "Things aren't always what they seem...."

When she finished, Karin said, "You mean to tell me...?"

"Alex thought he was asking for you. He wrote my name by mistake. It was you he meant to ask for, not me."

Karin looked pleased for a moment, then she frowned. Popping up out of the chair, she said, "Oh posh! I don't think Alex knew what he wanted. If he planned on asking for me, it was out of habit. Alex and I were finished long before that. Besides, I was never *that* serious about Alex. Back then I was young and foolish, I didn't know what I wanted. I fancied myself in love with him because he was the best man around at the time. I've grown up a lot, Katherine. Will has helped me see things better. Alex was my childhood beau, nothing more."

Katherine noticed Karin seemed a little preoccupied, and felt it was because of the news she had just given her, in spite of how well Karin seemed to be taking it. But when Katherine mentioned this, Karin jumped to her feet and pressed her opened palm flat against her chest, as if for emphasis. "Oh, it's not that way at all. If I am preoccupied, as you say, then it must be because it's so very hard for me to think of Alex at all." Her face lit up and she said, "I'm in love with Will, Katherine. I mean really and truly in love. He's such a wonderful man, and he understands me. I think it's because he's older. He's so understanding and kind. He doesn't mind my spending at all. He says I was born to be surrounded by beautiful things."

They talked on for some time. It was clear

to Katherine that Karin's new love was clearly a man of substance. When Katherine asked what he did, Karin said, "He's a very busy man. He has all kinds of investments and land. He even owns several ships...and a building in New York! Can you imagine that? He is such an intelligent man, a good businessman... everyone in Waco knows him. He's very much a leader there. He even knows the governor."

"Have you seen any of his holdings, met any of the people that work for him?"

"Heavens no. That sort of thing doesn't interest me at all."

"Does he ever discuss his business with you?"

"Whatever for?"

"Don't you want to know what it is that he does, exactly?"

"My dear sister, I am perfectly happy just to share what he has. What do I care about boring things like banking and finance and interest rates? He buys me lovely things and says all I have to do is look beautiful. Honestly, Katherine, why would I want to do anything else?"

Maybe Karin had a point there. Even as she said it, Katherine knew she wouldn't be content to live like that for a minute. "Karin," she said, "don't you ever feel the need to use your *mind*?"

"I use my mind, Katherine. What do you take me for, a cabbage head? I just use my mind in a *social* way," she said, and that was that.

Karin spent two nights, leaving the following morning when Will came after her. Katherine remembered meeting Will, but at the time she hadn't paid much attention to him. Seeing a very distinguished gray-haired man climb out of a coach driven by a uniformed driver and pulled by four matched chestnuts, Katherine's immediate reaction was that Karin had done exactly as she said she would do. She had her a rich man. Whether or not they married remained to be seen. "Take a look at that coach and those horses," Fanny said, coming up behind them. "He must be rich, but he's awfully old for you, isn't he?"

"How old is too old, Fanny? I love him and he treats me like a queen. I'd rather have that than youth."

Katherine stared in amazement at her sister. Who would've thought it? Karin sounded downright sensible. Katherine felt a thrill of happiness and hugged Karin, giving her a kiss on her cheek, happy that they had been given this time together, that they had been able to confide in each other, happy to see that things were going so well for Karin. For in truth, Katherine had never seen her look happier. "That's what's important," she said, going out to the porch with Karin to greet Will. Katherine saw immediately that Will was every bit as nice and attentive as Karin said he was.

Watching the two of them drive off, Katherine thought she had never seen Karin as relaxed and confident around a man as she was around Will. She mulled that over for a minute, then turned and went back into the house to roast the Java coffee in the oven. There were mattresses to be aired, corn to be boiled into hominy, grease to be rendered by frying potato peelings in it, and a hole in the henhouse that had to be patched. And those were just the morning chores.

The next few months passed quickly and quietly, each day very much like the one before, so that it was easy to feel life had become a bit monotonous. Often she would find herself waking up in the morning and asking herself, "Is this today or yesterday?" For the days did seem to blend, one into the other, until it was difficult to distinguish what unexciting event had happened on which uneventful day.

All in all, Katherine couldn't exactly say she was gloriously happy, yet she was content and satisfied with the way work at the farm was progressing. Hiram, the new hand had set up housekeeping in the old Crenshaw place a mile or so down the road. Honest as the day is long, he worked, as Fanny said, "Hard enough for two men." The rains had been good that spring and the corn was as tall as the eaves on the house, and now that July was here, it had turned hot and dry, perfect weather for the corn to mature.

She tried not to think of Alex, but so many memories of him were tied to her home: the creek where he'd taught her about blood bait, the tree where he always tied his horse, the initials he'd carved on the tree next to the barn, the hole he'd shot through the smokehouse door. *It would have been so much easier it I had never married him, never felt what it was like to lie in his arms, to become intoxicated from his near-ness.* She was a woman in love; a woman with natural desires; a woman without a man. No excuses could explain that away, no amount of work could compensate for it. She missed Alex. She missed being around him. She missed the way she felt around him, the things he did to her, the things he taught her at night when they were alone. She told herself she was behaving shamelessly, that there were names for women like her, but nothing seemed to help. Whenever Karin and Will came over, Katherine would find herself despondent for days after they left. How happy she was that Karin had found what she had always been looking for, that she and Will seemed so happy. How happy she could have been if she were still with Alex. Once the sadness began to ease, she would tell herself to make the most of what she had. *Be content with what you have, Katherine, stop dreaming about what might have been, what could have been.* And as always, whenever she told herself this she wondered if leaving him had been the right thing to do.

Of course she had no answer for that. She mentioned that to Fanny one afternoon when they were both scrubbing down the churn and milk pails, putting them in the sun to dry. "I'd say it was simple enough to answer," Fanny had said. "Ask yourself if you're hap-pier now than you were then. If you are, then you did the right thing. If you're not...well, that's for you to decide."

Whenever she remembered Fanny's words the pain of missing him would return. No, she wasn't happier without Alex. If she didn't force herself to work to the point of exhaustion she would have found herself crying more than she already was. As it was now, nights were the hardest for her. That was when the memory of him was the strongest.

One good point had come out of everything, and that was at least the slate had been wiped clean. There were no more lies between them. She hadn't heard from Alex and had no way of knowing how he felt about her leaving, but deep in her heart, she felt he missed her— if only a little. *I know Alex had grown to care for me, I know it.* And then she would ask herself, *If you knew it, why did you leave?*

"Do you think I should have forgiven Alex before I left?" she asked Fanny.

"Forgiveness isn't the same thing as going to the Farmer's Market. You don't plop a basket on your arm and go happily along, selecting the things that look good to you, passing over the things that don't. You either forgive, or you don't. If you believed the things he said, why couldn't you forgive him? He's your husband, the man you say you love. And yet you can't forgive him? I've seen you forgive friends who wronged you. And Karin too, more times than I could count. Why is it so much easier to forgive friends or family, or even strangers than the man you love?"

"I don't know."

"I had an uncle once. He was a man of the cloth. He told me that forgiveness when it was given was like a miracle, making everything whole, complete, and new again."

Hearing it laid out like that—like the squares of a quilt, it did seem simple indeed—nothing more than a matter of forgiveness. Funny thing about forgiveness—talking about it and doing it were two horses of different colors.

She considered her options. She could have waited to see how things would go between herself and Alex. Immediately she ruled that one out. There comes a time when you know it's time to quit, and that time had come. Staying would have made her bitter, and that would ruin both of their lives. She still had options: She could write him. *No, you made your move, Katherine. The next move is up to Alex.* Besides, what could she say now? I've decided to forgive you? He would laugh all the way from California at that one.

You could also admit that you might be a little to blame here as well.

She didn't like the sound of that one, so she dismissed it. Only that didn't work. Time after time, it kept coming back to haunt her. *You could also admit that you might be a little to blame here as well.*

She didn't want to be accountable. She didn't want to think of herself as being at fault. *You knew, Katherine. Deep down in your heart of hearts you knew there was something rotten in Denmark when that letter came from Alex asking you to marry him. You knew, but you wanted him so much you smothered the spark of doubt. That makes you a little accountable for some of your misery too, doesn't it?*

Katherine didn't want to think about that right now. But in spite of it all, a flickering light was beginning to glow dimly within her, a light which, telling her what was right, was also showing her where she had been wrong. The light wasn't strong enough to draw her undivided attention, but it did bewilder and add to her confusion. Like a candle in the sun, it went unnoticed in the light of day, but it came to her at night when she lay between sleep and consciousness, a shadowy torment which robbed her of sleep and good feelings.

It could be said that Katherine Mackinnon was beginning to realize that the most essential element of growth lies in human choice. It had been her choice, and her choice only, to leave Alex and therefore be unhappy, just as it could be her choice to continue this unhappiness by muffling herself in a cocoon of denial until the day she died. In other words, she had come to the end of a road. She would have to choose whether she wanted to turn around and backtrack a bit until she came to another road, or if she wanted to just sit there until she started to rust.

Or, as Fanny said, "Just because you burned your finger is no reason to put out the fire and freeze your arse."

Fanny always had a wonderful way of putting things that went right to the heart of the matter. What Fanny had said struck Katherine so funny that as solemn as she was feeling, she had collapsed in a fit of laughter.

It got to be a joke after that, for every time Katherine was falling back into her old stubbornness, Fanny would say: "Katherine, you're freezing your arse."

In spite of Fanny's reminders, there just didn't seem to be much joy left in her life. "Bitter fruit," is what she likened it to.

As always, Fanny had a response for that one too. "That's easily fixed. It's nothing more than a matter of maturing. All fruit is bitter before it turns ripe," she said.

Speaking of fruit, one afternoon, Katherine was out in the orchard gathering freestone peaches when Clarabelle Dudley walked up. Katherine had seen her coming, wandering through the burdened trees, closing in on her like a sidewinder tracking supper. It was, to Katherine, sort of a predetermined, yet enraptured voyage, where Clarabelle walked a course of solid resolution but checked every bit of fruit she passed along the way, going so far as to drop a few peaches that passed inspection into the basket on her arm.

"I've been hearing some astonishing things about you in town," Clarabelle said, ducking under a low branch and coming to stand in back of Katherine who was three rungs up on a ladder.

Katherine kept on picking peaches and dropping them into the large pockets of her apron. "What kind of things?" she asked.

"Of course, I don't suppose I am any more astonished than you are, being a married woman and having to live out here and make do without a man about."

Katherine paused and turned halfway around. "Why should that astonish either one of us? I've been making do without a man for most of my life."

"Well, of course you have, but now that you're married folks just naturally assumed you'd be living with your husband."

"My husband is a busy man and a lumber camp is no place for a woman."

"It's too bad you didn't know that before you went all the way out there and then had to come all the way back."

"I'm glad I went. And I'm glad I'm back."

Reading the irritation in Katherine's voice, Clarabelle frowned. "I must say you've taken on quite a big responsibility. I've never seen so many fields under cultivation...not even when your pa was alive. Folks were saying in town the other day that it was a big undertaking even for a large family, and here you are just two women and a hired hand. Of course, I'm not trying to discourage you any."

"That's good, because you're not," was Katherine's dry reply. "I wanted to see what this old farm could do and I'm doing just that. We've had a good, prosperous year. The land has been good to us." Katherine climbed down from the ladder and began pulling the peaches out of her pockets and putting them into the crate. Then she looked square at Clarabelle. "What brings you out here on a hot day like this?" she asked. "Were you appointed by the Ladies Sewing Circle to come out here and research a few topics for your next discussion?"

Clarabelle made a pathetic attempt to laugh. "No, of course not. I just stopped by for a friendly visit. I was on my way to visit my late husband's aunt. She lives in the old Mabry place."

"That's interesting, since you passed the road to the old Mabry place a couple of miles back," Katherine said.

Clarabelle tried to look surprised and missed. "Fancy that," she said. "In that case, I suppose I'd best be heading back the way I came." She turned and made her way toward her buggy.

Katherine couldn't resist calling after her. "Enjoy the peaches," she said, but if Clarabelle heard, she didn't let on.

Katherine moved the ladder over to another tree and began picking peaches, just as she had been before. Once again, she had just climbed to the third step when she heard someone come up behind her. Clarabelle was fast making herself a pest. *What could she possibly want this time. More peaches?*

Without turning around, Katherine said, "Did you lose something?"

"Yes, as a matter of fact, I did," said a deep, masculine voice. "My wife."

CHAPTER
TWENTY-THREE

A lot of men in the world might be missing a wife.

But there was only one person in the whole world who had a voice like that. *It can't be.* The branches overhead began to grow fuzzy and blurred, the sky overhead started to whirl. Dizziness gripped her and she reached for a branch to steady herself, misjudged the distance and missed, losing her balance. His arms were around her before she fell and she felt herself lifted. She raised her head and looked into the bluest eyes this side of paradise. "They say," she said weakly, "that a man surprised is half beaten. Do you suppose that applies to women as well?"

"God, I hope so," Alex said.

Alex. *Dear, beloved Alex.* The feel of his arms, the sight of his beloved face. She felt like weeping. She wanted to die laughing. She wanted to kiss him for coming. She wanted to shake him for taking so long. She wanted to beat him over the head with her bucket, just for the heck of it. The sound of his voice washed over her, strong and uplifting. The sight of him was something she never expected to see again, the smile on his face touching her like a blessing. She wanted to bury her face against his neck, wanted to tell him all the things that were in her heart, how much she had missed him, how sorry she was she left, how she was ready to forgive him, but the words froze in her throat and she wanted to scream from the agony of it. She didn't want it to be this way. She wanted there to be no past, no mistakes, no deception, no foolish pride. There was only Alex, here, where she had so often wished him, and herself, still frozen in misery and unwilling to forgive.

"Well," he said, giving her a slow smile, "here I was, missing a wife, and now one has dropped into my arms. I had no idea wives were so plentiful in these parts that they were falling out of trees. I should have come sooner."

She felt the constriction in her throat. She was still so stunned, all she could say was, "Put me down."

The humor in his eyes dimmed and then brightened. She knew what it cost him to force it now. "I come halfway around the world to see you and you tell me to put you down?"

"That's no more than I did," she said. "I went halfway around the world to get away from you. Besides, what should I have said? Drop me?"

He laughed.

She wasn't softened one bit. "You shouldn't have come," she said, wiggling and trying to get free. "Will you put me down?"

"Only if you promise not to run away again," he said, giving her a soft look. "Why did you leave me, lass?"

Lass. Oh Alex, why did you have to say it that way? "I thought it would be best. I've never fancied myself staying where I wasn't wanted."

"You were always wanted. You just didn't know it."

"Neither did you, apparently." She drew back her head and looked at him thoughtfully. "Why are you here?"

"To show you what it can be like between us, to teach you how easy it is to forgive, even when you think you can't."

She struggled again, and he lowered her to her feet, watching her back away from him and then look at him like he was a stranger, waiting.

Everything around her had grown strangely quiet. All around her she could hear the locusts buzzing. The sun overhead was still shining and very bright, a shaft of it slanting through the trees, making a rectangle on the orchard floor for Alex to stand in. And that was all he was doing, just standing there, looking at her in much the same shocked way she was looking at him. For a while, that was all she wanted to do. It had been so long since she had seen him, so long since she had felt a part of something. For a long time she had felt alone, as if the very world had found her lacking and retreated, pulling back to observe her from a distance. She realized that she hadn't really wanted to feel accepted, that in some small way she had still wanted to cling to her pain, withdrawing to herself, as if the pain alone could keep the memory of Alex alive. But he was here, standing just a few feet from her.

Alex looked at her, remembering that

morning over a year ago, when he had gone to her room and found nothing save a short, terse note. His first reaction had been to get rip-roaring drunk and stay that way for a week. Who knows? If Adrian hadn't found him and locked him up, he might still be drunk. When he sobered up, Alex found he was thinking straighter than he had in years. He hadn't been really and truly happy even before Katherine came to California and that, he knew now, was because he had never wanted to be a lumber baron in the first place. He had never wanted anything more than to farm and raise cattle and children on the best-looking spread in Texas money could buy. That was the reason he'd gone to the goldfields in the first place.

That wasn't the end of his surprises. When he'd told Adrian of his desire to go back to Texas, Adrian said, "I think that's the smartest thing I've ever heard you say."

"You do? Why?"

"Maybe it's because I'm tired of looking at your long face. Maybe I'm sick of fighting with you all the time." He grinned. "Or maybe it's because I want to do business with Victoria Talbot and you keep getting in the way."

Alex shook his head. "What are you trying to do? Buy out the competition?"

"You might call it that." Adrian laughed. "Hell's bells, man. You're my brother. Why wouldn't I want to see you happy?"

"There have been a lot of times in the past when you went out of your way to keep that fact well hidden," Alex said sourly, but Adrian was in a cheerful mood and merely clapped his brother on the back and suggested they go have themselves a drink.

They agreed on a price and Adrian bought Alex's share. It had taken time to get the ownership transferred and Alex's money in the San Francisco bank, but the minute it was done, he was ready to go after Katherine—on bended knees if that's what it took. Perhaps it had all worked out for the best. If Katherine hadn't found out, she would have never left him, and if she hadn't left, they would in all likelihood have spent the rest of their lives chopping wood instead of planting seeds.

Looking at Katherine now, he had trouble remembering anything except a desire to put things right between them, for what they had been robbed of could never be regained. Knowing he didn't want to get all bogged down in the past, he concentrated on the here and now. *First things first, and all that,* he reminded himself. "Katherine..." He took a step toward her and she almost turned away.

She almost turned away—but she didn't. She didn't know why. She couldn't bring herself to say the words he wanted to hear, words that would heal, but neither could she lash out at him and send him on his way. He had come for her and that said a great deal. The thought that he might really care for her was too new, too fresh to deal with now. She shook her head. "Let's don't talk anymore. We've both said too many things in the past, things that have hurt and left scars. You're back. That's as much as I can handle right now."

Alex was silent for such a long time she wondered if he had suddenly lost his voice. But then he lifted his head to look at her, seeing her bare feet, the leaves and twigs in her hair, smelling the bloom of ripe peaches that clung to her skin. His hand trembled as it came up to pinch the bridge of his nose. "I suppose you're right," he said with a weak laugh. "To tell the truth, I don't think I have the stamina to say anything either, at least not right now."

He looked off for a long moment, as if he was putting things right in his mind, then he turned and looked at her with a soft look. She was afraid of the feelings he touched within her. They stood for a long moment, unspeaking, unmoving. A silent plea so strong she wasn't sure if it was his thoughts she was reading or her own. For a moment they weren't two adults lashing out at each other with harsh words that were meant for pain. For a flicker of time the years fell away and they were standing again in the pasture where Katherine found the dead fawn and he had come to her, feeling her despair, giving her his strength and understanding. Dear God, she wanted it to be that way again. As if knowing her thoughts he lifted his hand to lay it gently along the hollow of her cheek. "This is the place," he said. "Isn't it?"

For a moment she didn't understand what he was asking, but then it stirred within her, a half-remembered breeze that carried the sound of her mother's voice, the words she whispered whenever she touched the curve of Katherine's cheek where Alex was touching it now. "The place," Katherine whispered, remembering. "Where obstinance makes it curve."

He smiled. "Strange that I should remember that now."

"Yes," she said. "Strange that you remembered something my mother said a long time ago. Something I forgot."

His face was a place of hollowed-out sadness that wrenched her heart. "That's what being married is, isn't it? One carrying on when the other is unable, one being strong where the other is weak, one remembering what the other can't?" He turned away, pausing just long enough to look back at her and say, "I'll be back."

She watched him go, the trees closing behind him, one by one, to cloak him like stretching fingers of fog. He was going. But he would return. She felt a deep aching sadness inside her, afraid he had come back too soon, that he had returned before she had suffered and grown enough, before time had a chance to turn her bitter fruit sweet.

Alex took up residence in the old Mackinnon place across the creek. He had been there a little over a week, keeping himself busy and dropping in on Katherine and Fanny enough to "wear out his welcome," but he didn't. It was one afternoon, the second week in August, when he rode over to Katherine's house. He found her in the backyard, winding the thorny branches of a climbing rose in a trellis she had just whitewashed. The heat and the close proximity of Alex had her in a dandy mood. It didn't take Alex long to find that out.

"Don't tell me you're back already," she said sourly.

"Okay," he said in good humor, "I'm not back."

"Good, then I can go on about my rat killing and not have to pretend you aren't here."

"Is that the same as ignoring me?"

Katherine looked at him through narrowed eyes and then snipped off a dead bloom in a manner that made him feel it could have just as easily been his neck. "It is," she said.

"Then you won't mind if I don't ignore you. That wouldn't be polite, you know."

"I don't want you to be polite. I don't want you to be anything...except gone. I've got work to do, Alex."

"Katherine!" Karin gasped, coming out the back door. "Where are your manners?"

Karin. How lucky can I get? Katherine mumbled something else under her breath and crossed her arms, looking at her sister. "What are you doing here in the middle of the week?"

"I have the most wonderful news to tell you." She stopped in front of Alex, giving him a looking-over like she was committing him to memory. "Hello, Alex. You've changed."

He looked at Karin briefly. "Hello, Karin. So have you." His eyes went back to his wife.

551

He realized suddenly what had just happened. For a moment Alex was too stunned to move. He had just seen Karin, the woman he had loved longer than he could remember and it hadn't done a blasted thing to him. He hadn't felt even the slightest quiver of attachment. Not even a flicker of interest. He had known he would ultimately see Karin again, and he hoped to prove to himself that he didn't love her as he once had, but he didn't plan on being knocked over the head with the surprise of it.

Maybe you didn't get a good look. Or maybe she didn't look good.

His eyes went over Karin, slow and easy. Nope, that wasn't it. She looked good. Real good. *But not as good as Katherine.*

Maybe it just hasn't had time to soak in that it's Karin you're looking at.

He couldn't help himself. He looked her over good and proper this time, from the yellow straw bonnet dripping with pink silk flowers and the smooth shimmer of golden curls clustered beneath the bow, over the pink dimity dress, the tiny waist, the slim hips, the parasol, now closed and balanced in her hand. All the way from Waco and not a smudge or a wrinkle or a hair out of place.

What are you feeling now?

Nothing.

Nothing?

A great, big, wonderful nothing. He smiled, feeling supreme satisfaction. The feeling vanished the minute his eyes landed on Katherine.

There she was, in her faded gingham bonnet, strings dangling—make that one string dangling, for the other was missing entirely—one braid, sloppy and coming loose, hanging down her back. His eyes traveled over the simple cotton dress—the blue washed out and faded almost to gray except at the seams—then down the sleeves which were rolled up, making him notice the scratches from the rosebush on her arms, the green stains on her hands. Strange, the things that make a man hear music and go weak in the knees. He took another quick look at Karin. *Nothing.* Then he looked at Katherine. *There it is again. The sound of music. The weak knees. It must be love.*

His eyes lingered on his wife's face. She wasn't taking all this scrutiny too well.

Katherine was still standing with her arms crossed, watching Alex and Karin drool over each other like two starved hogs eyeing the same slops. Unable to stand it any longer, Katherine said, "What wonderful surprise do you have for me?"

"Come into the house," she said, taking Katherine's hand, then seeing how dirty it was, she dropped it. "The surprise is in there."

No one invited Alex, but he tagged along anyway, telling himself that no one had told him to stay away either.

"Why didn't you write to tell me he was back?" Karin said, as they went up the back steps.

"I haven't talked to you since he came.

Besides, I didn't think it was important." Giving her a questioning look, she added, "Is it?"

Karin looked dumbfounded. "Heavens, no. Why would you ask that?"

"I don't know," Katherine said, stepping into the kitchen. "Why would I?"

"Well, fiddle-dee-dee, I don't want to get all bogged down in trivia at a time like this." She took Katherine's arm, careful to avoid her hand, and led her into the parlor. William Burnett was standing in front of the window, looking as handsome and distinguished as he had the day Katherine met him. Katherine looked around the room. Will was the only thing that had been added, but he wasn't a surprise, since Katherine had already met him weeks ago.

"Where's the surprise?"

"Right here," Karin said, releasing Katherine's arm and moving to take Will's.

Fanny walked into the room about that time. "You're giving him to us?"

Everyone laughed except Katherine, who felt like she was the only one left in the dark. "We're married," Karin said. "As of ten o'clock this morning I'm Mrs. William B. Burnett." She held up her hand to show her ring and Fanny backed away from the glare.

"That ain't a surprise," Fanny said. "It's a miracle."

This time Katherine laughed along with everyone else, running across the room to hug Karin. "I can't believe you got married without telling me," she said.

Karin laughed. "I didn't know myself until Will woke me up banging on my door at eight this morning and tossed a stack of boxes as high as a house in my front door and told me to put everything on, that he'd be back for me in one hour and he wouldn't take no for an answer. You wouldn't believe what he gave me."

"A wedding dress," said Katherine.

Will laughed at the surprised look on Karin's face, then he introduced himself to Alex. "Well," he said, upon finding out Alex was Katherine's husband, "I didn't know I'd be meeting my brother-in-law today."

"Neither did I," Alex said. "I could tie up half the afternoon asking you questions, but I guess Katherine can fill me in on everything later." Turning to Katherine, Alex said, "Love, do we have any spirits in the house? An occasion like this calls for a toast!"

Katherine was so dazzled by the sound of Alex calling her *love*, that Fanny, bless her soul, had to step in. "Dewberry wine is about it," she said. "We'll have to settle for that." Katherine invited Will and Karin to stay for supper, but Will said they were catching a stagecoach in Dallas and had to be on their way.

"We're going to New York City," Karin said. "Can you believe it? And then we're sailing for Europe."

Katherine had never seen Karin so happy, and she had never felt so happy for her. Life was harsh and cruel. Life wasn't supposed to be like this. Her eyes filled with tears—happy tears. Who would have thought it—here they were, nearly starving a few years ago, and look at them now. Katherine intended to go on and get all emotional thinking about all the hard times, when suddenly she remembered when Karin was being courted by that horrible old Ben Witherspoon. She began to laugh.

She laughed. And she laughed. She laughed until tears came streaming down her cheeks and she doubled over as if in pain. Alex, who was wondering over Katherine's sanity at this point, helped her to the sofa. Karin looked panic-stricken. Will looked completely baffled. Fanny looked like there wasn't a thing out of the ordinary going on.

"Whatever's the matter?" Karin asked, coming to sit beside Katherine.

"I was trying to get all sentimental, and then I started thinking," Katherine choked out between fits of laughter, "about the time Ben Witherspoon was courting you."

"Ben Witherspoon!" Karin said, "that old…"

"F…fossil," Fanny said, catching herself just in time. Everyone in the room started laughing.

"Remember how we hadn't had anything to eat that winter except pork?" Katherine said.

"And how old Witherspoon kept bragging about all his beef?" Karin said. "You started dropping hints right and left, your mouth watering…."

"And old Witherspoon brought us all that..."

"*Pork*," the three women said in unison.

By this time, even Fanny was laughing and the three of them sat on the sofa laughing and crying and hugging each other until Will looked at Alex and said, "I've got a bottle of good Kentucky mash in the buggy."

Alex was there first.

Some time later, Alex, Katherine, and Fanny stood beside the gate, watching Will hand Karin into a shiny new buggy when Karin remembered she had left her parasol. "I'll get it," Katherine said, running into the house.

She had just picked it up and started for the door when Will stepped into the room behind her. "I'm glad to have a chance to speak to you. I know you must think I'm too old for Karin, and you may be right. I have a daughter the same age as Karin and a son two years older. But I honestly believe I'm the right man for her. I love her, Katherine, and more importantly, I understand her. I know some people may think her flighty and too obsessed with money and the things it will buy, and perhaps she is—deprivation and loss of parents can do that to some people. But that doesn't matter to me. I'm a rich man. I can give her anything she could ever want and more. With me she feels secure for the first time in her life, and I feel ten feet tall knowing I've given her that."

By the time Will finished, Katherine was crying again. "Here now," he said, coming to take the parasol. "I didn't mean to upset you."

Katherine gave him her best rendition of a bear hug and kissed him on his clean-shaven cheek. "You haven't upset me at all, Will. You have, by making Karin happy, made me very happy as well. Thank you," she said, "thank you from all of us."

After Will left, she stood at the window and watched him hand Karin her parasol and climb in the buggy next to her. Never had she seen Karin so relaxed and radiant. How had she not seen it before—all the love shining in her face? The thought of the happiness in Karin's life made her even more aware of the hollowness in her own, and she turned away from the window and went upstairs before Alex and Fanny returned.

Two days later, Alex faced the sweltering one-hundred-and-four-degree heat and rode over to Katherine's. He had purposefully given her a couple of days away from him, hoping Karin's marriage might have some positive influence upon their strained relationship. But when he reached the Simon place, he couldn't find Katherine or Fanny, and seeing the wagon and Clovis were gone, decided they had gone into town.

He went back home and tried getting his mind on work, deciding to put the new roof on the tool shed, but after he smashed his thumb for the third time, he called it quits. Hot and restless, he headed down to the creek for a swim to see if he couldn't cool off and think things through. It was time to have a confrontation with Katherine and he wasn't sure how he should approach it.

As he walked through the trees lining the creek, he remembered how many times he had done this when he was growing up, and how many times he had hoped to catch a glimpse of one of the Simon sisters. And then he remembered one time when he had.

Lord, that had been a long time ago, but the memory of it was still as vividly painted across his mind as the day it happened. He thought about the way Karin had looked when he had seen her the last time, perfectly groomed, as always. He couldn't help wondering if Karin naked still looked as good as the memory he carried of her. He closed his eyes, seeing her as she had been that day, the sun warm upon her pale skin, the water sluicing from her body, the dusky tips of her breasts hard and pointed. He had loved her intensely from that moment.

He dipped his head, coming up on the other side of a branch and froze. *What the hell? Karin. Karin here?* He could swear she was, standing in the water, just as he'd seen her then. He blinked. She was still there. He closed his eyes for a moment, knowing she would be gone when he opened them. But when he did, she was still there. And then she turned, stepping out of the shadows into the sunlight and he saw this woman didn't have blond hair. This woman had auburn hair. Hair like his wife. In fact, she looked a lot like his wife. By God, it was his wife!

Alex couldn't move. He stood, transfixed, watching his wife walk into the deeper water, swimming and splashing, then swimming back to stand in the shallows, giving him a good view of what she kept hidden beneath all the prim buttons on her dress. The current carried the long strands of her hair to swirl like ribbons of shiny black silk around her hips and legs. He watched her standing in the sun-dappled shallows, where she washed her hair beneath the droopy, yellow-green branches of a willow tree, tiny iridescent bubbles of foam sluicing over skin as pale as a winter moon.

He remembered a time years ago, when a young boy had come to a place very near this one, and how he had stood, dry-mouthed, and watched a beautiful girl bathe in the warm waters of this same creek. In that boy's youth it had been commonplace to measure a girl's beauty by a physical measuring stick, to yearn for what he found dazzling, but fiery youth saw in only half-truths. Age had made the boy into a man and taught him to be practical, to look with the heart and not the eyes. That man had learned his lesson. He had not brought the faults of youth into his later life. He understood that youth had its pleasures, and although different, age had them as well. They weren't the same pleasures, but they were no less enjoyable. *This* was the lesson life had taught him. He had learned it, and gained a profit.

And wasn't that what life was all about?

Suddenly, uncontrollable laughter gripped him and he went weak in the joints. Laughing as hard as he was, he was powerless and too watery legged to stand, dropping to a half-rotted log before he fell over.

The sound of masculine laughter drifted over the tops of trees and across the water to where Katherine stood. Instantly, she dropped low in the water, holding her breath. She listened. Her fists clenched.

She knew that laugh.

Yanking an old sheet from the limb where she had left it, Katherine wrapped it around her body and made her way through the undergrowth, drawing closer to the sound. She broke through the brush and saw Alex sitting on a log, collapsed in a fit of uncontrollable laughter.

The bastard is laughing at me! The thought seared like a hot poker and she moved like someone had just applied it to her backside. Certainly there was more pride in her zeal than charity when she came up in front of him and said, in the most caustic tones, "Why don't you tell me what's so funny and then we'll both laugh?"

Alex looked up, seeing his angry wife, wet and dripping and another fit of laughter gripped him. "You won't b...b...believe," was all he manage to get out.

Katherine hadn't seen a thing funny so far. "If it concerns you," she said dryly, "I'd believe it."

When he could manage the breath to speak, Alex said weakly, "Sweetheart, come sit beside me. I've got something to tell you."

"I'll take the hilarity standing up, thank you."

"I don't really know where to begin," he said,

stretching his long legs out in front of him.

"What were you laughing at? Me?"

"You?" He laughed again. "No. I was laughing at myself... at my youth."

Katherine looked at him like he had gone over to the other side, to senility. "Alex, there wasn't a blasted thing funny about your youth, or mine either, for that matter."

"Oh, but there was. Come here," he said, patting the log beside him.

"No thank you," she said.

"I've got a story to tell you. Are you sure you don't want to sit down?"

"Positive."

So it began, the telling of his story. For over an hour, Alex talked on, telling Katherine of his earlier feelings for her, moving to those in-between years when she clobbered him and let him know she wanted no part of him. He went on to tell her about the day he saw Karin at the creek, and how in time even the thought of her that way couldn't hold him. "I read somewhere once that men spend the first half of their life making the second half miserable, and I believe it."

Katherine listened to every word, straight up to the moment Alex said, "and that's when you walked up and found me sitting here laughing like a fool." He dropped his head in his hands from exhaustion, rubbing his temples for a moment before he raised his head and looked at her.

"You know," he said, "it was strange seeing Karin again. It was like my past came back to me. I won't lie to you and say I didn't think about the way things used to be, the way she was everything I ever wanted, and how I prayed every night that God would make her mine." He leaned down and picked up a twig and began breaking pieces off of it, tossing them to the ground. Katherine's heart broke a little each time that twig snapped.

"How strange it felt to stand there looking at her the other day, seeing she wasn't quite the angel I remembered her to be. Time had changed her...and my feelings, too." He looked at her and shook his head. "Now don't you go getting all teary, lass.

"I'll have to admit it wasn't all one-sided. I could see time had changed Karin's feelings as well. You know, I felt like a fool standing there, wondering if we should try to talk about old times, knowing all the while that we had nothing to say. I looked at you, the woman I married, and I heard myself thanking God for unanswered prayer."

She took a step toward him and stopped.

"Katherine, I love you," he said. He lifted his hand up as if he were attempting to touch her to see if his hand would slice through thin air or touch something that was real.

"Katherine," he whispered, "what are you thinking?"

She took a swipe at her eyes with the back of her hand. "You big oaf! I ought to tell you I can't stand the sight of you for scaring me like you did just then—telling me all that teary stuff about Karin."

"Come on," he said, his voice light and cajoling. "Tell me what you're really thinking."

"I'm thinking it's a pity I'm your wife."

Seeing the hurt look in his eyes, she hastily said, "Because if I wasn't already your wife, I'd ask you to marry me." She breathed deeply to gain control. "Since I'm already your wife, I'll just have to think of something else."

"Oh, I don't know about that. When we got married I was such a fool. All I could think of was I was being forced to do something wrong, that I was making a big mistake." He looked into her eyes. "I'm not the fool I was then. This time I know what I'm doing. I want to marry you, Katherine."

She laughed, then seeing how serious he was, she stopped. "Is this for real?"

"It's a real as it can be."

"You're crazy. We can't get married. We're *already* married!"

"Is there a law against getting married again?"

"I don't think so, but…Alex, normal people don't get married twice."

"Who says we're normal?"

"True, but that's no reason to get married again. Why would you even consider it?"

"Because, *this* time I want to marry you for all the right reasons." He paused, getting down on his knees in front of her. "Marry me, Katherine. I love you with all my heart." He grinned. "And a few other organs as well."

Katherine looked at him, seeing the boyish grin, and the years that had separated them all ran together. She threw back her head with a throaty laugh. The sheet fell away from her body.

"Good Lord!" Alex said as he shot to his feet. "Good Lord a mercy!" His mouth went dry. He didn't know whether to grab her and run before she changed her mind, or let out a war whoop that would put a Comanche to shame. "Good Lord, Katherine, does this mean what I think it means?"

"Mackinnon, stop your grinnin' and drop your linen."

And that's precisely what he did.

EPILOGUE

Caleb Mackinnon sprang to his feet and began pacing the floor. "My God! How long does it take to have a baby? She's been in there all night. Isn't there something that doctor can do?"

Alex looked at Caleb, the youngest of his five boys. "These things can't be rushed, son. Birthing babies takes time. Your mother said everything was coming along as expected. It won't be much longer now."

"The first one always takes longer," said Rafe. He was the oldest son, already the father of three.

Caleb went on pacing. "I don't think I want any more," Caleb said. "I didn't know how much Julia would be going through, or I wouldn't have had this one."

"Nonsense," Eliza said, dropping down on the sofa beside her husband. "Birthing babies is the most natural and beautiful thing in the world. You couldn't deny that to Julia any more than you could deny it to yourself."

Alex watched Caleb. Of all his sons, Caleb was the most like him, right down to the same pale blue eyes and dark hair. He was acting about as nervous as Alex had when Katherine was birthing their first over thirty years ago. Only Alex didn't have five brothers and three sisters to give him advice. He thought about his own four brothers and how they always liked to tease, thinking how lucky he was that none of them were there when Rafe was born, or he would've gone through the same thing Caleb was enjoying right now. He watched Caleb's dark brow knit together as he rounded on his sister. "And what makes you such an expert, Eliza? You and Josh have only one child."

Eliza looked just like Katherine when she was a bit put out. "My Lord, Caleb. I'm only twenty. How many children do you think I should have?" Eliza asked.

"That's what happens when you're the baby of the family," Rafe's wife Amelia said. "I was the baby of our family. All my life I've been trying to catch up."

"Eliza has always been a slow starter. We thought she'd never learn to talk," said Cal. He was just two years younger than Rafe and not yet married.

"That's because the seven of you were always talking so much I never got a chance," she said. Eliza picked up a sofa pillow, holding it by the fringe as she hurled it at him. Cal laughed and caught it easily in one hand.

Alex settled himself back in his leather chair and picked up his glass of brandy. He looked around the big comfortable room filled with his children, pleased that all eight of them had come, bringing their families. His eyes went over the faces of his sons and daughters by marriage, thinking his children had done him proud when it came time for them to pick a mate. He loved each one of them as if they were his own.

The rumble if footsteps on the porch outside, the shriek of children laughing reminded him that he shouldn't leave out his twelve grandchildren either. It was a blessing, he thought, that his entire family was together like this for the first time in over five years. It made him feel there was something special about that little mite struggling to be born upstairs. Not many children came into the world surrounded with the love of thirteen aunts and uncles and twelve cousins, not to mention a doting old grandfather and a grandmother who insisted on giving each one of them a mule for their fifth birthday. He lit his pipe and exhaled a wreath of smoke, giving thanks to God. This was one Christmas he wouldn't be forgetting.

The shrieking wail of a baby pierced the conversation and the room grew suddenly quiet. Caleb sprang to his feet, just as a door upstairs opened, then closed. Tap, tap, tap came the sound of footsteps coming down the hall. A moment later, Katherine Mackinnon paused at the top of the stairs, a radiant smile on her face. "You can come up now, Caleb. Julia is tired, but she wants to brag a little before she goes to sleep."

"Yaaaa-hooo!" Caleb shouted, and he leaped the leather ottoman his father's feet were resting on to prove just how elated he was.

Alex watched him take the stairs two at a time, then he looked at Katherine as Caleb picked her up and swung her around, giving her a big kiss before he put her down and dashed down the hall shouting, "Julia honey, I love you."

Katherine laughed and looked at Alex.

"Come up here, Grandpa. I have something I want to show you."

Alex joined Katherine at the top of the stairs. "Is everything all right?" he asked. "Julia..."

"She's fine."

"The baby?"

"Everyone is fine." She smoothed the deep furrow between his brow. "Don't look so worried, my love."

"Then what's wrong?"

"Nothing is wrong, Alex."

"Why'd you tell me to come up?"

She put her arms around Alex's neck and kissed him softly, ignoring the hoots and whistles from below. "Maybe I just wanted to hear you tell me you're glad you married me."

He grinned. "I'm glad I married you," he said, nuzzling her neck. "Both times." He pulled back, looking into a face that was remarkably young for a woman who was on the downhill side of fifty. "I'll tell you another little secret, too. I love you, Katherine."

"I know you do." She took his hand in hers and led him down the hall, stopping at the room that joined Julia's. "I love you too, Alex. With all my heart."

Alex didn't speak, but he did look a little wary. After all, he knew his wife better than anyone. "Katherine, what in the blue blazes is going on? Why are you acting so strange, wheedling confessions from me, telling me you love me in the middle of a birthing?"

He had never seen her eyes so bright, or her smile either, for that matter. He put his hand on her forehead and she slapped it away, giving a soft laugh. "If you'll stop looking so suspicious, I'll show you why," she said, opening the door and leading him into the room. They passed the open door that led to Julia's room, seeing Caleb sitting on the bed beside Julia, holding her hand, kissing her forehead. Caleb's sisters, Alexandra and Noel, were standing next to Caleb, their backs to the door. Just as they passed, Alexandra turned and seeing her mother and father, she smiled and nodded, giving Noel a nudge. Alex still had a frown on his face when his two daughters came through the doorway, each of them carrying a tiny bundle that was mostly blanket and a tiny red face surrounded by thick black hair.

"Say hello to your grandsons, Alex," Katherine said, watching Alex's face as the babies were placed in their cradles.

"Two," Alex said hoarsely, hearing his daughters laugh as they left the room, closing the door behind them. "She had two? Julia had *two* babies?"

Katherine laughed. "They're commonly known as twins, Alex. Now close your mouth." She reached up and closed it for him, then shook her head. "Honestly, for a man who was a twin himself, I'm amazed at you."

"Well, I'll be," Alex said. And then again. "Well, I'll be." He stood over the two babies in the tiny cradles, his joy a secret thing, a look of awe upon his face. He gazed upon a part of him that was fresh and new, a part of him that was living and would go on living, his grandsons, posterity slumbering in their small bodies, the promise of his seed that would continue for generations.

His chest puffed out, he looked at his wife. "Do you think they'll take after me?"

Katherine slipped her arm through his and rested her head upon his shoulder. "You bred their father, didn't you?"

Then seeing the expression on her husband's face, she laughed and took his arm. "Aye," she said, "I think they will return the compliment."